PRISONER OF THE IRON TOWER

Also by Sarah Ash

LORD OF SNOW AND SHADOWS
Book One of the Tears of Artamon

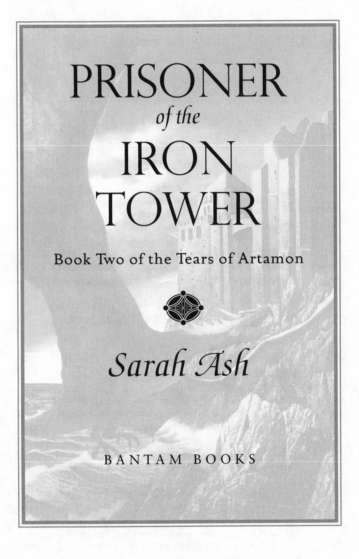

PRISONER
of the
IRON
TOWER

Book Two of the Tears of Artamon

Sarah Ash

BANTAM BOOKS

PRISONER OF THE IRON TOWER
A Bantam Book / August 2004

Published by
Bantam Dell
A Division of Random House, Inc.
New York, New York

Book design by Glen M. Edelstein
Map © 2003 by Neil Gower

Library of Congress Cataloging-in-Publication Data
Ash, Sarah.
Prisoner of the iron tower / Sarah Ash.
p.   cm. — (The tears of Artamon ; bk. 2)
ISBN 0-553-38211-X
1. Prisoners—Fiction. 2. Painters—Fiction.   I. Title.
PS3601.S523P75 2004
813'.6—dc22   2004041093

Manufactured in the United States of America
Published simultaneously in Canada

10 9 8 7 6 5 4 3 2 1
RRC

For Christopher
(who knows all too well what a deadline is!)

ACKNOWLEDGMENTS

PRISONER OF THE IRON TOWER would never have made it without:

The two best (and most rigorous!) editors an author could hope for: Anne Groell at Bantam US and Simon Taylor at Transworld UK and their respective teams.

My agents, Merrilee Heifetz of Writer's House and John Parker of MBA, for making it all possible.

Steve Youll for stunning cover art.

The talented Neil Gower for deciphering my scrawl and transforming it into such a wonderful map of New Rossiya.

My brilliant webmaster, Ariel, editor of The Alien Online (who would be better described as a web-magician for his skills in setting up sarah-ash.com).

My headmaster, Mike Totterdell, and colleagues at Oak Lodge School, for their support and encouragement.

And my husband, Michael, for being there (and all those cups of tea).

Thanks, everyone, you've been great!

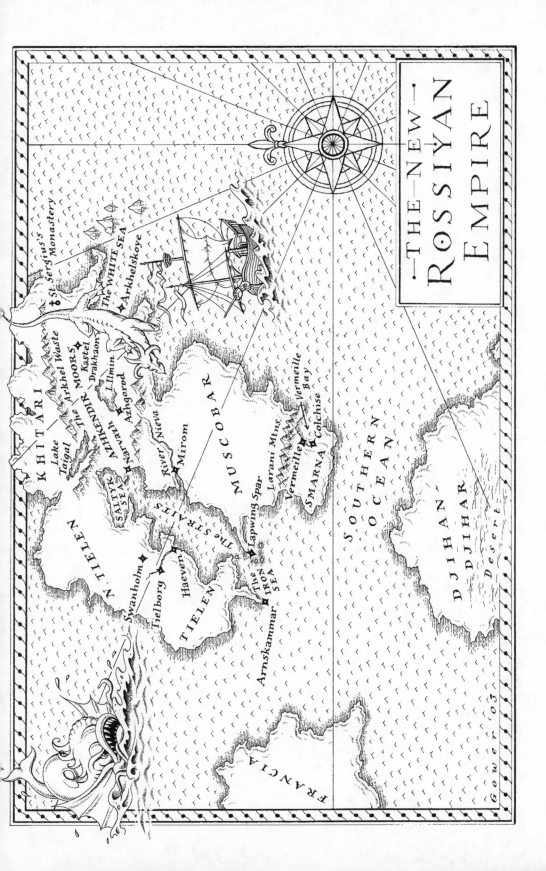

PROLOGUE

Gavril Nagarian, Lord Drakhaon of Azhkendir, opened the door to Saint Sergius's shrine. Candleflames from ochre beeswax candles shimmered in the gloom. The air smelled of bitter incense and honeyed candlesmoke.

The radiant figure of the Blessed Sergius dominated the ancient mural, staff upraised to defend his flock from the dark Drakhaon. Even the saint's face had been covered with gold leaf by the artist. In contrast, only the Drakhaon's eyes glinted in the candlelight, jeweled with chips of blue glass. The rest of his winged daemon-form had been painted black as shadow.

"Now it is finally gone, and I am alone." Gavril's words went echoing up into the shadows of the vaulted roof, where the angelic hosts stared down at him with their painted eyes. The strength suddenly drained out of him and he sank to his knees before the saint's stone tomb.

The heavy nail-studded door to the shrine was flung open with such force that it crashed into the stone wall. Candleflames wavered in the fierce draft and some blew out, guttering trails of smoke.

Warriors of his *druzhina* stood in the doorway. Foremost among them was Bogatyr Askold, first officer and commander of his bodyguard, who came striding down the aisle toward him.

"What have you done to yourself, my lord?" Askold's voice was harsh with grief and accusation. "What have you *done*?"

The others crowded around, so close he could smell the pungent damp of their fur cloaks and the sweat of their bodies.

Askold seized hold of Gavril.

Gavril tried to wrench himself free but, his strength exhausted, he could not break away.

"Forgive me, my lord, but it's the only way to be certain," muttered Askold, twisting one arm behind his back. Gavril heard the whisper of steel against leather as Askold drew a knife from his boot.

A flash of fear flickered through his mind. Did they mean to kill him? In this dangerous mood, his own men could turn against him. And then he winced as Askold drew the knifeblade across his wrist in one small, expert stroke.

The warriors crowded closer, staring as blood began to well up from the shallow incision and drip onto the flagstones.

Gavril stared too.

Red blood. Crimson-red. Human-red. Without a trace of daemon-purple.

A shuddering sigh echoed around the shrine.

Askold let go of him. "So the Drakhaoul is gone. And with it, all your powers."

"You broke the bond! You broke the bloodbond that binds us to you!" cried out scarred Gorian.

"You betrayed us!"

"I did what I had to," Gavril said wearily. "I did what should have been done centuries ago."

"Azhkendir was safe," said Barsuk Badger-Beard, his gruff voice unsteady. "No one dared attack us. But now that it's gone, who knows what will happen?"

"You call yourselves my *druzhina*?" Gavril raised his head and stared at them, challenging. "Then act like warriors!"

Eyes stared back at him, dark with hostility. He could see the glint of their unsheathed sabres in the guttering candlelight. If he did not win back their allegiance now, he was as good as dead.

"We've driven Eugene of Tielen out of Azhkendir. Now we must learn to fight without daemonic powers to protect us. To fight like *men*."

"Didn't you hear what Lord Gavril said?" A younger voice rang out, passionate with anger. Gavril saw Semyon, the newest member of the *druzhina*, his freckled face flushed red. "I swore to defend you, my lord. I haven't forgotten how you saved my life in the siege. My oath still holds."

"Aye, and mine too," said Askold. He knelt at Gavril's feet. "Forgive us, my lord."

Gavril knelt down too and placed his hands on Askold's shoulders, raising him to his feet. "We've much to do," he said. "Kastel Drakhaon is in ruins. Will you work with me to rebuild it?"

It was not until he left the shrine to walk across the monastery courtyard with Semyon and Askold at his side that he heard again the far-distant echo of the Drakhaoul's dying voice, each word etched in fire on his mind:

"Why do you betray me? Divide us and you'll go insane. . . ."

The old fisherman Kuzko and his wife found him lying on the seashore, so battered by the waves and the rocks that his clothes were torn to shreds. For days he wandered between life and death—and when he returned to himself, he no longer knew who he was. The sea had stolen his memories from him. The only distinguishing feature was a signet ring on his broken right hand . . . but the device had been worn so smooth by the sea and the rocks that it was impossible to tell with any certainty what it had been.

So they called him Tikhon after their own lost son, drowned years before in another night of terrible storms, and they nursed him slowly back to health. Many weeks later, when he could walk again, he began to help with a task or two: mending nets, carrying wood for the fire.

Everything had to be relearned, even speech; he was like a great child, limping slowly after Kuzko, speaking awkwardly, as if his tongue would not obey his brain. Yet he seemed cheerful enough in spite of his deficiencies—although sometimes he was suddenly overcome with a terrible wordless raging that could not be assuaged.

Tikhon was helping old Kuzko mend the boat, caulking a leak in the storm-battered hull with a stinking mess of oakum and pitch that Kuzko had boiled up over a driftwood fire. The wind blew keen and raw across the bleak island shore. There was nothing to be seen here for miles but sea and rocks. The sky was pale with scudding clouds. Until Kuzko noticed one cloud blowing toward them, darker than the rest, moving faster than the others.

"Storm coming," he shouted to Tikhon. "Best find shelter till it passes." He gazed up into the sky. This was no ordinary stormcloud; it was moving too fast, its course erratic and unpredictable. And as it tumbled nearer, the light began to fade from the sky and the shoreline turned black as night.

Tikhon stumbled after his adoptive father—but his damaged body betrayed him and, with a gargling cry, he fell on his face on the pebbled beach.

The old fisherman started back toward him. "Come on, lad!"

The dark cloud hovered overhead. Lightning crackled—and Kuzko dropped back, covering his eyes.

Tikhon let out another cry of terror as he cowered in the lightning's beam.

Kuzko watched, helpless, as with a sudden, sinuous movement, the cloud wrapped itself like a dark shroud around Tikhon. The lad convulsed, his body wracked by violent shudders, twisting this way and that as though struggling with some invisible shadow-creature.

And then the struggle ceased. The darkness had disappeared—and the sun's pale winter light pierced the scudding clouds.

Kuzko slowly picked himself up. "T-Tikhon," he stammered. The lad lay unmoving. Tears welled in his eyes. He had seen his son taken from him once—was he to have to endure it all again?

"Tikhon?" he said, extending a shaking hand to touch the boy's shoulder.

Tikhon's eyes opened. He sat up. Each movement was lithe, precise, controlled. He looked at Kuzko and said, "Where am I?" His voice was no longer slurred.

"Are you all right?" quavered Kuzko.

The young man looked down at himself, frowning. "I think so."

"You're cured. It's a m-miracle." Kuzko felt weak now. "Come, Tikhon, let's go tell Mother—"

"Tikhon?" The young man slowly shook his head. "I fear you must have me confused with someone else. My name is Andrei."

CHAPTER 1

Astasia Orlova leaned on the rail of the Tielen ship that was carrying her back home to Muscobar across the Straits. Cold seaspray blew into her face, her hair, but she did not care.

She was bearing Count Velemir's ashes back to Mirom. It was Feodor Velemir who had brought her to Tielen on the pretense that wreckage from her brother Andrei's command, the *Sirin,* had been washed up on the shore. She had gone, eager that there might be the faintest glimmer of hope that Andrei was not drowned but lying injured in some remote fisherman's hut, only to find that it had all been a ruse to display her charms to the Tielen court and council, to persuade them that she would make a suitable bride for Prince Eugene.

Well, Count, she thought, gazing into the rolling sea mist that hid the coastline of Muscobar from view, *you have paid the ultimate price for your treachery. You used me heartlessly. You lied, you twisted the truth to further your own ends, and now you are dead.*

But even now she was not sure she believed the evidence of her own eyes. What she had witnessed in the snowy palace yard had shaken her to the very core.

There crouched a dark-winged creature, veiled in a blue shimmer of heat. And—most horrible of all—the burning remains of something that had once been Feodor Velemir, Muscobar's ambassador to Tielen, lay in a charred, smoking heap at its feet.

Drakhaon.

In that one moment all certainties had been seared away.

"Altessa!" Nadezhda, her maid, came up to her, carrying a wool shawl. "You'll catch a chill up here in this bitter wind."

"Don't fuss, Nadezhda. I'm fine."

Nadezhda took no notice and draped the shawl over Astasia's shoulders. "Please come below and warm yourself."

"Not yet," Astasia said distantly. "In a while . . ."

The cloudy sky and the choppy sea mirrored her mood. She felt numbed. Whenever she tried to sleep, she saw the Drakhaon of Azhkendir rear up out of the darkness and then, oh then—

The one moment she could not forget, the moment when the dragon-winged daemon had turned its piercing blue gaze on her and she had recognized Gavril Andar.

Elysia Andar had tried to warn her, but she had refused to listen. Yet now she knew it to be true. Gavril, the one man she had ever allowed to hold her, to kiss her, was possessed by a dragon-daemon—

"Altessa."

She turned to see that one of the Tielen officers had come up on deck.

"We have received an urgent message from Mirom, altessa, that concerns you. Will you please come below?"

Reluctantly, Astasia followed him belowdecks to the captain's anteroom. Chancellor Maltheus had sent an escort of the household guard to protect her . . . or to prevent her from running away?

A group of officers were gathered around the table; they bowed as she entered.

"Is there a storm coming?" she asked, taking off the shawl. The fine mist of seaspray still clung to her hair. "Should we seek harbor and sit it out?"

"The message comes from Field Marshal Karonen, altessa. He reports there is rioting in Mirom. It seems that your parents have been trapped in the Winter Palace by a mob of dissidents who are threatening to torch the palace and all inside."

Astasia gripped the edge of the table to steady herself. "Dissidents?" she repeated.

"Your father has requested our help. It seems the situation is quite desperate."

"My father is asking for help?" Astasia said. If nothing else, this brought home the severity of the situation. Her father never asked for help.

"The Field Marshal is ready to lead a rescue force into the city, altessa. Just give the word and he will liberate the palace."

Astasia gazed warily around at all the Tielen officers. She could not help noticing the detailed map of Mirom that lay outspread on the table. They seemed so well-prepared. . . .

"We understand there has been unrest in the city for some months," said one.

"Well, yes—" she began, then broke off. How could she have been so blind? Maltheus had sent the soldiers with her as part of the invasion force. What better way to infiltrate Tielen soldiers into the heart of the city? Dissidents or no, Muscobar was about to be swallowed up into the growing Tielen empire.

"Prince Eugene is determined to quell any last stirrings of rebellion before your wedding takes place."

"Of course," she said coldly. They were still looking at her expectantly, and she realized that they were waiting for her command.

"Tell the Field Marshal," she said, knowing she had no choice, "to put down the rebellion—and with my blessing."

Astasia struggled up on deck against the prevailing wind, into a raw, red dawn. As the ship sailed up the broad Nieva, she noticed that the gilded dome of the Senate House had been reduced to a smoldering shell. And while at first she had believed the red glare in the sky to be the rising sun, surely no dawn could glow that brightly?

No, the West Wing of the palace was on fire.

She heard the crackle of the flames, the tinkle of breaking glass as panes burst in the heat; she saw the haze of smoke sullying the freshness of the dawn.

They were burning her home.

"No!" she cried aloud, gripping the rail to steady herself.

Now she could hear shouts from the shore; a confusion of people was swarming over the neatly clipped boxes and yews. Guards leaned from the windows, aiming muskets at the rabble, firing. A ragged rat-a-tat of fusillades answered.

"You must go belowdecks, altessa!" One of the Tielen officers came toward her, pistol in hand. "It's not safe up here!"

Screams carried on the wind, shrill above the rattle of gunfire. There were running silhouettes at the West Wing windows, dark against the blaze of the flames. Where were Mama and Papa? Where was her governess, poor, dear Eupraxia? She would be so flustered by the panic and the fire—

"There are people trapped in there!" she said to the officer, grabbing his arm and stabbing her finger at the burning building. "We must get them out!"

A musket ball whizzed over their heads, grazing the nearest mast, showering them with sharp splinters of wood.

"We're doing all we can," he said, hurrying her toward the hatch.

The battle for the Winter Palace lasted little more than an hour. Astasia crept back up on deck and watched as more and more Tielen soldiers swarmed into the gardens, driving the rebels before them, rounding them up at musket-point.

By now the West Wing was well-alight, and she saw looters risking the Tielen guns to carry away brocade curtains, pictures, fine porcelain . . . Too late, some servants formed a bucket-chain while others scooped water from the river. Flames burst through the roof. Rafters cracked and the whole structure collapsed inward with a crash like rolling thunder.

Shocked beyond speech, she stood with her hands clutched to her mouth. The clouds of acrid smoke carried the vile smell of burning: timber, molten glass, and, worst of all, human flesh.

"I've made some tea, altessa." She had not noticed that Nadezhda had emerged from belowdecks. "You've eaten nothing for hours. You need to keep up your strength."

"Mama," Astasia whispered into the billowing smoke. "Papa . . ."

"Tea with a drop of brandy, that'll warm you up." Nadezhda took her by the arm and steered her back below.

At about four in the afternoon, a party of Muscobar officers came on board and asked to speak with her. Sick with worry, she hurried to meet them.

"Colonel Roskovski!" she cried, so glad to see a familiar face that she wanted to run up and hug him.

"Altessa," he said, clicking his heels and saluting her. He looked haggard; he was unshaven and his immaculate white uniform jacket was covered in smears of soot. "Thank God you're safe."

"Is there . . . is there any news of my parents?"

"They are under the protection of Field Marshal Karonen," he said stiffly.

"But they're alive?"

"I believe so. Altessa—" he hesitated. "I have been obliged to surrender control of the city to the Field Marshal." She saw now that not only was he exhausted, but there were tears in his smoke-reddened eyes—tears of humiliation and defeat. "I am dishonored. I have failed your father."

"Not surrender, Colonel," she said, dismayed that such a proud and experienced soldier should openly weep with shame in front of her. "I'm sure you and your men did everything you could to save the city. But the odds were overwhelming. Without Tielen's help—"

"Altessa Astasia!" One of the Tielen officers came running up. "The Field Marshal requests a meeting."

Her heart began to beat overfast, a butterfly trapped in her breast. This was to do with her parents, she was sure of it. How would she find them? Even if they were physically unharmed, the last few days would have taken a terrible toll on Mama's nerves. And Papa . . .

"Colonel," she said, "please accompany me."

It seemed that there were Tielen soldiers everywhere: lining the quay as Astasia disembarked, guarding the Water Gate, and patrolling the outer walls where the rebels had smashed down the iron railings as they stormed the palace.

Even though the officers steered a carefully chosen path, Astasia saw soldiers carrying out bodies from the courtyards and piling them onto carts. Through an archway she glimpsed some of Roskovski's men cutting down a palace guard who was hanging from a lamppost, his white uniform red with his own blood.

"Were many killed?" she asked, determined that she should not be treated like a child.

"Enough," Roskovski said tersely.

She wanted to avert her gaze from the bodies, but found she could not look away. One bright head of hair, as fiery as a fox's pelt, caught her eye. One of her mother's maids, Biata, had hair of just that unusual shade. . . .

The woman's head lolled at an unnatural angle over the edge of the cart, eyes fixed, staring out from a wax-pale face. A trickle of blood from both nostrils darkened her lips, her chin.

"Biata?" But what point was there in calling her name when she was beyond hearing? And even as Astasia watched, the Tielens unceremoniously flung another body onto the cart, right on top of her. They were not distinguishing rioters from palace servants, they were just clearing away corpses.

Astasia started forward, outraged, and felt a firm touch on her shoulder.

"These men mean no disrespect," said Roskovski. "They're merely following orders."

"But it's Biata!" Astasia was ashamed to hear how high and tremulous her own voice sounded. She was trying to behave as the heir to the Orlov dynasty should. And yet all she felt was a cold, sick sense of dread. They had wanted to kill anyone who was associated with her family. It could have been her own body slung like an animal carcass into that cart.

"I would have preferred to spare you such sights." Roskovski shot a disapproving glance at the Tielen officer leading them.

The city now lay muffled in the winter dusk, eerily quiet after the din of the riot. Smoke still rose from the ruins of the West Wing; the choking smell of ash and cinders singed the evening air.

"Where are you taking me?" she asked the Tielen officer as they passed through the inner courtyard and entered the palace by an obscure door. A stone stair led into a dank subterranean passageway, lit by links set in the wall.

"This is no place to bring the altessa," protested Roskovski.

A smell of mold pervaded the air and the floor was puddled with water; Astasia lifted her skirts high, wondering uneasily whether she had walked into some Tielen trap.

"Is this part of the servants' quarters?" she asked, glancing at Roskovski for reassurance. "I don't remember ever coming here before."

Roskovski cleared his throat awkwardly. "This leads to the rooms used by your father's agents to detain and question those suspected of crimes against the state."

Astasia stopped. "The old dungeons from my great-grandfather's time? But my father had them converted to wine cellars. He wouldn't condone the use of such ancient, unsanitary conditions for—" She stopped. How naïve she sounded. There was so much she did not know about her father's rule as Grand Duke. Now she began to wonder what cruel tortures had been inflicted down here in the interests of the state, while, unknowing, she had danced at her first ball in the palace above. There was so much she had been shielded from. Had the rioters imprisoned her parents down here? Had they put them to the question? The sick feeling in her stomach grew stronger, as did the unwholesome smell. It was as if the dank water glistening on the walls and pooling on the floor were oozing in from the Nieva, bringing with it the city's stinking effluent.

At the end of the tunnel they came out into a small room. At a desk sat a tall, broad-shouldered man in Tielen uniform, poring over dispatches by lanternlight. When he stood up to greet her, he had to stoop, the ceiling was so low.

"Karonen at your service, altessa."

"My parents," Astasia burst out. "Where are they?"

Field Marshal Karonen cleared his throat, evidently uncomfortable. "That is why I requested your presence in this wretched place, altessa. This is where the insurgents imprisoned them. Now they are reluctant to come out, fearing further ill-treatment. I am hoping you might persuade them that the insurrection is at an end."

They sat side by side on a wooden bench, blinking in the lanternlight of a cramped, windowless cell. There was an unmistakably fetid odor of stale urine and unwashed flesh. How long had they been imprisoned here? At first Astasia did not even recognize her mother in the lank-haired, listless woman who stared blankly at her.

"Mama, Papa," she said, her voice trembling, her arms outstretched.

The Grand Duke half-rose from the bench.

"Tasia? Little Tasia?" he said, his voice trembling too.

"Yes, Papa, it's really me." Astasia flung her arms around him and hugged him tightly.

"Look, Sofie, it's Tasia," the Grand Duke said.

The Grand Duchess gazed at her, her face still expressionless.

"Mama," Astasia said, kneeling beside her mother, "we're all safe now."

"Safe?" the Grand Duchess said with a little shiver. "Did they molest you, Tasia? Did they lay hands on you?"

"No, Mama. I'm fine. But you're not. You must come out of this cold, damp place and warm yourself."

The Grand Duchess shrank back, cowering behind her husband. "No, no, it's not safe. They're in the palace. They're everywhere. They want to kill us."

"Mama, look who's with me." Astasia took her mother's chill hand and pressed it between her own. "It's Field Marshal Karonen of Tielen. He has taken the city from the rebels. He has rescued us all."

"Tielen?" said the Grand Duchess distantly. "Now I remember. You were betrothed to Eugene of Tielen, weren't you, child?"

"Come, Mama," coaxed Astasia. "Come with me. Wouldn't you like some hot bouillon? And clean clothes?"

The Grand Duchess glanced nervously at the officers standing in the doorway to the cell. Then she clasped Astasia's hand. "All right, my dear," she said in a wavering voice, "but only if you're certain it's safe."

Safe? Astasia thought as her mother ventured out of the cell, leaning heavily on her arm. *Poor, foolish Mama. If I've learned one thing in the past weeks, it's that nowhere is safe anymore.*

Astasia stood in an anteroom in the East Wing, gazing around her. Slander—hateful, obscene slander—had been daubed in red paint across the pale blue and white walls. The windowpanes had been smashed. And she did not want to look too closely at what had been smeared over the polished floors. The rioters had slashed or defaced everything in their path that they had been unable to carry away; everywhere she saw the evidence of their hatred. But at least the East Wing was intact and her parents were being warmed, cossetted, and fed by the few faithful servants who had not fled.

She was not in any mood to be comforted. Her home had been violated. She hugged her arms around herself, chilled by an all-pervading feeling of desolation.

Feodor Velemir had foreseen all this. Had she judged him too harshly? Had he anticipated the coming storm and sought to prevent it?

"Altessa."

She swung around to see the broad-shouldered bulk of Field Marshal Karonen filling the doorway.

"I have news of his highness for you, from Azhkendir." He came in, followed by several of his senior officers. The winter-grey and blue colors of the Tielen army filled the antechamber.

"News?"

"Prince Eugene has been gravely wounded," said Karonen brusquely, "in a battle with the Drakhaon."

The daemon-shadow of the Drakhaon suddenly billowed up, dark as smoke, in her mind.

"Ah," she said carefully, aware they were all watching for her reaction. "Wounded—but not killed?"

"We've lost many men, but the prince is alive. Magus Linnaius is tending to his injuries. The prince was most anxious to ensure that you were unharmed. He would like to speak with you."

"With me?" Astasia looked at him, uncomprehending. "But how?"

"It is called a Vox Aethyria."

When he showed her, she wondered if the Field Marshal had taken leave of his senses. She saw only an exquisite crystal flower—a rose, perhaps—encased in an elaborate tracery of precious metals and glass.

"It's very pretty, Field Marshal, but—"

"You must approach the device and speak very slowly and clearly. The crystal array will transmit your voice through the air to his highness."

"What should I say?"

"I believe his highness has a question he is most eager to ask you."

"Altessa Astasia."

Astasia, startled, took a step back from the crystal. A man's voice had addressed her from the heart of the rose. "What kind of trickery is this?"

"No trickery, altessa, I assure you," said Karonen, his dour expression relaxing into a smile. He turned the Vox toward him and spoke into it. "The altesssa is unused to our Tielen scientific artistry, highness. She is recovering from her surprise at hearing your voice from so far away." He beckoned Astasia to his side.

Astasia felt her cheeks tingle with indignation. She was not going to be shown up as an unsophisticated schoolgirl. She was an Orlov. What would her father have done on such an occasion? She approached the Vox Aethyria with determination and said loudly and clearly, "I must thank your highness, on behalf of our city, for sending your men to quell the riots and rescue my family. I—I trust you are making a good recovery from your injuries?"

Field Marshal Karonen nodded his approval and adjusted the Vox so that she could hear Prince Eugene's reply.

It was faint at first, so that she had to bend closer to the crystal to hear.

"Indeed; and I am in much better spirits already for hearing your voice, and knowing you are safe." Formal as his words were, she thought she detected—to her surprise—an undertone of genuine concern. *Does he care about me a little, then?* *"I had fully intended to lead my men to free the city myself, but fate decreed otherwise. Now I want nothing more than to meet you. I've had to wait far too long and, charming though your portrait is, it's a poor substitute."*

Astasia's throat had gone dry. She could sense what was coming next. *Am I ready for this?*

"We must meet, altessa, and soon. I have plans—great plans—for our two countries, but unless you are at my side, they will all be meaningless. Will you marry me, Astasia?"

"The altessa will not be disappointed, highness." The valet straightened the blue ribbon of the Order of the Swan on Eugene's breast, gave one final tweak to the fine linen collar, a last spray of cologne, and withdrew from the prince's bedchamber, bowing.

Eugene of Tielen forced himself to confront his reflection in the cheval mirror.

At first he had ordered all mirrors in the palace at Swanholm to be covered, unable to bear the ravages that his encounter with the Drakhaon had wrought. Now that he was almost recovered, he forced himself to look every day. After all, he reasoned, his courtiers were obliged to put up with the sight of his disfigurement, so why shouldn't he?

He had never been vain. He had known himself to be strong-featured—certainly no handsome fairy-tale prince from one of Karila's stories. But it still pained him to see the ravages of the Drakhaon's Fire: the scarred and reddened skin that pitted one hand and one whole side of his face and head. And his hair had not yet grown back as he had hoped, though there were signs of a soft, pale ashen fuzz, the rich golden hues bleached away.

How would Astasia react? Would she shrink from him, forced by court protocol to make a public show of tolerating what, in her heart, she looked on with revulsion? Or was she made of stronger stuff, prepared to search deeper than superficial appearances?

He squared his shoulders, bracing himself. He had conquered a whole continent; what had he to fear from one young woman?

He pushed open the double doors and went to meet his betrothed for the first time.

The East Wing music room had escaped the worst of the attack. Built for intimate concerts and recitals, it was crammed to overflowing with the military dignitaries of the Tielen royal household, leaving little room for the Orlov family and their court.

Astasia sat on a dais between her parents; a fourth gilt chair stood empty beside hers. First Minister Vassian stood silently behind her. Still in mourning for her drowned brother Andrei, her family and the court were somberly dressed in black and violet. A tense silence filled the room; the Mirom courtiers seemed too bewildered by the rapid succession of events that had led to the annexation of Muscobar even to whisper behind their black-gloved hands.

A blaze of military trumpets shattered the air.

"His imperial highness, Eugene of Tielen!" announced a martial voice.

The Tielen household guard came marching in, spurs clanking. Astasia felt her mother shrink in her seat.

"It's all right, Mama," she whispered, patting her hand, trying to suppress her own nervousness. Then she saw all the heads in the room bowing, the women sinking into low curtsies.

He was here.

She rose to her feet, pressing her hands together to stop them from shaking.

Prince Eugene came in, accompanied by Field Marshal Karonen. She noted that he too wore a black velvet mourning band. Was it as a sign of respect for their loss, or had he too lost someone dear to him in the fighting?

They had warned her about his injuries. She did not think herself squeamish, but she steeled herself nevertheless, hoping she would not let anything of what she might feel show on her face.

He stood before her, but still she stared at the golden Order of the Swan glittering on his breast, unwilling to meet his eyes.

"Welcome, your highness," she said, dropping into a full court curtsy, one hand extended in formal greeting.

She sensed a slight hesitation, then a gloved hand took hers in a firm grip, raising her to her feet. Still she did not dare to look at him, even as she felt him lift her hand to his lips.

Look, you must look, she willed herself, aware that everyone in the room was watching them with bated breath.

"You are every bit as beautiful as your portrait, altessa." His voice was strong, confident, colored by a slight Tielen accent. He still held her hand in his.

She could no longer keep her gaze lowered. She looked at him then, forcing herself to concentrate on his eyes. Blue-grey eyes, clear and cold as a winter's morning, gazed steadily back. But all the skin around them was red, blistered, and damaged. She was looking into the ruin of a face.

Gavril did this. She was so shocked she could not speak for a moment. *How cruel.*

"You flatter me, your highness," she answered, forcing firmness into her voice. She must not forget that this was also the man who had ruthlessly ordered Elysia's execution. "Please . . ." She gestured to the gilt chair that had been set for him beside hers.

He stepped up onto the dais, towering above her. He bowed to the Grand Duke and Duchess, to Vassian, and then sat down.

Astasia cleared her throat. This was the part of the ceremony she had been dreading the most—because it signaled to the world the end of the Orlov dynasty.

Her father rose from his chair and took her hand in his.

"My—my daughter has a gift for you, your highness," he said. His voice faltered. "A gift from the heart of Muscobar. Accept it—and with it, her hand in marriage, freely given, so that our two countries may be united as one."

Astasia took the jeweled casket her father was holding toward her and knelt before Prince Eugene, offering it with both hands raised.

The prince opened the casket. The Mirom Ruby glowed in his fingers like a flame as he held it aloft: a victory trophy.

"The last of Artamon's Tears!" His voice throbbed now with an intensity of emotion that startled Astasia. "Now the imperial crown is complete." He helped her to rise and took her hand, closing it over the ancient ruby clutched in his fingers.

"Today a new empire rises from the ashes of Artamon's dreams. Altessa, from the day we are married in the Cathedral of Saint Simeon, you will be known as Astasia, Empress of New Rossiya."

He drew her close and she felt—as if in a waking dream—the pressure of his burned lips, hot and dry, on her forehead, and then her mouth.

Field Marshal Karonen turned to the astonished court.

"Long live the Emperor Eugene—and Empress Astasia!"

After a short, startled silence, the cheers began. Astasia, her hand still in Eugene's, glanced at her father—and saw the Grand Duke surreptitiously wiping away a tear.

CHAPTER 2

"Would your imperial highness care to take a look?" The tailor wheeled the full-length mirror across the dressing room.

Eugene had permitted himself this one luxury: new clothes for the coronation, though he had stipulated—to the master tailor's profound disappointment—that they must not be in any way ornate or extravagant. He steeled himself and glanced at his reflection. He had chosen the uniform of the Colonel-in-Chief of his Household Cavalry for his wedding outfit: the gold-frogged jacket cut of the finest, softest pale grey wool, subtly decorated with braid. On his breast he would wear the Order of the Swan, suspended from a pale blue ribbon.

"If your imperial highness could raise your right arm so—" his tailor muttered through a mouthful of pins, making little marks with chalk.

Eugene had not believed himself to be vain; he had thought himself above such worldly conceits. But now, as he caught sight of his damaged face in the mirror, he knew he was as susceptible as any man. It was a face ghoulish enough to scare children on the Night of the Dead, one half still angrily red beneath the glistening film of new skin.

"Does the braid on the cuff please your highness?"

"The braid?" Eugene forced himself to concentrate on the details of the tailoring. "Why, yes. It's not too ostentatious."

There had been so many calls on his time, so many ministers and ambassadors to entertain from the world beyond the empire, that

Eugene realized he had hardly spent more than five minutes alone with Astasia since the betrothal.

This was not the best way to start a relationship with the woman he had chosen to be his empress. He had sensed Astasia stiffen as he embraced her, as his burned cheek brushed against hers. He could understand her revulsion; he felt much the same every morning as he faced his own reflection in the shaving mirror.

He must make time to pay her a visit; she would be chaperoned, of course, but it would still afford an opportunity for conversation.

In the meantime, he would send another betrothal gift. Amethysts would enhance the creamy pallor of her skin. He would ask Paer Paersson to select something rare and exquisite that would please her. He would have selected the gift himself, but he was due to attend a crucial meeting with Kyrill Vassian.

Eugene seated himself at a great gilt and marble-topped desk that had been rescued from the flames to sign and seal the documents presented to him by First Minister Vassian. Gustave hovered behind him, darting forward from time to time to shake sand to set wet ink, or melt a fresh stick of wax.

"So," Eugene said as he set his seal in the final blob of scarlet wax, "this concludes my part, I believe?" He stared down with a swelling sense of satisfaction at the written confirmation of his victory: Muscobar was truly his at last.

"Yes, highness." Vassian stiffly bowed his silvered head. "The lawyers have been awaiting these final documents. There will be plenty to occupy them, now that Muscobar has been swallowed up by New Rossiya." Still bowing, he left the study. Was that last comment a faint flash of defiance? The First Minister had seemed detached, coldly yet politely aloof, during the signing ceremony. Eugene could not help wondering if Chancellor Maltheus would have shown such detachment if the situation were reversed.

"Stand clear!" From outside came the shouts of workmen, and then a crash of falling masonry, followed by a rising cloud of dust: mortar and crushed plaster. Work on reconstructing the gutted wing had already begun, generously funded by the Tielen treasury.

"And the plans for the coronation, Gustave?"

"Are well in hand, highness. All the invitations have been issued, even to Enguerrand of Francia."

Eugene rose and shook his burned hand, which was stiff and sore from signing. The sudden flash of agonizing pain made him wince, but he turned hastily away, pretending to gaze out of the window so that Gustave should not notice. The pain slowly subsided.

"I want representatives from all five princedoms to attend—and be seen to attend. We will show the world—and Francia, in particular—how well New Rossiya's enlightened ideals can work for the good of the people."

"I can't marry him." Astasia sat frozen in front of the mirror. She could still feel Prince Eugene's lips on her own. Kissing her. And every time she remembered, she felt a shudder of revulsion. She despised herself for it. But she kept seeing again the unnatural red sheen of his burned face, the glisten of the fragile, new-formed skin that looked as if it would peel and flake away at the slightest touch, leaving a horrible oozing mess of raw flesh beneath—

She shuddered again. "I can't even bear to think of it."

There came a discreet tap at the door and, as it opened, she saw in the mirror the round, plump face of Eupraxia beaming at her.

"Praxia!" Astasia sprang up and, forgetting all rules of propriety, ran to fling her arms around Eupraxia's generous girth. "Dear Praxia, how I've missed you."

"Altessa." Eupraxia hugged her to her broad, lace-covered bosom. "Let me look at you." She gazed into her charge's face and Astasia saw tears glistening in her governess's warm brown eyes. "How pale you look. Where are those pretty roses?" And she gently pinched Astasia's cheek.

"I'm so much happier for seeing you and knowing you're safe, Praxia." Astasia caught hold of Eupraxia's plump hand and pulled her to sit on the little Tielen-blue sofa beside her. "I was afraid you'd been caught up in the riots."

"And if I hadn't been called away to the country to nurse my sister, I dread to think . . ." Eupraxia shook her head, making her little grey curls tremble like catkins. "But let's talk of happier matters, my dear. The wedding!"

Astasia forced a smile.

"What's this? You've snared the most eligible bridegroom in the whole continent and—oh no. You're not still pining for that unsuitable young Smarnan portrait painter, are you?"

"Certainly not," Astasia said vehemently.

"Then why the doleful eyes?"

"Because—oh, Praxia, I'm so ashamed to say it, but I can't bear for him to touch me. Am I so shallow that I can only see his disfigurement?"

"There, there." Eupraxia stroked her hair, just as she used to when Astasia was a little girl and had broken her favorite doll. "Your feelings are quite understandable. You've led a sheltered life. You've never had to tend to soldiers wounded in battle or look on such terrible injuries till now."

"It's true." Astasia had seen so little of the world until the last weeks of insurrection, fire, and bloodshed.

"What matters is what's inside, not outside. If the prince is a warmhearted man, a good man, you will come to ignore his outward appearance." As Eupraxia continued in this vein, Astasia nodded from time to time as though agreeing. But none of Eupraxia's words comforted her in the least. "Give it time, my child."

Astasia was infinitely grateful that Eupraxia had not chosen this moment to lecture her on her duty as sole Orlov heir. Her governess had neither been outraged by her confession, nor had she reacted hysterically as her mother Sofia would undoubtedly have done. Now, as Astasia rang for Nadezhda to bring tea, she felt more than a little guilty, remembering the many times she had defied her governess or had driven her to distraction with her whims and headstrong moods. In the last turbulent weeks she had begun to wonder whom she could still trust, and Eupraxia had proved herself a true and loyal ally.

She sat and sipped strong, sweet tea and offered Eupraxia some of the little sugared vanilla biscuits she had brought from Swanholm. It delighted her to see her governess smile appreciatively as she sampled the Tielen sweetmeats; she had always enjoyed such treats. Eupraxia inquired after her parents' health and Astasia inquired about Eupraxia's sister. But all the while, Astasia's mind kept wandering. *Is it so hard a thing, after all? To let him touch me, kiss me? To just close my eyes and pretend . . .*

But what kind of a marriage is built on pretense?

"Time, imperial highness," said Doctor Arensky, washing his hands in the basin provided and drying them on a linen towel proffered by his assistant. "Time is a great healer."

Eugene heard the doctor's words and understood only too well what lay behind them. He said nothing at first, but the breath he let out sounded like a sigh, ragged with despair.

"You were recommended to me as the most eminent physician in your field," he said. "Are you saying that there's nothing you—even you—can do for me?"

"Quite frankly, highness, you are most fortunate that the skin tissue has not become corrupted and there is no sign of necrosis. That would have led to a hideous and agonizing death."

"I've seen men die of gangrene." Eugene needed no reminding of the putrefying stench of a gangrenous wound. "And I have funded research at the University of Tielen into finding a remedy."

"Indeed, your highness's patronage is much appreciated in medical circles," Doctor Arensky said with a little bow.

Eugene, irritated beyond patience by Arensky's evasive manner, got to his feet and faced him. "I am in constant pain, Doctor. Whenever I talk, smile, eat—even when I kiss my little daughter. Every single facial movement a man can make, causes me pain. It is the same with the hand. Tell me the truth. Will the pain ever grow less?"

The expression of professional detachment faded and the doctor's eyes registered genuine surprise at the bluntness of his question.

"I wish I could offer your highness a miracle cure. But, apart from opiates or soothing unguents to dull the pain—"

Eugene made a dismissive gesture.

"Once the skin has been damaged by a fire of such intensity, it never repairs itself properly."

It was stark confirmation of what he had already suspected. "So this is the face that I must show to the world for the rest of my life." He stiffened his shoulders, straightening his back as if he were a soldier on parade, standing to attention before his commanding officer. "Nevertheless, I have decided to endow another post at the university in Mirom so that research may be pursued into afflictions of the skin and their possible cures."

"Your imperial highness is very generous," murmured Doctor Arensky, bowing low this time.

So that some other poor wretch may one day be spared the suffering Gavril Nagarian has forced me to endure.

But once Arensky had bowed his way from the room, Eugene

sagged, gripping the desk to support himself. He realized he had been sustaining himself with the hope that there might yet be some cure. Now he knew the truth: He must live with this burned face until the end of his days.

Yet in a few minutes he must attend an important meeting. He made a supreme effort to compose himself, to hide the crushing disappointment that had overwhelmed him. Soon he would be crowned Emperor—and the Great Artamon's successor could not allow himself to show the slightest sign of vulnerability.

As Eugene took his place at the head of the table, he scanned the faces of the dignitaries he had summoned to discuss the final plans for the coronation. Count Igor Golitsyn, a flamboyant dandy of the Orlov's court, had been appointed Grand Master of Ceremonies. Chancellor Maltheus was there, next to the ancient Patriarch Ilarion of Mirom who was attended by two of his long-bearded archimandrites. Their robes exuded a faint but distinct smell of bitter incense. Opposite them stood two envoys from Khitari; their beards were as long as the priests', but as fine as wisps of silk, reaching almost to the hems of their black-and-jade brocade jackets.

"Please be seated, gentlemen." As Eugene sat down, he saw that one chair was still empty. "But where is the Smarnan ambassador?"

The representatives from the Muscobite Senate glanced uncertainly at one another.

"I will look into the matter straightaway," said Gustave, hastily making for the door.

"Remind me of the name of the Smarnan ambassador, First Minister," said Eugene, trying to hide his irritation.

"Garsevani," said Vassian. Silence followed. Eugene was in no mood to exchange pleasantries; he was still brooding on Doctor Arensky's bleak prognosis.

"While we wait for news of Ambassador Garsevani," Maltheus said tactfully, "perhaps we might call upon the Master of Ceremonies, Count Golitsyn, to talk us through the rehearsal plans for tomorrow?"

The count rose, bowed to Eugene, and began to read from a leather-bound notebook.

"At nine o'clock, the carriages will set off from the Winter Palace . . ."

Golitsyn, although renowned for having penned several successful comedies for the Mirom stage, spoke with a singularly flat and uninteresting drawl. Eugene half-listened, trying to keep his mind from wandering; he could not help noticing that the elderly Patriarch was nodding off, lulled by the count's dreary tones.

"And then, at midday," droned Golitsyn, "a twenty-gun salute will be fired from the Water Gate—"

The door opened and Gustave came back into the room. He had been absent for almost half an hour. The Patriarch started and opened his watery eyes, blinking.

"Forgive me, highness." Gustave was breathless, as if he had been running.

"Well, where is he?" Eugene demanded.

"It seems that Ambassador Garsevani has been recalled to Smarna."

"Recalled?" said Maltheus, one bristling eyebrow quirked.

Eugene said nothing. There could, of course, be a pressing personal reason for Garsevani's sudden departure.

"It would have been courteous to send word," said Golitsyn, "but then, the Smarnans . . ."

Maltheus pounced on this seemingly innocuous aside. "What gives the Smarnans the right to behave so discourteously to his imperial highness?"

Count Golitsyn turned slowly to him with a knowing smile and a shrug. "I've a little villa down there, on the coast. Always take my own staff with me; the locals are bone-lazy. Too hot, you see; they spend most of their time idling in the shade, drinking and arguing."

"So are no Smarnan dignitaries to attend the ceremony?" said Eugene, unwilling to let the matter rest.

Golitsyn clicked his fingers and his secretary handed him the ledger containing the list of guests. The count ran his finger down page after page, concluding his search with a little shrug.

"Not one?" Eugene insisted. "Not even one of the ministers?"

"Well, there is the Countess Tamara, but she is a Muscobite by birth."

Eugene glanced at Maltheus, who gave an almost imperceptible nod. This sudden disappearance of Ambassador Garsevani could be interpreted as a snub. He hoped it was not an ill omen. He turned to the Patriarch, forcing the matter from his mind.

"And now, your holiness, to the seating plan in the cathedral . . ."

*   *   *

"You delivered my gift to the altessa?" Eugene emerged from the meeting well over an hour later than he had planned.

"Just as you instructed, highness," said Gustave. "And I sent your apologies with it."

"My apologies?" And then Eugene remembered. "Tea." He struck his forehead with his hand in frustration. "Tea with the Grand Duchess. And if Garsevani hadn't played us all for fools—" He started out down the corridor with Gustave following after.

"And now the altessa is at a fitting for her wedding dress," panted Gustave.

Eugene stopped. "So when will she be free?"

"Not until you've left for the dinner at the Admiralty, highness."

And so another day would have passed without spending any time with her.

"What did she say to the gift?"

"She said it was very pretty." Gustave's tone was guarded.

"But did she try it on?"

"Not in my presence."

"Ah." Eugene turned and began to walk slowly back toward his apartments. Perhaps Astasia was not impressed or excited by jewels. He wanted to send something to apologize for his lack of attention. Something more personal than jewels.

"Violets," he said. "To match her eyes. Gustave, can you find a little bunch of violets, no matter what the cost, and deliver them to the altessa? I'll write a card to accompany them."

"Violets in winter?" The secretary shook his head in bewilderment.

"I place great faith in your ingenuity, Gustave," Eugene said with a smile.

"He may be a Tielen, but he has exquisite taste, Astasia." The Grand Duchess exclaimed in delight over the betrothal gifts that had been accumulating on Astasia's dressing table. Eugene had sent a new treasure every day: a diamond-and-sapphire necklace yesterday with matching drop earrings; today a string of amethysts fashioned like violets. Earlier presents included black pearls, a gold-and-amber jewelry casket, and crystal bottles of attar from rare black desert roses. "You're such a lucky girl."

"Yes, Mama," said Astasia listlessly. The gifts were expensive, true, and each piece of jewelry beautifully crafted. Yet her mother was far more excited about them than she; she found it difficult to show much enthusiasm about cold stones, even if they were worth a small fortune. Yet, if nothing else, they had brought a flush to her mother's wan cheeks and a brief sparkle to her eyes. Sofia still woke at night, breathless and terrified, shrieking for the guard to come to her rescue. And though Astasia had found her mother's moods overbearing at times in the past, she was secretly relieved to see glimpses of the haughty Grand Duchess returning again.

But these gifts . . . she picked up one after another and then set them down again on the marble-inlaid table. They told her nothing of the man she was to marry except that he was very wealthy. He had probably not even chosen the gifts himself, but ordered one of his imperial staff to select them.

How little I really know about you, Eugene.

"Tasia, if there's anything you need to ask me about your wedding night, now's the time, while we're alone," said Sofia suddenly.

Astasia felt her face flame with embarrassment.

"Really, Mama, I—"

"He's fathered a child, so I don't think you need have any worries in that area, although there were some whispers—slander, I'm sure—when he adopted that Arkhel boy from Azhkendir . . ."

Worse and worse! Astasia closed her eyes, praying that Mama would not rattle on like this in front of some Tielen dignitary at the wedding.

"My little girl's going to be a woman, a married woman." Sofia embraced Astasia, hugging her close as tears coursed down her cheeks. Astasia hugged her back, desperately trying to think of an excuse to get away before Sofia embarrassed her further with more talk of the wedding night.

There came a little tap at the salon door and Nadezhda popped her head around.

"A gift from his imperial highness," she announced.

"Ooh!" cried Sofia excitedly, clasping her hands together. "What will it be, Tasia? A little amethyst tiara would go well with the necklace. . . ."

Nadezhda came in and, demurely bobbing a curtsy, presented Astasia with a delicate lace-bound posy of violets and snowdrops.

"Oh," said Astasia, surprised. "Flowers. *Real* flowers." The little posy appealed to her so much that she pinned it to the shoulder of her dress.

It was the first gift he had sent her that touched her heart. Violets in winter.

CHAPTER 3

It was the last of the five rubies, crimson as Smarnan wine, cunningly fashioned by ancient craftsmen in the form of a teardrop.

The fifth tear of long-dead Emperor Artamon was about to be reunited with its fellows for the first time in centuries. And for the first time in centuries, one man had dared to fulfill his dreams of an empire. Eugene of Tielen had battled to reunite the five princedoms of Artamon's shattered empire—and had won.

The coronation was tomorrow. The Emperor had attended his final fitting some days before. Adjustments had been made. The imperial crown must be finished before dawn—and to that end, the best jewelers in Tielen had been shipped across the Straits to Mirom and installed under armed guard in the East Wing of the Winter Palace.

Paer Paersson, the master jeweler, worked late into the night with his craftsmen to complete the setting for the Orlov ruby: a golden sea eagle, wings outspread, claws open to clutch the stone to its breast.

All the jewelers and their apprentices stood waiting to witness the final moment in the creation of their new Emperor's crown. They had labored for months, fashioning the settings from the most precious of materials: gold, pearls, and exquisitely cut tiny diamonds.

Paer Paersson carefully lifted the ruby from its box and, with skilled fingers, placed it in its setting. The others fell silent, watching respectfully. Only the ticking of the ornate clock on the mantel could be heard.

With a final twist, the master jeweler gently fixed the stone in position. He placed the crown onto a cushion of rich purple velvet and set it on the table in front of him.

"At last," he said, letting out a long sigh. "Send word to his imperial highness. Tell him it is ready."

The youngest apprentice sped away across the courtyard toward the imperial apartments.

In the candlelight, the rich rubies glowed red. The craftsmen of the Jewelers' Guild stood admiring their masterpiece in reverent silence.

The rubies glowed more intensely. Paer Paersson took off his spectacles and rubbed his tired eyes. Even without his spectacles he could see that the glow from the gems was growing brighter. And he could sense a sound so low it was almost a vibration—as if a heavy carriage were passing across the courtyard.

"Master Paersson," whispered one of the other craftsmen. "What's happening?"

The vibration had become a low buzz. The louder it grew, the more the brightness of the rubies increased. Five lights, like bloodstained flames, burned at the heart of each teardrop stone.

"Have you ever seen the like?" Paer Paersson leaned closer. The buzzing grew louder, the flames burned more brightly.

"Move away, Master Paersson." The jewelers began to back toward the door, bumping into one another in their confusion. "For God's sake, move away!" But Paer could not move; fear and wonder held him bound to the spot.

The room glowed like a furnace—and the heart of the furnace was the imperial crown.

Eugene of Tielen hurried across the courtyard toward the jewelers' workshop. He was so eager to see Artamon's rubies in the finished crown that he had not waited for Paer Paersson to bring it to him, but had come himself.

Now he halted, seeing a red glow illuminating the windows of the workroom. Was the room ablaze? He could not discern any trace of smoke.

Puzzled, he pushed open the door. The youngest apprentice, following close on his heels, let out a yelp of terror.

Each of the five rubies in the imperial crown burned in its filigree settings. And a deep buzzing filled the room, notes of five low pitches twining about one another like the droning of a hive of bees.

"Stay back, highness," Paer Paersson warned.

"But this is quite extraordinary. Artamon's rubies . . . *alive.*" Eugene moved forward, ignoring Paer Paersson's warning. "One of you go and fetch the Magus." He had to raise his voice to make himself heard as the hum of the stones grew steadily louder.

Suddenly five jets of crimson light shot out, one from each ruby, arcing upward toward the ceiling.

Eugene sprang back, shading his eyes. The craftsmen cowered away, hiding their faces. The apprentices whimpered with fear.

The five shafts of ruby-fire meshed together, fusing into a single column of light.

It pierced the ceiling of the craftsmen's workroom like a spear.

Eugene ran out into the courtyard, gazing up into the black of the night sky. The rubies' spearshaft of light went shooting upward into the starry heavens like a blood-streaked comet, illuminating the pale stones and columns of the Winter Palace in its glow. For a moment the stars themselves were stained red, as though with blood.

Servants and troopers of the Household Cavalry slowly gathered in the courtyard in awestruck silence.

And then—as suddenly as it had begun—the light died. The night air was chill, clear, and silent—except for the hushed murmurings of Eugene's astonished household.

Eugene stood staring up at the empty sky. The stars glittered again, cold and white-blue as the tiny diamonds Paer Paersson had cut for his crown.

A man appeared silently beside him in the darkness. And even in the uncertain starlight the prince sensed that it was Kaspar Linnaius, Magus and Royal Artificier. Eugene beckoned him to a secluded corner where they could not be overheard.

"Well, Magus?" he said quietly. "What does it mean?"

"In all truth, highness," came back the Magus's voice, calm and distant, "I do not know. I have never seen its like before. Perhaps we may take it as a good omen? A blessing from Artamon, bestowed on the first man great enough to restore his broken empire?"

"Oh come now, Linnaius, you know I am not in the least superstitious. You may circulate this pretty myth, if you wish, to reassure my people . . . but I need answers. Scientific answers." He approached the master jeweler. "Paer, is this the first time you have witnessed this phenomenon?"

Paer Paersson nodded his head, evidently still too shaken to speak.

"And perhaps the last," Eugene said pensively. "Linnaius, speak to our archivists in the morning. Send scholars out to all five prince-doms. I want to know if such a thing ever happened in Artamon's reign. I want to know the history of the rubies. I want this thoroughly researched."

The alarm bell of Kastel Drakhaon clanged out a frantic warning, shattering the night.

Gavril Nagarian clambered up the broken tower stairs, one pre-carious step at a time. Bogatyr Askold followed close behind.

The Kalika Tower had taken its share of the bombardment during the siege. Ragged holes gaped in the walls, letting in the cold night air. Yet still it stood, Volkh's tower, where other sturdier watchtowers had fallen in the attack.

Gavril reached the top and pushed open the door that led out onto the roof.

"What new mischief can it be this time?" grumbled Askold as they scanned the darkened horizon.

Below, servants and *druzhina* came hurrying out into the court-yard, pointing to the heavens.

A distant column of fiery light, thin as a scarlet thread, pierced the dark skies to the east. The crystalline brilliance of the constellations overhead flushed red as blood.

In that moment, it felt as if the fiery bolt of light speared Gavril's brain and a current of energy shivered through his mind. He strove to speak, but his tongue was frozen.

"What d'you mean, dragging us all from our warm beds for this, Semyon?" Sosia, the kastel housekeeper, chided. "It's just the north-ern lights, you silly boy!"

"I've never seen 'em burn bloodred before," muttered Askold at Gavril's side.

And just as suddenly as the column of light had appeared, it van-ished, leaving the stars sparkling diamond-clear above their heads.

"What d'you think it was, Drakhaon?" said Askold. "Some new Tielen weapon?"

"I don't know." Gavril found he had regained the power of speech.

His head cleared. "But whatever it was, we should stay on our guard. Eugene of Tielen won't forgive us so easily for defeating him."

Kiukiu was helping Lady Elysia sort through a pile of sheets and blankets that had been dug out from the rubble when the alarm bell began to clang—a harsh, terrifying sound in the cold of the night.

"Now whatever can the matter be?" Lady Elysia let drop the blanket she was mending and went to the window, raising the oiled cloth that had been nailed across the frame to keep out the worst of the drafts.

Kiukiu heard running feet, *druzhina* and servants calling out to one another. She could not move. *Please let it not be the Tielens,* she prayed silently.

"What *is* that light?" said Lady Elysia, peering out, her voice hushed with wonder.

Kiukiu went to get up and join her at the window—and her mind was suddenly filled with voices, children's voices, all screaming out in terror. "Oh," she whispered. "Who *are* you?"

She stands gazing out at a great expanse of moving water, bluer than Lake Ilmin. Children surround her, pulling at her hands, her clothes, their eyes wide with fear and despair.

"Help us, Spirit Singer. Set us free."

"I—I can't. There are so many of you . . . and I don't even know your names."

As she gazes at their pale, dead faces she sees that each child bears a red, ragged knife-wound across the throat. Horror numbs her. Who could have done such a terrible thing to these innocent children?

And then she senses she is being watched. Turning slowly, she sees a tall figure behind her, clothed in glittering darkness. It is watching her with two luminous eyes as slanted and strange as the Drakhaoul's— and a third eye, crimson as a bloodstained flame, burns on its forehead. And such a feeling of dread overcomes her that she cannot back away, even though every instinct tells her she must flee.

The children cry out again, clustering around her, clinging to her in fear.

"Please help us."

"Kiukiu." Someone was calling her name. The blue water faded from her sight, the children's piteous pleading grew fainter until she blinked and found herself gazing into Lady Elysia's anxious face.

"Are you all right, Kiukiu?"

Kiukiu nodded. She felt a little sick and disoriented. "What happened?"

"You fainted. Sit up slowly. That's right. Luckily the blankets cushioned your fall."

"I'm sorry." What must Lady Elysia think of her? "Sometimes I . . ."

Elysia nodded. "Gavril has told me of your gift. What did you see? Does it help to talk about it?"

Kiukiu hugged her arms about her body; she felt cold now, chilled to the bones. "Sometimes I hear echoes from long ago in the kastel. The stones remember . . ."

On a dark, lonely shore far from Mirom, Andrei lay asleep on a straw pallet in the fisherman's cottage.

A sudden spearshaft of light pierced his dreams, coloring them red as spilled blood.

He gave a cry and sat bolt upright.

It must be a flare, sent up by a ship in distress.

"Ship on the rocks!" Still half-asleep, he fumbled his way to the doorway and stared out into the night, scanning the empty sea.

A flaming column stretched from earth into the heavens on the distant horizon, staining the black sea red. A rushing sound suddenly filled his ears, as if a crowd of midges were swarming in his brain. Little flashes of fiery light flickered across his vision. His head spun.

"That's no distress flare." Kuzko, his voice thick with sleep, appeared behind him.

Andrei struggled to reply. Words tried to force themselves from his mouth, but when they came out, they seemed meaningless.

"Nagar's—Eye," he heard himself stammer. "Take—me—*home*."

"Yes, lad." Kuzko's hand came down on his shoulder. "And if only you could remember where home was, we'd get you back to your folks on the next spring tide."

And then the fiery column disappeared, as swiftly as if it were a snuffed-out candleflame.

Andrei blinked, rubbed his eyes. He turned to Kuzko.

"What did I say?"

"Take me home," repeated Kuzko.

"Before that."

"A place name, maybe. Not one I recognized. Nagar's Eye. Is that where you hail from, Andrei?"

Andrei shook his head. The name meant nothing to him. And the disappointment now seemed almost too great to bear. For a moment it seemed as if his memory had been unlocked. But whatever had been awakened by the fiery column had been just as swiftly extinguished.

Kuzko uncorked a stone bottle of spirits; he swallowed a swift mouthful, then passed it to Andrei.

"I've little enough left, but you look as if you could do with it, lad. Take a good swig. It'll help you sleep."

Astasia fretted on the foggy quayside, shivering in her warmest fur-lined cloak. She was waiting to welcome Karila and her entourage to Mirom.

Their arrival had been delayed because of the little princess's sudden indisposition. Her Great-Aunt Greta, the Dowager Duchess of Haeven, had sent a message to say that she had delayed the voyage of the royal barque because Karila had developed a nasty cough on the journey down from the Palace of Swanholm. And then they had encountered sea fog in the Straits.

It was strange, Astasia reflected, that she was soon to be stepmother to Karila, when their relationship was more akin to that of older and younger sisters. She had always dreamed of having a younger sister to play with, but Mama had never been robust enough to produce another child.

Palace servants brought a brazier of slow-burning coals and Astasia gratefully held her frozen hands to the warmth.

Wisps of fog began to roll across the city; the lanterns on the rigging of the great ships dimmed.

"You mustn't stay out here any longer," whispered Nadezhda. "You'll catch your death of cold. We can't have you sneezing your way through the service tomorrow. Just imagine—when his highness raises your wedding veil, he's not going to want to see a red nose and be greeted with a sneeze, is he?"

Astasia could not help smiling in spite of the cold. "But I must be here to welcome Karila to Mirom."

"Welcome her inside the palace, in front of a large log fire," insisted Nadezhda.

"Royal barque approaching!" came a shout from the lookout to the members of the new imperial bodyguard.

"At last," whispered Astasia, relieved that her freezing wait was nearly over.

Princess Karila's little entourage had just begun to disembark at the River Gate outside the Winter Palace when the night sky was pierced by a brilliant beam of fire.

"Holy saints preserve us!" Nadezhda hastily made the sign to avert evil. "It's not those insurgents again, trying to burn the palace?"

Astasia gazed up at the crimsoned stars. She had never seen anything like this before. It was at once strikingly beautiful, and oddly disturbing. . . .

Karila, muffled up in her fur-lined cloak, hat, and mittens, waited dutifully on deck with Great-Aunt Greta for the sailors to lower the gangplank onto the quay.

She had never made such a long journey away from Swanholm before.

"There's the Winter Palace, my dear, where we'll be staying," said Great-Aunt Greta, her breath issuing from her mouth in frosty clouds.

A spear of fire suddenly shot up into the night sky.

Karila gave a sharp cry. It was as if the crimson spear had pierced her throat. A wash of blood began to drip down from the wound, tingeing the whole world fiery red.

She dropped to her knees as a swirl of violent and incomprehensible images glittered and shifted in her mind.

An indigo sea washes onto a bone-white seashore . . .

"Whatever's wrong, child?" Great-Aunt Greta gripped hold of her and tried to pull her back to her feet.

Her throat felt as if it were choked with blood. She tried to speak, but all that came out was coughing.

The sailors on the Tielen royal barque had abandoned their tasks and were pointing up at the sky.

"Back to work!" shouted a military voice impatiently. "Have you never seen fireworks before?" It was a lieutenant of the imperial bodyguard, although from his accent, Astasia recognized him as a fellow countryman.

"Fireworks?" she repeated.

"I'll wager it's a rehearsal for tomorrow's celebrations by the Royal Artificier and his aides, highness. I—"

A shrill cry interrupted his words.

"Help! The princess!"

Forgetting decorum, Astasia gathered up her skirts and ran across the frosty cobbles toward the Tielen royal party, Nadezhda and the lieutenant hurrying after her.

As Astasia came closer, she could hear the dry, insistent sound of a child coughing. "What's wrong?" she asked, peering into the lantern-light. The coughing went on, rasping and painful.

"I said we should have stayed in Tielen," fretted an elderly voice, "but she was so insistent."

"Kari?" Astasia asked anxiously. The huddle of maidservants parted to let her through. She saw the elderly Dowager Duchess Greta supporting a hunched little form that shuddered and strained to draw breath.

"Ta— sia—" The child tried to say her name, but only began to cough again.

"We must get her indoors at once." Astasia went to pick up the little girl herself, but the young lieutenant gallantly stepped in and swung the princess up into his arms.

"I said the weather was too foggy, but she was so eager to come." The dowager duchess sounded as if she was at her wit's end as she followed the lieutenant to the River Gate where a carriage was waiting to drive them into the palace.

"When did this sickness begin?" Astasia offered her arm to the dowager duchess, who leaned on her heavily as they crossed the quay.

"Well, my dear, it's always a little difficult to tell with Karila; you know she's a sickly child. But this latest ailment has the royal physicians baffled."

Eugene looked down at his daughter as the Orlov's physician examined her. He tried not to breathe in a halting, sympathetic rhythm; he tried not to wince as the physician's sharp fingers tapped at the thin, misshapen back. Karila endured it all without complaint. Perhaps she was too tired to complain, or perhaps this had just become a normal part of her life.

"Papa," croaked Karila at last. Her hand rose, seeking his.

"Here I am." He took her hand and sat on the bed beside her.

"I can still be Tasia's bridesmaid tomorrow, can't I?" Blue eyes looked imploringly into his. He glanced up at the physician and saw him gravely shake his head.

"We'll see how you are in the morning, Kari." He kissed her flushed cheek. "Now you must rest."

Outside in the dressing room, he faced the Orlov's physician. He had heard plenty of Tielen doctors prognosticate gloomily since Karila's birth nearly eight years ago. He was hoping that a fresh opinion might offer hope of different treatments, different cures.

"Well?" he said, trying not to sound too hopeful.

The Orlov's physician took off his spectacles and rubbed his eyes wearily. He seemed to be searching for the right words.

"Imperial highness," he said eventually, "your daughter is very sick."

"Karila has never been well." Eugene tried to keep his temper in check.

"The malformation of her spine has compressed her rib cage, making it difficult for the lungs to expand—"

"Yes, yes. All this is well-documented."

"But her present malady is unusual, highness. It has all the signs of a kind of wasting sickness. But a wasting sickness unlike any other I have encountered in Mirom."

"Unusual?" The word carried a weight of warning. "How so?"

The court physician hesitated again. "Your highness will forgive me, but the reputation of the alchymical weapons employed by your army has reached to all parts of your empire. Is there any way the princess might have inhaled some noxious fumes?"

"Certainly not!" The answer was out of Eugene's mouth before he had stopped to think if the physician's suggestion could be in any way possible. Karila was fascinated by Kaspar Linnaius, but the Magus would never have allowed her anywhere near his laboratory when he was experimenting. No, there had to be some other explanation. "So what can you do for her?" he asked curtly.

"I can burn soothing vapors near her pillow to loosen the tightness in her breathing. And I shall prescribe some nourishing oils to build up her strength."

"But the prognosis—"

"Is not good."

"Papa . . ." The hoarse little voice called from the bedchamber.

Eugene hurried back to her bedside to see her sitting up, clutching the sheets to her.

"You must lie down, Kari. Try to sleep."

"They said it was fireworks, Papa, but it wasn't fireworks." She sank back on the pillows. "It was a dragon-path. Through the sky."

He felt a sudden chill. Karila and her dragons. At first he had thought she would grow out of her obsessive interest. But when the Drakhaon had invaded Swanholm, she had fearlessly confronted it. She had spoken with it. There was—though he had no idea why—a connection between them.

"A dragon-path, Kari?" he asked.

"To show . . . the way home." Her lids slowly closed; her voice faded.

He stood staring at her as she drifted into sleep, desperate to question her. Was it just some fancy of her fever, this dragon-path? Or was there some deeper revelation concealed in her drowsy words?

As he walked away from her bedchamber, he heard the dull strokes of the great bells at Saint Simeon's Cathedral striking midnight. The coronation would take place in twelve hours.

He must force his worries from his mind; his love for Karila made him vulnerable. Prince Eugene could afford to be indulgent toward his only child. Emperor Eugene of New Rossiya could not.

CHAPTER 4

The day of the coronation-wedding dawned bitterly cold and grey. But Astasia had been up long before dawn, submitting herself to the ministrations of her attendants, while ladies of the Mirom and Tielen courts gossiped and preened in the anteroom. Eupraxia was supervising her *toilette,* aided by Nadezhda and Astasia's maid of honor, Lady Varvara Ilyanova, the dowager countess's granddaughter and Astasia's closest friend since childhood. Varvara had recently returned to Mirom from the city of Bel'Esstar, bringing exquisite ivory lace for the wedding gown.

"You look so pale, Tasia," she said as Nadezhda laced Astasia into the gown. She leaned forward and playfully pinched her cheeks.

"Ow!" Astasia slapped at Varvara's fingers. "What's that for?"

"To give you some natural color. Eupraxia won't allow rouge, will you, Praxia?"

"Certainly not," Eupraxia said through a mouthful of hairpins. "Rouge is for ladies of easy virtue—and actresses." Her governess's cheeks were flushed already, Astasia noticed, and little pearls of perspiration dewed her cheeks and upper lip. Poor Praxia. All this was too much for her.

"All the ladies at Ilsevir's court are using it in Bel'Esstar," Varvara continued, her brown eyes glinting mischievously. "I have a pot or two here in my reticule. See? This one is called 'Pouting Pomegranate' . . . and this, 'Carnal Caress'—"

Eupraxia choked and spat out the hairpins onto her palm. "Enough, Varvara!"

In spite of herself, Astasia felt a smile begin to break through.

"That's better," cried Varvara gaily.

"Such a pity the little princess is not well enough to attend the ceremony," said Eupraxia, fixing the pearl-and-diamond wedding tiara in place in Astasia's dark curls.

"She'll be so disappointed." Astasia had been to check on Karila's progress and had been told the princess was sleeping. Poor little Kari, brought all the way across the Straits, only to fall ill on the eve of the festivities.

Astasia rode to the cathedral with her father, Grand Duke Aleksei, in the ceremonial Orlov carriage. The old carriage had escaped the rioters' wrath, and the proud sea eagles that perched on each of the four corners of the roof had been regilded to glitter in the foggy morning.

The great square around Saint Simeon's Cathedral was filled with row upon row of uniformed soldiers. Behind the ranks of grey-clad Tielen troops and White Guards of Muscobar, Astasia saw the people of Mirom, her people, silently huddled together, muffled up in greatcoats and fur hats against the cold. No one cheered. They just stared. Astasia pulled her white velvet cloak closer. Their silence was frightening.

They still hate us. They will always hate us.

Candles burned in every niche of the cathedral. The dull gold of the screen of icons around the altar gleamed like a winter sunset, sun sinking beneath lowering clouds.

Astasia was hastily ushered into a side chapel, away from the echoing murmur of the eminent wedding guests thronging the aisles. Dark-painted icons of haloed saints stared down at her, their faces emaciated, their eyes wild with holy revelations. The richly dressed courtiers of the new empire seemed small and unimportant beneath their stern gaze.

A glowing coal brazier gave off thin blue smoke, a welcome heat in the chilly cathedral. Astasia held her numb fingers to the glow to try to restore some feeling, as her bridesmaids crowded around, fastening then straightening the gold and lace train of her gown.

"Ready, my dear?" inquired the Grand Duke.

A last, wild desire to fling down her bouquet and run from the cathedral overwhelmed her. And then she looked into her father's eyes and saw a look she had never seen before: a look of pride, mingled with bitter resignation. He was a broken man, crushed by this double defeat. She could not run away now. She could not let him down.

"You are the last of the Orlovs," he said, leaning forward to kiss her forehead. She smelled spirit on his breath; he had needed courage to appear in public today and hand his daughter and country over to this foreign invader.

"Oh, Papa," she whispered, squeezing his hand.

A choir began to sing as Astasia appeared. Boys' voices soared into the echoing dome like a flight of white doves.

Flowers spilled from urns and gilded baskets: hothouse roses in white and gold, myrtles and lilies with their orange-stamened hearts. But the sweet scent of the flowers was swamped by the overpowering bitterness of incense billowing from swinging censers. Venerable, bearded priests, white-garbed for the wedding, mumbled prayers in every side chapel Astasia and her entourage passed.

He looks utterly confident, Astasia thought as Prince Eugene took his place before the altar, beside her. *But then, this is not the first time he has been married. . . .*

The choir finished their anthem. In the silence, the guests coughed and shuffled their feet.

The elderly Patriarch Ilarion, who had been standing near the altar, tottered forward to greet the bride and her father. A group of young girls standing by with baskets of rose petals ready to scatter, hurried to their places. The choir began the epithalamium and, before Astasia knew what was happening, Patriarch Ilarion had placed her hand in Eugene's and was pronouncing the words that made them man and wife before God. She could not even remember whispering, "I take thee, Eugene . . ." She could only remember gazing, mesmerized, into his grey-blue eyes.

And now he was leaning forward to kiss her. She could not, dared not, flinch away this time. She steeled herself. His hands were warm and firm on her shoulders as he drew her toward him. How strong he was. She shivered and closed her eyes as his mouth touched hers.

After, she found herself looking up into Eugene's eyes and saw that they burned with emotion. The intensity of his gaze made her forget the red, scarred skin that marred his face. No one had looked at her in that way before.

"Now you are mine, Astasia. You need never fear for your safety again," he said softly, each word charged with the same intensity of feeling that she saw in his eyes. "I will protect you."

And then he turned to present her to the congregation. She glimpsed her mother and Eupraxia sobbing into their lace handkerchiefs. Even Varvara was wiping away a tear.

I am his wife. Soon we shall have to do more than kiss. . . .

The thought sent a shiver through her whole body. How could she think of such a thing in the cathedral!

Eugene led her to the ceremonial throne beside his and, as her maids rearranged her heavy train, she sat down. Then he took the imperial crown from the shaking hands of the Patriarch and raised it high over his own head, then slowly lowered it until it rested on his burned scalp.

Trumpets blazed triumphant fanfares from all corners of the cathedral.

And as Astasia watched, she thought she saw a faint glow of fire radiating from the Emperor. Though it might have been caused by a sudden ray of sunlight penetrating the gloomy cathedral, catching light in the crimson depths of the five Tears of Artamon. . . .

Great tiered chandeliers—hastily imported from Tielen—lit the Hall of Black Marble with waterfalls of crystal light. Eugene had ordered an army of craftsmen to restore this room in the Winter Palace first so that he might officially receive the overtures of goodwill from the many foreign ambassadors and politicians who had attended his wedding and coronation.

Lavish refreshments had been provided: silver trays of glossy caviar piled on sparkling crushed ice were being carried around to the eminent guests. Eugene had decreed that the food and wines should represent the best each of the five princedoms could produce. All kinds of smoked and pickled fish delicacies represented Tielen: from pike and sturgeon to eel and river trout, all served on little squares of rich black bread with sour cream. Muscobar provided the finest vodka to drink with the caviar. Rich Smarnan wines were offered with rolled slices of dried beef, olives marinated in fiery oil, or little cakes of honey and nuts. But Khitari had supplied the most exotic selection; Khan Khalien had sent five of his most skilled cooks to prepare the dishes and, in their emerald brocade jackets and tasseled hats, they were exciting as much comment from the guests as the delicious spicy parcels and crisp crackers they had cooked. Only Azhkendir was poorly represented: All that could be found in the food halls of the Muscobar merchants were a few barrels of salted herrings and some jars of cloudberries and lingonberries from the moors. Eugene's chefs had avoided the herrings and, displaying considerable culinary imagination, had popped the berries into tiny shells of almond tuile, subtly adding florets of liqueur-flavored cream.

"It's hard to imagine any dish less representative of that harsh, barbaric country," Eugene heard Chancellor Maltheus declare as he crunched one of the dainty tartlets.

"May I offer my congratulations, imperial highness?" A tall man of distinguished bearing placed one hand on his heart and inclined his head in a brief bow.

"His excellency, Fabien d'Abrissard, the Francian ambassador," Chancellor Maltheus said, shooting Eugene a significant look from beneath his bushy brows. Relations between Francia and Tielen had been chilly since Eugene's father Karl had defeated a Francian invasion fleet some twenty-five years before.

"Let us hope," Eugene said smoothly, "that this heralds a new relationship between Francia and New Rossiya."

"Indeed," said Abrissard, equally smoothly, "Francia is most eager to place our relationship on a different—"

"Imperial highness!" A veiled woman suddenly pushed through the throng. "I come to beg for your protection, imperial highness!"

Instantly Eugene's bodyguard surrounded her.

She was dressed in widow's black, her rich chestnut hair bound back in a severe chignon. In her arms she carried a baby, an infant of no more than four or five months old.

Eugene saw—to his acute embarrassment—Fabien d'Abrissard raise one elegant eyebrow at this intrusion. Did the ambassador think the child was his?

"Protection for my son, whose father was killed in the recent war in Azhkendir." The woman's voice throbbed with emotion; he saw courtiers standing close by glance uneasily at one another.

"Lilias Arbelian," Chancellor Maltheus murmured in his ear. "One of Velemir's agents."

Eugene frowned. How had she gained admission to this prestigious reception without an invitation? And was the child another of Velemir's bastards?

"Award her an army widow's pension, Maltheus. The usual arrangement." He made to move on.

"Only now, imperial highness, can I tell the truth." She lifted her child, drawing back the delicate lace shawl from his little face. "This is Artamon Arkhel—Lord Jaromir's son."

A lightning flash of memory flung Eugene back to a bare wintry hillside in Azhkendir. Jaromir Arkhel gazed at him, asking eagerly, "Lilias? And the child? Are they safe?"

Blinking back sudden, unbidden tears, he put out his undamaged hand to touch the soft cheek of the little child.

"*His* son?" The baby's fine wisps of hair glinted gold, dark Arkhel gold in the candlelight.

He became vaguely aware that Maltheus was whispering, "She's an adventuress, highness. She was Velemir's mistress, then Volkh's. Don't trust her. . . ."

He did not trust her word—but he trusted Jaromir's. In all the bitter ashes of loss, one faint hope suddenly glimmered. He could not bring his dearest Jaromir back to life—but he could care for his son, and ensure that the boy's rightful inheritance was restored.

A plan began to form in his mind. Now that he was crowned Emperor, it was time to bring Azhkendir to heel.

"You presume much, Madame Arbelian, in giving your son an imperial name. Choose him an Arkhel name instead, and I will see you both want for nothing."

"Then let him be called Stavyomir," she answered, unabashed, "after his grandfather, Stavyor."

Eugene laid his hand on the baby's golden head. "I rename you Stavyomir Arkhel." The child did not whimper or flinch at his touch, but stared back at him with wide, wondering blue eyes. *Your father should be here at my side, little one, to share in the victory celebrations. His death will not go unavenged.*

"I must confess myself a little surprised not to encounter any delegation from Azhkendir at the celebrations," said Fabien d'Abrissard. "Until now," he added, gazing after Lilias Arbelian as she was ushered away by red-faced palace officials. He turned back to Eugene. "Indeed, rumor has it, imperial highness, that the Drakhaon and his household are still defying your claim to his kingdom."

How like a Francian to make such a malicious—yet apt—little dig in front of so many illustrious guests. Eugene stared levelly back at Fabien d'Abrissard, refusing to allow his indignation at the ambassador's insolent observation to show.

"I can assure you, ambassador," he said, "that the Drakhaon no longer presents any threat to the stability of the empire."

"And the atrocious weather conditions in Azhkendir have prevented Lord Stoyan from attending the ceremony," Chancellor Maltheus put in hastily. "Let me introduce you, ambassador, to . . ."

As Maltheus led the ambassador away, Eugene beckoned to Lieutenant Petter, his newly appointed aide. "Ask Field Marshal Karonen to attend me in my study," he said softly. "I have urgent instructions for the Northern Army."

"Return to Kastel Drakhaon, imperial highness?" Field Marshal Karonen looked at Eugene, his pepper-and-salt brows raised in an expression of incredulity.

"I learned some weeks ago from a secret source," Eugene said, rather relishing the dour Karonen's reaction, "that Gavril Nagarian has lost that certain advantage he held over us. I've been biding my time, Karonen, waiting for the right moment to crush that rebellious little country. And now that moment has come. The heir to the Arkhel lands was here, in the palace, tonight. Lord Jaromir's son."

Karonen's brows shot up again. "He sired a son?"

"His mother managed to smuggle him safely out of Azhkendir. She brought him here." That wispy hair of dark gold, those wide blue eyes, were all that he had left to remind him of slain Jaromir, who had been dearer to him than any brother. "It's time the Arkhels were restored as the rulers of Azhkendir and Clan Nagarian toppled from power." As he spoke, Eugene realized that he had been waiting for this opportunity a long time. "How soon can you mobilize your men?"

"The Northern Army is stationed on the border between Muscobar and Azhkendir." Karonen pointed to the map spread out over Eugene's desk. "The weather's still pretty chilly up there. No sign of a thaw yet."

"Issue extra winter rations, new boots, and gloves—and fire-sticks." Eugene felt the same glow of power and confidence he had experienced in the cathedral earlier that day. "This mission takes priority."

"And my orders?"

"Arrest Gavril Nagarian. I want him alive, Karonen. I want him to stand trial here in Muscobar so that the whole world can hear of his crimes against us and our empire."

Varvara and Nadezhda set to work to release Astasia from the tight lacing of her wedding dress. In the anteroom, the flower girls—the daughters of the noble houses of Tielen and Muscobar—chattered and giggled together, eating little quince jellies flavored with rose or lavender, and sipping sparkling wine. They were waiting for the next part of the ceremony, the singing of the traditional bridal song as the Emperor was brought to the Empress in the bridal chamber.

Eupraxia and Grand Duchess Sofia, exhausted by the long day's excitements, both reclined on velvet chaise longues, resting their swollen feet. Sofia's maid had brought a silver tray of little delicacies from the reception, as well as a crystal bowl of fruit punch, and the elder ladies were sampling the sweetmeats with enthusiasm.

Astasia let out a slow sigh of relief as the lacing was undone and layer after layer of frothy lace and sleek satin slid down about her ankles.

"My ribs ache from all that whalebone," she said, drawing in a deep breath without constraint for the first time since dawn.

"But you looked exquisite," said Varvara, stroking her cheek.

"These little almond biscuits are delicious," said Sofia, reaching for another.

"How clever of the pastrycooks to shape them into the emblems of the five princedoms," said Eupraxia, nibbling the sugared head of a swan.

"Eugene has such excellent taste," Sofia said, dipping her biscuit in her glass of punch. "Didn't he choose my lovely daughter as his bride?"

"Oh, Mama." Astasia hoped her mother was not going to start weeping again. She was apprehensive enough about her bridal night without having to deal with Sofia's emotions as well.

"Come and give your mother a kiss."

Astasia dutifully bent down to be smothered in her mother's perfume-scented embrace.

"I promised I'd pay a call on Karila, to see how she's faring," she said, extricating herself from her mother's arms.

"That poor, sickly little mite," said Sofia, dabbing at her eyes. "You'll give the Emperor strong children, healthy children, my dear. A son!"

Astasia fled, making toward the suite of rooms where Karila and her entourage had been installed.

Guards of the new Imperial Household Cavalry were posted at every door, staircase, and corridor. Eugene had decreed that the safety of the imperial family was of paramount importance, so she made slow progress, as every guard saluted her.

"Don't announce me," she whispered to the guard at Karila's door. "The princess may be asleep and I don't want to disturb her."

He nodded and quietly opened the door for her. In the anteroom, the Dowager Duchess Greta dozed in a chair beside the crackling fire. The bedroom door was ajar and, as Astasia tiptoed closer, she heard a man's voice.

". . . and then the Swan Maiden flew down to the prince's side. Spreading her snow-white wings, she spun around—and he saw she was no longer a swan, but a beautiful princess . . ."

The Emperor was reading his daughter a story. She could just see his burned head leaning close to Kari's golden curls as she snuggled up to him, gazing at the pictures in the book of fairy tales.

A feeling of shame overcame her. Karila didn't notice her father's disfigurement—or if she did, it was irrelevant to her. She saw only the father who loved her enough to find time to read a bedtime story on the day of his coronation. Yet she, his bride-to-be, had almost pulled away the first time he kissed her, partly out of fear that she might cause him hurt, partly out of an instinctive revulsion she could not repress. And she knew he had sensed her hesitation.

Now she felt as if she were intruding on a rare snatched moment of intimacy between father and child and was just about to creep away when Karila said drowsily, "You like that story too, don't you, Tasia?"

Eugene looked up and saw her. He looked surprised.

"I just came to see how Karila is—" she began.

"The doctors say she needs her rest," said Eugene, smiling at Astasia over Karila's head.

"I'm not at all sleepy, Papa."

"Sleepy or not, no more stories tonight."

With a sigh, Karila let herself be tucked in and kissed good-night. "You kiss me too, Tasia," she commanded in a croaky voice.

Astasia kissed her cheek and felt the heat emanating from the little body. The fever had not yet broken.

"Must be up early," murmured the child into her pillow, "to get ready . . . for the wedding. . . ."

Astasia met Eugene's gaze as she rose from the bedside. She saw him silently shake his head.

They went out into the anteroom where the dowager duchess still slept, her mouth slightly open, emitting the gentlest of snores.

"You saw how she didn't protest once?" Eugene said, keeping his voice low. "If she were well, she'd have demanded another story, and then another."

"I know," she said, remembering Karila's eager appetite at Swanholm. His concern for Karila touched her heart and she found she had drawn a little closer to him.

"Astasia!" The dowager duchess was awake. "Eugene! Do you young people have no respect for the old customs?" Astasia hastily moved away. "The bridegroom must be brought to his bride in the bridal chamber. And the flower girls must sing the wedding song; they've been practicing it for days."

Astasia knew she was blushing and was annoyed with herself. Yet when she glanced sideways at Eugene, she saw he looked as discomfited as she, almost like an overgrown schoolboy caught in midprank.

The sweet voices of the flower girls faded as they went singing down the echoing corridor, leaving Astasia and Eugene alone together for the first time. Astasia knelt down on the flower-strewn carpet and let some of the white petals drift through her fingers.

"Orange blossoms at the end of winter," she said wonderingly. "Even my father's gardeners have not achieved such a thing in the hothouse at Erinaskoe."

Eugene smiled, glad that his little surprise had pleased her. He excused himself and went into his dressing room to change out of his wedding clothes. When he came out again, he saw Astasia gulping down a glass of sweet musk wine.

Is she so terrified of what is to come that she has to fortify herself with wine?

With her dark hair unbound about her shoulders and her dark eyes gazing uncertainly at him, she could not have looked more different from golden-haired Margret. And the scent of her skin was different, exuding a cool, clear perfume that reminded him of bluebell woods in spring. Then he checked himself. What was he doing? He had vowed he would not let himself think of Margret tonight.

Astasia silently offered him a glass of wine. He drank it straight down. When he looked at her again, he saw she was shivering in her thin silk-and-lace nightgown.

"Come closer to the fire," he said, reaching out to her. "You're cold as ice." He took both her hands in his own and rubbed them to warm them, as he would have done for Karila.

"It always feels damp on this side of the palace, even in summer," she said. He could hear her teeth chattering. "I th-think it's the river."

"I will have my craftsmen take a look." Gently, he pulled her closer to him in the fire's flickering shadows. "Drafts and damp can be fixed." She did not resist, but rested against him so that he could feel her slender body shaking with cold . . . and apprehension. "They drained marshlands to build Swanholm, so they are skilled in these matters." He talked on about Swanholm, saying nothing of great importance, just talking until he sensed her begin to relax a little in his arms. She could not know that he was as apprehensive as she— maybe more so. It was not that she did not excite him; now that he held her close, it was that no matter how hard he tried, he could not keep the images of another bridal night, nearly nine years ago, from returning to haunt him.

"Don't be frightened," he said into the softness of her dark hair.

"I'm not," she said a little indignantly.

Margret had gently teased him until the awkwardness of their first night together had melted into laughter. But Astasia still seemed in awe of him, reluctant to respond to his caresses. Had some malicious Tielen courtier insinuated that he pined for Margret, that she could never replace her in his heart?

Or was she repelled by his injuries?

He swept her up in his arms and carried her to the great swagged bed, with its garlands of flowers. He would prove to her that he had banished the ghosts of his past.

He would prove it to himself.

CHAPTER 5

Gavril stumbles on across a hot, dark shore. Stars gleam red over-head, unfamiliar constellations, half-obscured by poisonous fogs.

Every step burns the soles of his bare feet. The air stinks of sul-phur; every breath he draws in sears his mouth, his throat, his lungs. In the distance, a cone of fire simmers; choking fumes and vapors drift past. Glossy foliage drips moisture onto the grey, glittering vol-canic sand.

The ground shudders beneath his burned feet, pitching him for-ward into the sand. The sea is sucked back from the shore. He can see it, boiling and churning, building high into one vast tidal wave that will sweep in with the next tremor and drown him—

Gavril woke with a start. But all he could see were the lime-washed walls of his bedchamber, white in the first light of dawn. He was soaked in sweat as if he really had been trapped on a burning shore by a volcanic eruption.

Since the night of the column of fire, the dreams had begun. They were always the same, always leaving him with the same sick, de-spairing feeling that tainted his waking hours.

Drakhaoul . . .

They had been one. They had thought and acted as one to defend Azhkendir. But at such a terrible cost to his own humanity that he had torn the dragon-daemon from deep within him and cast it out. Was this sultry volcanic shore the place it had ended its whirlwind flight? Was this the last it had seen of this world as it slowly, pain-fully, faded from existence?

"Ahh, Gavril . . ."
He could still hear its last harrowing cry.
It was the last of its kind. And I destroyed it.

Ever since the horrors of the Tielen invasion, Gavril had slept badly. During the day he worked alongside his men to repair the kastel, hauling stone, timber, and slate, laboring hard to repair the damage inflicted by Eugene's army. He pushed himself to the limits of his physical resources, scraping the skin from his knuckles, straining muscles till they ached.

He told himself that he was doing it to help his people—but in the darkest depths of his heart he knew he worked himself to the point of exhaustion day after day to try to forget the terrible things he had done when the Drakhaoul possessed him.

Only one of the kastel staff eluded him: Kiukiu.

Did she feel ill at ease in the Nagarian household now that she knew she was of Arkhel kin? Or did she—at some deep, wordless level—fear him for the injuries he had inflicted upon her?

There was a connection between them, a connection forged in blood. But he could not forget that he had hurt her, had nearly killed her. Whenever they passed in the kastel and their eyes met, he saw only forgiveness and love in her shy gaze—and found himself looking away.

He knew he loved her—but could he ever trust himself not to hurt her again?

"I should tell him." Days had passed since the night of the crimson light, but still Kiukiu had not brought herself to tell anyone of her vision. The shadow-creature had been so like the Drakhaoul . . . and yet how could it be? Lord Gavril had destroyed it.

Kiukiu set down the empty water buckets and rubbed her aching arms.

All water for the household had to be lugged from the old well in the stableyard, as the kitchen well was clogged with rubble.

She had hoped Lord Gavril might be back from Azhgorod today; he had ridden there with Bogatyr Askold and some of the *druzhina*, in search of materials that could not be found on the estate: lead, putty, and window glass. And as Azhgorod was a long day's ride from the kastel . . .

She began to wind the first bucket down into the well, hearing it clank hollowly against the dank, mossy sides until it hit the water far below. She leaned out over the ragged rim of the well to check that the bucket was full. The water was alive with ripples and her reflection broke up into spinning circles. *All those poor, dead children.* She shuddered as she strained to wind the heavy bucket up again. The Drakhaons of old had committed terrible atrocities as the Drakhaoul drove them to seek out innocent blood to feed their cravings. Like as not, the ghost-children were victims of the Nagarians' uncontrollable lusts. The rebuilding work in the disused East Wing must have disturbed the place where their bones had been buried. Except . . .

She heaved the bucket up onto the top of the well, cold water sloshing over the top and splashing her dress. She yelped and hastily pinched the water out of the thick folds of cloth.

Except for that endless span of blue. She had never in her life visited the sea, but she had seen it in Lady Elysia's portrait of Lord Gavril, the portrait that had caused her to fall in love with him long before she had ever met him.

"Kiukiu!" called Sosia from the kitchens.

She divided the well water between her buckets.

"Kiukiu, where's that water for the soup?" called Sosia again.

A small wisp of a sigh escaped. She wished she could stop herself thinking about Lord Gavril. Was he deliberately avoiding her? They had barely exchanged more than the briefest greetings in the past few days. But then, he had been so busy organizing the rebuilding work.

If he truly loves me, he'll speak when he's ready, she told herself as she braced her legs to pick up the buckets again. Or was that just the kind of foolish self-delusion that servant girls indulge in when telling love-tales around the kitchen fire?

"Why have you brought me here? Can't you hear my boy's blood crying out for vengeance?"

"Grandma?" Kiukiu recognized her grandmother's voice, shrill with fury and hatred. What was she doing here? She had left her in the care of the monks at Saint Sergius's monastery; the damaged kastel was far too drafty and damp for an elderly woman.

"And where's my granddaughter? Tell her I want to leave tonight."

She hurried to the courtyard to see two of the monks helping Malusha down from their cart. Brother Cosmas, from the Infirmary, looked utterly bewildered by her vehement protests.

"There you are, Kiukirilya," he said, his worried frown melting into a smile of relief. "Your grandmother insists she wants to go home. But Brother Hospitaler says she's not strong enough to make the journey alone."

"Nonsense!" insisted Malusha. "Kiukiu, go and get the sleigh ready."

"It's too late to set out now, Grandma," Kiukiu said. She would have to use her strongest powers of persuasion. "Come inside and I'll make you some tea. Tomorrow we'll plan the journey together."

The monks nodded gratefully at Kiukiu.

"Stay here?" Malusha cried. "I'd rather you turned me out on the moors."

"Just one night," Kiukiu pleaded.

"Then put me in the stables with Harim. I won't cross that blood-stained threshold." Malusha spat on the flagstones.

"There's a little drying room in the laundry. Warm. Near the stables."

"Near the stables? Well, I suppose it'll have to do. . . ."

Kiukiu realized from the heavy way Malusha leaned against her that, in spite of her show of defiance, her grandmother was utterly spent.

Kiukiu settled Malusha underneath the hanging sheets in a chair in the drying room and knelt down to tuck her blanket around her.

"Let me look at you, child." Malusha leaned forward and tilted Kiukiu's chin to one side.

Kiukiu instinctively raised a hand to cover her throat as her grandmother's gnarled fingertips touched the ragged scars left by the Drakhaoul.

"Why are you still here, Kiukiu? How can you bear to stay under the same roof as the man that mauled you?"

"You know very well," Kiukiu said defensively, "that the Drakhaoul drove him to it. It was the only way to save him. I wanted to save him." Why didn't her grandmother understand? "It was *my* choice."

Malusha shook her head. "And what do you think *he* thinks every time he sees you? Your scars remind him of a deed he'd far prefer to forget."

Then that's why he's been avoiding me. He's ashamed of what he did. Kiukiu's hand closed on the scars, pressing into them as if

her touch could somehow erase them from her body. She wished
Malusha had not put into words the fear that had been haunting her
for days.

Malusha gave a disdainful sniff. "I thought you said it was warm
in here. I'm chilled to the bone."

The fire in the little brazier that dried the linen had burned down
to glowing embers.

"I'll go fetch fresh kindling." Kiukiu fled, glad to have an excuse to
escape. As she hurried down the passageway she could still hear her
grandmother muttering virulent little curses against the House of
Nagarian under her breath.

Dusk had fallen. As she crossed the yard, she heard a soft, hooting
call. Out of the shadows Lady Iceflower came swooping down in a
shiver of snowy wings to land on her shoulder. She had waited for
dark, to follow her mistress from the monastery.

"You can't stay here, my lady," Kiukiu said, glancing uneasily
around for fear someone had seen her. Old feuds died hard and she
knew the *druzhina*'s instinctive reaction at the sight of an Arkhel Owl
would be to kill it. "It's the summerhouse for you."

She set out across the darkening gardens. Lady Iceflower seemed to
understand for she took off from her shoulder, circling above her head.

"Plenty of mice to eat," Kiukiu said, ducking under the broken
doorframe to enter. The owl alighted on a rafter above her. The summerhouse smelled of mouse droppings and rotting wood. This was
where she and Lord Gavril had hidden Snowcloud, tending to his injured leg. The summerhouse had become their secret retreat.

So why did her heart pain her so when she remembered those first
stolen meetings?

"You must stay here," Kiukiu told Lady Iceflower, "until Malusha
is well enough to go home."

Even as she spoke the words aloud, she remembered how heavily
her grandmother had leaned on her arm.

*She will need someone to care for her, and I am the only family she
has left. But that will mean leaving Kastel Drakhaon . . . and Lord
Gavril.*

"A toast, boyars!" roared Lord Stoyan, raising his goblet high.
"To Lord Gavril of Azhkendir, who drove the Tielen invaders from
our land."

"To Lord Gavril!" roared back the guests.

Gavril bowed his head to acknowledge the honor. The hall in Boris Stoyan's house was filled with the wealthy boyars of Azhgorod and their retainers; the firelit room was hot and filled with a fug of steaming mulled wine and the damp fur of their cloaks and coats. He raised one hand for silence and as glowing-cheeked faces turned to him, said, "And a toast to my loyal *druzhina,* who valiantly defended Kastel Drakhaon against Prince Eugene's armies."

He saw Askold's eyes gleam in the firelight as the boyars repeated the toast, cheering and stamping until his ears rang with the sound. The other *druzhina* nodded their approval and held out their goblets as serving girls came around to refill them. Dunai, Askold's son, seized hold of one of the girls and kissed her, only to receive a loud slap. This caused great amusement among the other *druzhina.*

"A ladies' man, just like his father!" crowed Barsuk, flinging his arm about the young man's shoulders.

Gavril stole a glance at Askold to see how he was reacting and saw, at last, the hint of a smile curling the Bogatyr's lips. "Young fool," he said, not without pride. "Deserves all he gets."

"A word with you, Lord Drakhaon."

Gavril turned around to see Lord Stoyan beckoning him to one side. Even though the boyar's face was flushed with heat, his eyes were still clear and shrewd.

"Any news from beyond the borders?" Gavril asked, keeping his voice low.

"Nothing, if you mean any sign of Tielen troops returning. But a caravan of merchants came over the pass from Muscobar on their way back to Khitari a week ago." Lord Stoyan drew him farther away from the noisy throng. "Their command of the common tongue was poor, but they said there had been rioting in Mirom. Half the city, even the Winter Palace, was set afire. It seems the Tielen armies arrived just in time to put down the rebellion."

"So Eugene's men have taken Muscobar." Suddenly Gavril sensed they were celebrating their victory far too soon. "Where is Eugene?"

Lord Stoyan gave an expansive shrug. "You and your men have dealt him a harsh blow. He's busy in Mirom, playing at emperor. He won't be back in a hurry."

The heat in the hall and spicy mulled wine had made Gavril's head muzzy. He went out into the night to take a few breaths of crisp, cold air.

Bright torches burned outside Lord Stoyan's mansion. Across the square he could see the shadowy outline of the Cathedral of Saint Sergius looming high above the wooden houses of the city, its spires blacker than the night sky. The muddy slush underfoot, churned up by sledges and horses, had frozen into hard ruts with the night frost. It was difficult to walk without slipping.

Gavril stopped a little way from the mansion. Roars of men's laughter and gusts of rowdy song carried from the shuttered windows. He was in no mood to join in the revelry tonight. Boris Stoyan's news should have reassured him. The Tielens were far too busy securing their valuable prize, Muscobar, to bother about an impoverished little kingdom like Azhkendir. But there was this nagging feeling of unease: *Were* they celebrating too soon?

Why am I worrying? Eugene has seen the Drakhaoul's power first-hand. And he can have no idea that I have cast the Drakhaoul out.

He turned to walk back to the mansion and heard soft laughter close by. In the yellow lanternlight he caught sight of a man and a girl, arms wound tight around each other. He recognized young Dunai by his fair braids, and the girl looked remarkably like the serving maid who had slapped him so loudly in the hall.

He walked on, but in his heart he felt a sudden emptiness, as if he had lost a vital part of himself.

Kiukiu.

How had it taken all this time for him to see how much he needed her? What must she think of him, always too busy, inventing excuses not to be alone with her?

The Drakhaoul was gone. He could not harm her, he knew it now, and he must do all he could to make it up to her.

He'd buy her a present. Nothing ostentatious—some blue ribbons, maybe, or some soft kid gloves to protect her fingers. And then he'd ride back ahead of his men; after tonight's celebrations they'd probably make a slow start in the morning.

The invasion was over and the Tielens were gone. It was time to start living again.

"I've brought you some porridge, Grandma."

But Malusha's chair was empty, the rugs cast onto the floor. Kiukiu set the bowl down and stared around, perplexed. Surely she hadn't gone to the stables? Her grandmother had seemed so frail, so tired, hardly capable of walking to the courtyard, let alone attempting a journey by sleigh.

Yet once Malusha had an idea in her head, she was stubborn enough to see it through, no matter what the physical cost.

Kiukiu hurried down the narrow passageway and went out into the stable courtyard. Sure enough, there was Malusha in Harim's stall, patting Harim's shaggy coat and whispering in his thick-furred ear. He was already harnessed, ready to be strapped to the sleigh.

Kiukiu found herself almost speechless with exasperation.

"Grandma, where *do* you think you're going?"

"Home, child. I don't belong here and you know it."

"But you're not well enough—"

"Harim knows the way; all I have to do is sit in the sleigh and he'll do the rest."

"Home to a cold cottage, all on your own?"

"All on my own? Have you forgotten my lords and ladies? They'll be waiting for me. I've already sent Lady Iceflower on ahead. I've neglected them long enough." Malusha's eyes glittered rheumily in the gloom of the stall. "I can't stay here. Here, where the Nagarians tortured my son."

"And I can't let you go alone." If Malusha refused to stay in Kastel Drakhaon, then she had no choice but to see her safely back to her cottage.

"But your heart is here, Kiukiu."

Kiukiu felt her face go warm with a sudden, uncontrollable blush. Were her feelings so easy to read?

"Y-yes, but he won't begrudge me a few days. Just a few days to make sure you're all right. . . ." She let out a little sigh. "I'll go ask Sosia for some provisions."

"We've precious little to go around as it is, Kiukiu." Sosia was rummaging through her remaining stone crocks. "Heaven knows, this is a lean month at the best of times and those Tielens ruined half my stores. Nobody wants to eat burned buckwheat or rye. . . . Here." She emerged from the pantry carrying two loaves of dark rye and some strips of dried meat. "That'll have to do. Take a stoppered jug and fill it from the ale barrel in the laundry; that one's not been spoiled."

"Thank you, Auntie Sosia." Kiukiu came forward to take the provisions and, to her surprise, found herself squeezed in a hard, swift embrace.

"You're a good girl, looking after that tetchy old woman with never a complaint."

Kiukiu nodded and backed hastily out of the pantry, unused to such a show of effusiveness from her aunt.

She drew the ale and went back to the stable courtyard to find Malusha already sitting in the sleigh, bundled up in old blankets and furs. Harim's oat-sweet breath steamed the air. Behind them, the *druzhina*'s steeds stamped and snorted in their stalls, impatient for exercise. One stall was still empty, she noticed, the stall of Lord Gavril's favorite horse, jet-black Merani.

"Ivar?" she called. The lanky stableboy came out from one of the nearby stalls, trailing his wooden rake behind him. "Did the Drakhaon leave no word of when he would return?"

"He's the Drakhaon; he does as he pleases." Ivar gave a shrug and turned away to continue raking out the stalls.

"Hurry up, child. The sun's already climbing high in the sky and the dark comes on soon enough!"

So there was not even the chance to say good-bye.

Kiukiu took Harim by the bridle. She led him out, the sleigh runners bumping over the muddy cobblestones, trying to ignore the dark ache in her heart. Perhaps it was for the best . . .

Good-bye? What am I saying? Am I leaving Lord Gavril forever?

"My poor bones!" Malusha complained, grabbing hold of the side of the juddering sleigh.

"We'll be on compacted snow soon. Hold tight."

Kiukiu led Harim the long way around, away from the burned, scorched ridge where so many Tielens had died. No one from the kastel chose to use the old road anymore; the scarred earth exuded a tainted air of desolation and death. The road wound upward above the kastel, past a ruined watchtower where a gang of *druzhina* whistled and chanted as they labored to repair the damage.

As the moorlands opened out before them, Malusha began to sniff the air.

"Best hurry. Thaw's coming fast."

And as if to confirm her words, a skein of grey geese appeared high overhead, their wild cries carrying on the wind.

Kiukiu squeezed in beside her grandmother and gave two sharp tugs on the reins. Harim put his shaggy head down and slowly set off across the snow.

The wind blew keenly across the moorlands and though there was no longer a bitter taste of winter to it, it still stung Kiukiu's eyes to watering. Yes, it was the wind, she told herself angrily as she stared out at the blear of cloudy sky through tear-blurred eyes.

Beside her, her grandmother said nothing, lulled into a doze by the movement of the sleigh.

Soon they would reach the wide tarn and the icebound beck that flowed into it from the distant Kharzhgylls. Harim would pull the sleigh so much more swiftly along the frozen watercourse.

Far ahead, something moved, a black speck against the blur of white. Kiukiu sat up, straining to see. Renegade *druzhina*—or Tielen deserters? Two defenseless women alone on the moors stood little chance, although they had nothing worth stealing except a loaf of bread and a jug of ale. Malusha had fallen asleep before she could weave a cloak of mist around the sleigh, and she had not yet taught Kiukiu that useful trick.

Kiukiu sat upright and clutched the reins tight, her palms sticky with sweat against the worn leather.

A lone horseman was speeding toward them. She felt her thudding heart trip a beat or two. The horse was black, jet-black. Could it—could it be?

"Kiukiu!" His voice carried to her on the keen wind.

Harim's ears twitched at the sound of his voice and his steady trot faltered. It was almost as if he were expecting her to halt him.

"Lord Gavril," she whispered. Her heartbeat thrummed in rhythm with the approaching hooves. There was no avoiding this encounter.

"Where are you going?" he cried as he drew near.

"I'm taking Malusha home." She steeled herself not to look at him, concentrating on the snowy track ahead.

"Why now?" There was bewilderment in his voice. "I—I thought—"

"Thaw's coming. We'll travel much faster before the ice melts." Kiukiu swallowed back any suggestion of emotion.

Lord Gavril pulled Merani around, forcing him to match Harim's pace beside the sleigh. Harim slowed to a stop.

"And you were just going to slip away unnoticed? Without even saying good-bye?" Lord Gavril swung down from Merani's glossy back and approached the sleigh.

Kiukiu's heart thudded faster, but she glared resolutely ahead, willing herself not to look him directly in the eyes for fear she would lose all resolve.

"There's been so much to see to . . ." Lord Gavril made an awkward, self-deprecatory gesture.

"You're the Lord Drakhaon," she said with a little sniff.

"I had to be sure," he said, almost as if speaking to himself.

"Sure?"

"Kiukiu—"

"Yes?" It was the way he pronounced her name. She found herself helplessly, recklessly, gazing into his eyes. *Say what's in your heart. Say it!*

Gavril gazed into Kiukiu's eyes and felt his courage fail him.

He had ridden ahead of his bodyguard to try to make sense of his feelings. He had chosen to go on alone, against Askold's advice, because he needed time to think. All the way back from Azhgorod he had been rehearsing what he would say to Kiukiu. And now—before he had fully worked it out—here she was and he was tongue-tied.

There was only one way to put it to the test.

He reached out and, taking her hand in his, drew her from the sleigh until she was standing close to him in the snow.

"My lord?" she said in a whisper. The icy wind whined about them and he saw that she was shivering.

"You're trembling, Kiukiu." Was she afraid of him?

"J-just cold."

He had to be sure that—in spite of her protestations—she would not flinch from him. And he had to be sure of himself, sure that the lust for innocent blood was finally purged from his system.

He drew her closer until he held her pressed against him, his arms tight around her. Slowly he felt the trembling cease.

"Look at me," he said.

She raised her head and looked steadily at him.

His hands moved to cup her face, tilting her mouth to meet his. Still she did not flinch away as his lips touched hers.

Astasia's kiss had been sweet, her lips cool as the delicate sheen of hyacinth petals. But to kiss Kiukiu was to taste the rich earth of Azhkendir; her mouth was warm and she kissed him back with a passion and intensity that surprised him.

"Are you going to leave me to freeze to death here?" inquired a testy voice from the sleigh.

"I have to go," Kiukiu said softly.

"I know." Still he held her close, reluctant to let go of her now that he knew how much she mattered to him. "Is there any hope for us, do you think?" he said at last, his voice unsteady.

"Arkhel and Nagarian? No good'll come of it," Malusha muttered to herself.

"Take no notice," Kiukiu said in a whisper, blushing beneath her freckles.

The blush charmed him. "When we've finished the work on the Kalika Tower, then I will come for you. Whether your grandmother likes it or not," he added.

A smile lit Kiukiu's face, sun piercing winter clouds.

"I'll wait for you," she said. "Gavril."

He found himself smiling too, happy to hear her say his name without any trappings of rank or class. Not Lord Drakhaon, just plain Gavril. What better confirmation that he was truly himself again?

"*Kiukiu!*" Malusha was fully awake now and glaring at them from her cocoon of furs.

"I must go." Kiukiu drew away from him, turning back toward the sleigh. Still he kept hold of her hand.

"Shall I ride with you?"

"No need. Harim will take good care of us."

"Travel safely, then." He let go of her hand at last and she climbed back into the sleigh. "We'll be together again soon."

She gave the reins a little tug, clicking her tongue. Harim raised his shaggy head and obediently lumbered off.

Gavril stood in the snow, watching the sleigh until he could see it no longer. The wind off the mountains still whined across the moorlands, but he no longer noticed its keen edge.

Merani gave an impatient whinny and nudged his shoulder. It was only then that he remembered the gift he had brought for her: a pair of soft-fringed gloves of brown kidskin that he had carefully placed inside his saddlebags, ready to give to her.

He smiled again. Now he had the ideal excuse to pay her a visit.

"I'll wait for you . . . Gavril." Each word glowed, as though etched in gold on his heart. She would help him forget the darkness that flooded into his dreams at night. She would show him the way to live a simple life again, free from the shadows.

CHAPTER 6

The hours of daylight grew longer. Wooden struts and props shored up bulging walls, ladders blocked the passageways, and the kastel echoed to the ring of hammers and chisels.

Gavril and Askold were at work repairing the wing that over-looked the gardens. And all the time Gavril was busy shoveling sand for mortar or carrying out buckets of broken plaster, his mind was free of the horrors that haunted his dreams. Besides, he felt a kind of companionship working side by side with his household, sharing the common aim of the restoration of their home. They were still in awe of him, but not in the way they had been when the Drakhaoul gifted him with its daemonic powers. There was still a bond between them, but it was a bond of shared adversity, strengthened and enriched by mutual respect.

Askold straightened, wiping sweat from his brow with the back of one hand. "Look, my lord," he said, jabbing a grimy finger down the garden. "There's someone down by the old summerhouse. A woman."

"A woman?" Gavril glanced around, hoping that it might be Kiukiu.

"Looks like your mother."

This was not the first time Gavril had glimpsed Elysia wandering alone in the neglected gardens. He sensed that the hint of thaw in the air had made her restless.

He wiped his hands clean of mortar and went out into the over-grown rose garden that had once been her delight. She was kneeling in the last of the snow near the ruined summerhouse.

"Look," she said in tones of delight. "Snowdrops."

Gavril helped her to her feet. "Shall I pick some for you?"

"No. They look so pretty here in their natural setting. Yesterday I found yellow aconites behind the summerhouse. Spring will soon be here—and the thaw." Then she placed her hands on his shoulders, gazing into his eyes. "I want to go home, Gavril. I want to be in my own house, with my own things about me again. I want to see the white lilacs in bloom in my gardens. And think of our poor Palmyre! She must be wondering if I've sailed off the edge of the world by now."

"All the way back to Smarna? It's so far to go alone."

A smile appeared, both sad and wry at the same time. "I fled Azhkendir once before, remember? With you just a little child."

"But what about the Tielens? It's been weeks now, and there's been no news from beyond the borders—"

She took his hand and pressed it firmly between her own.

"Smarna will be safe. From what I heard at Swanholm, Eugene was intent on conquering Muscobar. Why would he bother with an insignificant little republic like Smarna?"

Every time she said the name, memories came surging back—memories of the warm, wine-gold Smarnan sunshine.

"Lord Drakhaon!" Ivar the stableboy came hurtling toward Gavril and Elysia as if propelled from a mortar. "Oleg's found something in the cellar!"

"Oleg?" Elysia said with a knowing little smile at Gavril. "So the wine fumes have given him visions again?"

Gavril hurried on ahead and arrived just as Oleg emerged from the darkness of the wine cellar carrying a great canvas almost as tall as himself. He propped it up against the wall and began to brush away the thick veil of dust and cobwebs that covered it.

Gavril stared as the portrait of a young man was revealed. A young man who, except for the coal-black of his glossy hair, resembled him so closely he might have been gazing at his own reflection.

"My *father*?" he whispered.

The only portrait he had seen of Lord Volkh was the brooding, grim-browed painting that hung in the Great Hall, executed by some unknown artist of the old formal school. But the young man in this picture had been portrayed with a skillful, naturalistic touch. The artist had caught an expression at once charming, idealistic, and proud in the dark blue eyes.

His father stood on a white balcony overlooking a sun-bright bay, his black hair tousled by the breeze off the sea. He was informally dressed, his white linen shirt open at the neck. The only sign of his status was the golden chain around his neck from which a magnificent ruby pendant hung, crimson as vintage wine.

From the way the artist had captured the subject's smile, Gavril had no doubt that it was his mother's work. Wasn't this how they had met, the young Drakhaon commissioning his first portrait—and falling in love with the painter?

Volkh's eyes seemed so full of hope and optimism, unclouded by any premonition of what was to come. . . .

The portrait blurred as tears trickled down Gavril's cheeks. He let them flow, unashamed to be seen to weep for the father he had never known.

"I thought it was burned." He had not noticed old Guaram, who had been Lord Volkh's valet, till then; now the old man shuffled forward to inspect the canvas more closely. "That's what my lord ordered: 'Burn it. I can't bear to look on it anymore,' he said." He turned on Oleg, wagging an arthritic finger. "So what was it doing in the cellar?"

Oleg shrugged. "No idea. Someone must have hidden it."

"My portrait?"

Gavril heard the mingled emotions in his mother's voice: surprise and regret. He hastily wiped the tears from his cheeks with his sleeve.

Elysia had arrived, closely followed by Sosia and the serving maids.

"Mother?" Gavril said.

She stood utterly still, gazing at her work. By now word had spread, and the echoing din of hammers and saws ceased as the *druzhina* working in the Hall laid down their tools and came out to gaze at the portrait. Lord Volkh's name was whispered as they respectfully removed their fur caps before the image of their dead master.

"I was good then, wasn't I?" Elysia said at last, half-jesting. But Gavril could hear the profound sadness that lay beneath her words. He put his arm around her shoulders.

"There was no one to touch you, Mother."

"Flatterer!" She kept her tone light, but she would not meet his eyes, gazing steadfastly at Volkh. She went up to the canvas to examine it. "There's some damage here—and here on the corners. Probably mice, but it could easily be restored."

By now a little crowd had gathered in the hallway. It soon became obvious to Gavril from their murmured comments that the younger members of the *druzhina* had never seen the portrait before either.

"That splendid ruby," he said. "Didn't you wear a stone like that sometimes, Mother?"

Her hand crept to her neck, as though unconsciously feeling for the jewel. A deep blush colored her cheeks. "It was a wedding gift from your father. It should have gone to you, Gavril. And now . . ." Her voice dropped. "My jewelry is at the Palace of Swanholm with my paints and the rest of my luggage. I doubt I'll ever see it again."

"No matter," Gavril said, wanting to spare her embarrassment. "I'll commission a new frame for the portrait. It will hang in the Great Hall again."

The murmurs changed to nods and mutters of approval.

"And there won't be a Hall for it to hang in if you layabouts don't get back to mending the roof!" Askold's voice cut through the gossip like a whip-crack.

The servants scattered; the *druzhina* trooped back to work until only Gavril and Elysia remained.

"Smarnan light." Gavril still stared at the painting, recognizing the balcony on which Volkh stood and the view of Vermeille Bay beyond. He had been mired so long in the darkness of the Azhkendi winter, he had almost forgotten the intensity and clarity of the summer sun. Suddenly he found himself yearning to paint again—a yearning so strong it was like a physical ache.

But painting was a luxury he could only afford when the repairs to the kastel were finished. There would be views of the moorlands and the distant mountains in spring to capture, and the clear, cold Azhkendi light would be both inspiration and challenge to a painter who had not lifted a brush in many months. . . .

"It's time for me to go home," Elysia said softly.

A gateway gapes open, darker than a thunder-wracked sky. Little crackles of energy fizzle across the opening. And now he sees the bolts of energy are forked tongues, flickering from the carven mouths of great winged serpents whose coils tower above him, forming an archway leading into darkness. And high above, a serpent-eye, blood-red, transfixes him in its burning gaze—

Lying there in the darkness, Gavril tried to reason what the dreams might mean. Did they presage some cruel punishment to be inflicted upon him by the Tielens? His mother had told him the little she knew of Magus Kaspar Linnaius, Eugene's court alchymist, who had tried to kill him with subtle poisons. She was certain he possessed occult powers and had seen him control the wind with a twist of his fingers. If the scarlet thread of light that had caused such chaos in his brain emanated from Linnaius—

Except that the vivid dream-images had a tinge of Drakhaoul glamor about them.

It's . . . as if it has left its memories in my brain.

He could not sleep. He lay staring at the lime-washed walls, still half-wandering in the fire-riven dreamworld.

If only Kiukiu were here. She would hold him in her arms and stroke his hair and he could lose himself in her embrace. . . . But she was far away in Arkhel country, the other side of the moors, caring for her grandmother.

"You think you can live without me, but without me you will go mad. . . ."

"Two ice-breaking vessels sailed out of Arkhelskoye yesterday, my lord." The messenger was a sailor, rough-bearded and smelling strongly of tobacco. "The port master sends his compliments and invites my lady to make her way to the port in readiness for her passage to Smarna."

"So the thaw has really begun at last?" Gavril asked. The news was not entirely welcome. Not just because it meant Elysia would leave him and the parting would prove difficult for them both, but also because, if ice-breakers could sail out of Arkhelskoye, other ships— Tielen men-o'-war—could sail in. He must summon the boyars to discuss ways of protecting the harbors from unfriendly foreign powers.

"The thaw is well under way, my lord."

"I'll go and tell my mother."

Gavril came upon Elysia at work on the portrait of his father, painstakingly cleaning away the dust and grime, watched by old Guaram.

"The port's open," he said.

"Mmm. Good . . ." She seemed to only half-hear him, concentrating all her attention on the painting.

"You can go home, Mother."

"Then all the more reason I should finish this." She smiled at him and continued with her work.

One fact about the canvas had been bothering Gavril. Now that it had been cleaned of its shroud of dust and cobwebs, it was even more obvious.

"My father was Drakhaon, wasn't he, when he came to Smarna?"

"He was," said Elysia distractedly, picking at a loose chip of oil paint with a fingernail.

"Then why is there no sign of it?"

She turned to face him, her auburn brows drawn together in a frown.

"The Drakhaoul only leaves the Drakhaon's body at the moment of death to seek out his heir. Isn't that right?"

"I painted him as I saw him," Elysia said, gazing at the portrait. Her voice softened, her hand, still holding the fine brush, moved almost caressingly over the dark, painted locks of hair.

"But look. His eyes, his hair, his skin—all normal. Not even a glint of Drakhaoul blue—"

She sighed. "Volkh told me that in his case, it was different. The *druzhina* made him Drakhaon when his father, Zakhar, disappeared."

"My grandfather disappeared?" This was new territory. But then, there was so much about the Nagarians she had kept from him.

"Lord Zakhar set out on a voyage." Old Guaram now spoke up. "My father went with him. They never returned." The old man's voice quavered. "But years later, a black thundercloud came speeding over the mountains, swift as an eagle, seeking out Lord Volkh. It was the Drakhaoul. We knew then that Lord Zakhar was dead, and my own father with him."

"But why? Why did my grandfather leave Azhkendir?"

Guaram gave a rheumatic little shrug. "That question always haunted your father, my lord. He spent hours in the Kalika Tower going through Lord Zakhar's books, searching for clues."

"The books belonged to Lord Zakhar?" Gavril had puzzled over the books left open in his father's study at the time of his murder. The turbulent events of the past weeks had pushed them out of his mind.

Now he knew he must find them and examine again the cryptic scribblings in the margins.

"Mother, don't forget to pack," he called back over his shoulder as he hurried away.

"What is there to pack?" Her voice was dry. "I only have the clothes I'm wearing, remember? We left Swanholm in quite a hurry."

"Good morning, Lord Gavril!" A cheerful voice hailed him from high above. He looked up to see Semyon's freckled face grinning down from a rickety platform.

"Morning, Semyon." Gavril continued on beneath the scaffolding toward the doorway to the Kalika Tower.

"Drakhaon! The repairs aren't finished. . . ." Semyon came sliding down the ladder at breakneck speed.

"I'll be careful." The lower door had been blown off its hinges so Gavril had to clamber over shattered timbers to reach the spiral stair. A cold blast of air reminded him that one ragged hole in the tower wall still gaped open to the elements. He made his way slowly up the ruined stair, testing one step at a time.

As he opened the door to his father's study, a rush of memories overwhelmed him. He saw it glittering with Doctor Kazimir's tubes and alembics, transformed into a chemical laboratory as the scientist worked on the elixir to reverse the Drakhaoul's influence on his mind and body. And then the Tielens had come . . .

The *druzhina* had nailed up sheets of vellum to cover the broken windows so that the room was infused with a turgid sepia light, even at midday. At least the books and maps were protected now from weather damage—although it was necessary to light a lantern to read or write in the gloom.

There were still fragments of glass everywhere: colored shards from the shattered windows and fine, clear splinters from Kazimir's broken phials. Before the repairs, wind, sleet, and smoke had blown in, causing yet more damage to his father's maps and books; some lay open, sodden pages a mush of paper pulp.

"They must still be here," he muttered. "They must be."

The first time he had come to the Kalika Tower with Kostya, he had noticed the books lying on his father's desk. At the time he had wondered why Volkh had been so interested in titles such as *Through Uncharted Seas: A Sailor's Account of a Perilous Voyage of Exploration.* Now he wondered if his father and grandfather had also been cursed with the Drakhaoul's dreams and had been searching for clues as to their origins in these ancient volumes.

The top of the desk was covered in a layer of dirt, dust, and broken glass. Gavril began to brush the debris away. Beneath, he could just make out two or three volumes. The first was *Travels in the Westward Isles,* but as soon as he picked it up, he could see that a corrosive chemical of Kazimir's had leaked onto it, burning a great, brown-edged hole into the heart of the book:

> The tempest had blown our vessel so far from its course that we found ourselves far beyond the bounds of our maps and charts,

the page that lay open read.

> Almost dead for lack of fresh water, we sighted land toward nightfall of the third day and anchored in the bay of an uncharted island, lush with green vegetation and fresh springs of clear water.
> Having slaked our thirst and refilled our water casks, we made camp on the shore. In the dark of night, we were awakened by a terrible sound, like groaning or roaring. Some of the more superstitious men called on the names of the holy saints to protect them—

The rest was illegible. Gavril put the book down and picked up another, trying to suppress the growing feeling of frustration. As he brushed the dust from the cover, the title glinted dully in faded gold: *Ty Nagar: Legends of the Lost Land of the Serpent God.*

"Ty Nagar," Gavril whispered and felt a shiver, as though saying the name aloud invoked some latent enchantment long dormant in the dusty pages. He opened the book gingerly and, flicking through the first few pages, saw with a growing sense of excitement that most of the text was intact:

> The fabled land of Ty Nagar cannot be found on any chart or map. Although mentioned in the ancient chronicles of the Rossiyan Empire, scholars have long dismissed its existence as mere fable. However, as this account by Captain Hernin records, there may be some truth in the old chronicles after all. When his ship was blown

off course by a tempest, he and his crew found themselves sailing in uncharted waters far to the west. . . .

Gavril leafed on through the rough-edged pages until he spotted some paragraphs marked in red:

There lies one island far to the south, dominated by the cone of a volcanic peak, said by the people of these isles to be sacred to the powerful Serpent God of their ancestors. They will not go there, as they maintain that the island is haunted by hungry ghosts and ghouls who suck the blood of unwary travelers.

Another legend tells how the priests of the Serpent God, Nagar, built a great temple to their god, at the heart of which was a gateway to the Realm of Shadows. From this gateway they conjured powerful daemon-spirits to do their bidding—until Nagar himself, furious at such sacrilege, caused fire to reign down upon the temple—

Gavril turned the damaged page with great care.

—and its priests, slaying them all.

Here, for the first time, he spotted words scribbled in the margin of the text. Excitedly he raised the open book to the lanternlight, moving it first left, and then right, trying to decipher the lurching scrawl.

The burden has grown too heavy for me. The cravings are too strong to bear. I must go away and try to put an end to things, once and for all.

The burden. Gavril felt his heart beat faster as he recognized what the writer described but dared not name.

Beneath the books lay the crumpled star chart. Gavril smoothed it out and studied it. Now he saw it was not, as he had originally thought, a map of the skies over Azhkendir. Unfamiliar constellations were pricked out in silver and white on the ultramarine wash of sky. And someone had scribbled figures in the margin. Readings from an astrolabe, perhaps?

"Lord Zakhar?" Gavril muttered. Was it the Drakhaoul that had driven his grandfather to sail off on that perilous journey, never to return? A journey beyond charted territory to seek out a lost island known only in ancient legends? What had they hoped to find? Expiation? Or a final division?

"*I am the last of my kind.*"

Was the Drakhaoul trying to find a way home?

The third volume, *Through Uncharted Seas,* which lay open close by, was full of tiny slivers of broken glass, lethally sharp. As he shook the book to dislodge them, he felt one prick his finger.

"Ow!" A drop of blood dripped onto the yellowed page—mortal red, as if to remind him he was free.

The kastel bell suddenly began to clang again.

"What now?" Annoyed at the interruption, Gavril let the book drop and went to the door.

"My lord!" Semyon shouted from the stairwell. "The Tielens. We're under attack!"

"It can't be." Gavril stared down from the tower roof at the Tielen regiments surrounding the broken walls, a blur of blue and grey uniforms.

Had time turned back on itself? Had he only dreamed the destruction of Eugene's army? Or was this some ghostly force come to haunt him? They looked real enough from the top of the Kalika Tower.

In the courtyard below, Askold had mustered the pitifully small number of those *druzhina* fit enough to fight. Crossbows were loaded, aimed at the Tielens.

This time it looked hopeless. There were too many. All the Tielen soldiers bore firearms: muskets, carbines, and hand mortars. Now that he had rid himself of the Drakhaoul, the crossbows and sabres of his bodyguard would prove little use against the firepower of Eugene's elite troops. Even as he watched, shivering in the morning damp, he saw a group of officers detach themselves from the ranks and ride forward under a white flag of truce toward the archway that led into the courtyard. One dismounted and entered beneath the archway.

"Hold your fire!" Gavril cried.

Askold went to meet the newcomer.

"What do they want, Askold?" Gavril called down.

"You, my lord. They want to speak with you."

To speak with him. The words were so ordinary—yet he knew that he was in mortal danger. He looked down at his finger and the red blood oozing from the little cut.

They know. God knows how, but they know I am no longer a threat to them. Why else would they have taken the risk?

Wild plans of escape whirled through his mind. If he made for the secret tunnels under the East Wing, he could slip away unnoticed into the forest. But that would certainly lead to brutal reprisals—and executions. What kind of man would save his own skin and leave his household to face the consequences?

He had little choice but to see what it was the Tielens had to say to him.

As Gavril went out into the courtyard, Elysia came hurrying up to him. "Don't go," she said, catching hold of his hand.

He squeezed her hand as reassuringly as he could and walked out unarmed across the mossy cobblestones, heavyhearted in the knowledge that this time there was no Drakhaoul to save him or his people.

The Tielen officer—a young, brown-haired man not much older than himself—saluted briskly. He held a rolled parchment weighted with a blue wax seal.

"Lord Gavril Nagarian, I come in the name of the Emperor Eugene."

Gavril heard his men murmur the title in disbelief.

"His imperial highness has charged me to read you the following decree:

" 'We herewith order the arrest of the renegade warlord, Gavril Nagarian, sometimes known as Gavril Andar, for crimes against the New Rossiyan Empire.' "

Somewhere behind him he heard Elysia cry out, "No!"

" 'In his place we appoint Lord Boris Stoyan as Imperial Governor of Azhkendir, until young Stavyomir Arkhel is of an age to be proclaimed Arkhaon.' " The officer finished reading from the parchment and rolled it up again, tucking it inside his greatcoat.

"And if I decline the Emperor's invitation?" Gavril asked wryly.

"We have orders to counter any resistance with the utmost force. Your kastel is to be razed to the ground and all members of your household executed."

Gavril raised his head and gazed at the ranks of well-armed, mounted Tielen soldiers waiting outside. It seemed there was no choice but to go with them.

"What are these crimes my son is charged with?" Elysia demanded. "Defending his people against an invading army? What kind of a crime is that?"

One of the older officers who had been observing, dismounted and came into the courtyard; the other saluted him smartly, clicking his heels.

"Karonen, Commander of the Northern Army," he said brusquely, grey mustache bristling in the cold. "I understand, madame, that any legal proceedings against Lord Gavril will be merely a formality. The Emperor is not a vindictive man. He is merely anxious to restore the Arkhels to their rightful position in Azhkendir. I believe he mentioned the possibility of exile with regard to your son."

The *druzhina* began muttering among themselves.

"That's as may be," said Elysia, folding her arms, "but will my son be properly represented? If he is to stand trial, he must have lawyers!"

"My orders, madame," said Karonen with a hint of weary disdain, "are to escort Lord Gavril to Muscobar—or to destroy the kastel."

"Well, my lord?" said the first officer to Gavril.

"It seems," Gavril said, hearing the words issue from his mouth as if another were speaking them, "that I must come with you."

"Who is in command of the kastel garrison?" demanded Karonen curtly.

"I am." Askold took a step forward. He stared at the Field Marshal through narrowed lids.

"You will surrender your weapons to Captain Lindgren. He and his regiment will be stationed here; a further two regiments will be installed in Azhgorod, a fourth at Arkhelskoye, and a fifth on the eastern coast."

Askold stared at Karonen. "We are the Drakhaon's *druzhina*," he said slowly, stubbornly. "We are oath-bound to die in the defense of our master rather than surrender."

"Askold," Gavril said. "Do as the Field Marshal says. I want no more deaths."

Askold turned and Gavril saw scorn in his eyes. He stared at him as if he were a stranger.

"You dishonor us, Gavril Andar. You dishonor your own bodyguard."

His words cut Gavril to the heart. His own men—whom he was

trying to defend—didn't want his self-sacrifice. Locked into their ar-chaic warrior code of honor, they didn't understand what he was try-ing to do for them. For a brief while he had been their warlord, but now they looked on him as a weakling and a deserter.

"We're wasting time." Karonen signaled to two of the waiting sol-diers. They marched forward and placed their hands on Gavril's shoulders.

"My son needs warm clothes!" Elysia protested. "At least let me fetch him a coat—"

Karonen shrugged. He beckoned the soldiers to lead Gavril after him.

"I'll be all right, Mother," he said, forcing a bravery he did not feel into his voice.

"I'll be there, Gavril," she cried. "I have friends in Muscobar. Friends in high places!"

Gavril tried to look back over his shoulder, but the troopers were increasing their pace now, walking him briskly under the archway. The last thing he saw was the *druzhina* go slowly forward, one by one, to drop their weapons at the Tielen captain's feet.

CHAPTER 7

The Empress Astasia sat in front of her mirror listlessly brushing her hair. Nadezhda usually performed this task for her, but she had dismissed her early, wanting to be alone with her thoughts.

She was remembering her bridal night.

All the ladies-in-waiting had teased her with lewd tales about men's lusts and appetites. And it was not as if she had been ignorant of what was expected of her. But she had not anticipated this remoteness. Eugene had been courteous, even respectful, as though the act of consummation were some faintly embarrassing but necessary diplomatic procedure. He had murmured some affectionate words . . . but she felt they were spoken out of duty, rather than spontaneous feeling.

She had seen the portraits of golden-haired Margret, his first wife, at Swanholm. Perhaps he still held her in his heart and she could never hope to compete with the distant, dead beloved in his affections.

Or perhaps he will never see me as anything other than a commodity in a political transaction. At least Gavril loved me for myself alone.

"And where are you tonight, Husband?" she asked. "Oh yes, urgent affairs of state." All through dinner, he had had a distant and preoccupied look in his eyes. She had tried to make conversation, telling him that Karila's cough was much improved, but he had only nodded distractedly. Then he had made his excuses and left before dessert, kissing her on the top of the head just as if she were his elder daughter, not his wife.

The bristles snared on a tangle. Eyes smarting, she dropped the silver-backed brush and picked the knotted strands apart with her fingertips.

"I'm not crying," she told her reflection angrily. It was only a tangle of hair. "I'm *not* crying."

Her reflection stared back through the gauzy light of the candle-flames. She forced herself to smile, willing the tears to stop.

I am Empress now. I have a duty to my country and my husband.

"More coffee, highness?" asked Gustave.

"Why not?" Eugene stifled a yawn. He had stayed awake into the small hours to read the reports specially prepared by the Mirom Senate, fortifying himself with strong coffee. It was a task he had intended to delegate to Maltheus, but after a first glance, he had seen that he needed to understand fully for himself the chaotic state of the Muscobar finances that had led to the uprising.

It made sorry reading. The Muscobar economy seemed precarious, largely based on shipbuilding, exports of iron from foundries close to the Nieva, and herring. The Orlovs had drained the country of money to fund their lavish lifestyle. All the nobles owned large estates that were only just self-sufficient enough to feed the life-bound peasants who served them and worked their lands. Both the army and navy, starved of investment, had not enough revenue left to pay their men. There was no state schooling and the few hospitals were run by religious institutions.

"If your highness has no further requirements tonight?"

Eugene looked around and saw Gustave was still in attendance. "I didn't mean to keep you up so late, Gustave. I can see to myself."

By three in the morning, Eugene was rubbing his sleep-starved eyes as he outlined a plan to turn around Muscobar's economy. It would have to be negotiated with both Tielen and Muscobite councils, for it involved a substantial amount of investment from Tielen coffers to exploit Muscobar's natural resources and to develop manufacturing industries. It would mean persuading the Muscobar nobility to part with many of their peasant-servants to work in the new factories. Silk mills and looms could be established on each estate. Though this would not be an easy task. He would have to buy the nobility's support with promises of privileges and subsidies. They had been used to a life of indolence and luxury for far too long.

The flame in the oil lamp began to gutter and a thin thread of black smoke snaked upward; the wick was almost burned out and the light was too dim to read by.

Eugene rose from his desk and stretched his stiff back. He had heard Saint Simeon's clock strike three some while ago. It was too late to disturb Astasia. As a precaution, he had had Gustave set up his camp bed in his study, just as if he were on campaign. He kicked off his shoes and took off his jacket by firelight. He raked the embers of the dying fire and replaced the fireguard. He liked doing things for himself. So much less fuss.

The air was chilly now that the fire had died down; he pulled the blankets around him, emptied his mind of all extraneous thoughts, and let sleep take him.

At dawn Eugene woke and got swiftly out of his camp bed, fired with the plans he had been devising for Muscobar. It was a brisk morning and he was up before the servants had reached his study to make the fire. No matter. He had accustomed himself to cold mornings and to managing on little sleep on campaign. He even found this regime invigorating. Besides, he was looking forward to the meeting with the Senate today. His plan for Muscobar would encounter some opposition, but he was confident he could persuade even the most reactionary diehards that it was time to change. His enlightened ideals had brought prosperity and contentment to Tielen. And if Muscobar could be swayed, then maybe recalcitrant Smarna could be influenced as well.

Ever since the dissidents torched the Senate House, the members of the Senate had been meeting in the Admiralty, a magnificent colonnaded building painted white and brilliant blue, on the banks of the river.

Eugene rode to the Senate at the head of his bodyguard. To his pleasure, people going about their daily business in the streets stopped to watch the cavalcade pass by, and he distinctly heard cheering and saw smiling faces in the crowd. He acknowledged their greetings with a wave of the hand and a nod of the head, smiling back with genuine warmth. This could only be a good omen for the reforms he was preparing to put to the Senate.

"The free wine and beer on coronation night were much appreciated in the city, highness," murmured the captain of the bodyguard. "And the silver coin you gave to each child."

As Eugene dismounted and climbed the broad Admiralty steps, he could not but notice that the central pediment of the building was still ornamented with the two-headed gilded sea eagles of the Orlovs.

Inside he was greeted formally by representatives of the Senate and shown to a lofty council chamber whose painted walls and ceiling showed billowing seascapes dominated by magnificent warships and rosy-bosomed sea nymphs.

The senators all rose to their feet as he entered and took his place at the head of a great oval table, with Maltheus at his right hand. His bodyguard silently stationed themselves around the great chamber.

"Please be seated, gentlemen." As Eugene sat down, he noticed the chair to his left was still empty. "But where is Kyrill Vassian?"

The senators glanced uncertainly at one another.

"This is most unusual; the First Minister has never, in my experience, been late before, imperial highness," said one, evidently embarrassed. "I will look into the matter straightaway."

Eugene nodded. He had seen the glances exchanged and wondered briefly if Vassian's absence could be interpreted as a last silent protest against the annexation of his country.

Chancellor Maltheus rose to his feet and, after clearing his throat, began to address the Senate in the common tongue.

"Now that we are united in one empire, Tielen is ready to share the benefits of her experience in commerce and manufacture with Muscobar."

As Maltheus gave a brief outline of Eugene's plans, Eugene himself studied the faces of the listening senators, searching for any hint of approbation or objection.

"This is all well and good," called out a dark-bearded senator, "but how is this to be financed? With more taxes?"

"As soon as the First Minister arrives, the Emperor will address us himself on that issue," said Maltheus with extraordinary restraint, Eugene noted.

"And I see the Emperor has filled this chamber with his bodyguard," cried out another. "Is this to ensure we all vote in favor of the plan? Are those who abstain to be arrested?"

Eugene glanced up at Maltheus.

"The bodyguard always accompany his imperial highness wherever he goes," Maltheus said mildly. "They are all specially chosen men whose sole task is to protect the Emperor—"

The door opened and a man hurried in. It was the official who had gone to fetch Kyrill Vassian.

"There's been a terrible tragedy," he stammered. "The First Minister—" He held out a piece of paper to Eugene in a trembling hand.

As Eugene read aloud the handwritten message, he noticed it was faintly speckled with tiny spots of dark red:

> "I have dedicated my life to Muscobar and her people. But I have failed in my duty to the city of Mirom and to the House of Orlov. I can see no other course of action but to end it all. May God have mercy on my soul. Vassian."

Eugene looked up and saw the shocked expressions of the senators. "I take it he is dead?" he said quietly.

"And by his own hand." The official took out a handkerchief and wiped his sweating face, trying to conceal a shudder.

"You saw the body?"

The man nodded.

Patriarch Ilarion had begun to shake his head; the senators were muttering among themselves.

"A tragedy, indeed," Eugene said, sinking back down into his chair. He cast the blood-spotted note onto the polished table. If Kyrill Vassian had wanted to sabotage his plans for Muscobar as his final gesture, he could not have chosen a better—or more drastic—way to do it. Even with a suitable respectful pause to honor the dead, no member of the Senate would have his mind fully on the matters under consideration if they proceeded.

"I suggest we adjourn, gentlemen," he said, "and meet again tomorrow."

Maltheus turned to him, one eyebrow slightly raised.

"Now what?"

"We send our sincerest condolences to his widow and family. We assure Madame Vassian that she shall want for nothing. I suspect that an imperial visit would seem somewhat insensitive under the circumstances."

*   *   *

"Kyrill Vassian is dead?" shrieked Sofia. She collapsed onto a sofa, weeping noisily. "A suicide?"

"Mama, Mama, please don't upset yourself." Astasia was as shocked as her mother at the news, but Sofia's loud cries drove all other thoughts from her head.

"What will your father say? It will undo him utterly. He had such faith in Vassian."

"Mama—" This uncontrollable weeping would surely lead to a fit of the hysterics, and Astasia did not want Eugene to come in and see her mother in such a state. She began to back away toward the bellpull, ready to summon help.

"And poor, dear Elizaveta, she must be quite distracted with grief. What a disgrace for the family. That handsome boy of hers, Valery, now all his prospects are ruined. Why didn't Kyrill think of such a thing? Why?" Sofia had begun to breathe too fast, taking in little hiccups of air between sobs. Astasia hastily tugged the bellpull and hurried back to her mother's side.

"Remember what the physician told you, Mama," she said, "you must breathe slowly. Inhale—then let the breath out steadily."

Nadezhda appeared.

"Smelling salts, quick!" Astasia said, seeing her mother's lashes fluttering rapidly, her eyes sliding upward.

Nadezhda swiftly reappeared with a little silver and crystal bottle, which Astasia waved beneath her mother's nostrils. Sofia wrinkled her nose in disgust and let out a sharp sneeze. Her sobs slowly calmed and she fumbled for Astasia's hand, gripping it in her own. Astasia patted her mother's hand as soothingly as she could.

"Fetch my mother some brandy, please, Nadezhda."

Nadezhda gave Astasia a little glance of sympathy and knelt down beside the Grand Duchess, placing the glass firmly in her shaking hand, steering it to her lips.

All the while she was trying to calm her mother, Astasia had had no time to examine her own feelings. But now she could imagine all the horrible little details: the sound of a shot from the stables, Elizaveta hurrying out, the stableboy trying to hold her back, knowing what a terrible sight lay within . . .

And Valery Vassian . . . How would his father's suicide damage his

career? He had been one of Andrei's close circle of cadet friends from
the Military Academy, often the butt of practical jokes, but good-
natured enough to laugh them off. She felt ashamed of the times she
had teased him. Now that Andrei was not here to protect his friend,
she must take on that role herself. She would speak to Eugene as soon
as possible.

Sofia let out another sob.

"Oh, *Mama*." Astasia settled herself on the sofa next to her
mother. "You and Papa need a little rest, a change of air. It will do
you both good."

"Smarna's so far," sniffed Sofia. "Couldn't we come to stay at
Swanholm with you?"

Mama in Swanholm, ordering everyone about, taking charge before Astasia had had a chance to establish herself as mistress of the
palace? "The Straits can be very rough at this time of year," she said
hastily. "And you know how you hate storms at sea, Mama. What
about Erinaskoe? You haven't been there in over a year. The valley's
so pretty in the spring. Papa can potter in his glasshouses and you can
walk in the Orangery. Why not send word to the housekeeper to air
the rooms?"

All the flags in Mirom were lowered to half-mast to honor the late
First Minister. Most of the court and Senate put on mourning bands,
though Eugene heard some mutter that they could not respect a man
who had taken his own life.

Eugene made a strategic retreat to his study and called Chancellor
Maltheus to join him for a late lunch. Gustave arranged for a cold
collation to be served, with several bottles of Maltheus's favorite
Tielen beer.

"And if things had gone as we had planned," Maltheus said, draining his glass, "I'd be on my way back to Tielborg with the morning tide
to ask the Tielen council to fund and support your plans for Muscobar."

Eugene studied the little bubbles slowly rising through the clear
liquid to the top of his glass. He was still mulling over the consequences of Vassian's suicide.

"Do you anticipate much resistance?"

"Only from the nationalist contingent. I'll remind 'em we're all
part of one empire now," said Maltheus with a broad smile, "and

that there are benefits to be reaped for Tielen as well as Muscobar from this investment."

"And then there's Smarna . . ."

"Smarna!" Maltheus let out a derisive guffaw. "What an extraordinary lack of diplomacy: calling back their ambassador, staying away from the coronation. Everyone was talking about it."

"Precisely so. When we should have been celebrating the union of the five princedoms, one was notable by its absence."

Gustave knocked and announced, "The directors of the Mirom Charitable Society and the School Board are here to meet with you, imperial highness. I've shown them into the Nieva Room."

"Still on your mission to educate the poor?" Maltheus asked.

"A man should be able to write his own name—and read. How else can he hope to better himself? Come, Maltheus," Eugene said, placing his arm around Maltheus's broad shoulders, "come and help me start a small revolution of my own in Muscobar."

Men and women of the Charitable Society had gathered in the long reception room that overlooked the river and the river gardens. Eugene moved among them informally, listening to their suggestions, making a few of his own. Soon he realized there was considerable resistance to his plans.

"And where will we find the teachers for all these schools?" one woman asked in disapproving tones.

"Surely you can't intend to include the street children?" added another. "Not without delousing and bathing them all first."

"Especially the street children," Eugene said. "And the school day will start with a nourishing meal for them all just as it does in Tielen. No one can work efficiently on an empty stomach."

This information was received with astonished silence.

"A good barley soup costs little enough to prepare," volunteered a third woman, who had kept silent until now. The other two turned on her, lapsing into the Muscobite tongue, so that Eugene could not follow their argument.

At that instant, Astasia came into the room. The arguing charity workers stopped in midflow and sank into curtsies. Eugene looked at Astasia with gratitude over their bowed heads; perhaps she would be able to sway them with her winning smile and enthusiasm.

"I'm so sorry to interrupt." She walked up to him and said softly, "Can I ask a favor of you?"

Surprised, he nodded, wondering what request she was about to make.

"Vassian's son, Valery. He was a friend of my brother's. Could you find some way to give him a position so that he can support his mother and sisters?"

Why had she chosen this moment to make her request? It was just the kind of spontaneous, inappropriate interruption he might have expected from Karila.

"We will talk of it later," he said, trying not to show his annoyance. He took her by the hand and addressed the visitors. "The Empress is, I believe, very interested in our proposed education program."

He could sense that she was looking askance at him. He pressed her hand, saying, "I am so pleased to have your support, my dear."

And suddenly the unreceptive throng was smiling and applauding.

What magic had she wrought to persuade them?

Beyond the smiling faces, he saw Gustave in the doorway. He left Astasia to the appreciative reception and went to see what was the matter.

"Refreshments will be served now, as you ordered, highness," Gustave said in a loud voice, flinging the doors wide to admit liveried servants carrying silver trays of sweet wine and cakes.

Then he continued quietly, "I thought you might be interested to learn that a detachment of the Northern Army has just entered the city. They have an Azhkendi prisoner with them. They are taking him, as you ordered, to the Naval Fortress on Gunwharf Island."

Eugene left the Winter Palace by the River Gate and, accompanied only by two of his most trusted bodyguard, crossed to Gunwharf Island.

They arrived as a small, curious crowd gathered to watch the coach with its barred windows pass under the archway of the forbidding fortress.

"Do you wish to interrogate the prisoner yourself, imperial highness?" asked the commanding officer.

Eugene shook his head. All he wanted was to look again on the face of the man who had bested him and nearly brought all his plans to nothing.

He stood a little apart from his soldiers, to watch the prisoner emerge from the carriage.

The prisoner descended slowly, awkwardly, to the cobbles, hampered by his shackles. Pale and unkempt, with several days' growth of stubbled beard, he looked around him, blinking dazedly in the daylight.

The last time they had met, those blue eyes had stared at him, filled with hatred and anger as the Drakhaon swept down on him and his men from the wintry sky.

Now all he saw was a bewildered young man, alone and bereft of his powers.

He would almost have felt pity for his enemy had the rain not started to fall, the cold drops stinging his burned skin. He had to live with the pain of the injuries the Drakhaon had inflicted, to the end of his days.

Now Gavril Nagarian would learn what it was to suffer the bitterness of defeat.

CHAPTER 8

"Stop moping around, Kiukiu, and fetch me some beeswax."

Kiukiu started. Where did her grandmother keep the beeswax? In the earthernware jar next to the honeypot? Or alongside the wood varnish in the row of tarnished little glass bottles on the high shelf? As she stood staring up at the rows of jars and pots on the shelf she could think of only one thing.

Gavril Nagarian.

He had promised he would come for her as soon as the work on the Kalika Tower was complete.

"Do you want me to mend this gusly for you in this life or the next?"

Malusha was regaining her strength by the day, and as her strength increased, her tongue grew more tart. Kiukiu went up on tiptoe to reach a little black pot on the end of the shelf. Uncorking it, she smelled the pungent richness of the deep ochre beeswax gathered from her grandmother's hives.

"Here it is." She brought the pot to Malusha, who was bending over the wooden frame of the damaged instrument, fiddling with pliers and wisps of wire.

"If you want to call yourself a proper Guslyar, you'll have to learn to do all this for yourself. I won't be here forever and I want some peace and quiet in the Ways Beyond. I can't have you popping up whenever you've broken a peg or snapped a string. . . ."

Kiukiu slipped back into the shadows. It was best to let Grandma mutter and complain to herself while she carried out the repairs.

The heat from the fire was becoming stifling in the little cottage. She felt muzzy-headed. She needed fresh air.

She crossed the courtyard, stepping over the hens as they skittered around on the frozen earth. As she passed underneath the archway that led out onto the moorlands, she murmured the secret words Malusha had finally taught her. Mists parted in a swirl . . . then formed again behind her, concealing the cottage from view.

Malusha had insisted on maintaining the charmed skein of invisibility she spun around the cottage to hide it from passersby—not that there were any, Kiukiu reasoned, so close to the desolation of the Arkhel Waste.

Kiukiu stood for a while, dazzled by the paleness of the daylight. The moors were still white with snow, and the horned peak of Arkhel's Fang was half-hidden by a wreath of woolly snowclouds. But the air tasted sweeter and the wind that blew from the mountains had lost its keen bite. And here and there, spines of gorse and lingonberry protruded from the snow, darkly green. High overhead, a skein of grey-winged geese flew, returning to their summer nesting grounds.

Winter was slowly dying.

How long had it been since Gavril had kissed her good-bye? His absence had cast her life into shadow. The first spring light seemed muted; the slight hint of warmth in the air brought her no pleasure.

Kiukiu set out, her worn leather boots squishing through the slushy snow, tramping away from the cottage.

"I will come for you. . . ."

Kiukiu frowned up at the cloudy sky. How long did it take to finish work on the Kalika Tower? She had thought it would be a matter of days. Now the days had become weeks.

But he had promised. He had promised he'd come back for her. Unless . . .

Another skein of grey geese skimmed past overhead, startling Kiukiu with their forlorn cries.

"Why can't I fly like you?" she cried. "Why can't I fly straight to Kastel Drakhaon and find out for myself what's happening?"

At this rate of thaw, travel by sleigh would be impossible in a few days. And then the journey would turn into a long, dreary trudge across the moors, skirting the treacherous marshlands and quagmires that still lay icebound.

If only I didn't have this sick, sore feeling around my heart . . .

She turned and marched back into the cottage. Her grandmother glanced up at her from the coil of wire she was twisting to make a new string.

"I'm going back to Kastel Drakhaon," Kiukiu announced, "and nothing you say can stop me."

Something was wrong at the kastel. Very wrong.

Kiukiu pulled on the reins, standing up in the sleigh as Harim slowed to a halt.

The main road leading to the kastel was trampled to the bare earth as though many horses and heavy carts had passed over it. No fresh snow had fallen for several days now. She would have to dismount and lead Harim.

"What's happened here, Harim?" she whispered.

Looking down from the high road among the trees, she saw flags fluttering from the kastel towers, flags of grey and blue.

The colors of Tielen.

And now she noticed men at work on the scarred earth of the escarpment where Lord Gavril had attacked the besieging army. She let the reins drop and hurried to the edge of the road, peering down through the low-hanging branches of fir and pine.

What were the Tielens doing? Building new fortifications? Great mounds of raw earth had been piled up. They seemed to be tunneling deep into the ground; she could see shafts lined with planks of wood, pulleys from which swung huge buckets filled with earth. Sentries armed with carbines patrolled the perimeter.

Kiukiu felt a cold, sinking sensation in the pit of her stomach.

The Tielens had taken the kastel. Where was Lord Gavril?

"Hey, you up there!" A sentry had spotted her. He pointed his carbine directly at her. "Come down! Identify yourself."

"P-please don't shoot. I'm coming, I'm coming . . ."

The Tielen soldiers guarding the gate took charge of Harim and brought Kiukiu before their commanding officer, Captain Lindgren.

The captain had installed himself in the Great Hall. All the Nagarian portraits had been taken down. Where Lord Volkh had once stared sternly down from the dais, a new picture in an ornate gilded frame had been hung, garlanded with Tielen colors. Kiukiu kept gazing at it, recognizing the tall, imposing figure as Eugene of

Tielen. A flash of memory jolted her back to the barren, burned battlefield—and her first sight of Eugene, lying horribly burned outside the kastel . . . though this portrait depicted him clean-skinned and unscarred, staring proudly out as though scanning the world for new countries to conquer.

Beneath his royal master's portrait sat Captain Lindgren, engrossed in reading a sheaf of dispatches. He glanced up at Kiukiu and spoke in Tielen to the soldiers who had brought her in. Then he set the dispatches down.

"Who are you and what is your business here?" he said in the common tongue. He did not speak brusquely, yet Kiukiu felt her knees trembling.

"My name—Kiukirilya. I-I work here." She saw him reach for a brown-bound ledger, open it, and scan a list of names.

"Your name is not on this list. Can you explain why?"

"I've been away. Caring for my grandmother."

He shut the ledger with a snap and looked up at her, unsmiling.

"Can anyone here vouch for you?"

Her mind was in a turmoil. All she could think was: "What's happened to Lord Gavril? Where is he?"

"Anyone in the kastel?"

"My aunt. Sosia."

"The housekeeper?" He clicked his fingers to the soldiers. "Bring her here."

One of them left the Hall and returned with Sosia—a subdued Sosia, who followed him without a word of protest.

"Auntie?" Kiukiu cried, relieved to see her alive.

Sosia's eyes widened on seeing her. She shook her head as if in disbelief.

"Whyever did you come back, Kiukiu? You should have stayed with Malusha!" she cried in Azhkendi.

"I didn't know. I didn't know—"

"Please identify this young woman for me," interrupted Captain Lindgren.

"This," Sosia said, her manner suddenly meek and cowed, "is my niece, Kiukiu."

"Please confirm her role in the kastel household."

"Maidservant."

"Why was I not given her name before?"

"She was given leave to go care for her grandmother. I didn't expect her back so soon."

"If she is to stay, she must earn her keep," the captain said. "We have too many mouths to feed here as it is. I will not tolerate idlers. Is that understood?"

"Yes, Captain," Sosia said. "She can take up her old duties in the kitchens again."

"Young woman, please inscribe your name on the household role here."

"M-my name?" Kiukiu shot Sosia an agonized glance.

"Do your best," Sosia mouthed at her.

With reluctant fingers, Kiukiu took up the pen and dipped it in the inkwell. She had had so little opportunity to practice writing—let alone sign her name. When she laid the pen down again, the untidy, blotched result marring the captain's neatly inscribed list made her glance away, her face red with shame.

He took back the ledger and she saw him shake his head as he looked at her efforts.

"In Tielen, all children must attend school until they are twelve; obviously this doesn't happen in Azhkendir." But there was no censure in his words. "Well . . . all that will change now."

Was the interview at an end? Kiukiu shot another glance at Sosia.

"So my niece is free to go?" Sosia ventured. "Back to her tasks in the kitchen, that is?"

Captain Lindgren looked up at Kiukiu again. His expression was severe. "You must understand that no one leaves or enters the kastel without my permission. Written permission. Anyone caught breaking this rule will be severely punished. Is that clear?"

Kiukiu nodded.

"Now, you may both resume your duties."

Sosia took hold of Kiukiu by the wrist and hurried her outside.

"What's happened?" Kiukiu burst out.

"Ssh! Not here." Sosia pushed her toward the servants' quarters. Only when they were in Sosia's little room, with the door shut tight, did Sosia let go of Kiukiu's wrist. She had clutched her so tightly, her fingers had left red marks.

"Where is he?" Kiukiu demanded. "Where is Lord Gavril?"

"Oh, Kiukiu, such troubles here—" Sosia began to speak and burst into tears, wiping her eyes with a corner of her apron.

Kiukiu's imagination overflowed with terrible possibilities. "Is he dead? Tell me, Auntie!"

"Lord Gavril was getting ready to take his mother to the port. And then—*they* came."

"The Tielens?"

"They arrested him. They took him away, Kiukiu."

"Where?"

"To Muscobar, the Tielen commander said."

"Why didn't the *druzhina* defend him?"

"Lord Gavril forbade it. There were too many in the Tielen army. He gave himself up to stop them attacking the kastel."

Kiukiu just stood there, stricken.

"I must go to him," she said at last.

"You heard what the captain said. No one leaves without his permission. We're prisoners here, Kiukiu. Only Lady Elysia stands a chance—and she's been to see the captain every day since he arrived, begging for an exit permit."

"I know secret ways across the moorlands—"

"It's not just getting out, silly girl," Sosia said sharply. "It's getting in to Muscobar. These Tielens are sticklers for papers: orders, permits, everything has to be in writing."

"But I can't just stay here doing nothing when he's all alone in prison!"

"Think straight for once in your life, Kiukiu. Muscobar is far away. You have no money. You have no influence. You're a kitchen maid. A nobody."

Kiukiu scowled at her.

"And don't pull that sour face at me! If you want to stay here, you'll have to earn your board and lodging, same as the rest of us."

"Sosia! Come see what they've found in Lilias's rooms." Kiukiu recognized the shrill voice outside as Ilsi's and she felt a shiver of repulsion. Ilsi, the highest ranking of the maids in the kastel, had made her life belowstairs a constant misery.

"What now?" Sosia asked, raising her eyes heavenward.

"Come quick!"

Sosia opened the door and hurried out; Kiukiu trailed reluctantly after her, dreading the inevitable reunion with the rest of the kastel staff.

I don't belong here anymore. I belong with Lord Gavril.

*   *   *

Kiukiu hovered in the doorway, watching while the kastel servants crowded close to Ilsi.

"The men were digging through the rubble in Lilias's apartments," Ilsi gabbled, "and they dragged this out from under one of the fallen beams."

"Are her jewels in there?" Ninusha asked, her voice soft with desire. "She had such gorgeous jewelry. . . ."

One of the Tielen soldiers came up behind Kiukiu and pushed her aside. "I am to supervise the opening of this trunk," he announced. "Captain's orders. Any weapons found inside are to be confiscated."

The servants drew back, muttering to one another.

"He'll confiscate anything of value, you mark my words," whispered Ninusha.

Kiukiu edged a little closer, curious in spite of herself.

Dented and filthy with masonry dust, the trunk did not look particularly promising. The Tielen soldier unsheathed a knife and slid its thick blade between the lid and base, grunting with the effort. Suddenly, with a click, the lock broke and the lid sprang open, powdering the onlookers with a fine shower of dust.

"Ohhh," said Ninusha greedily. "Clothes . . ."

"Take them out," the Tielen ordered Sosia.

"All these dresses . . ." Sosia pulled out one after another from the trunk, until the flagstone floor looked like a waterfall of jewel-bright silks and taffetas. "One for each day of the month."

"More like every day of the year," murmured Ninusha, her dark-lashed eyes wide with longing. "How could she *bear* to leave them behind?"

"Serves her right," said Ilsi with a sniff, "for stealing another girl's fiancé."

"You were never engaged to Michailo!" cried Ninusha.

"We had a secret understanding."

"An understanding? Is that what it's called nowadays?"

Kiukiu knelt beside her aunt in the billowing folds of Lilias Arbelian's wardrobe, reaching out to touch the shining folds of silk. So soft, so luxurious compared with the rough linen of her own patched skirt . . .

"What should we do with them?" she asked wonderingly.

"Burn them," said Sosia. "Burn anything to do with that treacherous woman. If it weren't for her, our Kostya would still be alive. They're bad luck."

Ninusha let out a shriek of dismay. "Burn these? But they're—they're far too beautiful to burn."

"We lost our belongings in the bombardment, didn't we, Ninusha?" added Ilsi cunningly. "We've only got what we're wearing now. Right, Sosia?"

"If you think these are suitable for doing the housework in, then think again," said Sosia tartly. "These are lady's clothes. Besides, they'd have to be let out to fit you, Ninusha."

Ilsi gave a malicious little laugh as Ninusha colored crimson at Sosia's gibe. Kiukiu was glad that, for once, she was not the butt of Ilsi's spiteful humor.

"What's all the excitement about?" Lady Elysia appeared in the doorway. At once Ilsi and Ninusha dropped respectful curtsies, heads lowered. "Are you thinking of opening a dressmaker's, Sosia?"

"The men dug this trunk out of the ruins of the West Wing, my lady. They belonged to—" Sosia's words dried up, as if unwilling to pronounce Lilias Arbelian's name aloud in Lady Elysia's presence.

"To my late husband's mistress?" Lady Elysia said. The serving girls gawped at one another to hear her speak of Lilias in such blunt terms. But Lady Elysia seemed unconcerned, picking up a gown of milky jade taffeta from the pile and examining it. "She had good taste—and a skillful dressmaker." If she was distressed by the mention of Lilias's name, she did not show it.

"We were—unsure of what to do with them, my lady," said Sosia.

Kiukiu saw Ninusha give Ilsi a nudge in the ribs.

"We're all short of clothes, my lady," Ilsi said.

"Well, then, help yourselves!" Lady Elysia said gaily. "I'm going to choose something. This one in jade green, I think. All my clothes are still in Swanholm." And then she noticed Kiukiu. The brave merriment in her face and voice faltered a moment as she held out her hands to her. "Kiukiu, they didn't tell me you had returned. We must talk."

Kiukiu heard the whispering begin as she went over to Lady Elysia's side.

"When did *she* appear?" hissed Ilsi. "And where's she been?"

"Choose yourself a dress too, my dear," Lady Elysia said, pressing Kiukiu's hand warmly.

"Let the others choose first," Kiukiu said, eyes lowered.

"Blue is your color," Lady Elysia said, ignoring her. She knelt and pulled out a silk dress the rich blue of summer cornflowers. "This will suit you very well." She held it up against Kiukiu, who felt herself blushing at all the attention.

"It's lovely," she said softly, stroking the silk against her cheek. The other servants plunged greedily into the pile of dresses. Ilsi and Ninusha were already bickering over a dress of mulberry silk, tugging it between them. Even old Marfa, who looked after the kastel poultry, had grabbed a dress of heliotrope bombazine.

"Come," Lady Elysia said to Kiukiu. "Let's leave them to it."

Lady Elysia opened the door to the Drakhaon's chamber and beckoned Kiukiu inside.

Kiukiu felt her heart falter a little as she entered the familiar room. Lady Elysia laid the dresses on the four-poster bed. The rich tapestries still hung on the walls—as did the portrait of Lord Gavril as a boy that she used to dust so tenderly, hoping that one day . . .

"Sit down, Kiukiu. Would you like some tea?" Lady Elysia lifted a little kettle from the fire and poured steaming water into a ceramic pot, releasing the gentle fragrance of green Khitari tea.

"I-I should serve you, my lady—" Kiukiu stammered, embarrassed.

"You're my guest," Lady Elysia said, smiling. "Besides, you've traveled a long way today, if I'm not mistaken. You must be tired."

"I came along the River Karzh; it's still frozen over." Kiukiu took the bowl of tea and cradled it in her fingers. "It would have taken at least two days by the moorland road."

Elysia took up her tea and sat down opposite her on the other side of the fire.

Kiukiu sipped her tea and felt the ache that had stiffened her neck and shoulders soothed slowly away. She had not realized until then how tense she was. "Lady Elysia," she said, looking at her through the gauzy steam rising from the tea, "where are all our men?"

"The Tielens took away their weapons," said Lady Elysia. A sigh escaped her lips. "Then they put them in chains. Captain Lindgren has set them to digging mineshafts. It seems he believes the estate lands contain valuable mineral deposits."

"They're making them work—in chains?" Kiukiu set her empty

tea bowl down. The thought of the proud *druzhina* being forced to dig tunnels appalled her.

"If Emperor Eugene believes I'm going to sit here and do nothing to help Gavril and his men, he's very much mistaken." The sadness had faded from Elysia's expression, which was now one of stern resolve. "I'm taking the sleigh and going to Azhgorod tomorrow, Kiukiu, to petition the governor. Captain Lindgren has agreed to write me a safe-conduct letter and introduction to Lord Stoyan."

"Can I come too?" burst out Kiukiu. As soon as the words were out of her mouth, she realized how foolish they sounded. "No. Of course not. Why would Lord Stoyan pay any attention to me?"

"I fear," Elysia said distantly, staring into the flames, "that he won't pay attention to any of us. The matter is out of his hands."

Kiukiu slipped away when no one was looking with a bowl of scraps and leftovers gleaned from the Tielens' dinner. Months ago she had crept out of the kitchens, night after night, to feed Snowcloud, the young snow owl she and Lord Gavril had rescued. But now the scraps were intended for a different purpose.

First she slid into the stables, where she found Harim contentedly munching from a nosebag. "Time for you to go home," she whispered in his hairy ear. Checking to see no one was about, she led him out into the courtyard.

"Where're you taking that pony?" demanded someone from the shadows behind her.

"Go on." She patted Harim's sturdy rump hard and sent him trotting off into the dusk. "Go home to Grandma!"

"Kiukiu?"

She turned to see Ivar, the stableboy, watching her, arms folded, chewing on a haystalk.

"I'm sending him home to Grandma. The Tielens have no need of him."

"They're using ponies down in the mine."

"Well they're not using my Harim."

He shrugged. "Don't worry. I saw nothing." He went back into the stables, calling teasingly back over his shoulder, "But don't forget— you owe me a favor now, Kiukiu."

Kiukiu blushed. *So he wants me to kiss him,* she thought. *And his voice hasn't even broken properly yet!*

Now that Ivar had gone, she gathered up the bowl of scraps and set out toward the escarpment where she had seen the diggings.

She managed to slip past two sentries without being noticed and made her way through the fast-gathering dark toward the mine-workings where the Tielens were lighting torches.

Surely they can't still be working now that it's night? Then she remembered that it was always dark underground.

As she came nearer, she saw a group of Azhkendi men lying down around the dying embers of a fire. Were they sleeping? She thought she recognized the straw-fair hair of the nearest prisoner. Crouching down, she threw a pebble at his back, whispering his name. "Semyon! Semyon, it's me."

He rolled over and she heard the clinking of chains.

"What is it?" he asked. His eyes looked dull and glazed and he moved sluggishly, as though only half-awake.

"Food," she hissed, pushing the bowl toward him. "You look half-starved."

"Food?" he repeated dazedly. And then he grabbed the bowl and started to cram the scraps into his mouth, chewing ravenously. His blanket dropped away and she saw with horror how thin he was, all skin and bones.

"What's that noise?" It was one of the Tielens, who had spotted the movement. Kiukiu shrank back into the shadows, crawling out of sight.

By the torchlight, she saw him take the bowl from Semyon and hit him, hard.

"Hungry, are you?" The Tielen turned the bowl over so that all the remaining scraps fell out onto the earth. "Let's test how hungry you really are." Laughing, he ground them into the earth with the heel of his boot.

Kiukiu began to edge away, terrified lest she be caught. And as she retreated, she saw, through tear-hazed eyes, Semyon desperately scrabbling for the few scraps the Tielen had trodden on.

Azhgorod was the ancient walled capital of Azhkendir. Round watchtowers stood at every gate to protect the wooden houses crowded together beneath the black spires of the Cathedral of Saint Sergius.

In more southern climes, the last snows had melted and spring had come. In Smarna, the white lilacs would be in bloom in the gardens of the Villa Andara. But here in Azhkendir, the last throes of winter still gripped the country in a gauntlet of ice.

Elysia Andar shivered as her sleigh skimmed closer to the city— though whether from the chill of winter's last snows or from the powerful memories that came surging back to her, she could not be sure.

She had first come to Azhgorod in a troika jingling with sweet-toned silver bells, a young bride nestled close to her husband beneath soft white furs, unaware of the waiting shadows that lay ahead.

And now here she was, a quarter of a century later, her estranged husband assassinated, returning to beg permission to visit her imprisoned son.

Then, the black dragon standard of the House of Nagarian had hung from every watchtower and spire. Clansmen of the Drakhaon's *druzhina* rode as escort beside them. The people of Azhgorod clustered together, straining for a closer glimpse of their young Lord Drakhaon and his bride.

Now the blue and grey pennants of Tielen fluttered from the watchtowers, emblem of the empire of New Rossiya that had swallowed up Azhkendir and the other surrounding countries in its gaping maw.

The sleigh reached the main road and began to bump over rutted mud and churned snow. Elysia had to grab hold of the rail to hold herself steady.

Her sleigh-driver turned around.

"Looks like they're checking everyone in and out, Drakhys." Ivar had gone pale beneath his freckles. She had chosen Ivar, the oldest stableboy at the kastel, as her driver. All Nagarian men of fighting age had been put to work in Captain Lindgren's mine, even the *detsky*—the keep boys—none of whom were much above fifteen summers in age.

"Don't call me Drakhys, Ivar," she said. "They'd arrest us for that alone."

"Suppose they suspect—"

"Our papers are in order. They have no reason to refuse us entry. Just relax." Even though she forced herself to speak calmly to Ivar, her stomach was churning, dreading the encounter to come, yet fearing just as much being turned away at the gates.

They were close enough now to see soldiers in the uniforms of the army of Tielen manning the gate. Others patrolled the walls, carbines on their shoulders.

"Madame Elysia Andar." The officer glanced at her as he scanned the letter Captain Lindgren had written. His face was expressionless, giving nothing away. She was glad she had insisted the captain use her professional name. "I see you come from Smarna. A long way to travel in winter, madame."

"You will also see that I am a portrait painter," she answered pleasantly. "I go where my work takes me."

"And you seek an audience with his excellency, the governor." He frowned at the papers as though questioning their authenticity, then handed them back. "You may proceed."

Ivar's freckled face had turned bright red with relief when he clambered back into the driver's seat. She nodded but said nothing, not trusting herself to speak yet.

The narrow streets of the city were dark and gloomy, overhung with carved wooden balconies and metal shop signs. The street was hard with rutted ice. Ahead the way was blocked by two larger sleighs. And, from the shouts and cursing, Elysia guessed the coachmen had come to blows.

"Ivar, you'll have to find somewhere to leave the sleigh while I go on ahead on foot."

He glanced at her doubtfully. "A lady alone? In this big city?"

She laughed. His concern for her safety was touching. Though she suspected he was equally anxious about how he was going to maneuver the sleigh without accident.

"I'm used to big cities, Ivar. I spent many weeks in Mirom, remember? You go and find a place to stable the horses, then meet me at the Governor's Mansion. It's in the main square, opposite the cathedral."

She swung her feet out over the side of the sleigh, lifting the jade skirts of Lilias's dress to avoid the wet slush of ice and mud pooling in the ruts, and set off beneath the low-hanging balconies.

She let her memory guide her, hurrying as best she could over the slippery mush of frozen snow, past a covered market ripe with the earthy stink of onions, winter kale, and turnips, where tradesmen hollered their wares aloud, their breath steaming in the cold air.

The iron-tongued bells of Saint Sergius's Cathedral dinned out, filling the city with their clamor. Following the sound, she came out of the narrow street into the great square and found herself gazing up at the cathedral, a dark blur against the pallor of the sky.

The town residence of Lord Boris Stoyan, Chief Boyar of the Council of Azhgorod—and recently appointed Governor of Azhkendir by the Emperor Eugene—stood next to the Council House. It was a sturdy, unpretentious mansion, built in the traditional Azhkendi style, with carved wooden shutters and balconies, and a roof pitched at a steep angle to allow the snow to slide off. Only the Tielen sentries guarding the front door, and the blue and grey flag of Tielen hanging over the entrance, distinguished it from any other rich merchant's house in Azhgorod.

Elysia steeled herself and approached the entrance, papers in hand.

One of the sentries stepped forward to examine her documents.

"His excellency is very busy," he said in the common tongue, his accent clipped and awkward. "He may not see you today. You'll have to wait with the other petitioners."

"But I've come a long way to see Lord Stoyan."

The sentry opened the great door and curtly indicated that she should go in. "Wait in the first room on the left. The door is open."

"You'll make sure that Lord Stoyan receives my letter?"

"We have a system here. You must wait your turn like the rest."

The petitioners, all older men dressed in fur coats and hats, were huddled close to a little wood-burning stove. Elysia nodded to them, but they all looked away as if she were not there.

Where was Ivar? He had only been to Azhgorod once before, he had told her, to the Butter Fair. And then he had been eight years old. But why was she fretting about what had become of Ivar? He was old enough to take care of himself. Perhaps it was easier to worry about the little concerns of the moment than to remember the true reason for her visit.

The door opened and a neatly dressed maidservant came in.

"Madame Andar? Please come with me."

Elysia glanced up, surprised that she should be called so soon. The other petitioners looked at her resentfully and one or two began to murmur behind their papers.

Ignoring them, she swept out of the room, following the maidservant.

She was shown into a large, painted wood-paneled chamber. A fire of logs crackled in the great stone fireplace, filling the room with the sweet cidery scent of burning apple wood.

"So you are Elysia Andar." It was a woman's voice, cool and yet tinged with a familiar accent, which Elysia could not quite place.

Elysia turned, caught off guard, and saw a red-haired woman in the doorway.

"I-I'm sorry, madame, you have me at a disadvantage. Are you Lady Stoyan by any chance?"

The woman came closer. Elysia's instincts as a portrait-painter noted that she was plainly yet elegantly dressed in a gown of black and violet—the colors of mourning. Her hair was more russet than red, her skin was richly creamy, and her eyes were a languid yet intense green. In spite of the sober colors of her costume, Elysia detected a strong aura of sensuality . . . and something else, less easily defined, that made her feel distinctly uneasy.

"Lady Stoyan?"

The woman smiled, a teasing, knowing smile. "No. I'm not the governor's wife, madame. Or should I call you Drakhys?"

Elysia felt the heat from the apple-wood fire color her cheeks. Ignoring the sly dig, she pressed on. "I think there's been some mistake. I came here to see Lord Stoyan and my petition is for his attention only."

"You want permission from his excellency to go visit your son Gavril in prison. But why should his excellency grant you or Gavril Nagarian any favors?"

"I fail to see what this has to do with you, madame."

"My name is Lilias Arbelian, and my son is Stavyomir Arkhel. Now do you understand?"

Lilias Arbelian. Her late husband Volkh's mistress. Elysia stared at the younger woman who stood before her so calmly, evidently enjoying her little moment of triumph. Beside Lilias she felt dowdy, middle-aged, and desperately needy. And then there was the matter of the jade-green dress from Lilias's own trunk that she was wearing. Surely Lilias had noticed by now?

"Ah. My Khitari jade silk," Lilias said, staring at the dress. "Jade really doesn't flatter an older complexion."

Utterly embarrassed by now, Elysia felt a flush of heat redden her face and neck. She opened her mouth to reply, then thought better of it.

"I see you know who I am."

"Yes," Elysia said, recovering a little. "Altan Kazimir has told me a great deal about you."

To her satisfaction she saw a slight frown darken the limpid green of Lilias's eyes.

"I don't know what you hope to achieve from this interview, Madame Arbelian," she continued, determined to maintain her advantage, "but if you've nothing of significance to say to me, then I shall not waste my time—or yours—any longer. Please tell me when Lord Stoyan will grant me an audience."

"Perhaps I have not made myself clear." Lilias's voice had a hard-edged ring to it now, all the earlier sweetness gone. "Since my little son Stavyomir was named heir to Azhkendir by the Emperor himself, the governor and I have grown quite . . . close."

Quite close. Well, of course, Elysia thought, and she had been a fool not to observe how Lilias's mourning dress had been subtly altered to enhance and display the milky bloom of her full breasts. A flurry of tart comments filled her mind, but she forced herself to leave them unspoken.

"You may be unaware, Madame Arbelian, that I have good friends at the court in Mirom."

"Oh really? Well, I have been at the imperial court in Mirom and I find that old allegiances have altered considerably since Eugene became Emperor. First Minister Vassian, for example."

"Oh?" said Elysia uncertainly.

"Put a bullet through his brains. Such a tragedy for the family. They say he killed himself because he had failed in his duty to protect Muscobar."

The news of Vassian's suicide shocked Elysia. She had only met him on a handful of occasions, but she remembered him as a dignified, self-composed man, who, unlike many at court, had shown her courtesy and understanding.

"I'm so sorry," said Lilias callously. "I hadn't realized you knew him."

Another potential ally dead. Elysia tried not to let her disappointment show. "And I am sorry to hear that such a faithful servant of Muscobar is dead," she said, forcing her voice to remain steady. "But I must remind you, Madame Arbelian, that I came here to see Lord

Stoyan. My letter of introduction from Captain Lindgren is addressed to Lord Stoyan himself, not to you."

"Well now . . . what a shame that I discovered your letter was a forgery—and was obliged to destroy it." Lilias suddenly drew a paper from her low-cut bodice, moving toward the sizzling fire.

Too late Elysia realized what she was about. She darted forward, hands outstretched to try to wrest her precious letter from Lilias, but the younger woman moved the more swiftly. With a flick of the wrist, she cast Captain Lindgren's letter into the flames.

Elysia let out a cry and seized the tongs, trying to pull the letter from the fire, but it was too late. The paper had been consumed, crumbling to black ash.

"Shame on you, Madame Andar, for stooping to such a low trick. Did you think you would get away with it?" A little smile played about Lilias's full lips. "I believe it is a very serious crime to forge the signature of one of the Emperor's officers. I should report you to the authorities."

"It was no forgery and you know it." Elysia stood, still clutching the tongs like a weapon. She was so angry she did not trust herself to say more.

To her surprise, Lilias let out a piercing scream.

"Help me, help me!"

The doors burst open and two of the Tielen guard hurried in.

"She attacked me!" Lilias, her face twisted in anguish, pointed a trembling finger at Elysia. "With the fire tongs!"

"Drop the tongs, madame."

Elysia let the fire tongs slip from her grasp as the guards advanced. Lilias had begun to sob into a delicate lace handkerchief.

"Bravo, Lilias Arbelian," Elysia said, forcing as much cold contempt into her voice as she dared. "I had not realized you were such a talented actress."

"Come, madame." One of the guards gripped her by the arms and started to propel her toward the doorway.

"What shall we do with her?" the other asked. "Take her to the city jail?"

"Oh no, I am not a vindictive woman," cried Lilias. "Madame Andar was distraught to hear news about her son. I—as a mother— can understand how concern for one's child can make a rational

woman behave irrationally. Escort her from the mansion, please—
and ensure she is not readmitted."

But as the guards hustled Elysia out, Lilias said in a low voice in
Azhkendi, "Did you think I would help you and your darling son?
Understand that I will do everything in my power to ensure Gavril
never returns to Azhkendir!"

CHAPTER 9

"Gavril Nagarian, you are accused of treason against the Empire of New Rossiya."

After weeks of confinement in a subterranean cell, Gavril's eyes ached. He squinted into the pale daylight, trying in vain to identify a familiar face among his accusers in the courtroom.

The chief of the three judges leaned back in his chair, staring at him fixedly as the prosecuting lawyer read out the charges again.

". . . that you brutally murdered Count Feodor Velemir . . . broke your sworn pledge to Eugene of Tielen . . . The prisoner will stand to hear the sentence."

Weak and faint, Gavril forced himself to concentrate on keeping upright. His wrists and ankles were shackled so that he could do little but shuffle when prodded by his guards to move forward.

"Well?" The judge looked down at him dispassionately. "What do you have to say in your defense?"

His life depended on the outcome of this trial. And yet he knew in his bones that it was all a show. He had been judged guilty long before the trial had begun.

"I acted to defend my people." His voice sounded so quiet in the vast wood-paneled courtroom. "Eugene of Tielen attacked my kastel. Yes, I fought back—but only under extreme provocation."

"That's not the story we have heard these past days." The judge adjusted his pince-nez spectacles on his nose as he read from his notes. "We have heard from the few surviving witnesses that you ignored his imperial highness's requests for safe passage through Azhkendir. And when offered reasonable terms of surrender, your answer was to turn your fearsome weapons of destruction on the Tielen army in a vicious attempt to assassinate his imperial highness."

The facts were true, but so distorted in the Emperor's favor that they made Gavril appear a duplicitous villain.

The judge raised his head from his papers and gazed out at the crowded courtroom. "Over five hundred Tielen men were killed in that onslaught. Five hundred! Including the Emperor's oldest friend, General Lars-Gustave Anckstrom, a veteran soldier who risked his life in battle countless times for the good of his countrymen."

A murmur of outrage went around the courtroom. Gavril closed his eyes, wishing that somehow he might wake and find it all a dream.

"Only by God's grace was our beloved Emperor spared from annihilation—although the imperial doctors say he will bear the scars of that terrible attack to the end of his days. Gavril Nagarian, it is the opinion of this court that you are guilty on all counts. I have no alternative by the laws of the empire but to sentence you to death by public execution."

Gavril heard the words as if from a very great distance. He tried to make sense of them.

So Eugene wanted him dead.

"You will be taken from this court to the imperial prison, to await execution—"

"*Wait!*"

A man had risen to his feet at the back of the courtroom. Tall and broad-shouldered, he strode forward into the shaft of daylight.

"Y-your imperial highness?" The judge bowed his head, evidently confused by this unscheduled interruption.

A whisper gusted about the courtroom like a gathering wind.

It was Eugene. Plainly dressed, unadorned with medals or ribbons, the Emperor must have been sitting, listening to the trial, unnoticed by the rest of the court.

Gavril stared at his enemy, seeing all too clearly in the daylight the damage he had inflicted at the height of his frenzy. Half the Emperor's face had been scorched by Drakhaon's Fire, as had the hand he had raised to halt the trial. The wounds still looked raw and painful.

Gavril swallowed hard, sensing that Eugene must hate him as much for ruining his face as for defeating him in battle.

"History shows us that too many rulers have stained their reigns with the blood of their enemies." Grey eyes, chill as a winter sky, scanned the silent courtroom. "What will it achieve if I take this young Clan Lord's life? Too much blood has been shed already in this conflict. Let the court record that I revoke the death sentence. Let it be known that Eugene of Tielen has begun his reign as Emperor with an act of mercy, of forgiveness."

One by one, the people in the crowded courtroom rose to their feet, applauding the Emperor's speech.

Gavril blinked.

"We have heard the evidence from a number of medical doctors. We have heard of the prisoner's episodes of madness in his cell, causing his jailers to restrain him to avoid injury to himself."

The judge nodded slowly.

"We conclude, therefore, that Gavril Nagarian is afflicted with a grave and incurable disorder of the mind. A danger to himself—and to others. We recommend that he be taken to an asylum, where he may be cared for in complete security until the end of his days."

To the end of his days? Locked away to rot in a lunatic asylum? What mercy was there in such a sentence? Till that moment, Gavril had managed to keep control of himself. But now he lunged toward Eugene, screaming aloud his fury. "I'm *not* mad!"

His guards grabbed hold of him by the shackles, forcing him to his knees. But still he shouted out till his throat burned, twisting and struggling to escape their restraining hands.

"Don't do this to me, Eugene! I'd rather die. Kill me, but don't lock me away!"

One of the guards struck him, bringing him crashing down onto the polished boards of the courtroom floor. Rough hands restrained him, forcing him to stay down.

"Look at the wretched fellow," he heard Eugene say to one of his aides as they walked away. "Obviously quite insane. Let's trust our physicians will be able to calm his frenzy. . . ."

Footsteps. Coming nearer.

Gavril lay curled in on himself, numb with dread and despair.

What new torment had his captors devised to enliven his last hours before they removed him to the lunatic asylum?

His body was marked with fresh bruises where they had manhandled him out of the courtroom. His wrists and ankles were rubbed raw where the shackles had chafed away the skin. Yet the physical discomfort was nothing to his mental agony.

Was he insane?

It was true that there were whole days he could not recall since they arrested him weeks ago in Azhkendir, gaping blanks in his memory. But then, he had traveled blindfolded and shackled for much of the journey, first in a barred coach and then by sea, in the lightless bowels of a Tielen warship, so that he had lost all track of time.

The only certainty was that he was no longer a threat to Eugene. He had fought the Drakhaoul that possessed him, and he had won. But in ridding himself of the Drakhaoul, he had betrayed his people. They had looked to him to defend them—and he had destroyed the only means of defeating Eugene's alchymical weapons.

A key turned in the lock and the heavy door creaked open. Lanternlight illuminated the cell, so bright that Gavril flung his hands over his eyes. Voices conferred in a language he gradually came to recognize as Tielen. They seemed to be arguing. One, strong and commanding, soon overruled the others.

The door clanged shut. Gavril slowly opened his eyes, peering warily through his fingers.

A tall man, lantern in hand, stood gazing down at him. The bright glow of the lanternlight revealed the red, puckered scars marring his face.

"Eugene?" Gavril whispered, lowering his hands.

"At least you're lucid enough to recognize me." Eugene spoke in the common tongue, with just the slightest trace of a Tielen accent. "After your outburst today, I feared you were beyond help."

"So you came to see the dangerous lunatic—alone."

Eugene held the lantern up close to Gavril's face. Gavril shied away, eyes stung by the brightness of the light.

"Linnaius was right," Eugene said, lowering the lantern. "You have rid yourself of your powers. Or—more accurately—you have rid yourself of the creature that made you so powerful."

"What does it matter to you? You're Emperor now, and I'm your prisoner."

"You could have taken the whole continent for yourself. You could have seared me and all my armies to ash. You had the power to do it, Gavril Nagarian. *You* could have been emperor. And you threw that power away. I want to know why."

"It was destroying me!"

"Surely there was some way you could have come to control the creature?" Eugene leaned closer. "Impose your will on it? Subdue it?"

"You're implying that I was not strong enough to master it?" Gavril said slowly. "And that another, less weak-willed, could have forced it to obey him?" He began to shake his head. "You have no idea what you are saying. It winds itself into your will, your consciousness, until you no longer know who is in control!"

"Tell me where it has gone, and I will see your sentence is greatly reduced. A year in confinement, little more."

"Why?" Gavril stared up at the Emperor. "Why is it so important for you to know? Don't you understand what I'm saying? Sooner or later, it destroys you. It refashions its host, body and mind, to resemble the being it once was."

"I see little evidence of that refashioning in you now." Eugene held the lantern close to Gavril's face, gazing searchingly into his eyes.

"There are still traces." Gavril held up his shackled hands. "Look at my nails. See those streaks of blue? And my hair—though your doctors have shorn most of it away"—he ran one hand ruefully over the short prison crop they had given him after clipping his cobalt-streaked locks—"for reasons of hygiene. But the signs are fading fast."

In a distant part of his mind he found himself wondering why he was talking to Eugene, revealing what little was left of his mystery. Had he said too much? Or had he said just enough to condemn himself to the asylum for life?

"You still have not answered my question." Eugene's eyes probed his, grey steel now, hard and determined. "Where did the creature go? I have evidence it passed east over Swanholm. But after that, its trail went cold."

"I severed the link between us. Don't you understand? I don't know where it went." Gavril forced himself to control the desperation in his voice. "It told me it would die without a Nagarian host to sustain it. For all I know, it's already dead."

Eugene stepped back from him.

"You fool," he said, his voice quiet, expressionless.

Suddenly Gavril's confused mind made a connection. He understood why Eugene had come in secret to interrogate him.

"So *you* want to become Drakhaoul," he said, bitterness darkening his voice. "You have the whole continent of New Rossiya in your power; you have Astasia Orlova as your bride, and it's still not enough for you! Be thankful that the creature is dead. Be thankful that you don't have to endure the unnatural lusts and desires the creature imposes on its host—"

"I," Eugene said coldly, "have had greater men than you silenced for such insolence. I have stripped their families of everything—even their name."

Gavril felt a sudden fear chill his heart. For one moment he had forgotten that this man was Emperor and could destroy the people he loved with a single word. He had endangered his mother, his household, his bodyguard . . . and his faithful Kiukiu. They might be far away from this dismal prison, but none would escape the Emperor's wrath.

He swallowed. "Forgive me, your highness. I forgot myself."

"Well. It's gone . . . and there's an end to it."

But Gavril heard no hint of resignation in Eugene's voice. He did not doubt that Eugene, no matter what he had said to him, would send his agents to all corners of his empire and beyond to trace the Drakhaoul.

Nothing would be left to chance.

Somewhere nearby water dripped, a monotonous, repetitive sound, regular as the ticking of an ancient clock. For some time now, Gavril had felt as if there were a great weight pressing on his chest, a jacket of iron slowly tightening, stifling his breathing.

The weight, he had begun to realize, was the burden of his own fear—fear for the future and the life he would not be allowed to live. Instead, an eternity of imprisonment stretched ahead, a living death. Slowly he closed his eyes . . . and found he was flying.

In the weeks of confinement he had almost forgotten what it was like to fly. Chill, pure air streamed past him, through him—cleansing all the petty concerns of the world far below.

A dark ocean, cold and black as ink, stretched beneath him now. He hurtled aimlessly onward, borne on a tumultuous stormwind of despair.

And now he felt a rawness at the core of his being, as if he had been wrenched in two and lost a vital part of himself. And this soul-wound was bleeding his life away.

Somewhere far off, a distant voice howled its grief aloud.

"I am weary of this world."

And something awoke within his brain. Livid spatters of light exploded across his vision. A horrible twisting, shuddering feeling gripped his whole body. He fell to the floor, limbs contorting.

"I want to go back to my own kind."

"H-help—"

Little slivers of light pulsed through his mind, and with each new pulse his body convulsed again.

"Prisoner's fitting!"

Men's voices began to shout close by. The cell door was flung open. Vaguely, through the electrical storm ravaging his brain, he saw boots, heard commands.

"Get restraints! Hurry!"

"He could bite his tongue off. Put this stick in his mouth."

Hands grabbed hold of him, clamping hold of his head, wrenching his jaws open, forcing in a wooden rule till he began to gag.

"Hold his arms."

"No, don't touch him yet. Not till he's calmed down—"

There's something in my head! He tried to tell them what was wrong, but the wooden rule pressed down on his tongue and only inarticulate, gargling sounds came out.

And just as suddenly as it had burst into life, the kernel of brightness in his mind died down. He went limp, unresisting.

"The fit's passing. Now's the moment, quick—"

The guards pinioned his arms behind his back, trussing him so that he could not move.

"Send for a strong sedative. We can't have him throwing a fit like this in the carriage."

One of the men went hurrying away. Another bent down and—none too gently—prised the wooden rule from Gavril's mouth.

"Not mad—" Gavril said in a gasp. "Tell the Emperor—it's still alive. I can hear it—in my head."

He saw the soldiers glance at one another.

"Humor him," whispered one.

"Of course we'll tell the Emperor."

"He'll—reward you—"

"Here's the sedative." One of the guards knelt beside Gavril. "Now then, Nagarian, this'll calm you down."

"No, no drugs!" Gavril twisted his head away. He must stay conscious. Once they sedated him, he would be unable to tell Eugene what he had experienced—and his last hope of reprieve would be gone. "I'm perfectly sane—"

"Get his mouth open. Hurry."

They thrust the rule back between his gritted teeth. The pain was almost unbearable, but still he fought them. One fetched a funnel and forced it into his mouth, pouring the sedative in till it trickled, cold and bitter as poison, down the back of his throat. Coughing, he tried to spit it out.

"This one's a fighter. Hold him down. It'll start to work soon."

They tugged out the funnel from between Gavril's clenched teeth.

"I'm not mad!" he cried with all the force of his lungs. "I'm— *not—"*

Already his tongue felt swollen, sluggish. The words sounded slurred. And the brightness of the lights was dimming as if a fine veil of mist were drifting through the cell. His limbs felt heavy, unwieldy. The faces of his guards seemed to be slowly floating away from him, their staring eyes like lanterns glimpsed through mist.

"See? I told you. Gave him enough to fell a horse. He'll be out of it for hours. By that time he'll be on his way to the asylum. . . ."

"Don't lock me away. Please don't lock me away. . . ." The words formed in his dulling brain like soap bubbles—and popped before he could speak them.

He was falling back now, falling slowly back into soft clouds.

Not mad . . .

Arnskammar Asylum for the Insane was armored to withstand the storm winds that frequently pounded the remote cliffs on which it stood. The local inhabitants nicknamed it the Iron Tower, for the stone from which it was built was veined with ore. When wet with rain or tidespray, its massive walls glistened with the dour, brown sheen of newly forged iron. It had originally been a fortress, one of two built by the Tielen princes to defend Arnskammar Point, the most southern promontory of Tielen.

In these more stable and enlightened times, the Tielen council had converted one of the fortresses into a secure hospital in which to house those distressing cases whose insanity could not be cured by conventional treatment. Also, wealthy and titled families had been known to pay for the confinement of difficult relatives whose scandalous behavior had proved an embarrassment. The government was rumored to house dangerous prisoners of state there too, those whose anarchic ideas would make them a danger to society.

It was to Arnskammar Asylum that the Emperor Eugene had sent a prisoner in a locked, barred carriage. The patient's identity was to be kept secret; he was referred to only as Number Twenty-One. All that was known about him was that he was not a Tielen by birth and that he had—in his madness—committed a terrible crime against the New Rossiyan Empire.

"The late Count Velemir once hinted to me, Eupraxia," said Eugene as he and Astasia's governess stood gazing at the betrothal portrait, "that the relationship between my wife and Gavril Nagarian was considerably more than that of patron and artist. . . ."

Eupraxia's eyes widened; he saw a deep flush spread across her face and throat.

"There was never any evidence of impropriety, your imperial highness," she said staunchly.

"I am not seeking to smear my wife's reputation. My sources, however, tell me that Gavril Nagarian was once thrown out of a court reception for attempting to kiss Astasia."

Little pearls of perspiration glistened on Eupraxia's brow; she dabbed at them with a lace handkerchief.

"Yes, but my Tasia was blameless in the affair. The young man's behavior was unpardonable—"

"Thank you, Eupraxia. You may go."

When the flustered Eupraxia had withdrawn, Eugene sat back, mesmerized by Gavril Nagarian's portrait of his wife. Young though the painter was, he had managed to capture her elusive air of wistfulness. This was no mere formal likeness; it communicated something more profound, hinting at a greater intimacy than was normal between sitter and painter.

The girl in the portrait stared past Eugene, her dark eyes wistfully fixed on some distant, unattainable desire. Such freshness, such a sweet simplicity of nature shone through . . . and yet there was also an undeniable melancholy, doubly poignant in one so young.

She seemed so distant. He had put it down to a natural shyness at first and found it not unappealing. Now he sensed it had become a barrier to keep him at a distance. When he had consummated the marriage, he had tried to murmur words of tenderness to assure her of his good faith and appreciation. But she seemed not to hear, turning away from him and pretending to sleep.

Perhaps she harbored feelings for someone else.

Eugene frowned at the portrait. Even now he could not rid himself of Gavril Nagarian. His presence still lingered, tormenting him with doubts and unanswered questions.

The young man had shown great promise as a painter. Some said the line between artistic talent and madness was a slender one. But it was not the brief flowering of Gavril's talent that concerned him now, it was the unspoken text behind the portrait. A text that spoke of a relationship between sitter and artist that transcended the bounds of propriety.

What's this? Am I jealous of a wretched lunatic? I am ruler of five countries, Emperor of New Rossiya; I have no need to envy any man alive.

And yet, and yet . . .

Astasia has never once looked at me like that. Her eyes have never once gazed into mine with that soft, yearning sweetness. . . .

She doesn't love me. I had hoped that she might grow to love me when she knew me better. . . .

There was a discreet tap at his study door and Gustave appeared with a dispatch on a silver tray.

"This has just arrived, imperial highness."

Eugene broke the seal and swiftly scanned the contents of the neatly written report.

. . . to inform you that the patient has arrived at Arnskammar. His guards were obliged to administer heavy sedatives before transporting the patient as he was suddenly gripped by a fit of such extreme violence that it seemed almost as if he were wrestling with some invisible force.

Some invisible force . . . The dispatch dropped from Eugene's hand. An uneasy feeling gripped him. Was it possible that Gavril had lied to him about the Drakhaoul?

He locked the doors of his study. Then he uncovered the glittering crystal voice-transference device, the Vox Aethyria that communicated directly with Magus Kaspar Linnaius far away in his laboratory at Swanholm.

"Is Gavril Nagarian still possessed by the Drakhaoul? Is it in any way possible?"

The device crackled into life and the Magus's voice, calm and distant, replied.

"We are still ignorant of the true nature and provenance of this Drakhaoul-creature, highness. It is an aethyric being, incapable of existing long in this world without a corporeal host. But your daughter Karila appears to have communicated with the Drakhaoul the night it passed over Swanholm."

"Karila?" echoed Eugene. Suddenly he felt chill sweat dampen his forehead and palms. His beloved little Karila, in contact with this dangerous spirit? "Why was I not told of this before?"

"She only confided in me a day or two ago when she returned to the palace. She came to beg me to take her as a pupil."

"The child is seven years old!"

"Your daughter is gifted. Such unique gifts often reveal themselves at an early age. But I will do whatever your highness commands in this matter."

Karila, gifted in the magic arts? This was not at all what Eugene had expected.

"The frustrations of her considerable physical handicaps may have significantly enhanced her mental powers. . . ."

"You're saying she can communicate with these aethyric beings?"

"It appears so."

For a moment the absurd idea entered Eugene's mind that if he were to bring Karila to Gavril Nagarian, she could tell him if he were still possessed. . . .

And then the preposterousness of such a suggestion made him dismiss it. What kind of a father would take his little daughter to a mental asylum where the criminally insane were confined? The shock of the experience could damage her for life. No, there would have to be another way.

"Have you ever been to Arnskammar, Magus?"

Gavril listened to the wind buffeting the tower. Far below he could hear the smash of seawater against rocks. It was an oddly comforting sound, reminding him of those rare stormy days in Smarna when the cloud-churned sky would turn the blue waters of Vermeille Bay to choppy grey and wind would whip the tops of the darkening waves into a frenzy of white foam.

Vermeille . . . the Villa Andara, his childhood home. Would he ever see it again?

He rose from the bed and went toward the high, barred window, standing on tiptoe, straining to look out. All he could see was a grey, endless expanse of sea and cloudy sky.

His cell must be at the very top of the asylum tower. Another precaution to ensure escape was impossible. And now he would stay locked away here till the end of his days, never to see his mother again, never to stroke Kiukiu's soft hair or gaze into her eyes . . .

From now on he was just a number.

Number Twenty-One.

CHAPTER 10

Astasia awoke with the first light of dawn. She was alone in the great velvet-swagged bed.

"Eugene?" she said sleepily. When there was no reply, she left the warmth of the bed and, wrapping a brocade gown around her, padded in bare feet to tap on Eugene's dressing-room door. Still no reply.

The Emperor must have risen early again. He had no taste, it seemed, for lingering in bed, but preferred to keep to his strict military regime.

She opened the door to his dressing room and found herself staring into her own face.

The betrothal portrait.

When had Eugene ordered it to be moved here, to his dressing room? It had been on public display in the Hall of Black Marble, garlanded each day with fresh flowers. What did it mean? Did he wish to have it closer to him, in a more private place? Was it some sign of deeper affection? Or did he have it removed from public display for some less personal motive, such as the artist's disgrace?

She looked at it again and felt a sharp pang of guilt. It was Nadezhda who had first told her the outcome of Gavril Nagarian's trial and sentence. The next day the verdict was widely reported in the daily journals. The journalists had made much of the Emperor's magnanimity in sparing the life of the lawless young warlord whose barbarous attack on the Imperial Palace of Swanholm had nearly killed little Princess Karila.

Gavril was beyond her help; he had committed a terrible crime and must pay the price. But there might be something she could do for Elysia. She still felt a warm affection for the portrait painter who had been as cruelly duped as she by Count Velemir's political machinations. The very least she could do was to request a safe conduct home to Smarna for Elysia. An imperial pardon would be even better. Surely Eugene could not wish to avenge himself on her; her son was no longer a threat to him, locked away for life in his distant prison-asylum.

Another pang of guilt assailed her. She remembered a sunlit summer room, her hair stirred by a warm sea breeze. She remembered talking to a young man more easily, more frankly, than she had ever talked to anyone else. And she remembered his eyes, blue as the summer sea, smiling at her over the rim of the canvas as his brush dabbed skillfully at his palette. . . .

Forget him! she told herself, pulling her robe more closely around her. *The Gavril Andar I knew is dead.*

The Emperor and Empress sat together by the fire, sharing a rare moment of privacy after dinner. They lived their waking hours in public now—Eugene with his ministers and generals, Astasia attending function after function to represent her husband: opening a foundlings' hospital; welcoming the wives of the Tielen dignitaries to Mirom; attending a subscription concert to raise money for the veterans of the recent hostilities. Astasia's social diary was filled for the next twelve months.

Coffee had been served, strong and black as Eugene preferred, with a dash of spirits. Astasia had declined the coffee but nibbled one or two of the little almond biscuits as she sat beside her husband. *Husband.* How strange that word sounded, even now. She was joined by law to this tall, powerful man who was drinking his coffee like any other man, absentmindedly dipping an almond biscuit into the dark liquid and then quietly cursing as half fell into the cup, necessitating some hasty fishing with his silver spoon.

Even now Eugene was working; important papers had arrived tonight from one of his commanders in the field.

The fire crackled in the grate, the gilded clock (another Tielen import) ticked on the mantelpiece. Astasia picked up a third biscuit, then replaced it. Was this the moment to ask him about Elysia? The silence could almost be described as companionable—except that she was bored. Elsewhere in the palace, there was dancing tonight—a naval ball. She was still tempted to go back to join Varvara and her ladies in the ballroom, if it were not for the fact that her feet were red and sore. Her own fault. Why had she foolishly, vainly, insisted on wearing those new powder-blue shoes? The pointed toes were so pretty, but utterly unsuitable for walking the long corridors of the new convent school Eugene had set up for daughters of the army.

Yes, there was no doubt that Eugene was trying hard to win the citizens of Mirom with his new schools and hospitals. Something her poor, foolish Papa had neglected to consider. . . .

Eugene looked up from the dispatch he was reading. "Oh and Maltheus tells me the council has commissioned a wedding portrait of us both, to hang in the Great Chamber in Tielborg. You will need to warn your ladies-in-waiting to make your wedding gown ready for a sitting."

"A wedding portrait?" This was her chance. Heart beating a little faster, she said, smiling, "I know of an excellent portraitist, Eugene."

"Maltheus has already seen to it. He has brought in the services of Maistre Josse from Francia. He believes we have no portrait artists of suitable stature in Tielen."

"In Tielen, maybe so. But in Smarna—"

He set the papers down and looked at her, frowning. "What are you suggesting, Astasia?"

What, not whom. She felt the smile begin to fray a little at the corners of her mouth, yet she was determined not to be put off. "Elysia Andar."

His eyes looked on her coldly now, bleak as a wintry sea.

"She has lost her livelihood—and all because Count Velemir made her go to Tielen to deliver my portrait." Astasia heard herself babbling and tried to slow down, to sound mature and reasonable. "Why should she be punished for her son's crimes?"

"You must understand that it would be utterly inappropriate to employ Elysia Andar. So many of my people lost sons, husbands, and fathers in Azhkendir at her son's hands."

"She was a good companion to me, Eugene." Astasia persevered even though she sensed he was becoming irritated. "Could you not at least let her go home? As a gesture of goodwill on our wedding?" She rose and gently laid one hand on his shoulder. "For my sake?"

He gazed up into her eyes. Still he did not smile back at her. "Does it mean so much to you?"

She nodded, feeling like a child again, cajoling Papa for some little treat she had been forbidden by Mama or Praxia.

"Then a passage will be granted."

"Tonight? You will see to it tonight?"

"I will instruct Chancellor Maltheus tomorrow. It will be dispatched to Captain Lindgren straightaway."

"That is more than generous!" Astasia, delighted at her triumph, kissed him. Eugene caught hold of her wrist and held her close, gently yet firmly, before she could pull away.

"You have a warm heart, Astasia," he said, gazing intently into her eyes, "but take care. Now you are Empress, there are many who will seek to insinuate their way into your affections and take advantage of your kindness. Be careful, my dear."

Her earlier elation drained away as she saw he was in deadly earnest.

"And never allow yourself to be alone with anyone, no matter how well you think you know them. There are some fanatical individuals who would not hesitate to harm you—or Karila—if they thought it would influence me."

It was her first spontaneous display of affection, Eugene reflected as Astasia withdrew to prepare for bed. That soft press of Astasia's lips to his was the first kiss that he had not had to initiate. The first time she had not closed her eyes as she leaned close to his burned, disfigured face. And all for Elysia Andar's sake.

Astasia had left behind the book she was reading; he picked it up and saw it was a romantic novel, its prose trembling with high passion and peril. She was still a schoolgirl in so many ways, as charmingly wayward and naïve as Karila. Was it possible that this perplexing, charming child-woman could grow to love him?

But did he dare to let himself grow fond of her? In allowing her a place in his heart, he would make himself vulnerable. An emperor could not afford such a weakness.

And yet, she had kissed him. She would be waiting for him now, in their blue velvet-hung bed.

The clock struck eleven. He took up the novel and had reached the door when there was a smart tap and Gustave appeared, bearing a folded paper on a silver tray.

"Well, what is it?" Eugene said a little curtly.

"A matter that requires your attention, imperial highness."

Eugene stifled a sigh and opened the paper, hastily scanning the message, transcribed from a Vox Aethyria:

> From Governor Armfeld, Old Citadel of Colchise, Smarna.
> Negotiations have broken down with the Smarnan council. They refuse to accept the terms of the annexation. They maintain that ownership of the Ruby of Smarna does not legally entitle his imperial highness to impose Tielen rule. They refuse to levy the taxes which are paid by all other citizens of the New Rossiyan Empire.

He lowered the paper, tempted to crush Armfeld's message and hurl it into the fire. He had not anticipated trouble so soon—and in the smallest, least significant of the five countries.

"Will your highness send a reply?" Gustave hovered, ready to take dictation.

"I'll speak to Armfeld myself."

Eugene set out at a brisk stride, with Gustave hurrying along behind. It was not until he sat down at the Vox Aethyria that he realized he was still holding Astasia's novel.

And what had he just promised Astasia, that he would send word to Azhkendir that Elysia Andar was free to return to Smarna? He closed his eyes and rested his head against his hand. He had allowed himself to be swayed by his feelings—and, as ever, it had proved to be imprudent. Now if he reneged on his promise, Astasia would believe that her wishes counted for nothing. He would attempt to explain that it was a matter of national security and she would shake her dark cloud of curls, pouting her pretty mouth . . .

Besides, what real harm could Elysia Andar do in Smarna? Her activities would be much easier to monitor in Vermeille than in remote Azhkendir. She might even prove to be useful. He would just have to take extra precautions.

He turned to Gustave. "Before I deal with Armfeld, get me our embassy in Francia."

*   *   *

It was well past one in the morning by the time Eugene had dealt with the matters in hand to his satisfaction. As he rose from the desk, yawning and stretching, his hand knocked something to the floor. Bending down to pick it up, he saw it was Astasia's novel. It had fallen open at the place she had marked and as his eyes strayed down the page, he read:

"My palace, my whole court will be yours," cried the Tsar. "Oh, Elise, my dearest Elise, you will be avenged. Tears of blood will repay you for the tears you have shed. . . ."

He snapped the book shut, shaking his head. Such romantic nonsense. And yet powerful in the influence it must exert on its readers, even on Astasia. Had novels such as this colored her expectations of life? Did she secretly expect him to match up to the dashing, tortured heroes in her favorite fiction?

If so, I must be something of a disappointment. He approached their apartments, nodding to the sentries on guard as they saluted him.

In their bedchamber, he saw her lying asleep, her dark hair unbound, like black silk on the pillow. Even now, to look at her sleeping, her dark lashes, her delicate pale complexion made him catch his breath.

"Astasia?" he said gently, bending down, his lips brushing her cheek. "You forgot your novel."

She murmured something he could not quite catch and turned over, away from him, snuggling her face into the pillow.

He sighed and quietly began to undress, then slipped into bed beside her, making as little movement as possible so as not to disturb her.

It was the start of the Spring Festival in Tielen tonight. Eugene gazed at the sunlight sparkling on the distant Nieva. All week the young people would be dressing in white costumes to dance around bonfires and wander the streets until dawn, drinking and singing to welcome in the spring. Here across the water, in Muscobar, they did not burn spring bonfires or sing into the small hours. Instead, Astasia told him, they waited another whole six weeks till Kupala's Eve. So to honor his homeland's festival—and maybe to quench a pang of homesickness—he had ordered a grand formal dinner at the palace and a fireworks display on the Nieva to impress the citizens of Mirom.

"The visitor from Francia is here, highness," Gustave announced. "I've shown him into your private study, as requested."

Gustave had left the study door discreetly ajar so that Eugene could take a moment to observe the new arrival.

The young man seemed at ease, looking thoughtfully at an oil painting of sunset at sea, leaning forward from time to time as though to inspect a detail of brushwork or a signature, then stepping back to assess the effect again.

So this was Pavel Velemir, Feodor Velemir's nephew. The likeness was striking.

"I've always been particularly fond of that seascape," Eugene said quietly. "It was commissioned by my father."

The young man started and then, effortlessly recovering his self-composure, placed both hands on his heart, bowing low in the Muscobar fashion. A lock of honey-gold hair flopped down over his eyes and he flicked it back with a careless toss of the head.

"Your imperial highness."

"How like your late uncle you are," Eugene said, smiling affably.

"Other people have told me so too." Pavel Velemir smiled back, a smile of heart-stopping charm. He had not only inherited his uncle's good looks but also his pleasant, easygoing manner. "What miracles of restoration you have accomplished here at the Winter Palace, highness. From the tales coming out of Muscobar, it was feared that the place had been burned to the ground."

Eugene sat down at his desk and gestured for the young man to sit opposite him. "You were abroad at the time of your uncle's death, I believe?"

"I was in Francia. Grand Duke Aleksei sent me as undersecretary to our ambassador there. I have a certain skill with languages."

Eugene nodded indulgently. He knew the real reason for Pavel Velemir's placement in the embassy: at the time, his agents in Francia had alerted him to the arrival of a new spy from Muscobar.

"I'm looking for an agent to undertake a mission of considerable delicacy. You might be the ideal candidate."

"I'm flattered, highness." Another hint of that heart-stopping smile.

"But first . . ." Eugene unfolded a document he had kept to his side of the desk. "Am I correct in thinking that you have inherited nothing from your uncle's estates?"

The young man's smile faded.

"In fact, I understand that at the time of his death, the count's affairs were found to be in total disorder. What was it he left you—his art collection?"

"His rooms in the Winter Palace here were ransacked by the revolutionaries. The paintings that were not looted were defaced or burned." Eugene saw that Pavel Velemir had clenched his hand into a tight fist. For a moment Eugene was vividly, painfully reminded of another passionate, fatherless young man: Jaromir.

"So you have nothing."

The young man's chin jerked up defiantly, as if countering a blow.

Eugene smiled. He had not been so impressed by Pavel Velemir's good looks that he had failed to notice that his immaculate white shirt was frayed at the cuffs, or that the polished sheen of his riding boots could not quite conceal the fact that they had been mended once too often. Pavel was making a brave job of concealing his impoverished state, and that could only work to Eugene's advantage.

Eugene leaned forward across the desk. "Work for me, Pavel, and I will see that you never want for anything again. Do you know Smarna?"

"Of course. My mother used to take a villa on the coast every summer when I was a child."

Eugene allowed himself another smile. His sources had done their research well. "And you've heard that there's trouble brewing there? A rebellion?"

"What do you want me to do?"

"Become part of that rebellion. Convince them that your heart burns with the same passion for freedom as theirs. And then . . ."

"And then?"

"You're an intelligent young man. Exactly how you act on that information, I leave to your discretion. But fulfill my trust in you, Pavel, and you will go far. Rossiya is a new empire, a young empire— and I need men and women of promise to protect our interests. What do you say?"

Pavel looked at him directly. "I am honored, highness, that you have chosen me." His clear hazel eyes betrayed not the slightest trace of guile. Had he inherited Feodor's gifts for deception as well as his charming smile? "But wouldn't it help my mission if I had a strong motive to convince the Smarnan revolutionaries of my hate for Tielen? I need to engineer some public slight—and ensure it is witnessed by one or two influential people. That way it will be reported abroad in court journals and gazettes."

Good! thought Eugene, warming to him even more. *Not just a handsome face.* "I will leave the details to you. I imagine you can be quite creative when the situation allows." He rose; Pavel rose too. "And this is for you," he added, holding out the folded document, "Count Pavel Velemir."

Pavel stared at him a moment and then opened the document. "My uncle's title—and the deeds to his estates?"

"You may continue to call him 'uncle' if you wish, but he named you as his only son and heir in this second, secret will," Eugene said, intrigued to see that the news had made the young man flush an angry red.

Pavel Velemir refolded the will, meticulously smoothing down each crease. He looked up at Eugene, the angry flush gone from his cheeks, his hazel eyes calm and shrewd as he handed back the document.

"Imperial highness, I believe this could be the key to my public disgrace. Is there anyone you trust implicitly among the younger Tielen nobility, who could be made party to our plan?"

"You want me to transfer your uncle's estates as a gift to one of my court?"

"And when I protest volubly, you could have me thrown out."

"Then I would like you to join us for dinner tonight. My wife Astasia is most eager to hear the latest news from Francia." Eugene could not resist setting another little test; his sources at the Mirom court had warned him that before her betrothal, Astasia had been seen to dance with Pavel Velemir on more than one occasion.

"I'd be delighted, imperial highness." There was not even a flicker of reaction to the mention of her name.

Pavel Velemir walked swiftly along the gravel paths of the Rusalki Gardens. In the white-painted tubs, rare tulips bloomed, their heavy burgundy heads feathered with cream and gold. In Francia, the first roses were already in bud, but this far to the north, the spring flowers were only just opening.

He passed the Rusalki Fountain, which sprayed fanning jets of water high into the mild air. Courtiers out strolling in the afternoon sun stared curiously as he strode past, making for the River Gate. Young ladies-in-waiting whispered and giggled behind their lace-gloved hands.

So the gossip that had haunted him was right. He was not Feodor Velemir's nephew. He was his son.

He slowed. It was not as if he had never suspected his true parentage. But he was angry with his mother. Why had she never told him the truth? He was no child, damn it; he was twenty-three.

As to the circumstances of his conception, he could only guess. An early forbidden romance between his mother and her libertine cousin, Feodor.

He had reached the wild garden that lay beyond the austere formal parterres and tubs. Here the grasses grew high between alders and the fresh green of weeping willows, all artfully planted to give the impression of a natural river meadow.

He snapped off a slender alder branch and struck angrily at the tall grasses.

Throughout his years at Mirom's Military Academy he had been forced to endure the sneering comments of his blue-blooded, highborn fellow cadets.

He had fought more than one sabre-duel in defense of his mother Xenia's honor.

He slashed at a yellow iris, neatly severing the flower from its stalk.

There were officers in the Mirom army who would bear the scars of their insolence to their graves.

It was Uncle Feodor who had rescued him from the drab prospect of an undistinguished military career, steering him into the Muscobar diplomatic service. Why had he never acknowledged him as his son? To avoid shaming his mother? Had he planned to reveal himself at some later stage? Or was it just too inconvenient in his busy life to burden himself with the duties of a father?

Just when did you plan to tell me, Uncle Feodor?

Another iris flew spinning from its stalk.

But it was nearly time to dress for dinner. This was not the moment to let his feelings run riot. And the Emperor had singled him out from all his other agents for a crucial mission.

If he had learned one thing from his natural father, it was the art of deception. Was it not Feodor Velemir who had initiated him into the shadow-world of espionage?

He reached the River Gate; a young officer stepped forward to bar his way, hand extended.

"Your pass, please."

There was something familiar about his stance, his bearing. Pavel produced his pass and, as he handed it over, stared at the young man's face. "Good God," he said. "Valery Vassian."

"Pavel!" said Valery, obviously equally surprised.

"Lieutenant Vassian, if I'm not mistaken," Pavel said dryly, "in the *Tielen* Household Cavalry."

It had never been difficult to embarrass Valery when they had been cadets together, and Pavel noted with some satisfaction that, lieutenant or no, Valery was still easily flustered.

"We're all one empire now, yes?" Valery said, his voice a little overloud. "And it's the Imperial Household Cavalry. See this imperial purple trimming on the collar?"

"Of course," Pavel said easily.

"Quite frankly"—Valery dropped his voice—"and not wishing to insult old Duke Aleksei, the conditions are so much better than in our own army. Good pay—regular pay, Pavel!—and decent lodgings and food. Training in maneuvers, weaponry, strategy—we were treated shabbily in Mirom. Remember Colonel Roskovski?"

Pavel nodded, remembering all too well Roskovski's irascible outbursts and lunatic lectures on military tactics.

"Why do you think I joined the diplomatic service?" he said, relaxing a little. He allowed himself to remember that Valery had not been one of his persecutors at the Academy, and had suffered quite a few torments of his own.

"I see you're invited to dinner at the palace tonight, too," Valery said, stamping his pass and handing it back.

"Too?" Pavel looked at Valery, wondering if he might be the one to involve in his plan.

"The Emperor honored me with an invitation as well. And now that you're here, I begin to wonder if he's invited our whole year from the Military Academy."

*　*　*

The Emperor favored an informal approach to entertaining his dinner guests, borne of long years on campaign and an ingrained impatience with elaborate dining rituals.

So when Pavel and Valery met in the antechamber, a liveried servant presented them with a tray of crystal glasses filled with aquavit—a custom more usual at military dinners.

"To a brighter future, then," Valery said, raising his glass. "To the empire."

Pavel shrugged and clinked his glass against Valery's. The aquavit was clean-tasting, sharp in the throat as a breath of icy air. He glanced around the antechamber, wondering who else the Emperor had invited from his Mirom past.

The double doors at the far side of the antechamber opened. The murmur of conversation ceased as the guests drew back from the doorway, bowing.

The Emperor Eugene and the Empress Astasia, accompanied by two of her ladies-in-waiting, had entered the antechamber. Astasia was dressed in a watered silk gown of hyacinth blue. Sapphires and diamonds glittered at her throat and in her elaborately arranged dark hair. Yet in spite of her formal court attire, Pavel still saw the young girl in white muslin who had once so intrigued him.

Suddenly he was back at his first court ball, thrown in honor of Astasia Orlova's eighteenth birthday. In her simple white gown, she had seemed to him more exquisite than all the bejeweled women of the court—even the flamboyant beauty of the famed tragedienne, Olga Giladkova. With her cloud of soft dark hair and wide, violet eyes, Astasia had completely bewitched him. He and Valery had competed to partner her in dance after dance. It had not gone unnoticed at the time.

Was that why he had been sent back to Francia so swiftly afterward?

Astasia was coming nearer, welcoming the guests with smiles and polite little exchanges of greeting.

He shot a sideways glance at Valery and saw that the lieutenant's face had turned red. Valery started to fiddle with his stiff imperial collar as if it were too tight. Did he still have feelings for Astasia? Surely it was not the heat that had caused him to flush so deeply. . . .

"Lieutenant Valery Vassian; Pavel Velemir of the Muscobar Diplomatic Service," announced an equerry.

Vassian clicked his heels and saluted; Pavel bowed. As he raised his head, he saw Astasia gazing at him intently. It was only for a second; a moment later her expression was composed, her smile distant.

"Lieutenant Vassian, I am delighted to see you've joined the Imperial Household Cavalry." She extended her hand and Pavel watched Vassian fumble a clumsy kiss. "I had great respect for your father. I know you will serve the empire as dedicatedly as he served Muscobar."

Then she turned to Pavel.

"And welcome, Pavel Velemir. It seems so long since we last met in Mirom. I trust the journey from Francia was not too tedious?"

He took her hand and held it to his lips. In spite of the warmth of the late spring evening, her slender fingers were cool.

No mention of his uncle. Well, it was hardly surprising, under the circumstances.

"The weather was clement and the seas were kind, highness," he said formally.

"Did you attend the ballet in Lutèce?"

The question took him by surprise. "On several occasions."

Her violet eyes were suddenly alight with interest. "You must tell me all about it! I am determined we should invite the company to the new theater at Swanholm—" She broke off, glancing uncertainly at Eugene, as though sensing that she had stepped beyond the bounds of imperial propriety.

Eugene nodded indulgently at his young wife, then moved on, obliging her to follow.

Pavel let out a slow breath; he had the distinct sense that he and Vassian had just been tested by the Emperor.

"So where's your next mission?" Vassian took out a linen handkerchief and mopped his forehead. Pavel could tell he was forcing the polite conversation for even as he spoke, his eyes strayed after Astasia. "Back to Francia?"

Pavel gave him a brief smile. "Probably."

"Damn it," Vassian said in a sudden burst of feeling. "She's radiant, isn't she? Too good for the likes of us. And yet if things had gone otherwise for Muscobar, if Andrei Orlov hadn't drowned—"

The double doors opened again, revealing a candlelit dining table beyond. A delicious savory smell wafted out; Pavel recognized the bittersweet aroma of fennel and fish bisque.

"Dinner is served."

*   *   *

"It is my custom, as many of you know," the Emperor announced as servants discreetly and efficiently removed the dessert plates from the long dining table, "to reward those who have served the empire faithfully."

Pavel glanced up. This was his moment. In the golden candleglow, he saw that all the guests were looking expectantly at the Emperor. Astasia had inclined her dark head toward her husband.

She looks at him as if she worships him. Is she a skillful actress— or is that genuine, unfeigned affection?

"And it is my pleasure, this evening, to honor the loyal service of one whose actions preserved much of this beautiful palace in the recent insurrection—Colonel Anton Roskovski."

Eugene must have an ironic sense of humor, Pavel thought, to have chosen his old nemesis from the Military Academy. This should prove interesting.

"What?" muttered Valery Vassian to Pavel under the cover of the polite applause that greeted the announcement. "Rabid Roskovski?"

Pavel shrugged, watching the colonel rise to acknowledge the applause with a stiff military bow. Any moment now—

"Colonel, in recognition of your service to Muscobar and the empire, I am pleased to bestow upon you the house and country estate that belonged to the late Count Velemir. As the Count died without legitimate heirs, it seems to me only fitting that you should—"

"Without legitimate heirs?" cried Pavel, leaping to his feet and upsetting his chair. "That estate is rightfully mine!"

"Steady there, Pavel." Vassian rose too, catching hold of him by the arm. "You must have taken a drop too much—"

Pavel shook off Vassian's restraining hand and started toward Roskovski. Everyone was staring at him. "I am Velemir's nephew!" Pavel reached the head of the table. He could sense the stir among guests and servants, knew that at any moment now, he would be wrestled to the ground and thrown out.

"How dare you, sir!" spluttered Roskovski. If Eugene had forewarned him, he was more than adequate to the role of the insulted party. "How dare you make a scene in front of the Emperor and Empress!"

"I demand my rights!" Pavel shouted. "I'll duel you for it, Roskovski. Pistols at dawn in the Water Meadows—"

"I believe your fight is with me, young man," Eugene said coolly. "The Velemir estates are mine to dispose of as I choose. You are quite obviously not fit to take on the responsibility." He clicked his fingers and four of the Imperial Household Cavalry hurried in. "Remove this man immediately."

"You Tielen lackey, Roskovski! Call yourself a Muscobite—"

As the guards wrestled him to the polished floor, Pavel caught a glimpse of Astasia's pale face staring at him, her dark eyes wide with dismay. And for a brief moment, he felt ashamed.

What must you think of me, Astasia? One day, maybe you'll learn why.

Then one of the guards struck him a stinging blow on the chin and he sagged in their grip. As they half-dragged, half-carried him from the dining room, he heard the shocked whispers begin.

They flung him out onto the square at the front of the palace. As he picked himself up off the cobbles, he yelled out for good measure, "D'you think you can treat me like this, Eugene, and get away with it? You haven't heard the last of me. You haven't heard the last of Pavel Velemir!"

His jaw throbbed. That guard had hit him pretty hard.

And so my new career begins. With a jawful of jangled teeth and a swollen face.

Ruefully, he limped away in search of some ice.

CHAPTER 11

Gavril opens his eyes. It is past midnight in the Iron Tower and his cell is utterly dark. And yet he senses that he is not alone.

"Who's there?"

Eyes glimmer in the darkness, blue as starlight. And something blacker than the darkness itself rears up out of the night until it towers above his bed.

"I have returned, Gavril Nagarian."

"Drakhaoul?" His heart is pounding with fear and a wild, unbidden joy. "Why have you come back?"

"You could not live with me—but now you cannot live without me. Do you want to stay here until your body withers with age?"

Stay here until he is a frail old man too senile to remember how long he has been imprisoned, too damaged to care? He springs up from the bed. He turns to face his banished daemon, arms wide to embrace it.

"Take me, then. Take me away from this place."

The Drakhaoul enfolds him, close, closer, until he is drowning in an ecstasy of shadows . . .

His body spasms, arching in one final convulsion of possession— and from somewhere buried deep within him he hears that subtle voice whisper in triumph.

"Now you are mine again, Gavril. Now we act, we think, as one."

His sight blurs, then clears. Suddenly he can see everything in the moonless dark of the cell. He can hear the sounds of the night, from the wheezing snores of the prisoner in the cell below his to the tick of the clock in the exercise-yard tower. He can even smell the tobacco smoke wafting from the warden's pipe and the brine of the waves pounding the cliffs below the Iron Tower. Until now, he has forgotten how the Drakhaoul sharpens every sense.

"What are you waiting for, Gavril?" the daemon whispers. *"Go to the window. Tear out the bars. Feel the salt of the sea breeze on your face. Launch yourself out onto the wild wind . . ."*

Gavril opened his eyes, the Drakhaoul's soft voice still echoing in his mind.

It was raining. The drab brown of the cell walls enclosed him, lit by the dull dawn light that streaked the stones.

His world was bathed in a wash of sepia. The rain showered against the Iron Tower in erratic bursts—a dirty-colored rain, not silver shot with sunlight. The clouds hung low in the sky, layer upon layer, heavy with more rain to come.

So it had just been a dream. A cruel illusion of escape and freedom, made crueler still by the fact that it had seemed so real.

Gavril lay motionless, staring up at the square of rain-wet sky, striped with metal bars. Once, when he and the Drakhaoul had been one, he could have used the daemon's strength to wrench the bars from their sockets, then flown free on powerful shadow-wings. But now there was no hope of escape from this bleak prison. Even his name had been taken from him.

Gavril blinked in the daylight. The paving slabs glistened, wet and slippery underfoot. A warder was taking him to the exercise yard. Gavril walked slowly, dragging his feet, hearing the clank of his shackled ankles. The touch of the rain on his shaven head was cool and refreshing. There was a slight smell of damp earth in the air that reminded him of spring. He wondered what day it was. What month.

"I will come for you. . . ." He heard himself making the promise to Kiukiu that he would now never be able to keep. He pictured her going to the door of her grandmother's cottage and gazing out over the empty moors, day after day. Who was there to protect her, now that he was gone? What would happen if the Tielens came searching for her?

"Keep up, there." His warder sounded impatient.

As he walked, Gavril examined in his mind the events at Kastel Drakhaon. Every day it was the same; he found himself obsessively going over what had happened, trying to work out how he could have better planned the defense of his domain. The Tielens had out-maneuverd him; their military strategic experience was far superior to his own. Karonen had taken out his lookouts before they could even raise the alarm. By the time the warning reached the kastel, it was too late to run.

But where could I have run to? And what price would my people have been forced to pay for my cowardice?

"No! *No!*" It was a man's voice, almost incoherent with rage and despair. "Let go of me!"

Gavril's warder ran ahead through the archway. Gavril tried to run too, but the shackles tripped him and he fell to one knee. In the court-yard beyond he saw another prisoner struggling with several warders.

"I'm not mad! It's all a fabrication!" yelled the man. "I know se-crets! State secrets that could bring down Eugene's empire!"

"Silence, Thirteen." One of the warders struck him hard across the mouth and the prisoner's wild shouting changed into a yelp of pain. The next moment, Gavril saw him kick out and send one of the warders flying.

"I *will* be heard! I will—"

It took four warders to hold him down, kicking and writhing, on the wet pavement. The one who had struck him hit him hard once more, causing a fountain of blood to spurt from his nose. The pris-oner let out a gargling cry, but still twisted and fought in the hands of the warders.

"Enough!" Gavril started forward, with no idea in his head but to stop the beating.

"Stay back, Twenty-One." His warder glanced around. "Stay out of this."

"Let him be. Can't you see he's hurt?" cried Gavril, still coming on, fists clenched.

"And unless you want a taste of the same treatment, you'll stay back."

Gavril halted. He looked down at his clenched fists and saw the shackles around his wrists. He was as powerless as the wretched Thirteen.

"I want to see a lawyer." The protests began once more, more mumbled than shouted this time, from a bleeding, broken mouth. "I demand another trial. A fair trial!"

"Get him back to his cell."

Still protesting, Thirteen was dragged away. By now his coarse prison shirt and breeches were torn and stained.

Gavril's warder exchanged quiet words with Thirteen's warder, a little distance away. "This has happened once too often. Tell the director."

Thirteen's warder nodded and followed after his charge.

"Was it necessary to hit him so hard?" Gavril said, anger still simmering.

His warder did not reply.

"Well? Was it?"

His warder turned and stared at him, his eyes hard with hostility.

"What makes you think you have the right to express an opinion?"

Gavril stared back, at a loss for words. The prison clock struck the hour, a dull, unmelodious chime.

"Speak out like that again and you'll be disciplined. Severely disciplined. Now, back to your cell."

"And my exercise time?" Gavril demanded.

"You heard the clock. Exercise time is over."

In the darkness, Gavril lay awake, unable to sleep. Somewhere in the Iron Tower below, another prisoner was weeping, a crazed, droning sound that went on and on.

Had he been tortured to let out such wretched cries? Or was this the madness that set in after years of incarceration in Arnskammar? Surely he must stop soon. . . .

Gavril tried to block out the desolate sound of weeping, burying his head under the thin, scratchy blanket. If only he could sleep. But his mind was restless, churning over the thoughts and fears that the daylight kept at bay. The only escape was in dreams. He lived more in the world of his dreams than in the drabness of his cold, rain-chilled cell. In his dreams he was not a prisoner. In his dreams he was not Twenty-One, or even Gavril Nagarian. In his dreams he was free. . . .

Colors shimmer in the air around him, so vivid he can taste them: yellow, tart as lemon zest; purple, heavy with the musky sweetness of autumn grapes; sea-aquamarine, tinged with a hint of brine; fern-green and gold of anise-savored fennel . . .

Now he can glimpse translucent forms darting and swooping around him. He senses the beat of wings, fast and light as a bird's, stirring soft whirring vibrations in the scented air. Brilliant eyes glimmer close, staring at him with curiosity, then blink and vanish. He feels the kiss of gossamer-soft lips, breathing spice-scented breath . . .

He raises his hand to greet these fleeting apparitions, overcome with delight and wonder—and feels himself slowly borne upward with them, light as a drift of soap bubbles . . .

Gavril awoke to hear the splatter of wind-driven raindrops against the roof slates of the Iron Tower. His mind was still filled with swirling colors; his body still felt light enough to float. The Drakhaoul's memories must be seeping into his dreams again. The images were richly sensual, yet tainted with a disturbing aura of darkness. He did not want to be drawn back into the darkness.

In prison in Mirom he was sure he had heard the Drakhaoul's voice. But if the Drakhaoul was still at large in the world, why had he not heard it since that night? Madmen heard "voices" that told them to commit terrible deeds. Did that mean he was truly mad?

He pulled his blanket closer, listening to the incessant patter of the rain overhead. He wished he could dream of more comforting things. He tried to picture his bedchamber at the kastel: his father's hunting tapestries of red and gold; the warmth of the burning pine logs in the grate, the aromatic scent of the curling smoke evoking the green shadows of the great forest of Kerjhenezh that lay beyond the kastel walls. And Kiukiu kneeling at the grate to tend the fire; Kiukiu impatiently pushing aside a straying strand of golden hair as she raked the glowing embers, wiping a smut of ash from her cheek with the back of her hand. . . .

"Stay with me, Kiukiu," he whispered. He was cold, and dawn was still hours away. "Help me keep the dreams at bay."

Gavril sneezed a wracking sneeze that left him shivering.

"One more circuit." His warder lounged against the wall of the exercise yard, picking at a hangnail.

Gavril pushed himself on. His head ached, his nose was blocked, obliging him to breathe through his mouth, and his throat was sore. Just a head cold. How could a simple cold make him feel so wretched?

He sneezed again. Now his nose began to stream and he had no handkerchief. He stopped, obliged to wipe his nose on his sleeve like a little child.

"Keep moving, Twenty-One."

Elysia would have made him a hot drink of honey and lemon juice to stop the shivering. Palmyre would have brought him clean handkerchiefs, freshly laundered and ironed, smelling of lavender from the villa gardens.

He lumbered doggedly on, forcing one foot to follow the other. If they could just allow him one extra blanket to keep warm at night . . . But he had asked and been told bluntly, "No special privileges." So he must endure the damp and the cold as best he could. . . .

The sound of voices made him raise his head. Through cold-bleared eyes he saw two warders supporting a prisoner who walked with a strange, lolling gait.

"Time's up," said his warder, jerking one thumb in the direction of the Iron Tower.

Gavril stared at the prisoner. He moved like one who has forgotten how to walk.

"Left foot now," ordered one of the warders, but the prisoner did not seem to understand. "Left!"

The prisoner began to make some kind of reply, but the words came out all jumbled and slurred together. "Trying . . . am . . ."

He was close enough now for Gavril to see that the man's head had been shaved and bandaged. Blood had leaked out and dried brown on one side of the bandages.

"Right foot."

"Sh-shorry . . ." The man tried to raise his drooping head. Gavril recognized Thirteen, the prisoner he had seen shouting and demanding his rights a few days ago.

Gavril's warder placed one hand on his arm, trying to move him on. Gavril shook the hand off.

"What have you done to him?" he demanded.

"None of your business." The hand gripped harder.

"Those bandages. The blood." Gavril stood his ground. "Has he been tortured?"

"Shut your mouth!"

*   *   *

Gavril's cold turned feverish by nightfall. He huddled in the corner of his cell, cocooned in his threadbare blanket. In most prisons, inmates could buy comforts such as a brazier of coals to keep warm or extra blankets. But he had no money at his disposal and no family or friends nearby to pay for such necessities.

He could not keep from thinking about Thirteen. Those bloodied bandages, that shambling gait . . . Was it torture, or had Thirteen harmed himself in his rage and despair? His teeth began to chatter uncontrollably as he pulled his blanket tighter. If it was torture, when would it be his turn?

As hot and cold chills ran through his body, he tried to sleep. Fever-fueled images began to leak into his mind. He kept starting awake, only to see fleeting impressions of jewel-flecked eyes, daemon-eyes, staring at him in the dark.

"No," he heard himself mumbling. "Leave me be."

The air trembles. A thunderous darkness looms. A feeling of foreboding overwhelms him.

The bruised sky is rent apart. A ragged gateway gapes, as though some nameless power has ripped the very matter of this world asunder.

A sound issues from the gateway in wave after sickening wave, the sound of disintegration, a grinding and groaning that judders through him until he feels himself drawn helplessly toward the rent in the sky.

Then he is sucked into a whirling vortex; a chaos that crushes all consciousness from him—

And spits him out into a harsh, dry place. Light washes over him, the cruel, blinding light of an alien sun.

The gate still gapes behind him, darker than a thunder-wracked sky. Little crackles of energy fizzle across the opening. It seems to him that the bolts of energy are forked tongues, flickering from the carven mouths of great winged serpents, whose coils tower above him, forming the great arch of the door. And somewhere high above, a serpent-eye, bloodred, fixes him in its burning gaze.

The gate—still a chance of escape.

He flings himself back toward the darkness and the curling fiery tongues lash out, binding him, spread-eagled across the gate. They sear into his wrists and ankles, a white-hot agony.

"Let me go!" he roars. He screams his rage aloud, yet no sound emerges. He is mute.

There are forms, vague and shadowy, looming up out of the intolerable brightness of the unknown sun. Strange, deep voices issue from his shadow-captors.

"Do not approach it yet. It is still too strong. Wait till it weakens."

"See how it shimmers. Like a dragonfly in the sunlight."

"Let me go!" he screams again, but still his plea goes unheard. And now he feels his life force ebbing from him. The harsh rays of the sun are draining it fast. He is fading. . . .

"Its light is dimming. We will lose it!"

"Wait!" That one voice again, which buzzes in and out of his consciousness, is commanding.

This terrible sun is searing the luminous liquid from his veins. The air is too thin; it is poisoning him. He is drying to dust, like a fallen leaf.

"Dying . . . help me . . ."

Anguish bleeds through him. He is dying here, alone, torn from his kin, against his will.

"Send it back. Look—it is in torment."

"No!"

"The doorway is still open—"

"Then I will shut it."

The bloodred glare is extinguished. With a sucking sound, the gaping rent seals itself—and his last means of escape is gone.

Frenzied rage shudders through him. What do they want of him? What possible use can they make of him? They will pay for what they have done. If it is the last thing he does, he will make them suffer as he has suffered at their hands.

"By all the gods—what's happening to it?"

"Stand back." That cold, authoritative voice again.

"Can't you see? We're killing it! It's in some kind of death-throes. We should send it back. Before we have its death on our consciences."

"Daemon-spirit. Can you hear me? I can save you. But first you must give me your allegiance."

"Never!" he cries back with the last of his strength—although he has no idea whether his tormentor can hear him.

Eyes stare into his. Strange eyes, not luminous and dazzling like those of his own kin, but small, fringed by flesh and curling fronds of hair. Ugly eyes, hardened by a hunger for power and dominion. This creature with the small, ugly eyes wants more than his allegiance. It wants to dominate, to bend him to his will.

To make him his own.

"He's coming round."

Gavril could smell the breath of his captor, foul with the reek of raw onion. He tried to turn his head away, and felt strong hands pressing him into the bare boards until his spine protested.

"Hold him down. He may attack again."

"Let—me—go." He twisted his head from side to side, desperate to free himself, but still they held him pinned down to the floorboards.

"Twenty-One." This new voice came from farther away; it was crisp and businesslike. "I will give you a choice. If you give me your word not to attack my warders, I will order them to release you. If you cannot give me your word, I will be obliged to order them to shackle you and administer a sedative. Now—which is it to be?"

"No—more—sedatives," he heard himself begging. Begging! How low had he fallen? He swallowed back the feeling of self-loathing that rose in his throat.

"Release him."

The pressure on his arms and legs did not relax. "Is that wise, Director? You've seen how strong he is when he's in one of his fits."

"And I've also seen how drained he is when the fit passes. He'll hardly have the strength to drag himself to his bed."

The warders loosened their grip on him and moved away.

"Now just stay where you are a moment longer, Twenty-One. Skar—the appliance, if you please."

A lean, sallow-skinned young man came forward and placed a crown-shaped metal device on Gavril's head. He proceeded to adjust and tighten the device until it pressed hard into his temples. Director Baltzar bent over, peering at the contraption and checking it was secure.

"Take down the measurements, Skar."

"What are you doing to me?" Sweat chilled Gavril's body. He had the distinct impression that the director was planning some unpleasant medical investigation.

"Hold still, Twenty-One. I'm merely making some observations for my notes. Hmm. There." The metal band was lifted from his head. "That will be all for now."

Gavril sat up.

"Now, Twenty-One," said Director Baltzar in a calm and reasoning voice, "that is the second fit you have thrown this week. Is there anything you can remember that might have provoked the seizure? Think back—if you can."

"I have a name, not a number," he said sullenly.

"The number is to protect your anonymity, Twenty-One, and the reputation of your family."

"I have nothing more to tell you." Gavril was not going to reveal anything of his innermost self to this lackey of Eugene's, for all Director Baltzar's kindly manner.

"I heard him cry out, 'Daemon-spirit!'" put in Onion-Breath helpfully.

"No voices in your head? Voices telling you what to do?"

Gavril opened his mouth to reply, and then closed it.

"You can earn privileges if you cooperate, Twenty-One. How much exercise does Twenty-One take each day?" the director asked the warders.

"A turn around the inner yard in the mornings," Onion-Breath said.

"That's not enough for a young man like you, is it? I've seen how fit, supple bodies can decline in here without adequate exercise and fresh air. I have devised a healthy regime for our more compliant inmates that keeps the muscles toned—"

Gavril was hardly listening. One thought alone possessed him.

"Paint."

"Paint?" Director Baltzar echoed.

"I am a painter. I want to paint. I want paper, charcoals, pastels, watercolors—"

"Privileges have to be earned," grunted Onion-Breath. "Didn't you hear the director? Don't you think you should start by earning a shave? Look at you. You look like a wild animal."

"Give me the razor and I'll shave myself," Gavril said, glinting a twisted smile at him.

"And I was born yesterday."

"Good-day to you, Twenty-One." Director Baltzar turned toward the door. "Remember what I said."

Skar opened the cell door for his master and Gavril caught a glimpse of the landing and spiral staircase beyond. Instinctively, he rose to his feet, making a lunge for the open doorway.

Onion-Breath grabbed him in an arm lock and flung him back onto his narrow bed.

"He's not ready for privileges, this one," he said, shaking his head at Gavril as if he were a disobedient child. "He's trouble."

"Just let me paint!" Gavril cried after the director. "I want to paint!" The door clanged shut and he heard bolts shot, keys clanking as they locked him in again.

The next day Skar brought him a list of conditions. First he must agree to a shave. If he agreed to the shave, he would be allowed back into the inner exercise yard. If he completed the morning turn for a week without attacking any of the warders, he would be allowed some paper and a box of watercolors.

Gavril agreed. What had he to lose? But he wondered who had given permission for him to be allowed to paint again. The time lag meant that Director Baltzar must have consulted a higher authority. Had the permission come from the Emperor himself?

Gavril sat staring at the treasures laid out on the little wooden table before him, as a starving man stares at food. A ceramic mixing dish, several brushes of good quality sable and of different thicknesses, a lead pencil, a stick of charcoal, a jug of water, and a box of paints. He took out each little brick of compressed color, one by one, and examined it.

Madder lake, ultramarine, green earth, dark grey smalt, blue verditer, rich gamboge yellow, even—and he smiled wryly to himself—a square of brown dragon's blood. Fanciful name, "dragon's blood." That, he knew all too well, was dark and purple.

But it was a good selection, full of possibilities. It must have been sent all the way from Tielborg or some other Tielen city where there were artists and shops to supply their needs.

And there was paper too. Sheets of fine quality paper with just the right texture to absorb a little of the paint, but also let it flow smoothly in a wash. He picked up the stick of charcoal and snapped it in half, a better length for sketching. He held the half poised above a clean sheet of paper, then glanced toward the door and the little round spyhole. Were the warders watching him, waiting to see what he would draw? Were they hoping for some clue to his secret, most private thoughts that would help them to break his will and make him compliant?

But the urge to draw became too strong. Let them watch. They would never understand. He wasn't even sure he understood this compulsion himself. It was just something he had to do. Something that confirmed he was still Gavril Nagarian and not just a number.

The weak afternoon sunlight was fading and it was almost too dim to see. At Arnskammar, the setting of the sun meant another day was already over for the inmates of the asylum. Nighttime and the hours of darkness were for sleeping. Candles were a rare privilege to be earned only after months of untarnished behavior.

Gavril laid down his charcoal stick and looked at what he had drawn.

A great stone archway, carved out of twisted serpentine bodies, filled the first page. Winged serpents with cruel hooked claws protruded into the center of the arch, as though to rip to shreds anyone rash enough to venture underneath.

Once he had started to draw, it had seemed as if another will was guiding his hand. Only the skill, the bold style, the little details, were his own, giving substance to half-remembered snatches of dreams.

The second sketch detailed the top of the arch: a terrifying serpent-head, fanged jaws gaping wide, and a single eye staring malevolently. He had put one daub of color onto the drawing. A blob of vivid red, carmine and madder lake mingled, that made the single eye glow like a living jewel.

How can I have drawn it in such detail when I've only glimpsed it in dreams?

His suppertime bowl of soup had gone cold; little globules of fat glistened unappetizingly on top of the pale brown liquid. He had hardly noticed when the warder had brought it in.

Is it somewhere I visited as a child?

Or was it just his own fevered imagining, conjured from those words underlined by his grandfather in the ancient book in the Kalika Tower library?

Another legend relates how the priests of the winged Serpent God, Nagar, built a great temple, at the heart of which was a gateway to the Realm of Shadows. From this gateway they conjured powerful spirit-daemons to do their bidding. . . .

In the twilight, he lay down on his bed and stared at the barred window as the sky deepened from cloudy grey, streaked with little veins of sunset fire, to a rain-swept black.

A gateway to the Realm of Shadows . . .

Eyes stare into his, hungry for power and dominion. This cruel creature that holds him bound in chains of fire wants to bend him to his will. To make him his.

He cannot breathe the thin, barren air of this alien world. He feels his consciousness waning.

"You are mine, daemon. I conjured you from beyond the Serpent Gate. Now you will serve me."

I will never be your slave.

"Give me your powers, daemon. Obey me—or die." As his captor leans closer, he catches the alien odors of his strange body of flesh, bone, and blood. Strong, delicious odors of salt and metals, water and carbon. The promise of life, strength, continuance—

"Its light is fading," cries another voice. "It's too late."

"Not yet!" insists his captor. "Listen to me, daemon. I am severing your bonds, the bonds of fire by which I have bound you. Now you will do my bidding."

His captor stands so close now he can see the warm life-liquids pulsing through his veins, can smell their nourishing warmth.

I will never be your slave. But you will be mine.

His captor raises his hands in the air. At his command, the winged serpents' tongues uncurl their fiery hold from his tortured limbs.

"Free!" Released, he springs forward to embrace his captor. To unite aethyrial spirit with alien flesh.

For one nauseating moment, he feels his captor's flesh and bone rejecting him, shuddering uncontrollably at this obscene assault. Suddenly everything slows as he lets himself flow into his host, slowly merging until he is completely absorbed into this strange new body. Together they topple forward onto the ground. The host twitches and jerks in the sand and dust, trying to reject him, to vomit him out.

And now it is he who shouts aloud in terror, "Help me!"

The inner exercise yard was a small courtyard surrounded by high brownstone tower walls, blind except for narrow arrow slits.

Gavril paused for breath in his daily circuit and gazed up at the sky. It was spring, no doubt of it, even though there was no sign of leaf or flower, not even a weed pushing up through the courtyard cobbles. The sky high above was a delicate shade of blue, the color of speckled eggshells. The air felt soft and the fresh breeze smelled somehow . . . green.

"Keep running!" bawled his warder. "Your time's nearly up. You've got three more circuits to complete!"

Gavril bit his lip. No point aggravating his warders and losing his paints. For now he would play their game. He began to run again, forcing his unwilling body to move.

It would take a long time to regain his agility. The long weeks of confinement and the heavy dosing with sedatives had slowed his whole system.

Must keep fit. Must keep alert. Must sweat the drugs out of my body.

"Time's up!" It was not Onion-Breath today, but another he had nicknamed Lanky. Lanky was a tall, shambling man whose stooped frame gave no hint as to his considerable strength.

Gavril continued running.

"I said time's up!" Lanky tossed Gavril the threadbare square of linen that served him as a towel.

Gavril caught the towel and wiped the sweat from his face. Then he bent over, gasping to regain his breath.

"You're one of the lucky ones," observed Lanky morosely. "You've got privileges. There's some here as hasn't been outside in years."

"In years?" Gavril straightened up. "How so?"

"No friends in high places."

Gavril cast a glance behind him as Lanky led him away. To be incarcerated here in the same cell year after year . . . He shivered in spite of the sweat dampening his body. He knew he only enjoyed this taste of fresh air because Eugene wanted something of him. Eventu-

ally Eugene would tire in his search for the Drakhaoul, and his privileges would be withdrawn. And he would be left to molder here forever.

"Clean yourself up!" Lanky ordered, pushing him into his cell.

A bowl of tepid washing-water stood on the table with his little
ball of yellow asylum-issue soap beside it, "to last you half a year, so
be sparing!"

"Where are my pictures?" He had left them in a pile on the table.
Now they were gone.

The door clanged shut. Lanky had locked him in.

"My pictures!" he cried. He thudded his fists in fury against the
iron door. "Where are they?"

They must have taken them while he was in the exercise yard. For
what purpose? What could they learn from them? To anyone uniniti-
ated in his family history, they would be meaningless. He was not at
all certain he understood them himself.

But the very act of taking away the one thing that was significant
to him was a violation. He had staunchly endured innumerable petty
slights and humiliations since the life-sentence was imposed. Now he
saw that, for all the so-called privileges, Eugene had ensured that the
loss of his name meant the loss of his identity. His wishes counted for
nothing. He was no one.

"Damn you, Eugene!" he yelled till his throat was raw. "Damn
you to hell and all its torments!"

Director Baltzar handed the sheaf of drawings to the visitor.

"The man's mind is deeply disturbed," he said. "And yet he's evidently an accomplished artist. What a tragedy. Perhaps we should try
to persuade him to paint a still life . . . or some flowers?"

"So you do not subscribe to the view that this outpouring of violent and disturbing images is in some way therapeutic for a troubled
mind?" inquired his visitor mildly.

"Indeed I do not!" Director Baltzar said with more vehemence
than he had intended. "I fear it may encourage him to dwell more on
such dark fantasies. It may feed the flames."

"And his behavior?"

Baltzar sighed. "My warders report that he has been shouting and
banging at his cell door for hours. I am reluctant, in all truth, to bring
you to him while he is in such a volatile state."

"You have reduced his medication, as requested?"

"Much against my better judgment, yes. But as your instructions come from the Emperor himself . . ." He ended with a shrug, and then wondered too late if he had acted presumptuously in expressing a contrary opinion to the Emperor's special envoy.

"You are a medical man, Director. How do you interpret these drawings?"

Baltzar felt even more uncomfortable now. He sensed he was, in some way, being judged by his visitor. But in what respect? Surely not his medical achievements? His degrees—from several eminent universities—were displayed on the walls of his study. His dissertations on the disorders of the human mind, bound in brown vellum and tooled in gold, lay on the desk for all visitors to see and consult. Yet when he spoke, he found his mouth uncomfortably dry. He swallowed hard.

"I suspect they are the expression of some deep and unresolved conflict of the mind. These terrifying portrayals of great fanged snakes could be interpreted as his fear and resentment of authority."

"Hm." The visitor nodded, apparently satisfied with this interpretation, but Baltzar did not feel in any way reassured. "We have talked enough. Take me to him."

"What, now?"

"Now." The visitor's pale eyes stared directly into his own.

Baltzar blinked. He had been about to say something, but his mind was utterly empty.

"Wh—what was I saying?"

"You were about to take me to Twenty-One," said the visitor.

"Yes. Of course." Baltzar rang a little bell to summon the warders on duty.

Gavril lay listlessly on his bed. He had lapsed into a daze, staring at the clouds endlessly drifting past his high window. Even blinking seemed an effort.

Why had he been deluding himself with these crazy dreams of escape? There was no escape from Arnskammar. He was confined here for life.

Now he wished he had died in the defense of Kastel Drakhaon, fighting side by side with his *druzhina*.

Footsteps echoed on the landing outside. He did not bother even to raise his head. What was the point?

Keys jangled. The locks creaked and the door swung inward.

"You have a visitor, Twenty-One."

A visitor? Gavril turned over, in spite of himself.

A wisp-haired, frail old man entered the cell. Behind him Lanky shuffled from foot to foot in the open doorway, awkward and ill at ease.

"You may go now," the old man said.

"I'm not allowed to leave anyone alone with Twenty-One. Governor's orders."

"The governor's orders are that you return to the ward-room. I will send for you when I need you."

To Gavril's surprise, Lanky nodded and shambled away, shutting the door behind him.

"Good-day to you, Lord Gavril," said the visitor. The old man's eyes gleamed like quicksilver in the dull light of the cell. Gavril found he could not look away. Now he saw that the old man's frail appearance was only a shell, a carapace hiding a dazzling power-source from the everyday world. And that power, he sensed, was as cold and inhuman as a force of nature.

"Who are you?" he gasped.

"We have met once before, Drakhaon. Do you remember?"

Gavril shook his head.

"You broke through my defenses. No one has done that before. But then, you were so utterly determined to rescue your mother."

"You were at Swanholm?" Nothing but a chaos of memories remained from that frenzied flight, when he had swooped down on the enemy's stronghold to snatch Elysia from the Tielen firing party. When he could still fly . . .

"You owe your survival to the intervention of one individual. You were exhausted, your powers all but spent. If she had not begged me to stay my hand, you would not have left Swanholm alive."

Gavril still stared at the visitor. His memory was fogged in mists. One moment alone of that day remained, lit with a horrible clarity.

A dark-haired young woman stares at him across the smoking, charred remains of Feodor Velemir, her eyes wide with revulsion and terror.

She knows him now for the daemon-monster he has become. She knows—

"Astasia. Was it Astasia?"

"You still do not know me?" the old man said, not answering his question. "My name is Linnaius. Kaspar Linnaius."

"The Magus?" Elysia had warned him of the Magus's powers. And now here he was, trapped in this little cell, with no means of escape and no one to defend him. It was as if he were stripped naked. "What do you want of me?" His shoulder blades grazed the wall. He had instinctively backed away, without even knowing he was doing so. But there was nowhere else to go.

"You are of considerably greater value to the Emperor alive than dead, Nagarian, I assure you. I am only here to ask you a few questions, that is all." Slender fingers reached out to rest on his forehead, the back of his head.

Gavril shuddered at his touch. He felt as if his skin were brushed by dead, dried husks of insects. And then a little flare of Drakhaon pride, too long subdued by the physicians' drugs, suddenly rekindled. *"Get out of my head."*

He felt the Magus's fingertips snatched from his forehead as if singed.

"It is in your best interests to cooperate," Linnaius said quietly.

"The Emperor has taken everything from me. Everything! Must you take the last of my sanity too?" And then he stopped as a tidal wave of sensations, images, feelings rushed through his mind. He gripped hold of his head in both hands, overwhelmed.

He saw the faces of his *druzhina*, eyes bitter at their betrayal, as one by one they went to surrender their weapons to the Tielen soldiers. He saw Elysia, distraught, her hands desperately outstretched as if she could tear him back from his captors. He saw Kiukiu turning to wave to him as her sleigh set out across the snowy moorlands. He heard his own voice confidently shouting, *"I will come for you. . . . We'll be together again soon."*

"Ahh . . ." An aching moan of grief and loss welled up from deep inside him. He raised his head and stared at the Magus directly. "What have you done to me?"

"Unlocked your memory, that's all. The sedative drugs had dulled your brain."

And protected me from the torment of living with the knowledge of all I have lost.

"So did you find what the Emperor sent you here for?" He would not let himself be intimidated by Kaspar Linnaius, powerful though he knew him to be.

The Magus stared back at him a long time without answering.

"You spoke the truth to him, as you perceived it," he said after a long while. "That I can verify."

"Don't speak to me in riddles. Tell me what you found."

"Your Drakhaoul is indeed gone. But you are not entirely free, are you, Gavril Nagarian? It has left you a legacy of memories, spanning many human lifetimes . . . and maybe more, besides."

"More?" Gavril felt a tremor of unease, even though the Magus's diagnosis was ambiguously phrased.

"I cannot tell." Linnaius's pale eyes seemed to grow more translucent as Gavril gazed at him. Silver eyes—seer's eyes—probing deep beneath the surface of the everyday world. Time slowed as he found himself unable to look away.

Dazzled, Gavril blinked.

And found he was alone in the cell. Alone—and filled with the anguish of bitterly remembered loss.

Why had Linnaius committed this cruel act? What had he wanted him to remember? And how would he use it against him—and all he held dear?

CHAPTER 12

"What do you make of these, highness?" Linnaius gestured to a sheaf of watercolors that spilled out from an open portfolio, their imagery dark-drenched with blood and shadows. "They are all the work of Gavril Nagarian."

Eugene lifted sheet after sheet from the desk. His eyes ached from looking at the vivid swirls of violent color as he tried to make some sense of the chaotic images of nightmare and madness.

"So this is what Drakhaoul-possession does to a man's mind," he murmured. Snakes coiled and writhed around a tall archway; glittering daemon-eyes glowered from the smoke-wreathed cone of an erupting volcano. "The incoherent daubings of a madman." He cast them down on the desk. "There's nothing of use to us here, Linnaius."

"On the contrary." Linnaius drifted closer to the Emperor and, with one spindle finger, began to outline certain images. "We see here an island—or isthmus—dominated by a single volcano. This crescent-shaped group of stars in the sky looks more than a little like the constellation we call the Sickle in Francia. And look, highness, at this gateway. It stands within an ancient temple, a portal enwreathed in winged serpents, daemons or minor gods. One crowned serpent dominates the gate and in its eye socket burns a sacred flame, red as volcanic fire."

"You think these images are clues to the daemon's origins?"

The Magus raised one gossamer eyebrow. "I am certain that Gavril Nagarian knows more than he has revealed in these paintings. He resisted my attempt to probe his mind with considerable force."

Eugene picked up the watercolor and stared at it, tilting it from side to side, trying to make better sense of it.

"Then if he will not talk to us . . . he might open his heart to a friend?"

"There was one I glimpsed close to his heart—before he countered my intrusion. A young woman in Azhkendir. The name I caught was 'Kiukiu.' "

"Kiukiu? That's a woman's name?"

"Azhkendi names can sound crude to more refined sensibilities," said Linnaius fastidiously.

"Let's contact the garrison commander in Azhkendir by Vox Aethyria and see if he can find anyone of that name."

Linnaius was looking at him, his pale eyes veiled. Eugene sighed.

"You disapprove of my plan."

"I merely ask your imperial highness to consider what your true motives are."

"You know—" Eugene checked himself, unwilling to speak his darkest obsession aloud. "You know my wishes on that subject."

"And you know my advice, highness."

"But if it is true that the Drakhaoul can heal its host . . . Look at me, Linnaius." Eugene gestured with his burned hand to his damaged face. "Is it any wonder Astasia still shrinks from me?"

"Highness," Linnaius said, the slightest glimmer of a smile illuminating his pale eyes, "we both know that it is not only the Drakhaoul's healing powers you desire."

Now that Linnaius had called his bluff, Eugene felt a certain relief. He could speak freely.

"How can I keep the empire together if others wield greater power?"

A frown passed as fleetingly as a distant cloud across the Magus's face.

"Ask yourself, highness. If the Drakhaoul's power is so great, why are the Nagarians not rulers of the world?"

It was a question that had kept Eugene awake at nights. *"Unnatural lusts and desires . . ."* Gavril Nagarian had said.

"There is always a price to be paid," the Magus said, as if reading his thoughts.

Kaspar Linnaius threw a veil of concealing shadowsilk over his sky craft. He had deflated the canvas balloon sail, wrapped it up, and placed it in the wooden hull. No one would notice it now in the shadowy forest glade; a passing monk or charcoal-burner would see nothing but the lichened trunks of the great firs of Kerjhenezh.

He set out to walk the last quarter-mile to the monastery. His progress was slow; today he felt the damp of spring rain in his bones. He would need to concoct another phial of the life-preserving elixir that sustained him.

At last the whitewashed walls of the Monastery of Saint Sergius could be glimpsed ahead through the trees.

He passed fishponds, murkily green and still, and then came to an orchard of apple trees, their branches covered with a snowfall of blossoms. At the far end of the orchard he could see bee skeps tended by an elderly monk.

"Good-day to you, Brother Beekeeper. Where can I find the abbot?"

The white-bearded monk replaced the lid on the skep and straightened slowly.

So the damp is affecting your old bones too, Brother, Linnaius thought. *I'd offer you a draught of my elixir—but if you knew what went into its preparation, you'd be sure to refuse.*

"He's in his study; I'll take you to him. . . ."

"You'll understand, Magister Linnaius," said Abbot Yephimy, "that the brothers and I permit only the most devout and learned of scholars access to our precious archive." He gazed severely at Linnaius, who sensed he was being assessed and found wanting. "But since you come on the Emperor's business, I cannot deny you. Though I must insist you wear these archivist's gloves at all times when you handle the ancient parchments."

"Thank you, Abbot." Linnaius took the thin, white silk gloves and eased them onto his gnarled fingers. "The Emperor was confident that you would help in our researches."

"Please follow me."

Yephimy led Linnaius into the monastery library. It had a deep barrel-vaulted roof, with a gallery beneath lined with bound volumes. On the ground floor several of the monks were busy copying manuscripts, sitting at high, sloping desks surrounded by pots of ink and pens. Each desk was placed in a window embrasure to take advantage of the natural light of day, which was filtered by diamond-paned glass. Some of the copyists glanced up as they walked quietly past, and nodded to the abbot. The only sound was the scratching of nibs and the occasional dry cough.

At the farthest end of the library was a little nail-studded door; unlocking it, the abbot showed Linnaius into a room so small it was scarcely bigger than a monk's cell. No windows let in the daylight here; Yephimy used a taper to light the lanterns.

Every book on the dark-stained shelves was chained. And every book was an ancient volume, the leather bindings faded and stained. Yephimy selected one bound in dark leather, red as dried blood, and laid it on the desk with a clinking of the chain that secured it.

"I think this is what you're looking for, Magus," he said. "I believe this volume is unique. The only surviving copy, and we hold it here at Saint Sergius."

Linnaius waited until the abbot had withdrawn and closed the door before lifting his white-gloved hands to the precious book.

This hand-scribed copy of the Rossiyan Chronicles, entitled *The Glorious Life and Martyr's Death of the Blessed Serzhei of Kerjhenezh* was quite unlike any of the others he had researched so far. For one, it was written in the obscure Old Church Azhkendi, not the common tongue, and it would take all his considerable philological skills to make sense of the ancient language:

And so it came to pass in the eleventh year of the glorious reign of Artamon the Great that Volkhar, the fifth and youngest son of the Emperor, was shipwrecked off the southern coast of Djihan-Djihar and thought to have drowned. The Emperor and all his court mourned the young prince for three months, and none were seen to grieve more than his elder brothers—although it had been whispered by malicious tongues that, being jealous of Artamon's fondness for Volkhar, they had caused his ship to founder.

But a year almost to the day that the prince's ship went down, a merchantman put into port at Mirom and among its passengers was none other than Prince Volkhar. The Great Artamon ordered a week of celebrations to be held throughout his empire in honor of the prince's return. And he was even more delighted when Volkhar presented his father with a magnificent ruby as large as a goose egg, which he had discovered during his travels.

The Emperor showered the young prince with so many favors that his brothers looked on him with suspicion, fearing he would supplant them in their father's affections.

Such was the envy of the older princes that they fell to bitter feuding among themselves. In his despair and fury, Emperor Artamon declared the ruby must be accursed and bade Prince Volkhar return it whence he had found it.

The prince set out to do his father's bidding. But his jealous brothers waylaid him and took the stone from him by force . . .

Linnaius read on, turning the leathery pages with care. Thus far he had not seen any great variation from the other versions of the Rossiyan Chronicles he had consulted. The warlike exploits of Artamon were enumerated. The violent feuding between the princes was described in stilted archaic terms. And then the text reverted to the life of Saint Sergius, which the title had promised. After pages of pious deeds, Linnaius began to wonder if this manuscript would offer any new insights after all.

Then the history of Archimandrite Sergius seemed to leap forward suddenly:

And so the Blessed Serzhei wrestled with the daemons all that night and day. At last, feeling his strength waning, he called in his mortal agony upon the heavenly warriors *whose names must not be uttered except by the pure of heart.* Armed with the might of the Righteous Ones, Serzhei banished the daemons from Rossiya, and bound them in a place of torment for all eternity. Yet there was one who still defied him and all the hosts of heaven.

Linnaius leaned closer. "Ah," he said softly. "Just as I suspected." A secret text had been hidden behind the intricately hand-scribed words. He was well-practiced in prizing ancient scholars' secrets from arcane manuscripts, but it gave him a special satisfaction to unravel this one, which had been so cunningly concealed.

Some hidden texts could only be read by moonlight, others were revealed by a sudden shaft of lightning. Others still required the concocting of alchymical solutions that, when applied with the greatest care to the vellum, would force them to disclose their secrets—although one had to be careful that they did not also release a breath of lethal poison at the same time, to ensure that their innermost treasures were never revealed.

Yet this incunabulum was different. It was embedded within the words themselves, like a cypher. Linnaius had only to apply a sprinkling of mirror-dust (an old mages' trick) and the hidden text appeared, glimmering in the lamplight.

And as Linnaius leaned closer, he thought he heard a far-distant murmur of deep voices that sent a shiver through his body. It was a curse and a very powerful one too; centuries after it had been pronounced, the resonances still lingered, a warning to the unwary:

"Seven. They were Seven, the Dark Angels of Destruction.

"Accursed be the barbarous priests of Ty Nagar who first summoned these dread warriors to do their bidding. And thrice accursed be the sons of Artamon who sought the powers of the Seven for their own selfish ends and brought down their father's mighty empire.

"And blessed be Serzhei of Kerjhenezh, who called upon the Heavenly Guardians to help defeat the evil ones. With his holy staff, he bound them until the very end of time.

"Accursed be he who seeks to release them from their eternal imprisonment."

But now, to Linnaius's surprise—and he had thought that nothing could surprise him still—what looked unmistakably like the contours of a map, glowed faintly beneath the text.

Little phosphorescent stars appeared as the map slowly revealed itself. And brighter than the rest glimmered six stars of cobalt-blue.

Linnaius, entranced by the sorcerous artistry of the device, realized that he was looking at a chart of the heavens.

He began to sketch furiously, trying to set down as accurately as he could the position of each star. But fast as he worked, the map faded faster, almost as if it had guessed his intent.

Soon, to his frustration, it vanished, hidden once again behind the chronicles of Serzhei's life. And even though he sprinkled more precious mirror-dust onto the manuscript, nothing happened.

He looked at his hasty sketch. The chart he had copied had been drawn centuries ago; there was little to suggest any familiar constellations. Except that the six blue stars looked remarkably similar to the Silver Sickle.

He leafed on through the manuscript, doubly wary now, in case it concealed some powerful ward to protect its contents. But there was no further hint of thaumaturgy until he came to the final page. Here a laconic motto concluded the life of the saint:

> Though death stills my earthly voice, through her songs will I tell my tale to those yet unborn.

The first letter of the motto was illuminated with the most exquisite draftsmanship. It showed a woman seated, playing a many-stringed zither. A dark doorway yawned behind her, and emanating from the doorway the illuminator had drawn insubstantial shapes, some with human faces and weirdly beautiful, others grotesque and frightening: death-daemons whose hollow eyes and mouths were contorted into writhing grimaces of pain and terror.

"A Spirit Singer," Linnaius murmured.

Kaspar Linnaius scudded on in his sky craft above the moorlands of Azhkendir. Where there had been nothing but the bleak whiteness of snow, he now saw a vivid blur of different greens; reeds and rushes hemmed the boggy pools, and great banks of gorse were about to burst into fountains of yellow blooms.

All the moor beneath him was fresh green until he spotted the dark scar of the burned escarpment, the charred bank of earth where hundreds of Tielen soldiers had perished, incinerated by Drakhaon's Fire. Even if he had not known that this was the place of such terrible carnage, he would have sensed the grim aura emanating from it, the lingering taint of daemonic breath. Nothing would grow there for years.

Circling lower, he identified the pale blue and grey of the many New Rossiyan flags fluttering from the towers of Kastel Drakhaon and caught the sound of picks and shovels.

"Ahh," muttered Linnaius. "Lindgren's mine."

Captain Nils Lindgren had written to the Emperor, sending samples of minerals and salts he had discovered while exploring the Drakhaon's confiscated estates. The Emperor had passed the samples to his Royal Artificier for analysis, and Linnaius had been pleased to report the results of his findings: Azhkendir was rich in untapped mineral resources. The Emperor had then given the order to open up mines to exploit this new discovery to the fullest.

Far below, men were excavating, digging a tunnel deep into the hill-side. A cart appeared, laden with stones and earth. Workers heaved on ropes, putting all their strength to shifting the cart. Even from this height he could see that their ankles and wrists were shackled together. Armed Tielen soldiers stood around, directing the work. These prisoners, he guessed, must be the surviving members of Gavril Nagarian's bodyguard, the barbarous *druzhina,* condemned to hard labor for their part in the recent troubles.

The wind carrying his craft whined and squalled above the earth-works. One of the *druzhina* glanced up, eyes squinting against the light. All he would have glimpsed was a cloud, scudding low across the sky. But Linnaius, reluctant to risk being seen, began a slow de-scent at the edge of the forest, beyond the mine-workings.

He concealed the craft in a shroud of shadowsilk, making sure it blended into the background of rough bark and damp moss. Then he followed a winding path down toward the kastel. It was not long be-fore he was challenged by Tielen sentries. Lindgren had the grounds well-guarded, Linnaius reflected, as one of the soldiers led him to find the captain.

Nils Lindgren was in the Great Hall with one of his subordi-nates, correcting plans with rule and pencils. "Magus," he said, straightening up as Linnaius appeared, "you honor us." He laid down his tools and, clicking his heels together, saluted smartly. "Have you come to check on our progress?" He gestured to the plans laid out on the table. "As you can see, my engineers have been busy. This first seam is already yielding good results. We're going to blast a second tunnel later this week. I could give you a tour later, when you've rested from your journey. And I think you might be intrigued by these samples I've taken from the escarpment. They're unlike anything I've ever seen before." He held out a small stoppered phial containing a dark, crumbling substance that emitted a faint phospho-rescent glow.

"Thank you," said Linnaius, giving the phial a cursory glance be-fore slipping it into the pocket of his jacket. "I'll submit the contents to a full alchymical analysis." The young man's eagerness to develop the mining project showed in his eyes and the healthy, wind-burned glow of his complexion. And these resources could certainly be used to increase the new empire's military resources. "But that is not the prime reason for my visit. I've come to ask you if there is a certain young Azhkendi woman working in the kastel. She goes by the name of Kiukiu."

He saw a look of puzzlement cross Lindgren's face; the young captain had evidently not yet learned to conceal his feelings very successfully.

"I would like to speak with this young woman alone, you understand?"

Lindgren found his tongue. "But she's a scullery maid, just a peasant girl—"

"She is the one," Linnaius insisted calmly. "Bring her to me."

CHAPTER 13

"If I never see another turnip again, it'll be too soon," sighed Ninusha, scraping away one by one at an earthy pile of root vegetables.

"What rubbish you talk sometimes, Ninny." Ilsi flounced past and slammed down a pile of greasy pots in front of Kiukiu without a word. " 'Never see another turnip again,' " she mimicked in a singsong voice. "You should listen to yourself!"

"Look at my hands. My nails are always chipped and dirty. Why can't those Tielens give us some decent food to cook?"

Kiukiu glanced at her hands as she plunged the pots into the water. Her nails, so carefully hardened for playing the gusly, had become soft with all this washing and scrubbing.

"You're lucky there's any food to eat at all," came Sosia's reply from the pantry. "If it weren't for the Tielens bringing their army supplies, we'd have starved by now."

"But Tielen army rations—" Ninusha pulled a face. "Pigs eat better."

"Not Kastel Drakhaon pigs." Sosia came out and pulled up a handful of peelings from the floor and examined them critically. "You're wasting too much, Ninusha. Cut finer, girl."

"I am—*ow!*" Ninusha dropped the knife and sucked her finger. "Now see what you've made me do, Sosia. I'm bleeding!"

"Go find a cobweb to put on it." Sosia took up the paring knife and began scraping away at the half-peeled turnip Ninusha had abandoned.

It's as if nothing has changed, Kiukiu thought, scrubbing at a hard rim of dried soup-scum. *It's as if Lord Gavril had never come back. Did I dream it all?*

And then she felt a strange, unsettling sensation, as though a gust of cold, elemental wind had blown through the kitchen. The little hairs stood up on her arms.

A Tielen soldier appeared in the kitchen doorway. "Which one of you is Kiukiu?" he asked.

Kiukiu sensed the others were staring at her. "I am," she said, letting the pot sink back into the dirty water.

"You are to come with me. Now."

Kiukiu hesitated a moment, wondering what this meant. She was sure it could not be good, whatever it was. She dried her hands on her apron and followed the soldier from the kitchen.

"What has my niece done?" cried Sosia. "Let me accompany her—"

The soldier put out one arm as if to prevent her. "She is to come alone."

They passed Ninusha on her way back from binding her finger.

"Been a naughty girl, have you, Kiukiu?" whispered Ninusha. "Is the captain going to punish you?"

Kiukiu paid no attention; she felt again that unsettling sensation, as if every room of the kastel had been infiltrated by eddies of moorland wind. And as they approached the door to the Kalika Tower, the sensation grew stronger.

"In here." The soldier held the door open. "Up the stairs."

"In Lord Gavril's study?" She hung back, the sense of apprehension increasing. "Why?"

"Go on up," he ordered, giving her a little push.

Reluctantly, she began to climb the spiral stair.

Kaspar Linnaius opened the door to the Drakhaon's study. A little sigh of satisfaction escaped his lips.

Books. Maps. Star charts.

Even though the tower had been damaged in the bombardment, he saw that the empty windowframes had been patched with parchment and the holes in the wall filled. That alone told him that the contents of this room were of considerable importance to Gavril Nagarian.

"So this is where the great warlords of Azhkendir planned their campaigns."

He could not resist rubbing his hands together at the sight of so

many books. And here, on the desk, left open as though the Drakhaon
had been interrupted in the midst of his researches, lay several ancient volumes with underlinings and footnotes scribbled in red ink.

"Ahh," he said aloud, picking up the uppermost book and murmuring the words under his breath as he read:

> " 'There lies one island far to the south, dominated by the cone of
> a volcanic peak, said by the people of these isles to be sacred to the
> powerful Serpent God of their ancestors.' "

A little stain of reddish-brown, darker than the crimson ink,
spotted the margin; it looked like human blood. Linnaius read on:

> " '. . . the priests of the Serpent God, Nagar, built a great temple to
> their god, at the heart of which was a gateway to the Realm of
> Shadows.' "

"Nagar!" he murmured triumphantly. The same name that he had
read in the concealed text at the monastery. This could be no coincidence. The House of Nagarian could well be named after this ancient
Serpent God.

> " 'From this gateway they conjured powerful daemon-spirits to do
> their bidding—' "

The door opened and a young woman appeared. He looked at her,
sensing in spite of her drab servant's clothes a distinctive and radiant
aura.

Could she be one of the Azhkendi Spirit Singers?

But all he said was, "Come in, Kiukiu. I have been waiting for
you."

Kiukiu stared at the man. She had thought doddery Guaram was
the most ancient person she had known, but this wispy-haired stranger
looked so frail he must be even older than Guaram.

"Sit down." His voice, though quiet, was authoritative. Appearances
could be deceptive. Here was the source of that glamorous power she
had sensed. Who was he—and what did he want with her?

"I bring you news of Gavril Nagarian."

"Gavril!" She cried his name aloud before she could stop herself; too late she clapped both hands over her mouth. But there had been no news in such a long time—

"Please sit down."

"Is it bad news?" People told you to sit down before breaking ill tidings: sickness, disaster, death . . . *Let him still be alive,* she prayed silently.

"He is alive," said the old man, as though he had read her thoughts, "but he is confined in an asylum."

" 'An asylum'? Isn't that where they send people who are mad?" Tears of distress filled Kiukiu's eyes. And then she felt anger welling up from deep inside her. She knew only too well what the *druzhina* did to their prisoners. "Mad, or driven mad? Has he been tortured?"

"As to the cause of his madness, we hoped you could enlighten us, Kiukiu." The old man gazed at her with his cold, pale eyes. For a moment she felt dizzy, whirled high into a spiral of cloud and wind. Then she blinked—and found she was sitting down opposite the old man. How long had she been absent? And what had he done to her in that time?

"Who are you?" she whispered, gazing warily at him.

"My name is Kaspar Linnaius."

"Is it my fault, Kaspar Linnaius, that Gavril is . . ." She could not say the word "mad." "Is it because he drove out that daemon-creature to save me?"

"How did he drive it out, Kiukiu?"

"My grandmother Malusha helped him."

"Malusha," repeated Linnaius pensively.

Kiukiu had the horrible feeling that, in merely naming her grandmother, she had in some obscure way betrayed her.

"And what skills did your grandmother use to do what countless mages and doctors of science had failed to achieve?"

"How is this to help Gavril?" burst out Kiukiu.

"I have it on the authority of the Emperor himself," Linnaius said, suddenly formal, "that if you answer my questions honestly and truthfully, you will be granted a visit."

Kiukiu's mouth dropped open. Her heart began to flutter. All she could think was that she would see him again, after all these long months—

"So how did your grandmother cast out the daemon?"

"She is a Spirit Singer. A Guslyar, like me." Now she could not stop herself from answering his questions. *A visit*, her heart sang, *a visit . . .*

"And Guslyars cast out daemons?" The quiet, insistent questions kept coming.

"Guslyars can travel between this life and the Ways Beyond."

"So you are shamans?"

"I don't know that word."

"You talk to the dead?"

Kiukiu gave a shiver. "Sometimes they talk to us. They ask us to bring them across, back into life."

"I would like to meet your grandmother."

Kiukiu, the trance shattered, looked up at Kaspar Linnaius in alarm. What secrets had she blabbed out to this stranger? Malusha would be so angry with her.

"Gavril Nagarian needs your help, Kiukiu."

Kiukiu nodded slowly. "I'll take you to her."

Forgive me, Grandma, she begged silently. *It's just that I can't stop loving Gavril, no matter how hard I try. Can you remember what it was like to love someone like that?*

The cloudy waters of the monastery fishpond gave little hint as to what stirred beneath the lily pads; only the occasional telltale bubble burst on the surface.

Abbot Yephimy had been sitting patiently in the sunshine, waiting for a tug on his line for over an hour. He was in no hurry. The fishponds were at the farthest end of the monastery gardens and the abbot was relishing the solitude, listening to the twittering of the little birds fluttering to and fro in the nearest forest trees, the hum of the bees busy collecting pollen from the meadow flowers . . .

"Two pilgrims are here, asking to speak with you, Abbot," announced a voice suddenly.

Abbot Yephimy started and saw young Brother Timofei on the other side of the pond.

"Ssh! You'll frighten the fish."

"Sorry, Abbot." Timofei went bright red.

Yephimy sighed and laid down his fishing rod. His peaceful moment was at an end. In truth he knew he was fortunate to have snatched so long in the sunshine undisturbed.

Brother Timofei led the way back through the kitchen gardens; Yephimy cast a knowledgeable eye over the progress of their vegetables as he walked.

"Those early onions need thinning out, Brother Timofei. And the first crop of radishes are ready."

Spring radishes for supper with fresh bread, butter, and salt, Yephimy thought with pleasure as they approached the main courtyard.

"Who are these pilgrims and what do they want?" he asked.

"They say they wish to pray in Saint Sergius's shrine. But they're not Azhkendi."

Yephimy saw the visitors waiting at the door to the shrine. They wore black robes and their heads were cowled; it was not the habit of any religious order he recognized. The taller of the two leaned on a metal staff.

"Welcome to Saint Sergius, my brothers," he said warmly, opening his arms wide to greet them. They turned, and he saw with surprise that one was a woman.

"We are members of the Francian Commanderie, Abbot," said the man. He spoke the common tongue with an unfamiliar accent, which made him slightly difficult to understand. "Is there anywhere more private where we could talk?"

Yephimy took them to his study.

"Now, what is this really about?" he asked. Pilgrims did not usually request private audiences; they preferred to spend their time praying in the shrine.

"The leader of our order has been monitoring the disquieting growth of daemonic activity in this part of the world. We have been sent to investigate."

"Ah," said Yephimy, folding his hands together. "The Drakhaoul."

"Is that its Azhkendi name?" said the woman.

Yephimy frowned at her. "It has never revealed its true name. And your leader will be pleased to learn that the daemon has been cast out."

"Cast out, maybe, but not destroyed," said the man. "Members of our order tracked it along the Straits. We believe it may have gone to ground in Muscobar."

"What?" This was news to Yephimy. Disturbing news. "It's still at large?" And he had been so certain Malusha had banished it; he had witnessed its last desperate flight from the shrine.

"We believe so. And that is why the Grand Master of our order has commissioned the reforging of Sergius's Staff."

"Sergius's Staff?" Yephimy repeated, bemused. "You have Sergius's Staff? But how? The Chronicles state that it was shattered in Sergius's last battle with the Drakhaoul." He rose, staring at them with suspicion. "Exactly who are you—and what is this Commanderie?"

"We are Companions of the Order of Saint Sergius, Abbot," said the man. "Our order is dedicated to the destruction of all daemonic influences in the world. As for the staff, well, legend has it that the founder of our order, Argantel, fled Azhkendir with the shattered pieces and had it repaired in Francia. All the pieces—save one: the crook, which we understand you keep here, in the shrine."

"Lord Argantel was Sergius's friend," said Yephimy slowly. "But the Chronicles do not record what became of him." He did not know whether to believe these two strangers who spoke so knowledgeably of secret matters known only to the monks at the monastery. "So. Show me this relic."

The man placed his metal staff on Yephimy's desk and unscrewed the top. He tipped the shaft gently and out slid an ancient, charred length of wood, fragments bound into a whole with bands of golden wire.

Yephimy put out one hand and touched it. He felt a slight tingle in his fingers as though the ancient wood still vibrated with a vestige of the saint's power. He stared at it, overcome by awe . . . and a distinct pang of envy.

"This should be kept here, with Serzhei's bones." Yephimy looked at the two visitors hopefully. "Have you come to return it to the shrine?"

"You misunderstand our intentions, Abbot." The man's eyes hardened. "We are on the trail of this daemon. We intend to use the staff to destroy it."

"But there are others on its trail too," said the woman, "and what they intend endangers us all. Have you had any visitors here at the shrine, claiming to be scholars researching the Sergius archive?"

"Why, yes. One called Kaspar Linnaius was here recently, on the Emperor's business."

"Kaspar Linnaius?" The woman exchanged a glance with the man. They seemed concerned—and also excited.

"Were you aware, Abbot," said the man, his lean face drawn, "that some of the manuscripts here contain hidden texts? Texts that only the most skilled adepts can unlock? Texts that hide secrets better left unrevealed?"

"Of course I am." Yephimy felt as if he were being reprimanded for some ecclesiastical misdemeanor.

"And that one of your manuscripts may hide the location of the other four daemon-warriors that Sergius defeated and turned to stone?"

This was news to Yephimy. He felt humiliated that he had been revealed to know nothing of these treasures; first the staff, and now a secret map . . .

"Will you give us Sergius's golden crook?" said the woman. "So that we can defeat the daemon and send it back to the Realm of Shadows?"

Yephimy sighed. If he refused, they might suspect him of harboring some secret sympathy with the Drakhaoul. And yet, to hand over one of the shrine's most sacred treasures to these strangers . . .

"I cannot answer for my brothers without consulting them," he said. "But I offer you the hospitality of the monastery while we discuss your proposition."

The man leaned forward and placed his hand on the abbot's arm, staring intently into his face. "This matter is urgent. I beg you, Abbot, do not discuss too long."

"What have you done, Kiukiu? Why have you brought *him* here?"

Malusha stood in the doorway of her cottage as if trying to prevent them from entering. Her eyes were dark, narrowed in an expression of bitter hatred and distrust.

"Him?" Kiukiu rubbed her eyes. She had the oddest feeling that she had just flown across the moors from Kastel Drakhaon, skimming high like a grey-winged goose returning to its spring breeding grounds. "H-how did I get here?"

"What have you done to my grandchild?" Malusha hurried across the courtyard, scattering hens in front of her, and put her arm around Kiukiu. "What spell have you laid on her?"

Kiukiu slowly realized that Malusha was not talking to her anymore, but to Kaspar Linnaius, who stood silently beside her.

"This is Kasp—" she began.

"I know who he is," Malusha said, still staring frostily at Linnaius. "And what he is. But I don't know what brings him here when he's quite aware he's not welcome."

"I come on the Emperor Eugene's business," said Linnaius. "The same Eugene who was patron to Jaromir Arkhel while he lived, and is now godfather to his son, Stavyomir."

"His son?" Malusha seemed utterly confounded. "An heir?"

"The Emperor has named young Stavyomir the next Arkhaon of Azhkendir. I thought you might be aware of the fact, as you served the Arkhel family for so many years."

Malusha was silent a moment. Then she said, "I think you'd better come in."

"Why didn't you tell me, Kiukiu?" Malusha whispered angrily as Linnaius walked past them and into the cottage. "About the Arkhel child?"

"I didn't know for sure," Kiukiu whispered back, cowed by her grandmother's wrath.

"And now you've brought that cursed wind-mage here."

"I didn't bring him! He brought me."

"Don't argue, child. What does he want?"

"Information for the good of the empire," said Linnaius. In spite of his great age, his hearing was obviously still extremely acute, thought Kiukiu resentfully.

"It'd better be for the good," Malusha said, shutting the door hastily as one of the hens attempted to follow them inside, "seeing as how you had the ill manners to break through my veil of concealment."

The instant the Magus entered the cottage, there had been a stirring and a shuffling among the roosting snow owls perched high above their heads. Linnaius glanced up and Kiukiu saw him blink in astonishment.

"And now you've disturbed my lords and ladies," complained Malusha. "They're very suspicious of strangers and they get very moody at this time of year. You don't want to go startling them; they can be vicious when they've got a clutch of eggs to protect."

"Believe me, I have no intention of harming them," Linnaius said, fastidiously drawing his gown up to avoid a pile of owl droppings. "Or their chicks."

"So what is the information your Emperor wants from me?"

"You cast out the daemon-spirit, the one that calls itself Drakhaoul?"

"I did," said Malusha stiffly.

"That was a considerable achievement."

"I could not have done it if Lord Gavril had not wished it so," Malusha said, still coldly formal.

"But you did not send it back to the Ways Beyond?"

"And where would I have taken it in the Ways Beyond?"

Kiukiu sensed a growing tension between the two. A glowing stick on the fire suddenly snapped, sending a hiss of sparks up the chimney, and she jumped.

"It was not a dead soul, Kaspar Linnaius, seeking expiation for its sins." Malusha's voice grew softer. "Even that dread place of dust and despair that we dare not name is not its true home."

"Then"—Linnaius drew closer to her—"what *is* it?"

"Why do you need to know?" Malusha asked slyly.

"There seems to be a connection between the daemon and the Emperor's young daughter." For the first and only time, Kiukiu heard Linnaius falter. Was it possible that this cold, calculating old man still nourished a little warmth in his heart?

Malusha shrugged. "What's that to us?"

"She insists the daemon is still at large somewhere in our world. And now that there is an Arkhel heir for you to protect—"

"I cast the daemon out from Gavril Nagarian, but it was too strong for me. It fled before I could destroy it."

"Then this will interest you. I have learned from my researches that only one man was ever strong enough to imprison such aethyric daemons: Serzhei of Kerjhenezh."

"Your point, wind-mage?"

"I have not the skills to talk to the dead, but you and your grand-daughter—"

"Have you any idea of the risk in such a venture?" Malusha shook her grey head. "Serzhei is long dead. He has traveled far, deep into the Ways Beyond—"

"I'll do it," said Kiukiu suddenly, impulsively.

"You'll do no such thing!"

"I'll do it if you let me visit *him*," Kiukiu said to Linnaius.

"Him? Oh no. You're not still hankering after the Nagarian boy?" Malusha turned on the Magus. "What nonsense have you filled her head with?"

"A visit can be arranged." The Magus's pale eyes rested on Kiukiu.

Malusha seized hold of Kiukiu's hand and pressed, none too gently, on each of her fingertips in turn.

"Ow!" Kiukiu snatched her hand away.

"Soft as butter," her grandmother said disapprovingly. "When was the last time you did any practice, hm? As I thought."

"I couldn't play the gusly in the kastel," Kiukiu protested. "Not with all those Tielen soldiers around."

"I would prefer to interrogate Serzhei myself," said the Magus.

"And well you might, but what you're asking is not only dangerous, it's very difficult."

"So you're saying such a meeting is beyond your abilities?"

Kiukiu heard the challenge and knew that her grandmother would be unable to resist.

Malusha glared at the Magus. "Do you know nothing of our craft? I can only bring a dead spirit back to this world with a lock of hair, a bone, or some such thing to anchor it here. Unless you're willing to offer your body for it to inhabit? I thought not. And I'm not in the business of creating spirit-wraiths, so don't even ask." She glanced accusingly at Kiukiu, who felt her cheeks burning at the memory of what she had once unwittingly done.

Malusha had worked steadily since winter to repair her broken gusly; now she took it down from the shelf and unwrapped it from its brightly colored wool blanket. Kiukiu found a layer of fine dust had settled on her instrument; she gave a surreptitious puff to blow the dust away.

"Ha!" Malusha said, missing nothing. "So now we shall have to waste valuable time tuning this neglected instrument." She handed Kiukiu the little iron key she used to tighten slack strings. "And you'd better use a plectrum or you'll cut your fingers."

It felt odd to Kiukiu to sit and hold the gusly again after so many long weeks of housework at the kastel. Just to pluck the strings and feel the resonances reverberate through her body reminded her of what she had been forced to bury deep within her. Now she felt a sense of liberation. Here she had no need to pretend; she could be who she truly was: a Spirit Singer.

When the tuning was finally done to her satisfaction, she looked up from the gusly and saw her grandmother gazing at her intently, the firelight glinting in her eyes.

"We're going together, child. You've never had to travel so deep into the Ways before. There are dangers you've never even imagined in your darkest dreams."

Kiukiu nodded, secretly relieved not to have to go alone.

"And while we're gone," Malusha said, turning to Linnaius, "you can make sure the fire doesn't go out. And no mage-mischief while we're away, or my lords and ladies will peck your eyes out." She picked up the gusly and struck a slow succession of notes. "Kiukiu, copy me. This is the Golden Scale. We'll need it where we're going."

"The Golden Scale?" Kiukiu had forgotten until now that she still had much to learn. And she needed all her concentration to copy the unfamiliar sequence of pitches that Malusha was plucking. Yet she did discern a golden quality to the music they were creating. The air seemed to glow with the richness of the sound. A gilded mist filled the little room and the firelight grew dim, receding until there was only the throb of each note, as warm as rays of evening sunlight, and she was rising through sunset clouds in a glory of bronze and gold.

"I've never been here before, have I?"

"This is the deepest I've ever taken you, child." Malusha was skimming upward beside her, and now Kiukiu saw her grandmother as a tall young woman again, her braided hair brown, her voice strong and true, her back straight.

"We could be sisters," Kiukiu said with heartfelt emotion. "I always wanted a sister."

"Pay attention!" Malusha snapped. "Even here, you must be on your guard. Even here, Lost Souls can waylay and entrap you to feed on your life force. Never forget—we are intruders."

"A bossy older sister," Kiukiu whispered. And then the burnished clouds parted and a distant sound breathed through the air like a perfumed breeze.

"I can hear music," said Kiukiu, gazing around her. "Singing. Such strange, beautiful singing . . ."

"This is going to be harder than I thought."

"Why?" Kiukiu felt herself drawn toward the sound of the singing. She began to drift in the direction of the music.

Malusha stopped her.

"But I want to go and join in—"

"We're trespassing here to help your Lord Gavril, though heaven knows why; he doesn't deserve it for what he did to you. Now stay close and don't wander off."

Ahead of them, crowning a little hill, stood a high-walled garden; Kiukiu could see tall cedars rising above the weathered stones of the wall as well as oaks and white-flowering chestnuts. They reached the top of the hill and found themselves in front of finely wrought, gilded iron-work gates.

As Malusha raised her hand to push the gates open, two gold-armored warriors suddenly appeared, barring their way with crossed scimitars. Half-blinded by the light radiating from their faces, Kiukiu threw up one hand to shield her eyes.

"We are pilgrims from Azhkendir," said Malusha. "We seek counsel from the Blessed Serzhei."

"Serzhei's work in Azhkendir is complete," said one of the warriors. His voice rang out like a brazen trumpet call. "Why do you disturb his rest?"

"A daemon-warrior is at large in our world. It calls itself the Drakhaoul."

Kiukiu ventured a glance through her fingers at the warriors. Though light still shimmered around them like wings of golden flames, she managed a glimpse of their faces, at once terrible and beautiful, as they consulted each other with a look.

One slowly pointed to the ragged scars on Kiukiu's throat. Kiukiu gave a little cry when the scarred skin began to burn, as though a fiery liquid had been dripped onto her body. She looked down and saw the scars were glowing. Her hands flew, too late, to cover her throat.

"You bear the mark of a Drakhaoul."

"All the more reason for us to seek Serzhei's help," said Malusha dryly.

"You know well enough, Spirit Singer," said the first, "that such a thing is forbidden."

"Why?" burst out Kiukiu.

"You are trespassers here. You must return to the world of the living."

"Very well," Malusha said, though Kiukiu heard not the slightest hint of resignation in her voice. "Come, child." She strode off away from the gate, Kiukiu hurrying after.

"So we're just going to give up?" Kiukiu cried.

"You heard, Kiukiu, we're trespassers." But Malusha was not going back down the hill, she was skirting the edge of the walled garden.

"Ah." Kiukiu understood what her grandmother intended; here, in the Ways Beyond, walls were not necessarily a barrier to Spirit Singers. "But won't *they* come after us?" She glanced uneasily over her shoulder, expecting to see the winged guardians swooping down on them.

"Without a doubt. But is that going to stop us?" Malusha stopped and gazed up at the wall. "It shouldn't be too difficult to shin up here; there are plenty of toe-holds." And she started up the wall, grunting as she pulled herself aloft.

Kiukiu could not help giggling. Her grandma was climbing over the wall, just like a little girl scrumping apples!

"Don't dawdle," Malusha hissed from the top and disappeared over the other side. Kiukiu began to climb, and though the stones grated against her fingers as she clung on, she found she could clamber upward as easily as if she weighed nothing whatsoever. She jumped down, landing beside Malusha on gravel between the tall chestnuts.

They stood in a formal garden with knots and winding paths and intricately cut topiary. The sound of running water came from fountains playfully carved to resemble whiskered carp, which sprayed crystal jets into the air from their pursed mouths. Kiukiu recognized herbs growing in the beds as they walked past and heard the summery droning of bees among the cloudy banks of lavender.

"It's just like the monastery gardens back home," she said, surprised.

"Where else do you think a monk would want to be?" Malusha strode on, plunging into a dark maze of high yew hedges, with Kiukiu still lagging behind. "And keep up! I don't want to have to search for you too."

At the heart of the maze, they came into a round garden with a sundial at its center.

"Here it is always summer," said a gentle voice. Kiukiu saw a grey-robed man rise from a garden seat and come slowly toward them.

She did not need to shield her eyes when she looked at him, although no matter how hard she blinked, she did not quite seem able to focus on his features.

So this is our patron saint, Serzhei. Awed, Kiukiu found she had lost her voice. He seemed so mild-mannered for a vanquisher of daemons.

"We have come to ask for your guidance, Serzhei," said Malusha. Her tone was much more respectful now than when she had answered the warriors at the gates. "How did you banish the daemons from the world of the living?"

For a while, Serzhei did not answer, nodding his head as if lost in contemplation. All Kiukiu could hear was the splash of the fountains and the droning of the bees.

"I could not have banished them had I not called upon the Heavenly Guardians to help me. And even then, the one you name Drakhaoul burned me with his cold fire and I died, my task incomplete. But there is more. Let me show you."

He beckoned them toward the sundial. As they drew near, he placed both hands, palms down, on the ancient stone. Kiukiu blinked again as the center of the dial melted away. Tiny, jewel-bright figures, like the illuminations drawn by the monks in the library at Saint Sergius, moved across a painted landscape, complete with a tiny range of mountains and barques bobbing on a choppy sea.

"You must understand that the danger was too great to ignore. Artamon's sons were tempted in their arrogance to summon daemons to settle their bitter rivalry. It had to be stopped or all Rossiya would have been seared to an arid wasteland."

Kiukiu was staring at one of the figures; there was a dark glitter about it that she recognized only too well.

"Drakhaoul," she said softly.

"That is the name it devised for itself in Azhkendir, but it has an older, more ancient name. Once it was kin to the guardians you saw at the gateway."

"The ones with the golden armor?" Kiukiu found the idea almost impossible to conceive. "But they're *angels*—"

"Even angels can be tempted to fall from grace. The Drakhaoul and its kin were banished to the Realm of Shadows. But there was a gateway to that realm from your world, which powerful and arrogant magi breached using a ruby imbued with the blood of children."

"Child sacrifice," Malusha murmured. "The daemon's craving for innocent blood . . ."

"The Drakhaoul was once an angel?" persisted Kiukiu. "And priests killed children to make it serve them? That's horrible."

"It must be sent back the way it came," Malusha said slowly, as though reasoning out loud, "by opening this gateway, wherever it may be. But not by killing children, surely?"

"And where is this gateway?" asked Kiukiu. "Is it in Azhkendir?"

"How can I be sure, if I tell you, that you will use this information for the good of the living?" There was a darker hint of warning in Serzhei's voice now. "Or that others will not force it out of you and use it to fulfill their own selfish desires? For that is how it was with the sons of Artamon. You have seen the terrible damage that one Drakhaoul-daemon can wreak; imagine the devastation if more were let loose."

The drowsy air grew warmer, releasing wafts of scent from the herbs. And the buzzing of the bees among the blue lavender spikes grew louder. The hazy sky filled with the sound of beating wings.

"Oh no," whispered Kiukiu. "They've found us."

"Only the emperor's tears," Serzhei said, "will unlock the gate. But take great care. For others of its daemon-kin may seize their chance to escape and—"

"Enough!" The two guardian warriors from the gate alighted, one on either side of Serzhei. And now others appeared, hovering overhead, golden hair and wings flickering like flames. Alarmed, Kiukiu shrank back toward her grandmother. "You were ordered to leave."

"Forgive us." Kiukiu held her hands out imploringly to Serzhei. "We didn't mean to do anything wrong."

One guardian took hold of Kiukiu, the other, Malusha. At their touch, Kiukiu felt her scars begin to burn. "Why can't *you* help us?" she cried to them, filled with frustration that so few of their questions had been answered.

"Only one pure of heart may call upon the Heavenly Warriors to defeat the Drakhaoul." The guardian warrior's voice was stern.

"And you have defied us once already," said the other. "You must go now, and never return."

Kiukiu let out a little cry as she was lifted high into the air and the guardians bore them upward through the gilded sky on fiery wings.

*   *   *

Kiukiu opened her eyes.

She was sitting by the fire in her grandmother's cottage. The gusly lay silent on her lap. The fingers of one hand were deeply scored with the marks of the gusly strings. The other hand clutched protectively at the base of her throat where her scarred skin still burned.

"Marked by the daemon," she whispered, overcome with shame. "Tainted."

Beside her, Malusha stirred.

"I'm getting too old for this." She laid her gusly down. "Put the kettle on the fire, Kiukiu. Let's have some tea."

A man rose from the seat on the other side of the fire; Kiukiu jumped. She had forgotten that the Magus was still there, waiting for them.

"Well?" he said. "What did you learn?"

Kiukiu lowered her eyes, too ashamed to say.

"Make the tea, Kiukiu," ordered Malusha. "I can't abide talking with a dry throat."

Kiukiu busied herself at the range, putting in a blend of healing herbs for her fingers and restorative herbs to revive them after their journey in the Ways Beyond. She could sense the Magus's growing impatience; she knew Malusha would take a malign pleasure in making him wait.

And indeed, not until she had taken several long sips of her favorite herbal tea, sweetened with honey, did Malusha deign to answer his question.

"We've heard tales of an ages-old war between the Drakhaoul's daemon-kin and the Heavenly Guardians," she said, setting her mug down. "And unless you can find someone as pure of heart as Archimandrite Serzhei to summon them, no Heavenly Guardians are ever going to come to our aid."

"I'd guessed that much from the manuscript at the monastery," Linnaius said.

There was something odd about his lack of reaction, Kiukiu thought as she drank her tea, balancing the mug carefully in her sore fingers. Had this just been some kind of test? No matter what it was, she wished that her grandmother would not provoke him with her sly little digs and send him away, his promise to her unfulfilled.

"There was one other thing Serzhei told us," continued Malusha, almost teasingly. "Just as we were thrown out for our pains . . ."

"And that was?"

" '*Only the Emperor's tears will unlock the gate,*' " said Kiukiu. "But we never heard where the gate was. They wanted to keep it secret."

"Ah." This obviously meant something to the Magus.

"So?" Malusha said, her eyes bright in the firelight. "We risked much for you and your little Tielen princess, Linnaius. The least you could do is to tell us what it means."

" 'The emperor' most probably means Artamon," Linnaius said obliquely.

"It doesn't take a scholar to figure that one out! And what about this ruby? Imbued with the blood of children?" Malusha was no longer teasing, Kiukiu saw; she was in deadly earnest. "I'll not be party to any practice involving the killing of children, and neither will my Kiukiu."

"I'll have to pursue my researches further." Linnaius began to walk toward the door.

"You seem very keen to be on your way, wind-mage." Malusha eased herself up out of her chair. "There's more to this than you're telling, isn't there? And what about that visit you promised my Kiukiu? Have you seen the state of her fingers? She's ruined them— and all on your Emperor's behalf! Show him."

Kiukiu reluctantly raised her hand, showing her sore, swollen fingertips.

"You understand, I'm sure, that there are orders to be filled out and signed by the Emperor himself. Gavril Nagarian is a very dangerous man and he is confined in a place of the utmost security. But I will set the process in motion. I will return when I have more news." He turned on his heel to leave.

"The Emperor's daughter," Kiukiu said. "She's only little. She could be the one pure of heart."

"An innocent child?" Linnaius stopped as though this had not occurred to him before. Then he nodded and, opening the door, disappeared into the courtyard.

CHAPTER 14

Gulls drifted lazily overhead on the warm breeze. Elysia stood in the middle of the quay at Vermeille and closed her eyes for a moment, taking in a deep breath of Smarnan air. Oblivious of the noisy bustle around her—the unloading of bundles of furs from the merchant ship that had brought her from Arkhelskoye, and the loading up of barrels of Smarnan wine for the return journey—she just stood there, letting the familiar smells and traders' cries wash over her. Even the pungent reek from the fish market was all the more welcome for its familiarity.

Home. I'm home. She gazed around her, blinking a film of tears from her eyes. There was a richness to the light here, a warmth that gilded the red tiles on the cafes and taverns lining the quay, that enhanced the vibrant colors of their painted walls: deep sea-blue, pepper scarlet, and rich earthy ochre. No one paid any attention to the shabbily dressed, middle-aged woman who stood enraptured by a scene of such unsurprising ordinariness.

Finally she picked up her bag and set off along the quay. It was a walk of some two miles to the Villa Andara along the upper cliff road, but she had no money for a carriage and, after the long voyage, she was glad of the exercise.

And then she saw the soldiers. Tielen soldiers. They had set up a barrier at the end of the quay and were checking everyone in and out. Even though she knew she carried a pass stamped with the Emperor's official seal and signature, she still felt a shiver at the sight of those blue and grey uniforms. Even here in Smarna, the power of the new empire was making itself felt.

"In line, lady, like the rest," ordered a soldier, officiously waving her into a long queue waiting inside a roped-off area.

Elysia glared at him but did as she was told.

"Bloody Tielens. Think they own the earth," muttered a balding merchant in front of her. He was sweating in the morning sun and mopping at his shiny forehead with a handkerchief. "I've got business in the citadel. And now I'm late."

"How long has this been going on?" Elysia asked quietly.

"Since Tielen annexed Smarna. Isn't it the same elsewhere? Passes to come in, permissions to leave, extra taxes to pay—"

"I wouldn't know," she said, "I've just arrived from Azhkendir."

"Papers," demanded the officer on duty, waving his hand in her face. "Papers!"

She handed over her safe-conduct letter without a word and saw, with some satisfaction, how he stared at the Emperor's signature.

"Madame Andar. You may go." He folded up the paper and presented it to her with a crisp salute.

As she passed through the barrier, she could not help but notice that he had made a note of her name and had whispered it to one of his men, who went hurrying away toward the customs house.

So even here I am to be watched. The brightness of the Smarnan sunlight seemed to dim a little as she watched the Tielen vanish inside, doubtless to send a message to Eugene's agents that she had arrived in Vermeille.

And then she shrugged. What could she do about it? She turned her back on the Tielen soldiers and began to walk along the winding cobbled lane that led upward out of the harbor toward the cliffs.

Palmyre was pegging out a line of washing in the gardens of the Villa Andara. A good breeze was blowing off the sea and the wet sheets would soon be dry. She bent to pick up another handful of pegs from her basket, stuck one between her teeth, then saw two feet placed opposite hers on the other side of the half-dangling sheet.

"Shall I hold that for you?" inquired a familiar voice.

"Elysia?"

"The very same."

The pegs fell into the grass. Palmyre gave a little shriek of joy and tried to embrace Elysia across the clothesline.

"Why didn't you send word?" Palmyre ducked under the line of sheets and hugged Elysia properly, tears streaming down her cheeks. "If I'd known, I'd have—"

"Gone to a lot of unnecessary fuss and trouble on my account," said Elysia, laughing and weeping at the same time, "when all I want is a good cup of tea, Palmyre, and to sleep in my own bed, with the sound of the sea outside my window."

"Tea it shall be," Palmyre said, drying her eyes on her apron, "and anything else you desire."

Elysia sat on the terrace, Palmyre beside her, and lifted her face to the afternoon sun.

"I can't tell you how good it is to be back," she said. "And I can't quite believe it to be true. Pinch me, Palmyre."

"Oh you're back all right," Palmyre said fondly.

"I'm still not sure why Eugene let me go." Elysia's smile faded. "I wonder whether Astasia had some influence."

"The Empress Astasia?" Palmyre said in impressed tones.

"And he has Gavril." Elysia had made a pact with herself that she would not even allow herself to think of Gavril's plight until she was in a position to start petitioning for his release.

"So the stories in the papers are true?" Palmyre ventured. "He's been imprisoned?"

"For life. Yes." Elysia stood up and walked to the edge of the terrace. She leaned on the balustrade, gazing out at the blue of the bay, feeling the sea breeze stirring in her hair. The last of the white lilacs were in bloom and their sweet scent drifted to her from the wild garden below. "The first snowdrops were just opening, Palmyre," she said softly, "when they came and took him away. I haven't seen him since that day."

Palmyre said nothing. Elysia guessed from her silence that she was upset as well. Palmyre had been a second mother to Gavril—sometimes more of a mother, Elysia thought, remembering all the times when she had been away from home on a commission and Palmyre had made his supper, tucked him up in bed, and told him stories of sea monsters and mermaids that she had learned from her seafaring father.

"So how's Lukan?" Elysia asked, turning away from the bay.

"Lukan?" Palmyre lowered her voice. "Something's brewing at the university, Elysia, and he's right in the thick of it."

"Oh?" Palmyre's words suddenly made Elysia deeply uneasy. Lukan had always been a passionate believer in democracy. He would not have taken kindly to the imposition of imperial rule.

Palmyre glanced around, checking to ensure there was no one else within earshot. "The Tielens are not popular. There've been . . . rumblings."

"I hope Lukan knows what he's doing; he has no idea how powerful the Tielens have become. They'll crush anyone who dares to oppose them." Then Elysia shook her head, forcing laughter into her voice. "Listen to me! And when did my views become so reactionary?"

Palmyre was looking at her with an awed expression. "You must have been through some terrible times in the last months."

Elysia swallowed. Yes, she had seen things she could still not bring herself to talk about.

"Well, there's no point dwelling on what can't be undone," she said briskly. "I must look forward now." Resolute of purpose, she set off across the terrace steps that led down to the shore.

"Where are you going?" Palmyre called after her, dismayed.

"Oh, Palmyre. Haven't you guessed? To see my old, dear friend Professor Rafael Lukan. We have much to talk about."

In the heart of the Old Citadel of Colchise was a little tavern, much frequented by students and artists. Like many of the dwellings in Colchise, Vardo's Tavern had been hewn right into the side of the cliff on which the citadel stood; the doorway was surrounded by an exuberantly climbing rose, already blooming with a profusion of scented yellow flowers. The courtyard garden was strung with paper lanterns, whose soft, flickering lights had already attracted hovering moths in the warm dusk. Wonderful spicy smells of cooking wafted up from the tavern's kitchen: garlic, rosemary, and tomatoes stewed with chopped onions and bay leaves . . .

Elysia felt a sudden stab of anguish as she stood looking down at the crowd of students gathered below, drinking Vardo's cheap red wine, talking and laughing together. This had been a favorite haunt of Gavril's. How was it that she stood here tonight and he was so far away, locked up for life in some remote Tielen prison with madmen and murderers?

For life? Not if I have anything to do with it!

She tucked a wandering strand of hair back in place and went down the winding rocky steps into the throng of drinkers.

She heard Lukan's deep, resonant voice long before she located him. Even now, its distinctive timbre sent a little shiver through her. She and Lukan had been lovers for many years after she left Volkh Nagarian, and even though their passion had cooled with the passing of time, they had remained good friends.

"And now this Tielen self-appointed governor, Armfeld, has the nerve to ban public meetings in the university. Without any process of consultation with the faculty board."

A roar of disapproval rose from the other drinkers. She had arrived at an opportune moment. Anti-Tielen feelings were obviously running high.

"What can we do?" called out a girl's voice. "Can we allow them to silence us?"

"They have no rights—constitutional or otherwise—to overrule the faculty," Lukan said. "Not even the Smarnan council can intervene in university matters."

Elysia pushed closer to the alcove where Lukan was holding forth.

"They have no rights in Smarna, anyway!" yelled out a man's voice, young and impassioned. "Did we ask to be annexed?"

"*No!*" shouted the students.

"Did Smarna ask to be swallowed up by this imperialist dictator?"

"*No!*"

"So what are we going to do about it?"

Heavens, Elysia thought, still resolutely pushing forward to get closer to Lukan. *This sounds like a full-blown revolt. Do they have any idea what they are up against?*

She emerged right at the front of the gathering. There was Lukan, his craggily handsome face crowned by an untidy tumble of silvered black hair.

He looked up, about to speak again, and saw her.

"Elysia!" He leaped to his feet, knocking over glasses, and came straight toward her, seizing her in his arms and hugging her close.

She had forgotten how strong he was. Breathless, she looked up into his warm, dark eyes and felt, for the first time in so many weeks, a glimmer of hope.

"Look who it is!" he cried to the whole tavern, his arm around her shoulders. "Elysia Andar. Returned to us from the jaws of hell, isn't that right, Elysia?"

As Lukan steered her to a seat beside his, she was aware that everyone was staring at her now.

"Returned from Azhkendir," she said, "to fight for my son's release."

"So it's true?" Lukan said, his voice somber. "Gavril is in prison in Tielen?"

"And sentenced to life imprisonment."

"What's that got to do with us?" shouted out a student.

"More than you might imagine," she answered calmly, resolving not to lose her temper with hecklers. "I'm not only here to fight for Gavril. I'm here to fight for Smarna too, if need be."

To her surprise, a cheer arose at these last words. *What am I doing?* she wondered, panicking. *If Eugene's spies are here tonight, I'll be branded a troublemaker—and then what use will I be to Gavril?*

"Welcome back, Elysia!" cried Lukan, kissing her heartily on the mouth.

She gazed up into his eyes, glad for once to have a strong arm to lean against. For the first time in a long while, she knew she was not alone.

Elysia stood beside Lukan and the other members of the newly formed Republican Alliance beneath the citadel. Behind them were ranged hundreds of students. The morning was bright and a crisp breeze blew off the bay, fluttering the many Tielen and New Rossiyan standards that had been hoisted on every flagpole and turret of the Old Citadel. Of the crimson and gold flag of the Smarnan Republic, there was no sign.

Governor Armfeld had taken up residence in the Smarnan council chambers, high in the ancient citadel itself, overlooking Vermeille Bay. From the large numbers of troops he had deployed about the citadel, it looked as if he was making ready to defend his base in case of trouble.

A woman, grey-haired and smartly dressed, came briskly up to Lukan. Elysia recognized Nina Vashteli, Minister of Justice, and First Minister of the Smarnan council.

"Is this wise, Lukan? To confront the Tielens head-on? If they feel threatened, they may retaliate."

"Haven't you tried to negotiate? And how has Armfeld answered our requests? With bluster and prevarication."

"It's true that the man is no diplomat," Nina Vashteli said sourly. "First he tries to impose these ludicrous taxes, now he has the gall to close the university. We won't be treated like this!"

Elysia had noticed a stir of movement up on the ramparts.

"Look." She pointed. "Here comes Armfeld's response."

Shadowed against the brightness of the morning sun, a line of soldiers had appeared on the upper battlements. Sun glinted on the metal of their carbines.

"This doesn't bode well," murmured Lukan. He shaded his eyes against the sunlight, gazing upward as he assessed the opposition.

"Your gathering is unlawful!" shouted down one of the soldiers in the common tongue. "Governor Armfeld orders you all to go home."

This was met with jeering from many of the students.

"Let him tell us so himself!" one yelled.

Elysia glanced uneasily at Lukan.

"I am Professor Rafael Lukan," he called out. "Tell your governor that since he has closed down our university, I am obliged to lecture to my students out here instead."

A great raucous cheer arose at his words, sending the grey and white gulls lining the rooftops flapping and screeching into the air.

"And today's lecture will be on the virtues of democracy and republicanism," Lukan said, balancing himself on the rim of an old well to address his audience, "compared to the evils of autocratic rule and dictatorship."

"Stop!"

Lukan turned slowly around. Elysia looked up to see where the voice was coming from. A florid-complexioned man had appeared on the ramparts. He seemed agitated.

"You have no right, Professor Lukan, to openly incite these young people to rebellion. I must caution you that you are committing an offense of the highest treason against the New Rossiyan Empire."

"I am merely continuing with my classes, Governor. Order your men to reopen our university and we will clear the streets and trouble you no longer."

"But your lectures are seditious, Professor Lukan. I cannot allow you to preach revolution here in the streets—or in the university."

"Then at least let them discuss their differences with you, Governor," said Nina Vashteli.

"I had hoped better of you, Minister," Armfeld said. "Why do you ally yourself with these troublemakers? There is no place for discussion here. Go home. All of you!"

Elysia heard a disturbance in the crowd of students behind her. A young man, bespectacled and earnest, pushed his way through to Lukan's side.

"Look, Professor." He pulled a folded cloth from inside his jacket and shook it out. "The flag! Our flag!"

Crimson and gilded chevrons unfurled and glinted in the sun. In the center of the cloth, a gold-embroidered merman with a scaly tail held aloft a trident.

"Well done, Miran." Lukan clapped the young man on the shoulder. "Now we have our standard again."

Another of the students came running up, holding a broom handle. With a little improvisation, the standard was soon lashed to the broom. Miran climbed up beside Lukan and brandished it in the air. Another deafening cheer went echoing around the citadel walls.

"I'm warning you, Professor!" spluttered Armfeld from the ramparts. "Send these young people home, or I will be obliged to take action."

"Lukan." Elysia was growing increasingly apprehensive. She touched his arm. "The Tielen military is ruthless. They don't think as we do."

"They wouldn't dare fire on us," Lukan said, arrogantly confident. "We outnumber them, five to one."

"They have alchymical weapons. They don't need to outnumber us."

She saw him hesitate for the first time.

"Alchymical weapons?" He glanced down at her, his dark brows drawn close in a frown. "No. He wouldn't dare. There are women and children here."

"Governor Armfeld!" Nina Vashteli called up to the ramparts, her voice stern. "Can't we come together and discuss these matters in a more civilized way?"

"Tell your mob to disperse!" shouted back the governor. He pulled out a white handkerchief and began to mop his face.

"What is there left to discuss?" yelled a light, passionate voice. Elysia saw that another student, face concealed under a broad-brimmed hat, had leaped up beside the standard-bearer. "What do we want? Tielens out! Tielens out!"

"Tie-lens out!" Other students nearby took up the cry, thumping on doors to emphasize the rhythm. "Tiel-ens out!"

"N-now look here!" Armfeld tried to raise his voice, but it was drowned in the angry chanting.

Elysia saw how red the governor's face had become. The hand that held the white kerchief suddenly waved in one decisive, furious gesture. Shots rang out and little puffs of white smoke could be seen issuing from the barrels of the left-hand row of carbines.

The Smarnan standard wavered—and the young man holding it fell to the cobbles.

Suddenly the shouting died as Lukan caught Miran in his arms and lowered him gently to the ground. The other student jumped down to help support him. There was no sound in the citadel now but the distant crying of gulls.

"Oh no, no," Elysia heard herself murmuring. The bespectacled student lay pale and limp; blood gushed from a wound at the base of his throat. Without even thinking, she had taken out her handkerchief and pressed it hard to the wound in a pad. *If it's an artery that's been damaged,* she thought, remembering her anatomy classes, *strong pressure must be applied or he will bleed to death.*

"A doctor. Get a doctor!" cried out the other student, pillowing the boy's head against his knee.

Elysia's white handkerchief had already turned red with blood. Lukan handed her another, already folded.

Miran tried to murmur something.

"Hold on, Miran," urged the student. "Don't try to talk. Just hold on."

"We need to get him out of the street," Elysia said. *Hold on,* she echoed silently to the injured boy, trying not to remind herself that he was not so much younger than her own son; it could have been Gavril who lay here, bleeding his life out on the cobbles, felled by a Tielen bullet. . . .

A stretcher was improvised from a ladder draped with coats, and Miran was hurried into a nearby doctor's surgery. Elysia followed after, aware that the students were massing outside. The silence that had followed the shooting of Miran was now replaced by an angry buzz that grew steadily louder.

She remembered the crowd that had raged for vengeance outside the Winter Palace in Mirom. Innocent blood had been shed then too. There would be a riot now; she recognized the signs. And nothing Governor Armfeld could do would stop it.

"My brother has been shot. And why? Because he dared to hold up our Smarnan flag!"

Elysia peered out through the little window and saw it was the other student who had seized the standard and was standing at Lukan's side on the top of the well. The broad-brimmed hat she had been wearing lay on the ground, and dark auburn hair streamed unbound about her shoulders. Her voice throbbed with bitter emotion.

The citadel square had filled with protestors. And now Elysia saw weapons: axes, pitchforks, sabres, pistols. The Smarnans were by nature easygoing—but when they cared about a cause, they would fight to the death.

"Take care, dear Lukan," she murmured. "Oh please take care."

The spring sun shone on the imperial dockyards, but the brisk wind off the Nieva stung like a whip. Eugene, well-protected by his greatcoat, hardly noticed the cold. He was inspecting the warships of the Southern Fleet, which had put into Mirom after a refit in Tielen. And he smiled as he surveyed the new pride of his fleet, the iron-prowed *Rogned*. The fierce figurehead portrayed the fearless warrior-princess of ancient Tielen legend, gilded braids streaming behind her as she thrust her spear toward the waves.

"What do you think of her, highness?" asked Admiral Janssen, who had been accompanying him on his tour from the hold to the upper decks.

"She looks superb," said Eugene. "But how does she handle under sail?"

"Oh she's fast. She completed her trials with flying colors. Sturdily built—but with a good wind, she can outrun all the others."

"We may need her," Eugene said, nodding, "and sooner than we anticipated."

"Smarna?" Janssen's jovial expression became grave.

Smarna. Just the sound of the name was beginning to irritate

Eugene. It seemed to represent all that frustrated him in his efforts to unite the empire.

"The negotiations have broken down. Armfeld's latest report is frustratingly vague, but he may well need backup."

"Just give the word, highness," Janssen said loyally. "We'll be ready."

CHAPTER 15

Gavril stumbles on across a hot, dark shore. Stars gleam red overhead, unfamiliar constellations half-obscured by poisonous fogs.

"I've been here before . . . but when?"

Every step burns the soles of his bare feet. The air stinks of sulphur; every breath he draws sears his mouth, his throat, his lungs.

Yet even as he wipes the sweat from his brow, he is aware that he has never visited such an inhospitable, desolate place.

This dream from which he cannot awake must be woven from someone else's memories.

"It's through here. It must be." He hacks his way through the dense vegetation with an axe, chopping at great creepers that snap and sting his skin like whips. He has no idea what he is searching for, only that some desperate obsession forces him onward.

In the distance, a cone of fire simmers; choking fumes and vapors drift past. The sulphurous air is becoming hard to breathe.

Suddenly he trips over a tree root and topples forward onto his knees. He raises his head. He is kneeling at the foot of a great overgrown archway, its ancient grey stones smothered in mosses and clinging lianas.

"Is this finally it?" he asks. "The Serpent Gate of Ty Nagar?"

Closer to, he can make out the forms of twisting snakes carved into the old stones. Fanged mouths snarl at him, baring forked tongues. He lifts one hand to touch the carven scales.

"This is the Gate," answers the voice in his head, "but where is Nagar's Eye?"

Gavril looks up and sees the carven head of a great winged serpent crowning the gateway. It stares balefully back at him from one empty eye socket.

"Without the Eye, the Gate remains shut." The soft voice is choked with anguish. "Shut for all eternity."

"What Eye? What do you mean?" Gavril cries out, his shout sending a flock of fire-feathered birds shrieking up into the air from the overhanging trees. "Have you brought us all this way for nothing?"

Gavril awoke in darkness, overwhelmed by a black mood of despair—and yet it felt as if the despair was not his own.

Those names in his dream, Ty Nagar, the Serpent Gate . . . He had read them somewhere before.

He sat up on his hard prison bed, suddenly alert.

In my grandfather Zakhar's books. I've been reliving Zakhar's last memories. The Drakhaoul must have planted them in my mind. Has it also left me the memories of other, far older ancestors?

He heard a quiet footfall on the stair outside.

He gazed up at the dark stripes of night sky that showed through his barred window. The prison day began early—but it was nowhere near dawn yet.

Was I shouting out in my sleep again?

A key creaked in the lock and the door swung slowly open.

"Who's there?"

Someone held up a shuttered lantern, its single beam directed right in his face. Dazzled, he flung up one hand to shield his eyes.

"You're to come with us." Two warders had entered his cell.

"Now? But I'm not dressed—"

"Come as you are."

Has Linnaius told Eugene that I am of no further use? Dear God, is this to be the end? Have they come to take me to some secret place of execution?

"At least let me put my shoes on."

They hurried him down the silent staircase and out across one of the many inner courtyards. The night air was fresh with a fine drizzle; no stars or moon could be seen overhead. Gavril, dressed only in shirt and breeches, shivered in the damp. Somewhere, a prison hound bayed dolefully into the empty night.

They hustled Gavril into another tower. The room into which they brought him was empty except for an iron chair and a wooden trolley covered in a cloth. Gavril halted in the doorway, staring at the chair and the leather restraints fixed on the arms and feet.

"Torture?" he said. His voice came out in a hoarse whisper. "Do you mean to torture me?"

"Whatever gave you that idea?" Director Baltzar appeared. He was dressed in a brown overall and wore a bizarre headpiece with a single thick glass lens attached to it, not unlike a jeweler's loupe. "No, I've brought you here to cure you, Twenty-One."

"But I'm not ill!"

"Put him in the chair." Baltzar turned away and busied himself with unwrapping the contents of the cloth on the trolley.

The two warders began to drag Gavril toward the chair.

"Just what do you intend?" Panic overwhelmed him. He dug his feet in, resisting their efforts with all his strength. "Leave me be!" He rammed his foot into one of the warder's shins. The warder let go with a shout of pain, and hopped away, cursing.

The other kicked Gavril's legs out from under him and pinned him to the floor with the weight of his body.

"Stubborn to the end," Baltzar said with a shrug. "Hold him steady." He came up to Gavril and, even though Gavril squirmed and turned his face away, pressed a cloth to his nose and mouth. A strong chemical smell issued from the cloth and suddenly the room wavered as all the strength leaked from his body, leaving him weak and limp as a marionette.

A strong light shone above him. He blinked, unable to focus in its dazzling rays.

Where am I?

He tried to move his head—and found that it was firmly clamped. A thick leather collar had been buckled about his neck so that any movement other than blinking was impossible. He looked down and saw that his wrists were buckled to the arms of the chair in which he sat. Another wide belt secured him at the waist. When he attempted to move his feet, he found his ankles were secured as well.

A shadowy form appeared above him and leaned in close to raise one of his eyelids.

He recognized Director Baltzar.

"So you're awake," Baltzar said. His voice boomed hollowly, as if heard through water. "Good. This procedure only works if the patient is conscious."

Procedure? Gavril tried to narrow his eyes against the glare of the overhead lantern to see what Baltzar was about.

"Stand ready to swab, Skar," Baltzar said. "You know how profusely these incisions in the scalp bleed."

Gavril caught the glint of steel in Baltzar's hand as he leaned forward again. Behind him he saw an array of scalpels, probes, and tweezers laid out on the trolley.

"What—are you going to do—to me?" Each word came out so slowly, as his tongue and lips moved sluggishly against the effects of the drug.

"We are going to cut into your skull to free the pressure on the part of your brain that has been giving you these delusions, Twenty-One. You call it your 'daemon.' But from my extensive researches, I suspect it is the result of some injury or disease of the brain."

"No!" Gavril cried out with all his force. "The daemon is gone—"

"You will be so much more placid when we have finished the procedure. You may feel a little pain during the operation—but when it is done, I assure you, you will be an altered man." Baltzar's eye glinted through the single magnifying lens.

Terror surged up from deep inside Gavril in a black, choking wave. He had heard of the technique of trepanning and its frequently disastrous results. This self-styled doctor intended to cut into his brain. When he had finished with him, he would be no more than a drooling idiot, incapable of remembering his own name.

"Help me!" Gavril shouted, though he knew there was no one who could come to his aid. "Help—"

And then he felt the tip of the cold steel blade slice into his scalp. Something warm trickled down one side of his forehead—and was wiped away.

They are cutting into my head. They want to excise my daemon— but all they will do is amputate my memories, my dreams, all that goes to make me who I am. Why is there no one to help me?

And now he heard the sound of a small drill boring into his skull, felt the terrible juddering as the bone resisted the bite of the metal. Until, with a sickening crunch, the tip went right through, penetrating the soft tissue of his brain.

The lantern-lit room imploded in a chaos of colored shards and dark stars. And then there was only the darkness.

CHAPTER 16

Every day Andrei forced himself out onto the long expanse of empty grey sands that stretched into the distant horizon, shrouded in sea fog. And every day he managed to walk a little farther, as his damaged body slowly, miraculously, repaired itself.

One evening, much like another, Kuzko and his adoptive son sat on either side of the fire as Irina cleared away the remains of the fish-and-onion stew they had eaten for supper.

"You'll be wanting to go find your own folks soon," Kuzko said with a sigh, lighting his tobacco pipe.

"If only I knew where to start looking." Andrei stared into the flames. "Or who they are . . ."

His name was Andrei. That much he remembered. But no more. There had been no clues in the waterlogged shreds of clothing that had clung to his body; the sea had washed them clean of any distinguishing marks.

"We know you're a sailor and we know you're from Muscobar." Kuzko drew on his pipe, letting out a slow, reflective puff of smoke. "Otherwise we'd have had trouble understanding each other, hm? But Muscobar's a big country with plenty of ports up and down the coast. We're out on the farthest tip here on Lapwing Spar. Land's end, with only the Iron Sea beyond. Far from anywhere. Nobody bothers much about us . . . and we don't bother them."

Andrei frowned, concentrating his gaze on a stick, forked like a stag's horn as it glowed white-hot, and then suddenly crumbled away to ash.

His memory, like the little island, was still shrouded in impenetrable fogs. Sometimes, in dreams, he knew he glimpsed familiar, well-loved faces and he would wake, calling out to them, arms longingly outstretched . . . only to find that the elusive memories had vanished again and he was calling out in gibberish.

"Now that spring's on its way, I'm planning on going over to the mainland for provisions." Kuzko tapped out the tobacco dregs and reached for his pouch. "Irina's been nagging me for days. . . ."

"You're running out of baccy, otherwise you wouldn't bother to make the journey, would you, old man?" called out Irina. "Never mind whether we have enough tea for the samovar!"

"I'll get news at the tavern," continued Kuzko, ignoring her. "Now that the thaw's under way, the merchantmen'll be stopping off at Yamkha again. Any wrecks, up and down the coast, they'll know. You come along too, Andrei. Maybe someone'll recognize you there."

Andrei shivered. And it seemed as if somewhere deep within his mind, a voice whispered, *"No, not yet. It's too soon. . . ."*

Director Baltzar looked down at his patient. Twenty-One sat slumped in a chair, staring dully ahead. Skar stood behind the chair.

"Twenty-One?" Baltzar said crisply.

The patient did not even respond to the sound of his voice.

"How long has he been like this, Skar?"

"Since he came round, Director."

Baltzar stroked his chin pensively.

"But there have been no more fits? No more shouting out?"

"He doesn't seem too aware of anything."

"Any fever?" Baltzar lifted the bandages around the patient's skull, exposing the blood-encrusted stitches where he had sewn up the surgical incisions.

"A little oozing, a little pus from the wound, but it seems to be responding satisfactorily to treatment."

Baltzar bent over the patient and lifted one of his eyelids. The man's pupils were dilated.

"Gavril Nagarian," Baltzar whispered, "can you hear me?"

Very far away, a voice calls his name. But he is lost, wandering along an endless grey road where everything is shrouded in fog and nothing is familiar. And then there is only the monotonous grinding throb in his head, a horrible sound that vibrates throughout his whole being.

Lost. Never get home. Wherever home is . . .

Never.

"Nagarian?" echoed Skar. "Is this the Azhkendi lord? The one who tried to kill the Emperor and his daughter?"

"You didn't hear that!" snapped Baltzar. In his desperation to elicit a response from the patient, he had committed an unpardonable breach of confidentiality. "Remember the contract you signed? Everything you witness within these four walls is to be treated with the utmost discretion."

"Understood." Skar nodded. "But, Director, do you think the operation may have damaged him? By now, they usually show some sign of consciousness."

"Are you impugning my methods, Skar?" demanded Baltzar. "I hardly think it's your place, as my assistant, to question my clinical—"

"Director." Skar pointed at Twenty-One. "Look."

A single tear rolled slowly down the patient's immobile face.

"He's crying."

Andrei waded back through the shallows, the cold, brackish tide lapping against his sea boots until he stood on the bleak pebbled shore, gazing after Kuzko's boat, the *Swallow,* bobbing its way out across the choppy waters of the Iron Sea.

This was where it had happened. This was the place the lightning bolt from the rolling stormclouds had struck him.

That sizzling flash of blue fire had restored his powers of speech but scoured his memory clean of all except his first name. He could have a wife and children mourning him, yet he had no recollection of anyone but Kuzko and Irina.

"Why can't I remember?" Andrei yelled to the distant horizon. *"Who—am—I?"*

A bolt of lightning suddenly scored through his mind.

"Ahh . . ." Dizzy, he staggered back up the beach, one halting step at a time, until he fell to his knees, panting, clutching at his head.

It was as if something within him was struggling to escape.

* * *

Irina hummed to herself as she pegged her wet washing to the line. There was a good drying breeze today, not so fierce it would tug the clean clothes from the line. The breeze would set Kuzko and the *Swallow* on a fair course for Yamkha—and the sooner he was gone, the sooner he would return with the much-needed supplies.

A man's voice cried out from the shore.

Above the wet sheets and shirts she caught sight of Andrei coming back up the beach, saw him stumble and fall.

Poor lad. He'd made such good progress, but he still needed more time to regain his strength. The sheet she was pegging up was left dangling as she set out to help him. Then a sudden sea mist, grey as smoke, gusted across the narrow spar of land. Bewildered, she blinked, trying to peer through the billowing fog. Andrei was still lying sprawled on the sand.

"Andrei!" she called, her voice shrill with alarm. He made no reply.

Her heart started to thud. Why must the lad have a relapse now that Kuzko was gone? She hadn't the strength to drag him back to the hut all on her own.

The sea mist swirled about her, yet not so thickly that she could avoid seeing Andrei start to twitch and writhe.

"Another fit?" The lad needed her; that was all that mattered. She gathered up her heavy worsted skirts and hurried down the shore toward him.

Andrei lay helpless on the sands, unable to move.

"*When I found you, you were damaged almost beyond repair. And so was I, cast out from my rightful lord . . .*"

Patterns of light pulsed across his sight. "*But I read in your blood the trace of Artamon's seed. It called to me. It revived me. So I have remade you, refashioned you as best I could. Yet you still resist me. Don't fight me, Andrei, let me help you.*"

Was this some kind of island spirit? It spoke of healing. What did it want of him? All he wanted was to remember who he was. Words formed in his mind—slow, clumsy words.

"Why—can't I—remember? Tell me—who I am."

"Andrei?" called a quavering voice.

Andrei opened his eyes to see the wrinkled face of an old woman bending over him.

"There now," she said as if she were soothing a child. "You were having a bad dream."

Kuzko had been gone for five days now, Andrei reckoned. Irina seemed unconcerned, busying herself feeding her chickens and working at her sewing.

"He'll have met friends. He'll be back when he's ready. Gives me a chance to clean up after him, the old curmudgeon. . . ."

Sometimes she forgot herself and called Andrei "Tikhon," the name of her drowned son. He never corrected her. It was such a solitary life for her here at land's end. The nearest neighbors were over a two-mile's walk away across the dunes.

A sudden shiver of restlessness went through Andrei. He set out from the cottage and walked up through the reeds into the dunes. A glimmer of pale, high cloud hid the spring sun. Beyond the calm, lapping green of the empty sea, the horizon was hazy with mist. The air felt softer today, milder. High overhead flew a skein of wild geese, honking exuberantly as they set out for their spring feeding grounds.

Two weeks ago, walking at this speed would have exhausted him. Today he felt exhilarated, hardly noticing the last, lingering stiffness in his mended legs.

"Ahoy there, Andrei!"

He spotted Kuzko's little boat and hurried down the shingle to help Kuzko pull it out of the shallows up and onto the beach.

"Thanks, Andrei," said Kuzko, clapping him on the shoulder and gazing intently into his face. "Andrei, lad—" he began, as though about to ask a question.

"And about time too, Kuzko!" called out Irina. Kuzko let his hand drop away, turning to face his wife as she hurried down from the hut to greet him.

Andrei was eager, desperately eager to ask Kuzko what news he had gathered in Yamkha, but there were sacks of provisions to be unloaded first and a little keg that smelled strongly of spirits.

"Careful with that keg," Kuzko warned with a wink.

"Did you remember my thread and needles?" Irina fussed around them. "And the beeswax for polishing? And—"

"All in good time, woman," growled Kuzko. "You can brew us up some tea." He tossed her a bag. She caught it and sniffed it, a broad smile slowly lighting her worn face.

"Real tea!" She hugged Kuzko to her and planted a kiss on his mouth.

"Cost me a small fortune, that did. Don't waste it, now!"

Kuzko's weather-wrinkled cheeks were red with a glow that spoke of hours whiled away in the tavern, and his eyes were bloodshot. Irina drew away from him, tutting.

"We don't have a small fortune. So how exactly did you pay, Kuzko?"

Kuzko shuffled from foot to foot, suddenly embarrassed.

"A little favor I agreed to do," he muttered. "For an old friend."

"Favor?" Irina repeated loudly.

"You remember Baklan?"

"Baklan, the smuggler? Oh, Kuzko, you promised me you wouldn't risk it again. You're too old."

"It's only a little consignment to be delivered to Gadko's. Andrei'll give me a hand, won't you, lad?"

Andrei nodded, not entirely sure what he was agreeing to.

"And if you get caught?" Irina was still cross; her foot tapped against the earth floor.

"A few barrels of aquavit in an old fishing smack? Who's going to pay attention? There's greater concerns out there, Rina."

Later when the provisions had been stored safely away in stone crocks and jars, they sat down around the fire with mugs of strong, black tea sweetened with Irina's apple jam.

"So," Irina said, "what's the news in Yamkha?"

"Big news!" Kuzko rolled his eyes. "Seems old Duke Aleksei's been deposed. There was a riot in Mirom and half the city burned to the ground. Some are saying the rioters collaborated with the Tielens, others that the Tielens sailed down the Nieva and bombarded the city."

"Mercy on us," Irina said, setting down her tea. "The Tielens?"

"They're in charge now." Kuzko noisily drained his tea to the dregs and wiped the last drops from his mustache with his sleeve. "We have an emperor. Emperor Eugene."

"What does that matter to us out here?"

"Could mean more taxes. Customs duties. And there's talk of a census. I saw Tielen soldiers—only a handful, mind you—at the harbor."

"And what did Duke Aleksei ever do for us?" Irina said with a shrug. "What did the Orlovs care for us, the little people? They spent all Muscobar's money doing up their fine palaces. We're well rid of them, I say."

"Oh we're not quite rid of them yet, Rina my love. Eugene's made Aleksei's daughter his empress. Empress Astasia."

Andrei listened, the mug of tea going cold between his fingers. The names, the names . . .

"Didn't old Aleksei have a son too?" Irina asked.

"Young Andrei? The night of that terrible storm in the Straits, his ship, the flagship, went down, all hands lost." As Kuzko was speaking, Andrei realized he was looking searchingly at him again as he had earlier on the shore. "They say she had too many cannons and the weight sank the ship. Truth is—nobody knows because it seems nobody survived."

"Terrible," whispered Irina, staring into her tea mug. "What a waste . . ."

Aleksei . . . Astasia . . . Orlov . . .

"Where did the ship go down?" Andrei demanded. "Was it far from here? And what was she called?"

"The *Sirin.*"

A shiver ran through Andrei's body. "I know that name," he said slowly.

"Andrei," began Kuzko awkwardly, "I've been thinking. They say nobody survived. They say all the crew drowned. But—"

"You think *I'm* Duke Aleksei's lost son?" Andrei got up, knocking over his stool. He clutched his head, as if he could wrest the memories from his locked brain.

"Stands to reason, lad. The storm that night washed you up here, on this very beach."

"Then why—why can't *I* remember anything?" And Andrei, overcome with bitter frustration, flung open the hut door and went out into the darkness.

The night was as dark as the foul-smelling pitch Kuzko used to caulk the hull of his little boat. Andrei stumbled, unseeing, along the shingle, blind, deaf to the mean blast of the wind off the lightless sea, or the menacing rattle of the incoming tide fast clawing its way up the pebbled beach.

"Why!" he yelled at the black sea, straining his throat until it was raw. He dropped to his knees on the damp stones, sobbing with frustration. "*Why* can't I remember?"

"*Why do you need to know?*"

The voice was softer than the whisper of the tide.

"Who's there?" Andrei jerked around. "Come out! Show yourself!"

"*I am the one who healed you.*"

It was that voice again, the one that had haunted his fevered dreams when he was hovering between life and death.

"I'm going mad. Hallucinating."

"*Think of me as your spirit-guardian . . . if it helps.*"

"I don't believe in spirits. Angels or daemons."

"*I can help you unlock your memory. But only when you are ready.*"

"Do it. Do it now!"

The voice fell silent and all he could hear was the chitter of stones swirled around by the encroaching tide.

And then the fog in his mind melted away and a flood of memories rushed in.

Faces flickered before him in the dark like phantasms: Astasia, his sister; his father Aleksei, careworn with affairs of state; his mistress Olga, with her bewitching smile . . .

He stood on the quay on a grey, windswept morning. His royal-blue naval uniform glittered with golden buttons and epaulettes, but the collar was damnably tight.

His mother and father were there, shivering in the fierce wind off the River Nieva. And his beloved sister, dark-eyed Astasia, came running forward, flinging her arms about his neck to hug him as if she would never let go. . . .

And now he was in a little boat, being rowed out toward a great warship anchored midstream. Her wood-and-iron hull towered above him; a rope ladder was lowered for him to scramble up. As the oarsmen brought the little boat around, he gazed up and saw her figurehead: a gold-feathered bird with the face and bare breasts of a voluptuously beautiful woman. He read the name: *Sirin,* Spirit-Bird of Paradise.

Andrei opened his eyes and found himself sprawled facedown on the cold shingle, with a froth of tide lapping close to his head.

"I am Andrei Orlov." He spoke the words out loud.

Slowly he drew himself up to his feet. "I *am* Andrei Orlov!" he shouted with all the force of his lungs across the black sea.

CHAPTER 17

"My lord." Kuzko and Irina went down on their knees on the dirt floor of the hut.

"I'd be dead if it weren't for the two of you. You saved my life. I'll never forget that." Andrei went to help Irina up.

"But you're the Grand Duke now." Kuzko kept his eyes averted, staring embarrassedly at the floor.

"As for that . . . isn't my father Aleksei still alive?"

"Oh dear, dear," whispered Irina, throwing her apron over her face. "And I said such things. About your family. Forgive me, my lord, forgive me."

"If the Emperor Eugene believes me dead . . ." The implications were too immense for Andrei to take in all at once. He only knew that the Tielen tyrant who had usurped his father's throne would not be pleased to see a rival claimant return from the grave.

He took Irina by the arms and gently eased her down into her chair by the fireside. "Listen to me. What you've learned from me tonight must stay our secret. As far as we're all concerned, I'll revert to being Tikhon, a shipwrecked sailor."

Kuzko nodded, gnawing on the stem of his pipe.

"But I need to find out how the land lies in Mirom. Any chance of a trip up the Nieva to Mirom for supplies, Kuzko?"

"Won't you be recognized?"

"Not with this beard," Andrei said wryly, stroking the curly growth darkening his chin.

"I haven't traveled that far since I was a young man. It's a long journey, my lor—Tikhon." Kuzko corrected himself. "And who's going to look after my Rina while we're gone?"

"There'll be a generous reward for your kindness." The magnanimous words were out of Andrei's mouth before he had thought. If he was penniless Tikhon, how was he to gain access to the revenues from his estates?

"I can't pretend that wouldn't be appreciated," Kuzko said gruffly. "But there's also the question of your health. It's hard work sailing a little boat like my *Swallow*. The spring tides can be treacherous out in the Straits—and she's not built sturdy like a warship."

Gavril lay immobile, staring at the sky through his high, barred window. Clouds drifted past. He could not even lift his damaged head from the pillow. Every time he blinked, the cell wavered and contracted before his eyes, leaving him as nauseous and dizzy as if he were on a storm-tossed ship.

From time to time, a terrible throbbing pain pulsed through his temples. He dreaded its return, for with the pain came hallucinations: grotesque and disorienting. He thought he saw Director Baltzar and his lean-faced assistant bend over him, wielding saws and scalpels.

"We slice the top of the skull off, like the shell of a boiled egg," he heard Baltzar say as the saw blade began to grate into his head and his own warm blood began to drip down into his eyes, *"and then we scoop out the diseased parts of the brain—"*

And then the dripping blood became a crimson curtain, blinding him. They prized off the top of his skull and exposed his raw, pulsing brain to the cold air—

"Help me," whispered Gavril. "I can't go on like this."

"Mirom," murmured Andrei. The *Swallow* had just rounded a bend in the broad Nieva, weaving in between great merchantmen and warships, just another little fishing smack amid so many others bobbing on the swirling waters. And now the prospect of the city lay before them, half-hidden by the forests of masts and sails.

As the *Swallow* slowly drew closer to the city, the ravages of the citizens' revolt and the Tielen invasion began to reveal themselves. The spires and star-spangled onion domes of the Cathedral of Saint

Simeon still glittered, gold and azure and crimson, against the cloudy sky. But the great dome of the Senate House was blackened like a roasted eggshell, cracked and half-open to the sky.

And as the strong current of the Nieva propelled them onward, the ruined facade of the West Wing of the Winter Palace loomed up on the right bank. Fire had seared to the very heart of the building, leaving a roofless, charred shell.

The view of the fire-blackened ruin blurred. Andrei turned away, angrily dashing his hand across his eyes. Buildings could be restored and rebuilt. But the people who had died in the revolution, they could not be brought back. And his inheritance, his right to succeed his father as ruler of Muscobar, how could that ever be restored?

Andrei's plan was to seek out an old, influential friend of his father's and confide in him. First Minister Vassian seemed to be the most suitable choice; Vassian's eldest son, Valery, had been in his year at the Military Academy and had, he suspected, been quite seriously smitten by Astasia's charms.

And yet, as he made his way from the quayside toward the more affluent quarters of the city, he felt a growing sense of unease. Everywhere he looked he saw Tielen soldiers, the Tielen tongue was spoken on every street corner. Even if he was permitted an audience with Kyrill Vassian (which was far from certain, given the shabby state of his clothes and untrimmed beard), did the First Minister still wield any influence in Tielen-ruled Mirom?

Vassian's town house was an imposing mansion, its stucco frontage painted in pale blue and white, the colors of a spring sky. As he approached, Andrei saw that all the blinds were drawn. He halted, confused. What did this mean? Was the family away? Had Eugene sent them into exile?

He decided to go around to the servants' entrance. Even if the family was not at home, they would have left a housekeeper and a maid or two to care for the property.

After knocking and ringing the bell several times, all without reply, he had just decided to give up when he heard footsteps echoing hollowly within, and the door opened a crack.

"What is it?" demanded a surly voice.

He would have to bluff his way in. "I heard there was work in the gardens," he said, improvising. "Spring planting—"

"Well, you've had a wasted journey. The house is shut. Good-day." And the door slammed in his face.

Andrei stepped back. He was unaccustomed to such churlish treatment. His first instinct was to pound on the door again and demand to speak to someone in authority. And then he looked down at his shabby clothes and remembered. He was Tikhon, son of a poor fisherman. No one would let him near the First Minister.

Slowly he made his way back to the front of the house. In his mind's eye he saw the blinds open, the sparkle of candles at every window, the First Minister and his wife Elizaveta in formal evening dress, standing at the open door to welcome their guests . . .

"Such a tragedy." A bent old woman stopped beside him to gaze at the house, shaking her head as she spoke.

"A tragedy?"

"Didn't you hear? It was a bad business. I used to do their washing, you know," she said confidentially. "His wife found him in the stables. Dead."

"Dead?" Andrei repeated, astonished. "I had no idea the Minister was ill."

"It was suicide," she said. "He blew out his brains." She patted his arm and then shuffled on, still muttering to herself, "That poor woman . . ."

Andrei turned away. The blank windows behind him had hidden this horrible secret. What had caused Kyrill Vassian, a venerable and astute statesman, to fall into such black despair that suicide seemed the only honorable solution? Who else remained in Mirom from Vassian's ministry whom he could approach for advice? How many Orlov supporters had died in the revolution?

At a loss as to what to do, he wandered the streets of the city like a vagrant, head down, the collar of dead Tikhon's jacket pulled up to avoid the slightest risk of being recognized. He skulked in dingy alleys, drawing back into dark doorways whenever he saw anyone approaching too close.

Now a morbid desire gripped him. Here he was, little better than a ghost haunting the streets of his home city. He had to know how Mirom had commemorated the drowned heir to its ruling family. Had the city fathers erected a memorial to the lost crew of the *Sirin*? Had young women wept and left flowers and tearstained letters of farewell beneath it?

He searched the avenues of the fashionable Admiralty Quarter where prosperous merchants and naval officers lived.

The statues of his august forebears stood in tree-lined squares here, most prominent among them, the monument to his Great-Uncle Nikolai Orlov, who had died at sea in a skirmish against the Tielens. But where was the memorial to Andrei Orlov and his valiant sailors? He too had died at sea, sailing to confront the Tielens. But because they had perished in a storm, had he and his men been deprived of their heroes' memorial?

The unjustness of it brought a bitter taste to his mouth.

Or were there to be no more monuments to the Orlovs now that Eugene was Emperor?

He began to ask passersby if they knew where the *Sirin* Memorial was to be found. Some looked at him blankly. One or two spat when he mentioned the name of Orlov. The owner of the newsstand outside the Nieva Exchange looked at him quizzically.

"The Emperor's commissioned a bronze statue to stand in the Winter Palace Square. And can you guess who it will be?" The news-dealer gave him a wink from one rheumy eye. "Himself, of course!"

Andrei turned away. His heart felt cold as stone. The city where he was born, which he had been destined to rule as Grand Duke, had forgotten him.

He sat down on a bench beneath the trees opposite the ornate fa-cade of the Grand Theatre and watched seagulls squabbling noisily over a crust of bread.

What did I do with my life here? Frittered it away on gambling, pretty actresses, and parties. Andrei the Good-Time Boy? No. Andrei the Wastrel; Andrei the Good-For-Nothing. Small wonder no one's cared to erect a memorial to me; what was there worth commemo-rating?

A playbill, blown by the wind, landed at his feet. He picked it up and read:

Olga Giladkova, recently returned to Mirom from her triumphant winter season in Smarna as Leila in *The Corsairs.*

A memory of long-lashed eyes, smoky-grey, gazing into his, a husky voice murmuring, "Don't forget me, Andrei. You know I will always be your friend. . . ."

"Olga," Andrei said aloud. The need to see her again overrode every other thought in his mind. Olga could be trusted with his secret. Olga would never betray him. When they had become more than friends, she had shown him the secret entrance to her dressing room, used to avoid the crowds of admirers who pursued her after every performance.

"What a secretive lot you actors are!" he had whispered as she led him, his hand in hers, along the dark tunnel.

"Every actor needs a quick escape if his performance has not found favor with the public," she had whispered back.

"And every actress needs a discreet way to smuggle in her admirers?"

Andrei slowly limped toward the alleyway that led around the back of the theater. Away from the sculpted statues of voluptuous muses and floral garlands that adorned the splendid facade, the rear of the great building was plain brick, shabby and neglected, with dead weeds poking from cracks in the mortar. If there were a matinee today, the little door might be unlocked.

He glanced around to see if anyone was watching. He was alone. The rusty latch to Olga's little door was stiff, but after a few tugs, the door opened inward.

Andrei fumbled his way along the damp, dark passageway, remembering to count the number of paces, as Olga had taught him. Thirty-one, turn to the left, nine, stop and feel for the handle.

Silently closing the door behind him, he sniffed the air, recognizing the familiar musky scent of Olga's favorite tobacco. The secret passage brought him into a tiny, chilly room housing a water closet and rose-painted porcelain hand-basin. Through the velvet-curtained doorway lay her dressing room. His heart began to beat faster. He raised one hand to draw the curtain aside just enough to take a swift look inside. If Masha, her dresser, was there, he would have to wait till Olga was alone.

Inside he glimpsed the gilded mirror surrounded by the soft glow of candles, the cluttered dressing table strewn with pots of greasepaint, rouge, and powder. A woman was sitting at the mirror, humming to herself as she dabbed at her face with a powder puff. And what an unforgettable face: strong-featured, the mouth overlarge and generous, deep-set grey eyes, dark as a November evening. A slight haze of blue tobacco smoke perfumed the air from a slender cigar left burning on a saucer.

"Olga," Andrei said, moving so that she could see his reflection in the mirror.

The powder puff dropped from her hand.

"Who are you? And how did you get in here?"

He saw her hand move toward the little silver bell, ready to summon help.

"Don't you recognize me, Olga?" His voice trembled, in spite of himself. "It's me. Andrei."

"Andrei is dead," she said to his reflection. But her hand stayed where it was—close to, yet not touching, the bell. "Are you his ghost?" She asked the question as if the idea in some way intrigued her.

"Do I look like a ghost?"

"You look like a man who needs the attentions of a good barber. If you are Andrei, ghost, then prove it to me. Tell me something only Andrei could know."

Andrei swallowed hard. What shared secret lay buried in his faulty memory that might convince her? He saw her hand inch closer to the bell. If she rang for help, all was lost.

"For my last birthday you sent me a copy of *The Forbidden Tryst*, the first play I ever saw you in. I opened the little package in front of my family—and my mother was scandalized when a lace-trimmed scarlet garter fell out."

There was a pause. Suddenly her grave expression transformed into an expansive, welcoming smile. She rose from her dressing table, arms wide, and hugged him close.

"My lost boy! Where *have* you been? Making us all so sad! You should be ashamed of yourself." She held him at arm's length. "And, my darling, you badly need a bath!"

"Sorry," he said, grinning through the tears that had filled his eyes. "This wasn't quite the reunion I had planned." And then he remembered. "Olga—you mustn't tell a soul. No one knows I'm still alive. This must be our secret."

"You can trust me; you know that." She went to the outer door and bolted it. "There. Now even Masha will have to knock to be let in."

Suddenly the dressing room wavered before his eyes and Andrei was forced to grab at the dressing table to steady himself.

Olga poured him a little glass of spirit from a squat bottle. "Here, drink this. It's *karvi* from Smarna. It'll warm you up."

Andrei swallowed the whole measure of *karvi* in one gulp and felt the strong spirit glow its way down his throat.

"Thanks. I'm still not quite recovered."

"Sit down. And tell me where you've been all this time."

He lowered himself stiffly onto a threadbare armchair draped with a flower-embroidered shawl. He had not wanted to reveal his weakness to her.

"The *Sirin* was blown onto rocks in the storm. I was pulled from the sea by an old fisherman and his wife. They nursed me back to health. But the sea took my memory. They called me Tikhon. By the time I remembered my real name—" He faltered. "Eugene was Emperor."

Olga reached for another slender cigar and held it to the candle-flame until the tobacco glowed.

"So what do you plan to do?" she said, taking in a deep breath of the musky smoke.

"To go see my family."

"The shock could kill your father."

"Why so?"

She blew an elegant little ring of smoke from her red lips. "He is a broken man, Andrei. It's rumored that he's had a stroke. He's gone to Erinaskoe to recuperate."

A stroke. His father Aleksei had always seemed so strong, so robust. He could not imagine him weakened by illness.

His distress must have shown in his face for she drew closer, her voice softer.

"You didn't know? I should have realized. Forgive me, Andrei."

"So I am to remain incognito all my life? Or invent a new identity? It sounds like the plot of one of those absurd melodramas you delight in appearing in."

"You have a new identity already: Tikhon." She let her fingertips touch his cheek, stroking his beard.

"Olga!" he said, angry that she would not take his predicament seriously.

"And now you're cross with me," she said, pouting.

"I've risked my life coming to you. Trusting you with my secret. No one else knows but you."

"I'm flattered. The whole affair is deliciously dangerous. But I have some advice for you. If—and when—you must break the news to your family, do it gently, a little at a time. Lay a trail of clues . . . let them build up their hopes again day by day, week by week. And Andrei—" She laid her hand on his shoulder, all the earlier playfulness gone from her voice. "Be careful how you go about it. Your very existence could be seen to pose a threat to the new empire."

"You think Eugene—"

"Put yourself in his place."

"Even if I were to openly pledge my allegiance to him and the new empire?"

Olga was silent a moment, considering what he had said. "Is that what you really want, Andrei?"

"You were born to rule, Andrei. But it is still too soon." The voice, dry and sinuous as Olga's cigar smoke, drifted through Andrei's mind. He started, glancing up, wondering if he had inadvertently spoken his thoughts aloud.

"All's far from well in this new empire," Olga said, stubbing out the last of her cigar in a tobacco-stained saucer. "You know I've just come back from Smarna? The first night we played Solovei's *Blood Masquerade,* remember it? The one where the corrupt king is assassinated by the rebels in the middle of a masked ball? Well, there was a riot! The whole theater went mad with excitement, cheering and screaming when the king is shot. We had to bring down the curtain. After that, the Tielen governor closed the theater for two days. And he forbade us to perform the play again. We had to content ourselves with harmless romantic nonsense like *The Corsairs* and *Soraya's Secret*—"

Someone tested the door handle. Andrei leapt up.

"Madame Olga," a woman's voice cried, rattling the handle. "Time to get ready!"

"One minute." Olga rose too. "You must go, Andrei. Much though I love my faithful Masha, she is utterly indiscreet and babbles my secrets to anyone and everyone without thinking."

Andrei hurried into the chilly little washroom. His leg was less stiff now that he had rested it. Olga opened the door, letting in a dank breath of stale air. Andrei turned to go—and then turned back on impulse, kissing Olga hard on the mouth.

"Ugh—that beard tickles," she said, grimacing. But she did not pull away.

It was so long since he had kissed a girl, any girl. Yet the feelings the kiss stirred were disturbingly powerful. He wanted the sweet, tobacco-scented warmth of her body. He did not want to let her go.

"Madame Olga!" shrilled Masha's voice from beyond the dressing room door. "We're running late!"

"Let them wait!" cried back Olga.

"And if anyone asks—" he whispered in her ear.

"Trust me." She gave him a little push into the secret passageway and blew him a kiss as she latched the door, leaving him in darkness.

The pure, delicate voice soared higher, each little cascade of notes like clear water falling, or a lone thrush fluting in the still, close air before rain.

Celestine de Joyeuse, the celebrated Francian singer, stood with one hand lightly resting on the fortepiano. She was much younger than Astasia had imagined from her illustrious reputation—not more than twenty-four or twenty-five. She was dressed in a gown of rich mulberry silk, with a single orchid pinned in her golden hair, and looked to Astasia quite the epitome of fashionable Francian elegance.

The song came to an end and for a moment the last perfect notes hung in the air. Then the applause began. Astasia clapped and clapped, unable to restrain her enthusiasm. Celestine sank into a deep curtsy, one hand clasped to her breast, murmuring her thanks before rising and gesturing to her accompanist.

The fortepiano player rose, unsmiling, and bowed his head. A tall, gaunt young man with pale skin and long, straight dark hair, he had more the air of an ascetic or a monk than a musician. Astasia thought she caught a secret, subtle little glance that passed between singer and accompanist. *Can they be lovers?* she thought, thrilling at the idea.

"And now, we would like to perform for you the song 'October Seas,' set to the words of your celebrated poet, Solovei."

More applause greeted this tribute to Mirom's favorite author.

That Francian accent is charming, thought Astasia, sighing as she remembered how hard she had striven to learn to pronounce the Francian tongue. *Celestine de Joyeuse must have a gift for languages as well as music. . . .*

Astasia glanced at her husband as the recital continued. Eugene was staring beyond the illustrious Celestine with a distant, slightly frowning expression. She could sense he was not enjoying himself. She had hoped that the visit of one of the most celebrated musicians of the day might change his opinion of the art and might even give them something to discuss together. Eugene had already confessed to her that he had no ear for music. Give him a rousing military march to whistle and he was happy. This music was too subtle, too refined for his tastes. And then the artistry of Celestine's singing overwhelmed all other thoughts, and the music—wild, soulful, and free—possessed her.

During the applause, she saw Gustave appear and make his way toward them. He whispered something to the Emperor she could not catch.

"Ah," said Eugene. He nodded and leaned toward Astasia. "Forgive me. Some official business I must attend to." He rose—and the rest of the audience rose too. Court etiquette. "Demoiselle de Joyeuse," he said, "you have enchanted us with your delightful voice. Please do not think me rude; state affairs intrude upon my pleasure and I must attend to them."

"Your imperial highness honors me." The singer sank into another deep curtsy as Eugene left the room with Gustave at his side.

The recital continued, but Astasia could no longer concentrate on the music or surrender to its spell. She knew it must be some matter of import to have drawn Eugene away from such a prestigious gathering.

Two senior officers were waiting for Eugene in his study, tricornes respectfully held at their sides.

"Trouble in Smarna, highness." Eugene recognized the elder of the two as Henrik Tornberg, Commissar-General of the Southern Army. "A rebellion."

"What kind of rebellion?"

"They've declared themselves a republic again. The rebels have attacked our men garrisoned in Vermeille. They have taken Governor Armfeld hostage."

This was unacceptable. Though Armfeld was a damned fool to allow himself to be captured so easily.

"Maps, Gustave."

Gustave unrolled a map of Smarna on the desk.

"This rebellion must be put down immediately," Eugene said, pinpointing Vermeille with one finger. "Any hint of weakness on our part would be fatal for the empire at this early stage."

"From what we can gauge, highness, the rebels' stronghold, the

Old Citadel of Colchise above Vermeille, is vulnerable to attack by sea."

Eugene studied the coastline, pensively tracing the wide sweep of Vermeille Bay with one finger. Wasn't Vermeille where Gavril Nagarian had grown up? Could there be some connection between the Smarnan rebellion and Gavril Nagarian that his agents had failed to identify?

He looked up at Gustave.

"Is this anything to do with Nagarian's imprisonment, Gustave?"

Gustave gave a little shrug.

Eugene had no time for recriminations now. Swift action was essential.

"With a fair wind, Admiral Janssen could make Vermeille in three days with the Southern Fleet," he mused. "Gustave, get me the admiral. How are our men in Vermeille holding up against the rebels, Tornberg?"

"Well enough, highness."

"Tell them reinforcements are on their way."

Tornberg saluted and hurried away, followed by his adjutant.

Eugene gathered up the map and went with Gustave to the communications room. His empire of New Rossiya was young and the bonds that forged it were all too fragile. He had anticipated resistance to his rule—but not in sleepy Smarna, the least politically active of the five princedoms.

"Admiral Janssen, highness," Gustave said, pointing to the Vox Aethyria.

"Janssen?" Eugene cleared his throat. This was no time for any show of indecision. "Take the fleet to Vermeille Bay. There's trouble in Smarna."

"And how shall we respond to this trouble, highness?" came the crackling reply.

"Crush it. Show no mercy. Even if it means razing the whole citadel to the ground."

CHAPTER 18

Kuzko and Andrei sailed the *Swallow* into harbor at Varangaya, close to the wide mouth of the Nieva estuary.

The port was famous for its flourishing leather and fur trade—and yet there, among the merchantmen anchored in the harbor, towered a Tielen warship, a standard of sky-blue and gold glittering from its topmost mast in the gusting sea wind.

"See that?" Kuzko jerked his thumb toward the ship. "That's the flag of the new empire. Though it looks like the old Tielen flag to me."

They tied up with other little boats at the far end of the quay, well away from the big ships. The sun was setting beneath a low-hanging canopy of dark grey cloud, and the last streaks of green and gold lit the harbor buildings with a strange, lurid glow.

"Wind's on the turn," said Kuzko, sniffing the air. "You can only smell the tanneries when it's blowing from the north."

The stink of rotting herring mingled with the raw reek of hides from the tanneries made Andrei's eyes water.

"Ever been to Gadko's?" asked Kuzko. Andrei shook his head. "That's where we're bound with our little 'delivery.' "

At last, Kuzko's business was concluded and the barrels handed over with a nod, a wink, and a secret handshake.

The taproom at Gadko's was dark and overheated, the air a dingy yellow fug of tobacco smoke. Andrei followed Kuzko as the stocky old man elbowed his way through the throng of drinkers: shaven-headed merchants from Khitari, traders, Tielen sailors on shore leave. In his worn coat and seaboots, he was indistinguishable from any other fisherman.

He was tired. So tired his bones ached. He had overestimated his stamina, and the limp in his shattered leg had become more pronounced as the day wore on. He slumped down in a darkened alcove away from the firelight and rubbed it hard, as if the friction would lessen the dragging, bone-deep ache.

"Here you are, lad." Gadko placed a frothing mug of hot cumin-spiced ale in front of him. "On the house. That'll set you right."

"Thanks." Andrei drank it down, feeling the heat seep into his body, dulling the nagging pain.

In the corner closest to the fire, an old man started to croon a Muscobar love song, tapping out a rhythm with the bowl of his pipe against his mug. Another took up a balalaika and began to strum along. One by one, others set down their mugs and joined in; even Kuzko added his rusty bass to the refrain until the smoky air vibrated with their voices.

"Silence in the name of the Emperor!"

A gust of wet night air blew in. Andrei glanced up and saw that five burly Tielen sailors had entered the tavern. They all brandished clubs.

"I said silence!"

The balalaika chords stopped abruptly, but the singers continued on for a bar or two before their voices trailed away.

A man in a neat grey uniform came forward into the firelight. He carried a gold-tipped officer's baton.

"Shore leave is canceled. All crewmen are to return to the *Olava* straightaway."

A general groan arose. The five heavies began to push their way into the crowd, clubs raised menacingly.

"The Emperor has promised extra rum rations for every man who is on board within the hour. . . ."

One by one, Tielen sailors emerged, making their way reluctantly toward the open door.

"I've plenty of rum here!" came a slurred voice from near the fire. "Tell the Emperor what he can do with his extra rations—"

Jostling ensued. A man suddenly went flying across the floor, to land in an ungainly tangle of arms and legs near the door. Two of the

Tielen crewmen scooped him up and dragged him out into the night; Andrei could hear him swearing and protesting as they hustled him across the quay.

The Tielen sailors made one last tour of the tavern, glowering at anyone who stood in their way.

"Shore leave canceled?" Andrei had sensed tension in the air. "Is Muscobar under attack?"

"Careful, lad," cautioned Kuzko.

But Andrei no longer cared who heard him. "What's going on?" He slammed his ale mug down on the table. Heads turned. Suddenly he became aware that everyone was staring at him.

"Time to go, Tikhon." Kuzko rose and began apologizing loudly. "You'll have to excuse my boy. He was injured in the recent fighting. He gets confused sometimes. . . ."

Eugene woke with a start. It was not yet dawn, but his soldier's instincts told him it was time to rise. He went to the window and drew back the heavy folds of blue velvet to gaze out at the wide Nieva, a faint glimmer in the fading night.

The Southern Fleet had set sail for Smarna. The rebellion would be crushed before it had a chance to spread. He had ordered that no news of the uprising be published in Muscobar until the citadel was back under Tielen command and Armfeld released. He had little doubt that the rebels, poorly armed and untrained, would soon surrender under the barrage of Tielen cannon.

So why did he feel this continuing sense of unease about the whole affair? Gustave, pragmatic as ever, had murmured to him that his misgivings were a natural reaction to this first challenge to his rule as Emperor.

"There will always be a few who resist your authority," Gustave had said calmly, "and you must be prepared for such rebellions. Even the Great Artamon had to put down the uprising in Khitari when Khan Konchak sacked his garrison at Lake Taigal and executed his tax collectors. . . ."

But he needed Smarna. In his father's day, Smarna had proved a vital defensive link in driving back the Francian war fleet.

He went back to the window. A fresh, pale spring light sheened the eastern horizon. The spires of the city churches glimmered like spears of gold piercing the rising mists. The sun would shine on Mirom today—

but what was the weather like out in the treacherous Straits where the fleet was assembling?

"So when do we set sail?" asked a sleepy voice from the bed. Astasia had woken up.

Eugene stopped pacing a moment. " 'Set sail'?" The question came out more irascibly than he had intended, and he saw her blink almost as if he had shouted at her.

"For Karila's party."

He had forgotten Karila's birthday! He had been so preoccupied with the worsening situation in Smarna that it had slipped his mind. He saw that Astasia was looking at him, waiting for his reply, and he felt a stab of guilt.

I promised Kari we would come home to Swanholm. She was too ill to attend the coronation; how can I break my word now?

"She's expecting us to be there."

My only daughter is growing up, and I have not been there to share these precious weeks with her. A deeper-buried fear still nagged him. *And if her health continues to give cause for concern, these weeks may become all the more precious. . . .*

"Wind's tricky this morning," Kuzko said as they left the shelter of the harbor and ventured into open sea. "Weather's on the turn."

The waves were choppy, flecked with milky foam.

"Shall we wait for fair weather?" Andrei glanced uneasily up at the cloudy sky.

"Na," said Kuzko. "I've handled my *Swallow* in worse."

A strong gusting crosswind suddenly caught in the patched sail and tilted the little *Swallow*, lifting her prow right out of the water. A great Tielen warship was sailing toward them and they were being blown right into her path.

"Tikhon!" yelled Kuzko, leaping to tug on the ropes.

The tall warship's ironclad prow cut a swirling furrow through the grey-green water, towering high above them, drenching them with cold spray. Andrei grabbed hold of the tiller and pulled with all his strength.

"Harder!" Kuzko roared through the din of the churning waters.

"The wind's against us," Andrei yelled back. All his efforts seemed in vain. They were being driven right beneath the warship's prow; they would be smashed to matchwood.

"No use," he cried. "I can't control her! I can't—"

A jagged flicker, lightning-blue, burst in his brain and went fizzing down into his arms, his hands. Suddenly he felt his muscles pulsing with strength. He tugged at the tiller.

The *Swallow* bucked and yawed wildly. The cresting wake caught her and spun her aside.

"Hold fast!" Kuzko's voice carried faintly to him as a wave drenched the deck. Blinded by the water, Andrei gripped the tiller, leaning into it with the weight of his whole body until he could shake the wetness from his hair, his stinging eyes.

"I've got her!" he cried, voice raw with triumph. "We've made it! We've—"

Only then did he see the second shadow looming up to their left. Another warship in full sail, bearing down on them fast. To the lookouts on high, the little fishing boat beneath their bows would be invisible in this wind-whipped sea.

Kuzko stood, mouth agape, staring up at the mighty ship.

"Jump, old man!" Andrei let go the tiller and flung himself at Kuzko, trying to push him over the side into the sea.

The second warship smashed into the *Swallow*. Andrei was flung into the sea even as he grabbed at Kuzko. Splintered timbers flew up into the air. And then there came the hollow roar of the sea as Andrei went under. Freezing water squeezed the breath from his body. Blackness flooded his mind. He came up again, choking on the salt-bitter water, arms flailing, gasping for air.

"Kuzko! *Kuzko!*" Against the crash of the waves, his voice was as thin as a seagull's cry. He trod water, trying to stay afloat as the wash from the great ships came billowing back toward him. Now he saw there was a third—and a fourth approaching close behind. A war fleet. If they weren't drowned, they'd be crushed by the heavy vessels.

"An—drei . . ." The cry was so faint he scarcely heard it. Turning his head, he caught sight of Kuzko clinging to a plank, grey head just above the water.

"I'm coming!" He took in a lungful of salty air and struck out toward him. "Hang on!"

Skar tramped up the winding stair in the Iron Tower to check on the progress of his patient. Twenty-One's condition had been giving him some cause for concern. He had developed a slow-burning fever since the operation, and had been alternately mumbling and shouting out incoherently. Often he pawed at the dressings on his head, picking at them, then tearing them off as if they were some kind of infected scab.

Skar unlocked the cell door and placed a lantern on the table.

"Bright. Too bright." Twenty-One rolled away from the light, muttering and hiding his eyes.

"I've brought your medicine," Skar said.

"No—more—medicine." His speech was badly distorted.

"I've mixed it with honey to make it taste good," Skar said patiently, as if humoring a child.

Twenty-One peered out at him suspiciously from behind his fingers. His skin glistened with a feverish sheen and his eyes burned overbright in their darkened sockets. With his shaven head, crisscrossed with half-healed scars, and sunken cheeks, he looked to Skar like one of the damned.

"Here. Drink it all down."

Twenty-One's hands shook so much that Skar took back the glass and held it to the man's lips himself. He still seemed unable to drink properly, and some of the willow-bark infusion dribbled out down the side of his chin.

"Bitter," he mumbled.

And then his head jerked up and his whole body went rigid. He seemed to be listening with great concentration.

"Help me!" he cried out. He lurched off the bed and half-fell, half-shambled, one leg dragging, head raised toward the barred window.

Skar watched, fascinated. He had heard nothing.

Twenty-One raised one shaking hand toward the bars.

"Can you—hear me?" His body, exhausted by the effort, gave way and he fell to the floor.

"It—is—close by," he said as Skar tried to hoist him back onto the bed. "Why doesn't it answer me? It is—so close."

And then he started to weep: great gulping sobs. "I—cast it out. It—will never come back. Never. Never."

Skar found himself embarassed by this uncontrolled display of emotion. He picked up the lantern and withdrew, leaving the damaged man wailing and cursing.

*   *   *

Andrei struggled against the pull of the current and the dragging undertow from the wake of the Tielen fleet. He did not ask where this extraordinary burst of strength came from; he just fought the waves. He had nearly drowned once before. He was not going to let the sea claim him again.

Kuzko's head bobbed closer. Andrei made a grab for him. Kuzko's face was pallid with cold and fear and his eyes rolled wildly in his head.

"Catch hold of me!" Andrei tried to roll onto his back so that he could begin to pull Kuzko along with him, his face tipped upward, out of the freezing water. But Kuzko clung grimly to his plank. "Let go."

"My *Swallow*," Kuzko gasped.

"Let her go." A wave smacked into them and they went under. Andrei dragged Kuzko back up, coughing out a lungful of seawater. Glancing behind he saw a fifth warship sailing toward them, white sails filled with the wind, cutting through the bucking waves.

"Help me." Andrei closed his eyes, not knowing to what power he was praying, only that he could see no way to swim clear of the clean, cruel might of the metal-clad prow, churning the waves to foam.

Deep within him, he felt something stir. His heart twisted then cracked open within his breast. Stars exploded across his vision. A wordless cry burst from his mouth as a dark whirlwind enveloped him.

The warship ploughed on toward them, carving its foaming furrow through the waves. Andrei gave one last desperate tug at Kuzko's waterlogged body, trying to lift him from its path.

And suddenly they were rising, water cascading from their sodden clothes, rising from the sea as the great ship's prow hit the plank.

Andrei found himself hovering above the waves, clinging onto Kuzko's dangling body.

"Make for land."

Land. He cast around—and saw a flat grey shoreline beneath a rugged headline a mile or so away.

"I can't; it's too far—"

"Don't fight me!"

The voice urged him onward.

Wingbeats echoed in his head, throbbed through his whole body. Dark wings bore him upward, onward across the sea. His dazed mind was dazzled with a sparkle of stars. Was he drowning—and dreaming with his last conscious thoughts before the sea took his life from him? Or had a dark angel swooped down to bear him and Kuzko to the Ways Beyond?

"So how is he?" Baltzar asked, sliding back the observation shutter in Twenty-One's door and peering in.

"Worse," Skar said bluntly.

Twenty-One lay unmoving on the bed.

"Since his last outburst, he's lapsed into a stupor. Nothing seems to rouse him. It's almost as if he's given up the will to live."

Baltzar frowned at the prisoner.

"And the infection?"

"The wounds are healing cleanly on the outside. But I fear the infection has gone deep and invaded his brain."

Baltzar snapped the shutter closed.

"And what will we tell his imperial highness if he dies on us?"

"Would his imperial highness care?" said Skar with a shrug. "Plenty of prisoners die before their sentences are up. Prison air is not so wholesome. Diseases spread too rapidly for us to control."

Baltzar had been biting his lip. He knew this prisoner was different from the rest, life sentence or no. He knew the Emperor was still interested in his progress. Had his medical experiments gone too far this time?

"He could have caught typhus," Skar said.

"Yes," Baltzar said, nodding. "An outbreak of typhus. Tell the other warders to avoid this part of the tower and tell them why. We can't have a major outbreak on our hands. We'll keep this one in quarantine. Then if the inevitable happens—"

"A lime burial to avoid the infection spreading."

"A hygienic necessity."

Two passengers on the deck of the Francian ship following close in the wake of the Tielen war fleet saw the little fishing boat crushed by the man-o'-war. As the captain dispatched a rescue party and the Francian sailors lowered a rowboat, the passengers watched from the rail of the upper deck.

"Jagu." The woman clutched at her companion's arm, pointing. "Look. What in God's name is that?"

Jagu raised the eyeglass he had been using to observe the Tielen fleet and focused it on the wreck of the fishing boat.

"Whatever it is, it's not of this world." He passed her the glass.

"There were two men in the water. Now I see only one—and *that* abomination."

The sailors were gaining on the wreckage now.

"The angelstone," urged the woman. "Use the angelstone."

Jagu pulled out a crystal pendant from inside his shirt and held it up high. The clear crystal muddied and turned black as ink.

"A warrior-daemon," the woman whispered, "from the Realm of Shadows. This could be the one. If only Abbot Yephimy had not been so stubborn, we could have had Sergius's Staff . . ."

"Turn back!" yelled Jagu to the rowers, but they were too far away to hear his voice.

"Twenty-One. Can you hear me?" Skar bent over the prisoner. There was no response. He lifted the man's wrist, feeling for a pulse. When he found it, it was so faint and irregular it was hardly there. He looked so gaunt, his skin grey and pallid, his eyes sunken in their bruised sockets. Days of fever had exhausted him; his weakened body had no resources left to fight the infection in his brain.

Skar stood up and gazed at his patient. That rattling, wheezing sound in the throat did not bode well at all.

Twenty-One was dying. He must alert Director Baltzar.

And then he thought he heard the prisoner whisper something through cracked, dry lips. At first it sounded like nothing more than a guttural sigh. But then he thought he heard a name, though it was no name he recognized. Probably nothing more than the last jumbled utterances of a fractured mind.

"Drakhaoul . . . help me . . ."

The black-winged daemon halted in midair as though listening. It shuddered.

Suddenly it let out a wailing cry, inhuman and desolate. Then it began to plummet toward the waves, losing its hold on its human burden.

"Does it sense us?" Jagu said. "Does it know we are near?"

For a moment daemon and man disappeared below the surface. Then a whirlpool began to churn the waves. The sailors shouted out and cursed, gripping the sides of the rowboat as it was thrown sideways, almost capsizing. And out of the spinning water, Jagu and Celestine saw a shadow rise, dark as smoke, and speed away, low across the waves.

Andrei hit the water. The force of the impact knocked the breath from his body.

Blackness.

And then he was being lifted by many hands, strong hands, and let down onto the wooden boards of a ship.

He dragged himself to his knees, retching up a lungful of briny water. He was freezing, drenched to the skin, shivering till his teeth clacked together—but somehow still alive.

His rescuers returned, carrying someone else. They laid their burden down beside him. Pushing his wet hair out of his eyes, he saw Kuzko lying next to him, inert, limp, unbreathing.

"Kuzko!" Andrei prized the old man's mouth open and tried to blow his own warm breath into him. After a while, exhausted with the effort, he sat back on his heels and pressed on Kuzko's still rib cage in the hope of forcing it into some semblance of movement. The old sailor's head lolled back, mouth gaping.

"Come on, Kuzko!" Andrei laid his head against the damp chest, listening for a heartbeat. "Don't desert me now, old man!"

It was no use. Somewhere between the sea and the ship, Kuzko's spirit had fled its body. All his frantic efforts had been in vain.

Andrei laid Kuzko's body down on the deck and with clumsy, numbed fingers, closed his eyes.

One of the sailors came up and wrapped a blanket around Andrei's shoulders. Andrei's heart felt as though drenched with a cold and bleak despair. Kuzko had saved him from the sea. Why had he not been able to save him in return? And how could he break the news to Irina? First the sea had taken her son, and now her husband.

He crouched down beside Kuzko's still body and wept.

Shadow-wings, fast beating outside the Iron Tower . . .

"Who's . . . there?"

Eyes glimmered in Gavril's cell, blue as starlight. And something blacker than darkness itself reared up, towering above his bed.

"*You called to me, Gavril Nagarian.*"

"Dra—khaoul?" So many times he had dreamed this, and now he was so weak he could hardly whisper the words he wanted to say. He tried to lift one hand to welcome his banished daemon, but the effort was too great and his hand flopped back uselessly onto the bed.

"*What have they done to you?*"

"I—don't know. So weak. So *wrong*—"

"*You could not live with me—and now you cannot live without me.*"

"Take me. Take me away from this terrible place."

The Drakhaoul enfolded him—close, closer—until he was drowning in an ecstasy of shadows.

"*Now you are mine again, Gavril. Now we act, we think, as one.*"

His sight blurred, then cleared. He could see again.

"*Where shall we go?*"

"Home . . ." Gavril's heart burned with a sudden longing. "My home."

"To Azhkendir?"

"No . . . to Smarna."

Skar was crossing the inner courtyard on his way to check on his dying patient when he saw the skies darken. Stormclouds were blowing toward them across the Iron Sea. A sudden cold wind whined about the asylum walls. Then blue lightning shivered across the sky and struck the Iron Tower.

Skar felt the shock as if it had pierced his body. He dropped to one knee, gasping.

Director Baltzar ran out into the courtyard. He gripped Skar by the shoulders, pulling him to his feet. "What in God's name—" he shouted above the whine of the wind, pointing to the tower.

Skar looked up. Stormclouds, black and electric-blue, swirled about the top of the tower. Little crackles of energy lit the darkness. "A lightning ball?" he shouted back.

A sudden explosion rocked the tower. The iron bars burst asunder and stones rained down into the courtyard. Skar pushed the astonished Baltzar out of the way just as a huge block of masonry crashed down where they had been standing. Other warders hurried out into the yard, roused by the commotion.

Skar raised his eyes to gaze at the broken tower. For a moment he saw—or thought he saw—a great winged creature, darker than the rolling stormclouds, launch itself from the jagged top of the tower and go skimming off across the dark sea.

He blinked, rubbing his lightning-dazzled eyes.

The clouds were dispersing, blowing away as swiftly as they had come.

"The p-prisoner," stammered Director Baltzar. "Twenty-One. No one could have survived a direct lightning strike."

The tower stair was strewn with rubble. Twenty-One's door had been blown off its hinges. Through the doorway they could see daylight and feel the fresh breeze off the sea.

Skar gingerly entered the room and found himself staring at the open sky through a great gaping hole blasted in the tower wall. All the roof tiles had gone and only a few broken beams remained overhead. Scorch marks blackened the stones. Wind whistled through the gap.

"Where is he, Skar?" asked Director Baltzar, gripping hold of the doorframe. His face was pale as gruel. "Where is our prisoner?"

The imperial barque lay at anchor on the River Gate quay; Eugene could see the New Rossiyan standard fluttering from her topmast. All was ready for the voyage to Tielen. And yet he still lingered here in his study, reluctant to leave for no good reason that he could explain to himself.

If we don't sail soon, we'll be late for Kari's birthday celebrations. But sending her birthday greetings through the Vox Aethyria would prove a poor substitute. *What kind of father am I?*

If only there was some news from Smarna. If only he had been able to take command of the whole operation himself. It was not that he didn't trust Janssen; it was just that he preferred to be with his troops, in the heart of the action. And then there was this odd sense of foreboding that had troubled him all day. Premonition, or seasoned soldier's intuition? Whichever, it had never deceived him in the past.

"Highness."

Eugene did not even turn from the window; he recognized Gustave's voice.

"Yes, yes, they're waiting for me. I'm on my way."

"There's some new intelligence just arrived. From Arnskammar."

"Arnskammar?" Eugene spun abruptly around. "Let me see."

It was a letter, sealed with the official seal of the Asylum Director. Eugene cracked open the seal and hastily scanned Director Baltzar's neat handwriting:

To his imperial highness, Eugene, Emperor of New Rossiya.

It is with the utmost regret that I write to inform you of the demise of the prisoner known as Twenty-One. A terrible storm hit the coast and lightning made a direct strike on the Iron Tower in which the prisoner was confined.

Eugene lowered the paper slowly, not bothering to read the rest.

"Gavril Nagarian, dead?" he said softly. "Can this be true? Or is this some new piece of Azhkendi spirit-mischief, designed to deceive us?" He looked at Gustave, who stood patiently waiting for instructions.

"No one must know of this," he said, "not until I have had it verified by independent investigators. Send a letter to Baltzar informing him that no one in the prison is to breathe a word of this on pain of death."

Gustave bowed and hurried away.

But if what Baltzar writes is true, then I have lost the last surviving link to the Drakhaoul and its arcane origins. . . .

"I need verification," he said aloud. "Proof that Nagarian is truly dead. Proof, if need be, from the Ways Beyond."

CHAPTER 19

Andrei stands on the observation deck of the Sirin, *telescope in hand, scanning the calm, moonsilvered sea for enemy warships.*

Out of nowhere, a wind comes spearing across the sea and smacks into the ship, setting the waves violently churning.

The night sky boils black with stormclouds.

"All hands on deck!" Andrei bellows, straining his voice to be heard above the roaring of the storm.

The warship bucks and rolls, caught in a maelstrom of wind and wild-whipped tide.

The deck fills with crewmen, hauling on ropes, shinning up masts, frantically trying to furl the sails.

Andrei fights his way toward the quartermaster at the wheel, pulling himself, hand over hand, up the tip-tilting deck.

"Hold her steady, man. Steady! Or we'll hit the rocks."

"It's no use, Commander—"

The prow smashes into the rocks.

Timbers splinter, metal buckles. Ice-cold spray and fragments of shattered timbers rain down on the terrified crew.

"Abandon ship! Abandon ship!"

Scrambling across the deck toward the rail, Andrei is flung off balance. The ship heaves. Water gushes in.

"She's going down!"

He's sliding now, sliding helplessly down the slippery deck, down toward the icy sea.

"Must save my crew. Must make sure they're safe."

He makes a grab at the rail, clinging on with one hand.

"Commander! Jump! Jump!"

A groaning sound fills his ears, the groaning of the hull as it grinds against the rocks.

"She's going down, Commander! Save yourself!"

She's sinking fast, too fast for him to reach the boats.

The wind slams the sinking ship into the rocks again. Towering waves crash down, drenching him, cold and bitter with the taint of salt. Gasping at the chill of the water, he flings off his heavy uniform coat, sabre and belt, and pitches into the black vortex of water. . . .

"Andrei?"

"Drowning . . . I'm drowning!" He flailed wildly, fighting the deadly pull of the ravening sea.

A hand caught hold of his. "You're safe now." The calm voice penetrated the roar of the storm, the creaking of his shattered ship.

Andrei sat bolt upright and found he was staring into a pair of gold-lashed eyes. Soft daylight lit the little cabin and the simple bunk on which he had been sleeping.

"I—I'm so sorry. I was dreaming."

"It must have been quite some dream," his companion said, gently releasing his hand.

He nodded, still staring into her soft blue eyes. "I know you. You sang in Mirom last winter. Celestine—"

"De Joyeuse. I'm flattered you remember me."

"Celestial in voice as well as in name," he said. "How could I forget?"

"The daemon-creature that attacked you," she said, ignoring the compliment. "That would be enough to give anyone nightmares."

"That was not what I was dreaming about. My ship went down in the Straits some months ago. The old man, Kuzko, rescued me. And now—" Andrei choked at the memory. "Now he's dead."

"You don't talk like a common sailor, Andrei." She was looking at him curiously.

He felt himself suddenly overwhelmed by the desire to unburden himself and tell her everything.

"Where are you bound?" he asked.

"Why, to Swanholm, to sing for Princess Karila's birthday at the request of the Emperor's wife, Astasia."

"Astasia," he repeated. At last he saw a way to make himself known to his sister. And he felt dangerously close to tears. "Demoiselle de Joyeuse," he began in the Francian tongue, "may I confide in you?"

"The captain has just informed me we'll reach Haeven by morning." Jagu ducked down as he entered the little cabin to avoid hitting his head. He set down a bottle of red wine on the table and proceeded to pour with a steady hand. "So we've a day or two in hand before we're expected at Swanholm." He handed Celestine and Andrei a glass of wine and lifted his own in a toast. "To your miraculous survival, my Lord Andrei."

"Miraculous?" Andrei took a sip of the wine and nodded his appreciation: It was dry, yet enriched with just enough musky sweetness to soften the back of the palate. "If you hadn't sent out your men to the rescue—"

"I was thinking more of the creature that plucked the old man from the waves," Jagu said.

Andrei set his glass down. "You saw it, then?"

"What was it, Andrei?" said Celestine, gazing earnestly at him.

"It healed me. Whether it was a spirit that haunted the place where I was shipwrecked, or it sought me out for some purpose of its own, I don't know. All I know is it healed my body and restored my mind."

"It healed you?" echoed Celestine, glancing at Jagu. "Did it ever reveal its purpose to you?"

"Not on Lapwing Spar, no. But in Mirom it spoke to me. It said, 'You were born to rule. But it is too soon.'"

"Born to rule," said Celestine thoughtfully. "And then it abandoned you?"

"I don't know why. For a moment I thought I heard a distant voice crying out for help." Andrei gulped down his wine, trying to block out the memory of those last chaotic moments when he thought he was drowning again. "But it might have been Kuzko." His voice faltered and Jagu refilled his glass. "Where was Eugene's war fleet going in such a hurry?"

"We asked ourselves the same question," said Jagu, his pale face stern. "Who knows where Eugene's ambitions will lead him next. . . ."

"Our countries have always been allies, Andrei," Celestine said in Francian. "Your command of our language is excellent. We understand each other well, do we not? You have been deprived of your right to rule Muscobar by this new regime. Yet your family also claims descent from the Emperor Artamon. Had matters gone otherwise, you could be emperor of all Rossiya."

As soon as he had heard her speak the words aloud, Andrei knew they were true. The spirit that had healed him had also awoken that ambition simmering deep within him. He had as much a right to rule all five princedoms as Eugene of Tielen.

"I could be emperor," he said slowly. "But how? I have no country, no name, no troops at my disposal. The Muscobite army and navy have been absorbed into Eugene's forces."

He saw Celestine and Jagu consult each other with another glance. Then Celestine turned to him and said, "We believe our master, King Enguerrand, would be very interested in meeting you."

The old covered market in Colchise had become a temporary hospital for the casualties injured in the clash with the Tielen garrison.

Elysia returned to help bathe and bandage the walking wounded. Many were students, but there were older townspeople as well who had joined the fight.

"Would you like some tea?"

Elysia straightened up from the gashed temple she was bandaging and shook a stray lock from her eyes. It was the student girl with auburn hair. She smiled.

"Thank you, I'd love some. And so would my patient here." He was the baker's apprentice from Vine Alley, a good-hearted boy with unruly black curls. "What's happening at the citadel?" Elysia took the mug of tea gratefully and drank. Her back was stiff with bending over her charges, and from the slight throbbing over one eye, she could sense a headache looming. "It's gone very quiet out there."

"Still a stalemate," said the girl. "The Tielens have retreated and barricaded themselves in. They're refusing to talk terms unless we surrender. They're in for a long wait!"

"And your brother?" Elysia laid a hand on her shoulder. "How is he?"

"Miran?" The girl's fierce expression faded and Elysia saw fear in her eyes. "Still fighting. I—I hope."

"Raïsa!" A man with hair the same rich red-brown as the girl's came pushing through the throng toward them. "Miran's asking for you."

The girl gave Elysia a look that betrayed so much hope that her heart bled for her. She squeezed the girl's hand. "It'll be all right," she said, praying that it would be.

"Coming, Iovan!" called Raïsa, and hurried away.

"That young hothead Iovan Korneli is out for blood."

Elysia turned to see Lukan behind her, slowly shaking his head. "How so?"

"He's got a grudge against the Tielens. Seems some Tielen merchant cheated his father in a business venture some years ago. The old man lost all his money and had to sell the family home. Or that's the way Iovan tells it. Now that Miran's been shot, he's out for revenge."

"Lukan, is there any civilized way to stop this? Before Eugene loses all patience and sends his armies to crush us into submission?"

"Dear Elysia, such talk might be judged treasonable!" Even though he spoke lightly, she detected a grim note underlying his words. "Can you imagine Iovan Korneli and his friends agreeing to a civilized solution? It's a stalemate."

Andrei gazed out across the Straits from the long jetty at Haeven. The salty wind had dropped, but a fresh breeze still tousled his hair.

The sun was setting and had half-sunk beneath the low clouds, illuminating the western horizon with a vivid dazzle of stormy gold.

So much had happened, he could not yet take it all in. The Francians had treated him with kindness and understanding; they had even listened to his concerns about Irina and had made him a loan of money to send to her by a trusted courier. And what had surprised him the most was that they had accepted him without once questioning his story. He had no papers to prove his identity, not even an unusual birthmark. He could be an impostor, a pretender to the Orlov dynasty, plotting to dupe the Francian government.

"Andrei."

He looked around and saw Celestine de Joyeuse approaching, a lavender gossamer shawl wrapped about her throat against the evening damp. The soft shade made her blue eyes appear even more luminous in the twilight. She smiled at him.

"What a dramatic sunset," she said. "Does such a sky herald more stormy weather to come?"

Storms in the Straits. He remembered the terrible tempest that had sunk the *Sirin*. There had been no warning that night, not even a sunset such as this. "No," he said. "The weather can prove fickle off these shores, even for the most experienced sailor."

"I have news for you from King Enguerrand." She handed him a sealed letter.

He broke the seal and stared at the strange dashes and symbols, perplexed. "Is this some new Francian alphabet? It means nothing to me."

Celestine let out a soft laugh. "It is encrypted. Jagu has the codes to decipher the encryption at the tavern." She slipped her hand beneath his arm. "Let's go back now before I catch a chill out here and spoil my voice."

To our royal cousin, Andrei Orlov of Muscobar, from Enguerrand of Francia:

We are most heartily relieved to hear of your miraculous rescue. Please rest assured that news of your survival will not be revealed until you judge the time is right to do so.

We extend the hand of friendship to you and assure you of a warm welcome at our royal court. We also have new intelligence of events that took place toward the end of last year, which will both disturb and intrigue you.

Our representative in New Rossiya, Ambassador d'Abrissard, will soon arrive in Haeven. He has some proposals to make, which we believe will be to our mutual benefit. . . .

Andrei was rowed out through a brisk dawn breeze to meet with Fabien d'Abrissard on board ship.

"Eugene's agents are everywhere," the ambassador said as he welcomed Andrei into his paneled stateroom in the stern. "Here, at least, we are on Francian territory. Coffee to warm you this chilly morning?"

"Thank you." The square windowpanes afforded a view over the Straits: an expanse of rain-grey sea and pale clouds.

The ambassador clicked his fingers and his secretary poured Andrei coffee in a delicate white and gold cup. After living so long in a poor fisherman's cottage, Andrei had grown unused to such refinements and he handled the flimsy china nervously.

"And our guest might appreciate a dash of brandy." Had Abrissard seen his hands tremble? The ambassador's expression gave nothing away; although his lips smiled at Andrei, his manner was cool and detached. The secretary added a measure of brandy to Andrei's cup and discreetly withdrew, closing the door softly behind him. For a moment the only sound was the lapping of the water against the ship as it rocked gently at anchor.

"Were you aware that the power behind Eugene's empire is one Kaspar Linnaius, a renegade scientist wanted for crimes in Francia?" Abrissard asked.

Andrei shook his head.

"We have reason to believe that this same Kaspar Linnaius was responsible for the sinking of your ship."

"Sinking the *Sirin*? But how? She went down in a storm."

"A storm that came out of nowhere on a calm night?"

"Why, yes—"

"A similar event occurred some years ago in the reign of Prince Karl, when the Francian fleet was wrecked by a disastrous storm."

"But what possible proof could you have?" burst out Andrei.

"The testimonies furnished by two of Linnaius's students," said Abrissard smoothly. "They confirmed that this self-styled 'Magus' can command and control the winds."

"That's preposterous."

"We have a witness. The night of the storm, one of the grooms at the Palace of Swanholm confirms that he saw Linnaius create a storm that brought down trees in the parkland. I should emphasize now that this intelligence is of the highest confidentiality."

Andrei sat back, trying to grasp the full implications of what Abrissard was saying.

"This should not be so difficult for you to accept, Andrei Orlov," said Abrissard in the softest, smoothest of voices. "You, who have been touched by a daemon."

"You're implying that Eugene ordered Linnaius to sink my ship? Doesn't that count as assassination?" At first, the news had left him stunned; now anger began to burn through.

Abrissard shrugged eloquently. "In war, such terms do not apply."

"And my sister has married this man!" Andrei could sit still no longer; he rose and strode to the window to gaze out at the sea. A watery sun had begun to show beneath the clouds, catching the tops of the waves with flecks of silvery gold.

"You're ambitious, Andrei Orlov. Do you care about the future of Muscobar?"

"Of course I do!" Andrei said hotly.

"Then come to Francia. King Enguerrand assures you of the warmest welcome at his court. He has plans—great plans for the future. Those plans will include you, if you so wish." Andrei turned and stared at Abrissard. He heard what the ambassador was saying—and yet not putting into words. Francia had old scores to settle with Tielen.

"You were born to rule, Andrei," the daemon-spirit had whispered to him in Mirom. Now he began to see that that ambition might be fulfilled with such powerful allies at his side. If it were not for the fact that Astasia had married Eugene.

"And my sister?"

Abrissard's proud gaze grew colder. "Your sister has committed herself to Eugene. It may be difficult to persuade her to change her allegiances."

CHAPTER 20

Gavril felt warm sunlight on his closed eyelids. He opened his eyes and saw a cloudless sky above him. He lay on grass, coarse and springy; as he turned his head, he saw little tufts of white clover and daisies in the grass, and smelled their faint honeyed scent.

"Where am I?"

"*Near your home. But you need human nourishment to sustain you.*" He heard the Drakhaoul's voice resonating within his mind like a dark breath of fiery wind. He had never imagined he would feel so glad to hear that voice again.

"How long have I been here?" It was an effort just to form the words. He was so tired he just wanted to lie back in the sun and drift back into unconsciousness.

"*Long enough for me to heal the injuries to your brain. But you are still weak from loss of blood.*"

Gulls circled high overhead, white against the brilliant blue of the sky.

"Why did you come back?" he asked drowsily.

"*Your need was too great.*"

Sleep washed over Gavril. When he awoke again, the sun had moved across the sky toward the west. It was late afternoon.

He sat up and began to take stock of his bearings. "*Near your home,*" the Drakhaoul had said. Was he on the cliffs above Vermeille Bay? He tried to get to his feet but his legs were so weak that he crumpled back to his knees in the grass.

"What's he doing here?"

"Looks like he's been injured. Could be one of the rebels from the citadel."

Voices sounded close to Gavril. Prison warders? He threw up his arms to protect his head.

"It's all right, son. We're not going to hurt you."

Slowly he realized that they were speaking Smarnan. He opened his eyes and saw two men—vineyard workers, from the look of them—bending over him in the golden light.

"You've taken a nasty cut to the head there, boy. Have you been in the fighting?"

"Fighting?" Gavril repeated, confused.

"Fighting the Tielens."

"Tielens." Gavril's fists clenched at the hated name.

"Can you walk, son?" The older of the two nodded to the other, and between them they hoisted Gavril to his feet. "Where are you making for?"

"Vermeille."

The two workers glanced at each other.

"I wouldn't go back there right now. Not in your condition. Vermeille is swarming with Tielen soldiers."

"He can come back with us tonight, Jarji, can't he? He can sleep in the barn."

They hoisted Gavril up onto their ox-drawn cart and jogged back through the warm dusk to the vineyard.

The vineyard women made a fuss of him, tutting in horror over his wounds and insisting on feeding him soup fortified with their own rich red wine to "build up his strength."

It was so good just to sit in the kitchen, feeling the warmth from the fire on the range and to smell the hot peppery steam rising from the spicy meat soup. Good to hear the chatter around him in his native language. Good, above all other things, to know he was free.

"How's things in the citadel?" Jarji asked him suddenly.

Gavril blinked, at a loss to know what to say.

"How can you ask him that?" said Jarji's wife, Tsinara. "It's a wonder he can remember his own name with a head wound like that. What did you find out down at the village?"

"Professor Lukan and the students have taken Governor Armfeld hostage. They're threatening to shoot him if the Tielens don't withdraw. But now they say an imperial war fleet's on its way."

One of the workers came into the kitchen.

"Haven't you heard? The fleet's been sighted off Gargara. It's making straight for Vermeille Bay."

Listening to their conversation, Gavril began to realize that Smarna was not a safe place to be.

"Vermeille Bay?" It was the first time he had spoken in a while and they all stared at him. "But if they fire on the citadel, it'll be a massacre."

The sun-gilded sands of the Smarnan shore swarmed with Tielen soldiers. Warships, anchored out in glittering Vermeille Bay, had trained their powerful cannons on the Old Citadel of Colchise perched high on the cliffs beyond the pink and white stucco villas.

Elysia stood on the balcony of the Villa Andara and watched the guns from the warships blast the citadel. Tiles shattered to flying shrapnel, flames spurted from roof timbers, clouds of smoke besmirched the clear blue sky. The ancient walls began to crumble under the relentless bombardment.

"No. Oh no," she whispered to the bright morning air. "Raïsa. Iovan. Lukan."

The cannonfire shook the villa to its foundations, deafening as overhead thunder.

A man came stumbling into the orchard garden below.

"Elysia!" he cried in a voice rough with fear and exhaustion. "Help me!"

"Lukan?" She grabbed up her skirts and went hurrying down to the garden.

He had collapsed to one knee in the dewy grass. As she reached him, he raised his face to hers and she saw blood trickling from a jagged gash above one eye. "They're after me."

"Can you make it to the villa? Here. Lean on me."

The guns thundered again and she felt him flinch, his weight heavy against her shoulder. She braced herself and started slowly forward, a step or two at a time. The cannonfire made her heart thud like a kettledrum in her chest. Suppose they turned the guns on the houses next? They would all be blown to pieces.

"Why?" she said, breathless herself now with the effort of supporting him. "Why has Eugene attacked us?"

They reached a wrought-iron bench beneath the balcony and

Lukan sank onto it. She sat beside him and pressed her handkerchief to the gash, trying to stanch the blood.

"Eugene is a tyrant. He doesn't believe in negotiating."

His voice came faintly now, and she saw from the greyish pallor of his skin that he was near to fainting. He was too heavy for her to carry into the house on her own. What would revive him most efficiently, brandy or water?

"Just because Eugene got his hands on some ancient ruby from the Smarnan Treasury, he thinks it gives him the right to own us all. . . ."

Brandy, she decided as Lukan rambled defiantly on. He needs brandy.

"We must fight to remain independent. It's our birthright. . . ."

Another violent barrage of cannonfire shuddered along the cliffs. From where they sat they could see the fiery explosions, the jagged, broken walls of the citadel, with smoke pouring out as the fires took hold.

Shouts erupted at the far end of the garden. Elysia recognized the clipped tongue all too well. "Tielen soldiers!" She rose in alarm. "Inside, Lukan; quick."

The handkerchief dropped as she was hustling him in at the garden door. Too late she glanced back as she locked the door and saw it lying there by the bench, stained bright red with Lukan's blood. Too late to go back for it now.

"I thought I'd given them the slip." Lukan slumped against the wall, one hand clasped to his gashed head. "Let me out at the front, Elysia. If they find me here, God knows what they'll do to you and Palmyre."

Elysia was busy with her keys, unlocking the door to her studio, trying to steady her shaking hands. "You're not going anywhere in your condition."

The door swung open and she pushed him inside, hastily locking it again behind them.

Canvases lay stacked in piles against the walls. Easels had been draped with dust sheets to protect the unfinished works that lay beneath. Dim light seeped in through long linen blinds; the air was pungent with the smell of oil paints and turpentine, tinged with the dust of long months of neglect. Elysia had not yet confronted the task of cleaning up in here.

Men called to one another in Tielen.

"Quick. Under this dust sheet."

She pushed Lukan down, forcing him to crawl behind a pile of tall portrait canvases and draped more sheets on top. Booted feet came clattering up the wide steps.

"Open up!"

A man stood high on the rocky promontory, gazing out across the sea.

He stood motionless, tensed for action. But within his heart and mind there blazed a cold and vengeful rage.

He could see them in the bay below, the imperial war fleet, sent to crush the rebellion in Colchise.

"Eugene!" he cried, his voice strong, rasping raw with anger. "This time you've gone too far. You took my freedom, my name— but you shan't take Vermeille!"

The rage burned more fiercely within him, flooding through his veins with galvanic power. The Emperor's war machine would show no mercy to the Smarnans.

"But they have a chance if we go to their aid."

He slowly stretched his arms wide. Blue light crackled and hissed from his clawed fingertips.

He stared at the phosphorescent flickers of light, the physical manifestation of the daemonic energy he felt pulsing through his body. Such terrible power . . .

Far beneath him waves crashed against the jagged rocks, sending up bursts of white spray. If he had misjudged, he would fall to an agonizing death, his body smashed against the rocks.

"We are Drakhaon."

He took a step back, steeling himself. "Then don't fail me now." And crouching low, he ran toward the edge of the cliff and leaped into the void.

"Open up!" This time the Tielen soldiers used the common tongue and there was no mistaking their intent. One battered on the villa door; from the din it sounded as if the butt of a carbine was being used.

Elysia met Palmyre in the hall.

"Listen to that! If they've damaged the paintwork, they'll have me to deal with," Palmyre said, rolling up her sleeves.

"Stall them," Elysia whispered. "Tell them I'm ill." She hastily re-treated to the upper landing, where she could watch what was happening.

"Coming, coming," called Palmyre loudly, bustling back down the corridor. She reached with a shaking hand for the door handle and opened.

Tielen soldiers stood there: big lads, raw-shaven, in their blue and grey uniforms.

"Move aside."

Palmyre positioned herself so that her generous figure filled the doorway, arms folded across her chest. "What do you want?"

"You're harboring a rebel. We saw him come this way. We must search your house."

"There are no rebels here."

"Then how do you explain this?" He dangled the bloodstained handkerchief under her nose.

Palmyre took in a deep breath. "I can't let you in without my mistress's permission. I'm only the housekeeper."

The Tielens glanced at one another. The one who was acting as spokesman colored a deep red. He couldn't have been much more than twenty, Elysia thought, brashness barely concealing his lack of experience.

"Then fetch your mistress."

"She's ill in bed."

"Too bad." He nodded to the others.

"Stop!" Palmyre cried, raising her arms wide to block their way. They took no notice, rudely barging past her into the hall. Elysia hastily pulled a silken *peignoir* over her day-dress and tugged the pins from her hair, letting it tumble about her shoulders.

"Two of you take the stairs and search the upper floors," the Tielen ordered. "And you two follow me." He had kept to the common tongue, Elysia realized, so that Palmyre should not mistake his intent.

She took a deep breath and went to the head of the staircase just as two of the soldiers came running up, taking two stairs at a time.

"What is the meaning of this intrusion?" she asked in a faint voice, one hand clasped to her forehead as if she had a headache. They hesitated a moment, glancing uncertainly at each other.

"Take her downstairs," said one.

"You. Come with me." The other raised his carbine, pointing it at her.

It would not be wise to provoke him, Elysia decided, doing as she was ordered.

She came downstairs just in time to see the young officer fling open the double doors to her salon. His men followed, their boots leaving smears of mud all over her precious Khitari carpets.

The windows of the salon overlooked the bay. As Palmyre and Elysia stood helplessly watching the soldiers thrust bayonets into the sofas and cushions, they could see the Tielen fleet still firing upon the beleaguered citadel, could see flames rising from houses in the shelter of its walls.

The Tielen soldiers paused a moment to watch as another salvo crashed into the citadel.

"Our lads've breached the walls!" one said, grinning at Elysia. "It's all over for you Smarnans now."

Elysia, lips pressed together to avoid speaking her true feelings, could see only too well. The beach was covered with running men, line after line of grey and blue uniforms, bayonets fixed, advancing relentlessly on the citadel.

And then a shadow passed across the sun, dimming the spring brightness of the morning.

"What's that?" The Tielens gazed up at the sky.

Elysia moved toward the windows, peering apprehensively out at the bay.

"Dear God," Palmyre whispered, "what *is* that?"

Swooping down from the peerless blue sky came a dark cloud, moving swift as the wind, casting its shadow over the soldiers on the sands. Even as they stopped to gaze up at it, a terrible brilliance emanated from it—a glittering breath of flame so bright it seared Elysia's eyes.

For a moment the whole sweep of Vermeille Bay was irradiated in a surging blue tide of light.

"Ahh." She clutched at the sill, eyes clenched shut against the cruel brightness, water leaking from her lids. When she opened them at last and blinked away the streaming tears, she saw at first only the dark-winged shadow circling over the bay. Through her dazzled sight she could not be certain, but it seemed to her that she was seeing the impossible.

"Gavril," she whispered. "Oh, Gavril, is it you?"

The Tielens had fallen silent, transfixed, mouths gaping open. For where there had been hundreds of Tielen soldiers on the sands, there was nothing now but billowing smoke and a blanket of choking grey cinders blowing away into the air. And the dark-winged creature was swooping back across the waves, straight toward the Tielen fleet.

The masts of the Tielen warships lay below him, a forest of white-draped tree trunks.

The cannons were silent now.

As he swooped over them, he could hear human voices crying out in fear. They were moving the cannons, trying to angle them upward to bombard him. Cannonballs whistled toward him.

A cruel laughter welled up inside him as he swerved to the right and then to the left, snaking across the sky. Exhilaration powered him, and an insatiable desire for revenge.

The shots went wide. Some cannonballs fell into the waves, some thudded back down, smashing into the Tielens' own ships. The cries of fear changed to anger and panic.

Eugene's fleet was at his mercy. He could exterminate every Tielen crewman, every officer. And the Emperor would be left with no significant sea power to defend his empire.

Princess Karila sat watching the children invited to her eighth birthday party as they played blindman's buff.

She had tried to join in with the party games, but her twisted body had let her down. Too slow to keep up, she had tripped on the hem of her new blue gown and fallen flat on her face. Some of the younger children had pointed and laughed until they were shushed by their titled mothers, and bewigged servants had rushed forward to pick her up and dust her off. Bruised and humiliated, she had swallowed her tears—refusing to cry in front of the rude little boys—and limped back to her gilded chair.

Her great-aunt, Dowager Duchess Greta, clapped her hands in vain for silence. "These games are too boisterous! Let's play a different one now."

"No!" jeered the young guests, too caught up in the excitement of the chase.

Karila stifled a sigh. She gazed at her birthday cake: an elaborate confection of sponge cake, vanilla cream, and pink sugared rosebuds. Her stomach fluttered, queasy at the thought of so much cream and sugar.

Great-Aunt Greta instantly misinterpreted her look.

"Time for cake!" she cried, clapping her hands again.

"Cake! Cake!" shouted the children, jumping up and down.

The fluttering in Karila's stomach increased. If only Papa could be here. But now that he was Emperor, imperial business had kept him far away in Mirom with her stepmother, Astasia.

Her eyes strayed to the pile of presents, Papa's foremost among them: an exquisitely carved and painted musical automaton of a girl holding a little gilded cage containing a songbird. When wound, the mechanical girl pirouetted and the bird opened its little beak and fluted a strange, wistful tune. And he had promised another magical surprise for her—

"Time to cut your cake, Princess!" Papa's majordomo wheeled the extravagant cake on a little trolley in front of her and placed a knife in her hand.

"Don't forget to make a wish," whispered Great-Aunt Greta.

Karila sighed again as she placed the tip of the knife in the center of the vanilla cream. Her wish would be the same as it was every year. She closed her eyes and wished with all her heart.

Please make me whole. Make me like other children.

She pressed hard with the knife, feeling it sink into the soft sponge. The children cheered.

Then a bolt of star-blue flame flashed through her mind. Suddenly she was burning hot.

"Child, my child . . ."

"Drakhaoul!" she whispered. "You're alive!"

The knife clattered to the floor, spattering her dress with specks of cream and jam. And she felt herself falling, falling—

The Tielen soldiers tore down through the gardens of the Villa Andara, their search for Lukan abandoned.

Elysia and Palmyre watched them from the salon, amid a snow of feathers from the slashed cushions.

"Nothing I can't fix with a good upholstery needle," Palmyre said. She sat down abruptly on the ripped sofa. Her face was white underneath a glisten of sweat, and her breathing was shallow and fast.

"We both need a glass of brandy," said Elysia, going straight to the crystal decanter on the salon table.

"What was it?" Palmyre said faintly as she sipped her brandy. "What was that creature? It just flew down from the skies and destroyed them."

Before Elysia could reply, the door opened. Elysia whirled around—but it was only Lukan.

"What happened?" He hurried to the windows and gazed out. "Two of the men-o'-war are going down in flames, and the others are heading out of the bay. And the Tielen soldiers—"

"Brandy," said Elysia, handing him a glass. Lukan swallowed the generous measure she had poured him, in one gulp.

"I'd best go down to the citadel." He gave her back the empty glass. "They'll need me there."

"Not with your head gashed open!"

"Your brandy has magical restorative powers, Elysia," he said, flashing her a smile.

"But that creature. Suppose it's still out there?" cried Palmyre.

"Creature?" He stopped, seeing Elysia's expression. "You don't think it could be—"

"How could it be? He's imprisoned so far from here." Tears clouded Elysia's eyes, tears of sudden hope. The thought that he might be free again glowed like a bright star in her breast.

"Nonetheless . . . Gavril come back to defend his countrymen?" said Lukan. "There's only one way to find out. Keep all the doors locked and barred, ladies. Don't let anyone in but me."

"Why is there no word from Janssen?" muttered Eugene. He had delayed the departure for Swanholm, unwilling to leave until he had official confirmation that the siege of Colchise had been brought to an end.

He started to pace the polished boards of his study again. From time to time he stopped and gazed out to the broad Nieva. Ships passed to and fro on the fast-flowing river and the sight of their masts reminded him only too vividly of his own Southern Fleet, engaged at this very moment in a bloody battle with the insurgents in Smarna. He spun the great painted globe he had brought from his palace at Swanholm until his fingertip rested on Smarna.

Such insubordination had to be quelled—and swiftly.

His agents assured him that the leaders of the rebellion were academics, mostly artists and philosophers. Idealists, all, with little or no military experience. So when he dispatched the fleet, he had expected a few minor skirmishes—and a swift, contrite capitulation. Not a full-blown siege.

"Imperial highness." Gustave appeared in the doorway.

Eugene swung around.

"News from Smarna, highness." It couldn't be good. Gustave, who usually maintained an inscrutable expression, looked shaken. "The Southern Fleet . . ."

"Tell me!"

"It has been destroyed."

"Destroyed?" Eugene repeated. He stared at Gustave's blank face. "Impossible!"

Gustave proffered a paper. His hand shook. "I took down every word from Admiral Janssen over the Vox Aethyria."

" 'Tell—the Emperor—attacked,' " Eugene read the missive aloud. " 'Regiments ashore—wiped out. Few survivors. Three men-o'-war holed, three more on fire—two sinking. Retreat?' "

"Let me speak to Janssen." Eugene crushed the paper in his hand and pushed past Gustave, making for the office where several Vox Aethyrias were monitored, each device tuned to a different part of the empire.

Two undersecretaries were working in the office; both leaped up and bowed as Eugene strode in and seated himself at Gustave's desk.

"Janssen? Janssen! This is Eugene. Answer me. What in God's name is going on?"

"*—highness—it came—from nowhere—swooped down over the bay—*"

Eugene felt his skin chill as if a draft had seeped in from off the river.

" 'It'? What do you mean 'it'?"

"*—great, dark-winged—*" The admiral's words came indistinctly and Eugene had to crouch close to the device to catch them. "*—sheet of blinding light, like blue flame—*"

Eugene's skin suddenly burned with a shiver of fire. The terror he had experienced on that wintry escarpment outside Kastel Drakhaon returned, as it did still in the dead of night. He felt his scarred face and hand tingle at the memory of that cleansing blue flame.

"No," he murmured, "it can't be. He told me it was destroyed. *He gave me his word!*"

The sunlit glitter of the sea below dimmed. Suddenly all the power drained from Gavril's veins. He began to spiral down toward the surging waves far beneath. His mind, his will, was being torn in two.

"What's wrong?" he gasped.

Mortal terror overwhelmed him. He heard the roar of the rolling waves, felt the sting of the cold seaspray on his skin as he hurtled helplessly downward.

"Don't let me drown!" he cried. "Save me, Drakhaoul!"

"*Don't fight me . . .*" At last the Drakhaoul's voice crackled to life in his brain. "*Drained . . . don't know how long . . . can sustain . . . Make for land.*"

He felt his fast-tumbling body hit the waves. He shut his eyes tight, dreading to feel the sea clutch at him, pulling him under. Saltwater filled his throat and lungs. Down he sank, too weak to strike back up toward the surface.

CHAPTER 21

"Karila!" Eugene cried, running down the candlelit passage toward his daughter's bedchamber. His heart beating erratically, he flung open the door and went in.

"Imperial highness." Marta, Karila's governess, rose from her chair and curtsied. Her face was pale, her eyes dark-shadowed as if she had not slept in a long while.

"How is she?" Eugene heard his own voice as if from far away. "I came as fast as I could."

"The doctors think she is past the crisis."

Karila lay in her golden swan bed, fair hair spread in a tousled aureole about her head. Eugene knelt beside her. He watched to see if the sheets rose and fell regularly with her breathing, as he had watched so often before.

Yes, she was still breathing. Thank God.

How many times, in his worst imaginings, had he come to her bedchamber to find her lying cold and still, his child, his only child, all that Margret had left him? His heart was torn between the impulse to pick her up and hug her close, and terror lest such an action should disturb her healing sleep and provoke a relapse.

"Eugene?"

He blinked away the tears that misted his vision to see Astasia in the doorway.

"She's sleeping," he said softly.

There was a rustling sound as Karila moved her head.

"Papa . . ."

"Papa's here, Kari." Eugene took Karila's hand in his own, feeling how hot and damp it was.

"Papa." The sticky fingers clung tightly to his. "I saw it. I felt its breath."

"Hush, now," Eugene said, smoothing a strand of hair from her forehead. "Nothing to worry about. Papa's here now. And Tasia." He glanced up at Marta accusingly. "She's still feverish. Rambling."

"It called to me," whispered Karila. "It called me its child. Drakhaoul's child . . ." And then as if the effort had utterly exhausted her, her eyes closed and she fell back onto the silken pillows.

"Kari!" Eugene still clasped hold of her hand, pressing it between his own. "What do you mean?"

"Eugene." He felt Astasia's hand touch his shoulder, a gentle yet firm pressure. "Eugene, she doesn't know what she's saying. We should let her sleep."

"Yes," said Marta sternly, "she needs her sleep."

"I'll stay with her," said Astasia.

"No need for that, imperial highness, I'm well used to caring for the princess." Marta spoke with a certain chilliness, which did not escape Eugene's notice. Marta had been Margret's maid and confidante; it was inevitable, he supposed, that she should resent anyone he chose to supplant her mistress—even though Margret had died in childbirth eight long years ago.

He slowly let go of Karila's hand and stood up.

"Call for me if there's any change in her condition. No matter what hour of day or night."

"Have I ever failed to do so before, highness?" Marta said. But there was no resentment in her voice this time.

Eugene went to take Astasia's arm, but she drew away from him and walked swiftly from Karila's bedchamber.

"Astasia?"

She did not reply, but kept on walking. She was obviously upset by Marta's snub. He knew he should go after her and soothe her hurt feelings, but first there was the matter of the Drakhaoul.

Astasia hurried into her dressing room and locked the door behind her. She stood, back pressed up against the door, angrily sniffing away tears. She poured cold water into a bowl and splashed her face, dabbing at her reddened eyes with the corner of a dampened hand-kerchief.

What's the matter with me? Why do I cry at every little slight, every insignificant upset? I knew this was not going to be easy.

She untied her cloak and sat down at her dressing table.

Eugene had not come after her. But what had she expected? He probably thought she was being petty and childish, and he had far weightier matters on his mind. Why should he notice if his wife's feelings were wounded?

Besides, it was not so surprising that Marta had acted coldly toward her. Hadn't she cared for Karila since her mother died? And she suspected Marta had never forgiven her for sneaking Karila out of the palace on that illicit sleigh ride—

Marta's protective feelings toward Karila were understandable. But Eugene's reaction—

Astasia's fingers strayed to a pot of sugared almonds: vanilla, rose, and violet. She selected one and popped it in her mouth.

When the news of Karila's collapse had come, Eugene had abandoned everything. They had traveled day and night to reach Swanholm as fast as possible.

At least he cares for someone. She looked up and caught the shadow of a wry grimace in her reflection.

"Yes. He cares for *her* daughter," she whispered.

The flower-perfumed sugar coating the almond, usually her favorite sweet, tasted odd. Sickly. She spat the almond out into her palm.

A horrible thought entered her mind. Suppose someone was trying to poison her?

"No, no . . . I mustn't think this way. I'm just tired after all the traveling." Why would anyone hate her so viciously as to want her dead?

Drakhaoul's child? Eugene hurried toward Linnaius's laboratory, not even seeing the salutes of the guards he passed at each doorway. His thoughts were in ferment. Was she just in the grip of a vivid fever dream? Or was she still linked in some inexplicable way with the Drakhaoul?

"Oh Kari, Kari," he muttered as he crossed the outer courtyard. "What did you mean?"

As he approached the Magus's apartments, the lanternflames suddenly glowed with an intense brightness and the outer door swung slowly open to admit him.

A large telescope was positioned at an open casement window. On the desk, star charts had been unrolled: maps of the heavens, with the constellations marked out in silver and gold on a background of rich cobalt-blue.

"Welcome home, imperial highness." The Magus appeared from behind the telescope.

"Gavril Nagarian swore to me that the Drakhaoul was dead!" Eugene cried.

The Magus nodded.

"And Director Baltzar reported that Gavril Nagarian was killed in a freak storm that struck the Iron Tower last week. So how is it that our fleet has been destroyed by something that—judging by the reports—is the Drakhaoul? What's happening, Linnaius?"

Linnaius gazed at him, his expression disquietingly calm.

"Has Baltzar furnished you with any physical proof that Gavril Nagarian is dead? Surely there must have been some fragments of charred flesh, bone . . ."

Eugene leaned over the star charts toward Linnaius. "You said the Drakhaoul could not survive without a human host."

"I still know too little about this aethyric daemon that calls itself Drakhaoul. Karila said it was dying when it passed over Swanholm. I can only conjecture that it may have bonded with a new host."

Did Linnaius not understand what was at stake here? The pride of his navy had been destroyed. He felt the defeat as acutely as if a limb had been blown off in battle.

"And if my Southern Fleet had not been decimated, I could have let matters rest. But hundreds of men—good men—have died in Smarna. It has to be the Drakhaoul. Karila said so herself, tonight."

The Magus looked at him, all attention now. "What precisely did she say?"

"She said it called to her. It called her its—" he stumbled over the word, not knowing until then how much it had disturbed him, "its child. What in God's name does she mean? My own daughter!"

"So she is still in communication with it?" The Magus stroked his chin with spindle fingers. "Then who better to tell us who is behind this Smarnan business? Let me search her mind—"

"She has a high fever!" This plan had already occurred to Eugene and he had dismissed it. He could still feel Karila's hand clinging trustingly to his; it would be unpardonable to force a sick child to use her nascent powers while she was so weak. "There must be another way to determine if Gavril Nagarian is dead."

"Then there is no alternative but to look in the Ways Beyond," said Linnaius.

Chiefs of staff were waiting for Eugene in the Walnut Anteroom. Spread out on the desk was a detailed map of the continent. An old map, Eugene noted wryly, showing each country in a different color: Tielen pale blue, Muscobar mustard yellow, and Smarna, rebellious Smarna, in an inappropriately innocuous shade of rose pink.

Little lead models of battle tents and ships marked the positions of the New Rossiyan armies and fleets deployed around the empire. Colonel Soderham, a silver-haired veteran who had lost a leg in Prince Karl's Francian campaigns, was moving the models about the map.

"What are these forces here?" Eugene pointed to two model tents close to the border between Smarna and Muscobar. One was painted with the Tielen swan, the other with Muscobar's two-headed sea eagle.

"That's General Froding's Light Infantry, imperial highness," said Soderham.

"Froding?" Eugene looked puzzled. "What's he doing in Muscobar? I thought he was supposed to be down in Southern Tielen on maneuvers."

"Ah, but if you recall, highness, Colonel Roskovski asked if we might hold a joint exercise on Muscobar territory. To get the men used to working together."

Eugene remembered Roskovski's reputation rather too well; when the Tielen army invaded Mirom, the irascible Muscobar commander had put up a disastrously ill-planned defense. He suspected that a man of Roskovski's arrogance would not listen to advice, even from the experienced and genial Froding.

"Pull Froding's men out of there. Leave Roskovski guarding the border, if he must, but send one of our dragoon regiments garrisoned in Mirom to keep an eye on him."

"Straightaway, highness." Soderham saluted and murmured to one of his adjutants, who immediately sped off.

"And Froding?" Soderham asked, leaning over the map, ready to move the Tielen tent on Eugene's command.

It was time to test his theory. If he had learned one thing about Gavril Nagarian in their last conflict, it was that his instincts to defend his people would override any concerns about his own safety.

"Let's give the Smarnans something to keep them busy. Little forays and retreats—take a town here, a village there." Eugene felt a sudden yearning to be back in the field with his men. He relished this kind of cat-and-mouse strategy, keeping the enemy guessing where he would strike next. "Tell Froding to split his men up into raiding parties. And keep them on the move."

Astasia was still staring at the bowl of sugared almonds when there came a discreet tap at the the door. She hastily dried her eyes.

"Come in."

A Tielen lady-in-waiting appeared. She had the translucent complexion and ice-blond hair of those born in the far north, and her eyes were of the palest grey-blue.

"Where is Nadezhda?" Astasia asked, surprised not to see her own maid.

"His imperial highness has asked me to attend to you while you are at Swanholm," answered the woman. "I have assigned Nadezhda tasks more appropriate to a lady's maid." Even though her manner was polite, there was a frostiness about her that did not endear her to Astasia in the least.

It would have been considerate to have consulted me about this first, Eugene, thought Astasia, as the tears threatened to flow again.

"And your name?" She tried to stop her voice from wobbling.

"Countess Lovisa. I am cousin to his imperial highness on his late father's side." Her tone of voice grew frostier still. "I was presented to you at the coronation."

"Of—of course." But there had been so many Tielen courtiers presented to her that day, she could not possibly be expected to remember them all!

"I've come to tell you that the musicians from Francia have arrived, highness."

"Musicians?" Karila's sudden illness had completely put the musicians from Astasia's mind. She had, in a moment of presumptuousness, it now seemed, taken it upon herself to invite them to Swanholm to perform for Kari's birthday. She had been planning to tell Eugene of her little surprise, and now events had overtaken her.

"Where are they to be accommodated?"

"Accommodated?" She blinked her tears away, determined not to show any weakness in front of the countess. "Surely the lodging of our visitors is not my responsibility."

"Indeed, no. But for Fredrik, our majordomo, to make appropriate arrangements, it is essential for him to know who is expected and when."

Now her abilities to manage a great house were being openly criticized!

"And Demoiselle de Joyeuse asks if she might be granted a few moments of your time to discuss which of the various programs they have prepared you think would be most suitable." Countess Lovisa handed her a paper sealed with an ivory ribbon.

Astasia opened the paper and saw not the expected list of songs, but a brief message:

> If your imperial highness could vouchsafe me a minute or two in private, I have some news of personal significance to impart.

Astasia closed the letter before the countess could steal a glance at it.

"Have her shown to the Music Room, please. I will meet her there in a few minutes."

News? Astasia felt a sudden conspiratorial thrill. She went into her dressing room and dabbed cold water on her lids to try to disguise the signs that she had been weeping.

Celestine de Joyeuse was standing at the window in the Music Room, one hand resting on the exquisite marquetry of the fortepiano lid, gazing out at the park beyond. On seeing Astasia, she sank into a deep curtsy.

"What a charming room. If the acoustics are as pleasing as the decorations, this should prove a delightful musical experience."

"Please rise, demoiselle," Astasia said, smiling.

"I am so sorry to hear of your stepdaughter's indisposition, highness. Would you prefer to postpone the recital?"

Astasia was only too aware that Countess Lovisa was still hovering behind her.

"You can leave us now, countess," she said pointedly.

The countess bowed and slowly withdrew.

Astasia waited until she heard the double doors click shut. Then she hurried over to the fortepiano.

"You said you had something to impart to me," she said, keeping her voice low. "Something of personal significance."

The singer nodded her head. "Great personal significance."

"So what is it, Demoiselle de Joyeuse?" Astasia felt even more uneasy now.

Celestine looked at her from clear, cool blue eyes. "Is there nowhere more private?"

Astasia looked back at her uncertainly. *Never allow yourself to be alone with anyone, no matter how well you think you know them.* Eugene had warned her. *There are some fanatical individuals who would not hesitate to harm you or Karila if they thought it would influence me.*

Celestine seemed to notice her hesitation. "And you are right to be wary. You have no reason to trust me, Empress. For all you know, I could be an assassin sent by the Francian court to seek revenge on the House of Tielen for past defeats." She gave Astasia a radiant smile. "But I assure you, when you hear the news I bring, you will feel quite differently toward me. That, at least, is my hope."

Celestine's angelic blue gaze promised startling revelations. And Astasia found herself desperate to know what Celestine had to tell her.

"I have little skill at the keyboard," she confessed, "but if I were to attempt to accompany you, perhaps you could tell me the news you bring between verses?"

Celestine shot her a shrewd little look. "An ingenious idea." She lifted a book of songs from the top of the fortepiano and began to leaf through the pages. "Do you know 'The Waterfall'?"

Astasia settled herself on the seat and took a look at the music. She pulled a wry face. "Too hard. All those running notes in the left-hand . . ."

"This one is just right. 'Summer Evenings.' A beautifully simple melody, a deceptively simple accompaniment. And in my native tongue, which is not so familiar to the Tielens, I believe," she added with a mischievous little smile.

"I've never played this one before," Astasia stared at the notes, biting her lower lip in concentration, "so not too fast, demoiselle, I beg you."

"Don't forget the key signature," whispered the singer after her first attempt faltered on a clumsy dissonance.

Astasia felt herself blushing. "I wish I'd devoted more time to practicing my sight-reading," she said, ashamed. This time, the opening phrase flowed more smoothly and Celestine began to sing.

"In summer . . . when the swallows swoop overhead . . ."

At first Astasia could only think about placing her fingers correctly on the keys. And then she thought with a sudden thrill: *I'm making music with this gloriously gifted singer!*

"Empress," sang Celestine, "your brother is alive."

Astasia's fingers stumbled. She stopped playing. She stared at Celestine. "Andrei—*alive?*"

"Shall we keep the song going?" suggested Celestine gently.

Astasia tried to focus on the notes in front of her, but all she could see was a blur. Wrong notes and slips proliferated. *Andrei is alive.* Her fingers skittered wildly over the keys until, in an agony of excitement, she played a crashing chord and sprang up from the keyboard.

"Where is he? In Francia?" She could not hold the questions back any longer. "How is he? And how do you know?"

"He is in remarkably good health, all things considered," Celestine said. Her expression was serious now. "He lost his memory after his ship went down."

"He was badly hurt?" Astasia could not keep the distress from her voice. Even though she was Empress now and knew she must act with composure, this was her brother they were discussing, her brother whose death had made her cry herself to sleep night after night. "Tell me the truth!"

"We rescued a man from the wreck of a fishing boat. It was your brother. It seems that he was washed ashore nearly dead, and was nursed back to health by an old fisherman. The old man had no idea who he was, and renamed him Tikhon."

"My poor Andrei." Astasia felt sick and cold. Andrei, barely alive, clinging to life on some desolate wintry shore. "He must think we abandoned him." The thought was almost too hard to bear. "I must see him. Where is he?"

Celestine did not speak straightaway. She gazed earnestly into Astasia's face.

"My dear Empress, your brother finds himself in a very difficult situation. Your husband has taken the throne that was rightly his. If he were to come forward now, what would the Emperor do?"

"I'm sure Eugene would welcome him to court," Astasia said in a rush of emotion. "For my sake."

"Think again, imperial highness." Clear blue eyes looked at her frankly. "Some dissident elements might see your brother as a significant rival to your husband's authority. His reappearance could cause considerable damage to the stability of the empire."

"But Andrei would never do anything to hurt me," protested Astasia.

"The consequences could be disastrous," said Celestine with a firmness of tone that surprised Astasia. She spoke more like a seasoned politician than a court musician. "He was very reluctant to have me tell you the news—let alone your parents—for fear it would place you all in an impossible situation."

"But my parents should know. Papa has been a broken man since the news came of his loss. And Mama—"

"Even so, highness."

Astasia began to wonder if there was some other reason for Andrei's reluctance to declare himself. Was Celestine hiding something from her?

"Have his injuries changed him in some way? Tell me the truth, demoiselle."

"His physical injuries have healed quite miraculously."

"So where will he go? He can't stay in a fisherman's hut." Astasia had begun to devise possible ways for Andrei to assume his rightful place at court. Suppose she hid him away at her parents' country estate in Erinaskoe until she could explain to Eugene . . .

"His wish," Celestine said, "is to see you once more and then to begin a new life. Far away from Muscobar."

"How far?" Astasia stammered. All her joy at hearing the news he was alive was fast seeping away. She could not understand why Andrei wanted to go so far away from his family.

"I have a letter for you." Celestine slid finger and thumb into her décolletage and discreetly extracted a thin sliver of folded paper from beneath her lace fichu. Astasia opened it, feeling the paper still warm from the heat of the singer's body.

> Dearest Tasia,
>   I am so eeger to see you and our parents. Demoiselle de Joyeuse will reashure you, I hope, that I am once again sound in mind and body. Let us meet soon.
> Your loving brother, A.O.

The writing—big, bold, and untidy—was unmistakeably Andrei's hand. So were the misspellings. She shook her head over it affectionately. "He was never much of a scholar." And then she had an ingenious idea. It was inspired by the latest romance she had been reading: a stirring tale of passion, deception, and intrigue . . . but Celestine did not need to know that.

"There is to be a masked ball here at Swanholm for Dievona's Night—a Tielen spring tradition, it seems. If I could arrange for you and your accompanist to be invited as members of my party—"

"For Dievona's Night?" Celestine considered the proposition. "Well, my next recital is to be given in Bel'Esstar. The weather is clement and the seas are calm. If we delay our departure to attend the ball, I think we shall still make Allegonde in good time." She looked at Astasia and smiled. "That's a most ingenious solution, highness."

"I shall provide identical costumes," Astasia promised.

"And then you and I will secretly exchange masks for a little while, allowing us to smuggle your brother in, disguised as Jagu."

Astasia smothered a delighted giggle. "Just don't let anyone ask Andrei to play the fortepiano, or our charade will be discovered!"

Celestine laughed too. "And I will be Empress of New Rossiya! Or will I? For who'll be able to guess?"

"We must wear powdered wigs to hide our hair color, in the style of the court of Bel'Esstar."

"Great confections of white curls, topped with galleons—or doves." Celestine was giggling too.

"I don't know how to thank you, demoiselle." Astasia had not felt so dizzily happy in a long time; she reached out and clasped the singer's hands in her own, pressing them warmly. Since Varvara left court, she had lacked a friend, a woman of her own age to confide in. It was going to be such fun planning this escapade—and at the end of it, she would see her dearest Andrei again.

"Please, highness," said the singer, pressing her hands in return, "call me Celestine."

In her dreams, Karila could run as fast as any normal healthy child. . . .

How blue the sky is. And how warm the wet sand oozing beneath her bare feet. She runs along the white sands, darting in and out of the lapping tide, agile as the little crabs she sees scuttling to hide as she approaches. A flock of birds flies screeching overhead, their feathers bright as flame; one feather comes drifting down out of the sky and she jumps high to catch it. She holds it up to see the colors shimmer in the sunlight: It is streaked scarlet, orange, and gold. Laughing, she sticks her treasure in the woven belt around her waist. The other children will be so envious!

And then she hears the sound of distant gong-drums. Slow and solemn, pounding out a strong rhythm.

She gazes out across the sea. Other children run down onto the shore.

"Who is it?"

She can see a boat skimming over the sea toward them, its crew rowing to the steady beat of the drums.

One of the older boys gives a cry, pointing. "Look—it's a serpent-boat. Hide!"

Now she can just make out the carved head of a serpent on the prow, painted in green and gold, with a staring bloodred eye and ravening jaws.

Another boy grabs her by the wrist. "Quick. Let's go!"

She lets herself be dragged up the beach into the shelter of the trees. "Why must we hide?" she asks. "Are they bad men in the serpent-boat?"

The boys look at her scornfully. "Don't you know anything?" says the older one, keeping an eye on the shore as the drumming gets louder.

"She's only little," says the other. He squats down beside her. "Haven't you heard about Nagar?"

She shakes her head.

"Every year the priests come from the Sacred Island. Every year they choose children to go back with them. Special children."

"Why?"

The older one makes an impatient grunt. He is still watching the shore.

"To serve the Serpent God."

The Serpent God glares fiercely from the prow of the approaching boat.

"Suppose they don't want to go?"

"If the priests choose them, they have to go."

"Can they come home again?"

She sees the boys glance at each other.

"No one ever comes home from the Sacred Island."

Never to come home again? She stares at them, horrified.

"Does the Serpent God gobble them up?" she asks.

The older boy shrugs. "Who knows? Now keep quiet. They've landed."

Men with shaven heads have jumped down from the serpent-boat and are pulling it up the beach. Their white robes gleam whiter than the sand.

"Ti—lua! Ti—lua!"

She starts. She can hear her sister calling her name.

The boys put their fingers to their lips. "Don't answer," the older one whispers. "Don't give us away."

Linnaius silently opened the secret door that lead into Karila's bedchamber. Marta sat in a chair deftly stitching a tapestry on a needlepoint frame by the light of the fire. The Magus sprinkled a few grains of sleepdust onto his palm and gently blew them toward her; within a moment or two, the needle dropped from her hand and her head nodded sideways.

Linnaius crept toward the princess's swan bed. Karila stirred in her sleep. "Serve . . . the Serpent God . . ." she murmured.

Linnaius blinked in surprise. Was she dreaming? What did she know of Serpent Gods? He extended his hand toward her forehead—and then halted.

Eugene had expressly forbidden him to search her mind. Yet if his theory was correct, Karila was the key to the secrets her father so yearned to unlock.

His hand stole out again, fingertips resting lightly on her forehead. He closed his eyes, concentrating. He would not intrude too far; she would not even remember. . . .

Except there was not one mind here, but two! Two girls, one fair, one dark, staring at him, their faces blurring, merging, one into the other's, blue eyes fading to black, and black to blue.

This was too complicated for him to unravel. This needed the skills of a shaman, used to walking with spirits and lost souls.

He gazed down at Karila. She seemed quieter now, as if his touch had calmed her, charming the last vestiges of fever from her body. But this other soul residing within her, this dark girl who made her dream of Serpent Gods, must be slowly draining what little strength she had. And with her weak constitution, she needed all her energy to keep alive.

"Sleep well, little one." He gently stroked her golden hair. "I'll keep watch over you now."

The physician's news was encouraging: Karila's high fever had broken and she was sleeping peacefully. This had not prevented Eugene from going to check for himself before dealing with the affairs of the day. It was not that he did not trust Doctor Amandel, it was just that he needed the reassurance. Then he sat down at his desk to read his dispatches. The first was from Admiral Janssen.

The casualty list of those dead or missing in action at Vermeille Bay made depressing reading. Many were still unaccounted for. And as for Governor Armfeld . . .

"Let the Smarnans shoot him," Eugene muttered. "He's no use to New Rossiya now."

They had lost the flagship *Rogned,* the pride of his fleet, and four men-o'-war. Two had gone down in flames in Vermeille Bay and two more had sunk as they attempted to flee the assault. The rest were limping back to the nearest Tielen dockyards at Haeven, many in need of weeks of repairs.

The loss of the *Rogned* grieved him the most. He had supervised the designs himself; he had visited the dry dock in Haeven frequently during her construction. The most advanced ship of her kind, she had proved as vulnerable as the rest to this vicious attack from the air.

And now with Janssen's fleet out of commission, New Rossiya was unprotected on its southernmost shores.

He could not keep his eyes from straying to the map his cartographers had recently drawn of his new empire. Never before had it looked so clear: whoever held Smarna could control the Southern Ocean beyond Vermeille Bay, with its new trade routes—and protect the Straits from attack by sea. Smarna was still of vital importance. And Smarna still arrogantly proclaimed its independent status as a republic.

But he would win it back—by whatever means.

Kiukiu was hanging out washing behind Malusha's cottage, the wooden pegs clamped between her teeth. Her fingertips were healing and she felt stronger today, heartened by the warmth of the bright spring sunshine. There were even flowers in Malusha's kitchen garden as well as a dusting of pink and white blossoms on the apple trees.

Yesterday it had come again, that unsettling shimmer of daemon-blue, faint and very far away.

Malusha had felt it too.

"That cursed dragon-daemon is still at large," she said, shaking her head. "That's twice now we've both sensed it."

Kiukiu nodded. Had the Drakhaoul taken possession of a new host? Was such a thing possible? And then a cold wind gusted across the moors, making the wet clothes flap violently, spattering her with drops of water. Her arms were suddenly pitted with goose bumps. She gazed up into the sky, rubbing her chilly arms, to see if a rainstorm was on its way.

A small cloud flitted across the blue sky.

"The Magus!" Had he come to redeem his promise? Was she to see Gavril at last, after all these interminable weeks of waiting? She ran around to the front of the cottage, almost tripping over the hens, and gazed eagerly about.

"Kiukirilya." The voice came from behind her. She jumped. Kaspar Linnaius had appeared seemingly from nowhere.

"I wish you wouldn't do that!" She put one hand to her breast to try to calm the wild thudding of her heart. Only then did she think it was maybe not so wise to speak disrespectfully to such a venerable Magus.

"Is your grandmother in?"

"Where else would she be?" she said. "She doesn't leave the cottage these days." She went to lead him inside—and felt Linnaius's hand on her shoulder.

"I have news," he said.

"Oh?" She swallowed hard. News never meant anything good these days. Had her request been turned down?

"The Emperor has graciously agreed to grant you permission to visit Gavril Nagarian."

"Oh!" She let out a shriek of excitement. "Thank you, thank you, Magus!"

"You undertook a perilous journey to help his imperial highness. In recognition of that service, he has asked me to take you to Arnskammar." There was even the slightest glint of a smile in the Magus's pale eyes. "Just as soon as you have performed one more task."

"Another task?" Kiukiu was unprepared for this new condition. "Right now? I—I haven't finished hanging out the washing—" Her words died away under his stern gaze. "No. Of course the washing can wait. I'll just tell Grandma—"

"Tell me what, precisely?" Malusha appeared, arms tightly folded.

"I have the Emperor's permission to take your granddaughter to visit Gavril Nagarian."

"That's as may be, but you haven't got mine."

"Oh, Grandma, please—" burst out Kiukiu.

"And," said the Magus evenly, "I also have been granted permission to take you to young Stavyomir Arkhel in Azhgorod."

"I can take myself, thank you very much, I'm not so decrepit I can't drive my own pony cart over the moors."

Why must her grandmother always be so stubborn? Kiukiu gazed at her in frustration, wondering what would possibly make her change her mind.

"Then it would be a wasted journey," said the Magus, "for no one is granted admission to the household without a special permit from the Emperor."

"Please, Grandma," pleaded Kiukiu. "You know how much this

means to me. Let me go to Arnskammar—and then you can visit the baby."

Marsh ducks flapped overhead in a ragged "V," quacking rowdily.

"It would be about the right time to sing the Naming Song." Malusha seemed to be talking to herself, staring toward the hazy ridge of the Kharzhgyll mountains. "And if he's nearing six months in age . . ." Her gaze hardened, fixing on the Magus with stern intensity. "You can take her to Arnskammar, foolish girl that she is, but no good's going to come of it. You'll only upset yourself again, Kiukiu."

"I know," Kiukiu said defensively. Why did Grandma always have to spoil things?

"And you," Malusha stepped down and came close to the Magus, jabbing one finger at him, "you take good care of my granddaughter. If anything happens to her, I'll summon something up from the Ways Beyond that's beyond your worst nightmares."

"Grandma, please," murmured Kiukiu, horribly embarrassed. If Malusha kept on baiting the Magus in this childish way, she was certain he would just shrug his shoulders and leave.

"Go get your cloak, Kiukiu. It's cold in that sky craft of his."

Kiukiu sped indoors. Her cloak was made of pieces of worn blanket that she had stitched together. It was far from elegant, but it would keep her warm.

She heard a shiver of wings and Lady Iceflower alighted on the back of Malusha's chair, staring at her with suspicious golden eyes.

"You can't come with me, Lady Iceflower," Kiukiu said. "You have to go greet the new Arkhel lord. But watch out for his mother, Lady Lilias." She raised her voice so that it carried outside. "She's a nasty piece of work."

The owl let out a small, curious hoot and swiveled her head right around, watching Kiukiu intently as she put on her well-darned mittens.

"I'm ready." She picked up her gusly and went toward the door. Her stomach twisted with sudden apprehension. She was going to visit Gavril—and she must steel herself to see the changes that prison had wrought in him.

"Wish me luck, my lady. I'm going to need it."

CHAPTER 22

Gavril clawed his way out of the sea and crawled slowly up the sandy beach.

Each waterlogged breath was an effort. Water bubbled in his throat, streamed from his nose and mouth. His lungs were filled with it. He coughed and retched until his rib cage ached.

Some salty seawater came up, frothing onto the sand—and with it a foul black slime that seared his gullet. The taste, bitter as caulking tar, tainted his mouth and breath.

He stared down at what he had vomited up: a black oily puddle polluting the silver sand.

So it begins again.

He tried to raise himself but his head pounded with the sounds of the shore, the rush and fall of the waves against the sand, even the distant mew of gulls wheeling high overhead.

Must find shelter. Can't stay here . . .

He let himself drop back down onto the sand. The soft silvered grains grated against his cheek. He had no strength left. All that remained within him was this sensation, as if his innards had been scoured with burning coals.

"Water," he whispered. His lids drooped, seared by the brightness of the sun, and a burnished darkness that stank of flame and smoke enveloped him.

Raïsa Korneli reined her mare Luciole to a halt on the sands and shaded her eyes against the wine-gold dazzle of the setting sun. Lukan had given the order to separate so they could search the little coves and beaches that lay beyond the headland for Tielens, and she would do anything for Lukan.

They had rounded up a few stragglers in Vermeille—terrified survivors who had witnessed the annihilation of their fellow soldiers and had willingly surrendered. But there were more, she knew it—desperate men who must have watched their fleet abandon the attack and sail away, leaving them to fend for themselves.

She jumped down from Luciole's back and tied the reins to the branches of a stunted sea pine. Taking her pistol, she primed it and set off down the sandy track that wound down toward the beach.

The sky was still a brilliant blue, but the sea beneath was darkening as the sun sank, touching the farthest waters with gold. And the evenstar had already appeared, low in the western sky.

Such a day. At dawn they had woken to the crash of Tielen shells and grenades against the citadel walls. Death had seemed inevitable. She had seized the Smarnan standard from the hands of a dying student and had clambered up on the broken battlements to swing its tattered, bloodstained shreds defiantly at the Tielen soldiers massing the beaches. She had felt shrapnel and shards of splintered stone whistle past her head, powdering her hair with dust. Exhilarated, angry beyond reason, she had screamed her defiance at the Tielens.

And as she stood wielding the great standard, she had witnessed the unimaginable. The destruction of the Tielen armies on the sands far below.

A cool breath of wind, salt-tinged, stirred her hair. It felt good. Good to be alive. Good to smell and taste the freshness of the sea-stung air. The colors of the twilight seemed so much more intense because she had come so close to losing it all.

Bees were still busy in the dunes, droning around the honey-scented spikes of sea holly.

"Take care, Raïsa," Lukan had said, letting his hand rest on her shoulder. "These Tielens are dangerous." His dark eyes gazed into hers. "Call for help if you find any survivors." She hardly heard what he was saying. "Don't tackle them on your own."

Her imagination began to weave scenes of high drama in which she flung herself in front of him to save him from a Tielen bayonet, falling to lie dying in his arms, his warm tears dripping on her face as he whispered, "I always loved you, Raïsa, and now it is too late. . . ."

She moved swiftly on, scanning the empty sands. Seagulls strutted and preened near the tide's edge, digging with their sharp beaks in the wet sand for worms. She wanted to capture a Tielen for Lukan. What better proof of her loyalty to the cause—or her loyalty to him?

She knew these little coves and beaches from childhood. She knew every hiding place in the cliffs, every bramble-choked cranny from the games she had played with her brothers. ("Tomboy Raïsa," they had teased her, "you should have been born a boy!" And she had tossed her unruly hair and answered: as if she cared!)

And then she saw him. Not hiding behind a rock. Lying sprawled, as if drowned and washed up by the merciless tide like driftwood. It could be a trap. She crept closer, clutching the pistol tight.

No trap. This one looked way beyond help.

Cautiously she prodded him with the muzzle of the pistol.

"Hey! Wake up!"

There was no response, not even an involuntary twitch of muscle. She dropped to her knees beside him in the sand.

His waterlogged clothes were shredded to tatters. She could see terrible scars on his head, but they were not fresh wounds. And even though his clothes were stained by seawater, she could see no signs of Tielen colors. A sailor, maybe, young and good-looking . . . A deep sigh swelled in her breast. He was about the same age as her brother Iovan. Too young to drown.

She reached out her left hand, still holding the pistol in her right, and felt for a pulse at the side of his throat.

She detected a faint throb of life beneath her fingers.

Her drowned sailor gave a groan. She snatched her hand away as if scalded, sitting back on her heels and leveling the pistol at his head.

"I've got you covered, Tielen!"

He gave a sputtering cough and convulsed, spewing up a mess of seawater and slime onto the sand. She drew back, disgusted.

"Don't try any tricks." She held the pistol in both hands to keep it steady. Why were her hands trembling? She had faced the enemy on the broken battlements of the citadel. She had seen the naked aggression in the Tielens' eyes as they charged toward the barricades. This was just one man.

"Don't—shoot." The words came out on a rasping breath as he slumped back onto the sand, eyes shut. "Not—Tielen. From Smarna."

"Smarna?" she echoed, voice taut with suspicion. "Prove it."

His mouth twisted into the semblance of a wry smile. "Proof? My word. That's all—the sea has left me."

"So where do you come from? Identify yourself."

"Vermeille. I came home when I heard of the revolt." He spoke in fluent Smarnan, without a trace of a Tielen accent. And then the water bubbled in his throat again and he rolled over, retching exhaustedly.

Raïsa watched, still wary. He seemed in no fit state to attack her, but it could be a ruse to lure her into a sense of false security.

"Water . . ." The word was faint, as dry as if all moisture had been seared out of his body.

She hesitated, then backed away toward Luciole, who was standing patiently by the pine tree. A quick rummage through her saddlebag and she found her leather water bottle, half-full. She went back to the sailor. He lay still now. Kneeling beside him, she tugged the stopper from the water bottle with her teeth.

"No tricks," she said. "There's water here. Drink." She raised his scarred head, propping him against her knee. Awkwardly, she poured some of the tepid water into his mouth. Some slopped out down his chin, dripping onto her riding breeches. The water had been sharpened with a measure of Smarnan eau-de-vie to disguise the taste of old leather, a huntsman's trick her brothers had taught her.

The sailor's eyes suddenly opened again and he gazed directly up at her. She blinked, astonished to see how brilliantly, radiantly blue they were.

Trick of the twilight, she told herself, trying to quell the sudden feeling of unease that shivered through her.

"You're a—woman."

She clapped a hand to her shirt. Had it gaped open, revealing her secret? She had bound her breasts tight and cut her auburn hair short to fight beside her brothers on the barricades. How had he known?

"You saved me. What is your name?"

"Raïsa." What was she doing, telling him her name? Yet there was something about him that compelled her to answer.

"Raïsa?" His voice was still hardly more than a dry whisper. He raised one hand to touch her cheek and she felt a shiver of heat run through her.

"Raïsa!" Someone shouted her name, shattering the strange intensity of the moment. She looked up guiltily and saw horsemen with flaming torches riding onto the beach, her brother Iovan at their head.

"Here, Iovan!" she called back, waving.

They urged their horses across the sands until they formed a semicircle around Raïsa and the sailor.

"What's this the tide's washed up?" Iovan dismounted, pistol in hand. "More wreckage from the Tielen fleet?" He slowly lowered the pistol until it was pointing directly between the sailor's eyes.

"No!" she cried, leaping up. "He's Smarnan!"

"Is that what he told you?" A grim smile twisted Iovan's broad mouth. She heard the click as he primed the pistol.

"Iovan!" She grabbed hold of his arm. There was a flash and a deafening crack as the shot went wide, skimming low over the shore toward the sea. The horses started, rearing in panic. One of Iovan's men swore.

"For God's sake, Raïsa." Iovan shook her off with a violence that threw her tumbling onto the sand. "I could've killed you!"

"Since when do we shoot strangers on sight?" She struggled back to her feet. "What's got into you, Iovan? At least give the man a chance to speak for himself. Look at him. He's no threat. He's half-drowned!"

He gripped hold of her by one shoulder, fingers gnawing into her flesh. "We're at war, little sister, or had you forgotten?" In the torchlight she saw the desperation and exhaustion in his eyes.

"How could I forget?" She forced the anger from her voice. And then she asked the question she had ridden out from Vermeille to escape. "Miran? Is he—"

"Still holding on by a thread. So the doctors say . . ." He let go of her.

It was the shooting of Miran, the youngest of the three Korneli children, that had triggered the revolt in the citadel. Miran, her favorite brother—bookish and gentle, more interested in philosophy and poetry than in warfare—had been the first casualty of the siege.

"Iovan!" shouted one of the men. "Do we continue the search?"

Iovan passed one hand over his dirt-smeared face as if trying to collect his thoughts.

"No. It's too dark now. Let's take the prisoner back to the citadel. We'll interrogate him there."

*   *   *

"Water . . ." Gavril heard a voice pleading from the sulphurous clouds of his fevered dreams. After a while he came to realize that the croaking words were issuing from his own throat. He opened eyelids as stiff as old parchment and gazed blearily about him.

It must be near dawn, he reckoned, as a pale shaft of jagged light fell on him through a broken-paned window.

"Water . . ." His lips could barely frame the word. His tongue, leather-dry, clacked against his palate. His mouth seemed filled with cinders. It was as if all the moisture in his body had been seared away, leaving him a desiccated shell.

He had forgotten the terrible toll the attack would take on his body. Now he knew again the reality of the thirst that could never be quenched by water alone.

All around him lay sprawled figures. Sleeping, he hoped, not dead. One man near him gave a grunting snore and turned over on his side. Weapons lay piled in corners. The smell of sweaty feet and unwashed bodies hung stale in the air. This chamber was being used as an improvised barracks. And then he saw it. An earthernware water pitcher. So close, all he had to do was reach out—

Metal bracelets bit into his wrists, arresting his efforts with a jerk. He was shackled, hand and foot. He could not even crawl toward the prize he craved.

"Water . . ." He tried again. Even to enunciate that single word cost him enormous effort. If he didn't get water soon, he would die.

A door clanged open.

"Dawn muster! Wake up!" a voice bellowed. "On your feet!"

The sprawled figures slowly began to move. Groaning and yawning, men stretched stiff limbs, scratched themselves, sat up.

"Out in the courtyard! Quick!"

They shuffled around Gavril, clumsy with sleep. No one seemed to care he was there.

"Another suspect! Chain him up!"

Gavril recognized the snarling voice of Iovan, the rebel who had tried to shoot him the night before.

A man was flung onto the floor close by; two of the militia grabbed him by his arms and clamped shackles onto his wrists and ankles.

"Claims he's from Muscobar. Claims he's come to join the rebellion." Iovan aimed a vicious kick at the man's back; the prisoner jerked but did not cry out.

These are my countrymen . . . and they are behaving no better than the Tielen invaders. What's happened to us? Gavril closed his eyes, sickened at what he had seen, sickened by his own weakness.

"Stop, Iovan! That's enough."

It was the girl, Raïsa, who had found him last night on the beach. She would help him. If only he could muster the strength to call to her.

"Raïsa. Water . . ."

The next moment, someone thrust a tin cup of water into his hands.

"Here."

He drank, water streaming down his chin, soaking into his tattered shirt. He didn't care. Yet the more water he gulped down, the more his body craved. "More." This burning thirst seemed unquenchable. She refilled his cup.

"The citadel is crawling with Eugene's spies," Iovan was saying loudly. "Put them all up against the wall and shoot them. That's the only form of negotiation Eugene understands."

"Minister Vashteli is ready to interrogate the prisoners," announced one of the militia.

"The one who says he's Smarnan first." Iovan came and stood over Gavril. "Unshackle him."

The militiaman knelt to unlock the shackles around Gavril's wrists, leaving his ankles chained together.

"You. On your feet."

Still dripping, Gavril got unsteadily to his feet.

"Look at him! He's too weak to plead his case," Raïsa hissed to Iovan.

Iovan shrugged.

"At least give him something to restore his strength."

"And then you'll stop nagging me?" Iovan pulled a metal flask from inside his jacket. "Here. Smarnan brandy."

Gavril took a quick swig from the flask and winced as the brandy scorched his parched throat. His senses sharpened a little. "My name," he said slowly, "is Gavril Andar. Rafael Lukan will vouch for me." There was no point complicating matters further by giving his Azhkendi name and title.

"Andar?" Raïsa echoed. "But Gavril Andar disappeared last year."

"I told you not to trust him," Iovan muttered.

"Lukan's with the Minister now." Raïsa turned to her brother. "Let Lukan decide the matter, Iovan."

"Bring him to the council chamber, then." Iovan kicked out at the water pitcher, sending it rolling into a corner.

The council chamber, high in the Old Citadel, had been hit in the bombardment. Tarpaulins had been draped to cover a gaping hole in the roof, and piles of debris, tile shards, shattered beams, and plaster had been swept to the side of the chamber.

A tall man and a woman were talking together in low voices; they turned as, ankle-chains chinking, Gavril shuffled into the chamber.

"Lukan!" whispered Gavril, unable to restrain his emotion at the sight of a familiar face after so long in prison. "Lukan, it's me."

Lukan stared at him, a frown of puzzlement creasing his face. "Gavril?" he said. He came closer. "*Gavril?*" Then he gave a shout that echoed around the broken rafters and hurried up to Gavril, flinging his arms about him and hugging him. "Welcome home!" He held him at arm's length. "But—dear God, what have they done to you?" Gavril saw concern in Lukan's dark eyes. "I hardly recognized you at first, with your head shaved—"

This was in no way the happy homecoming he had dreamed of so often in the bitter cold of Azhkendir. He was too aware of Iovan standing close by, stroking the barrel of his pistol.

"How shall we tell your mother?" Lukan was saying. "We don't want it to come as too much of a shock—"

"My mother?"

"Yes, she's up at the villa right now."

Elysia was here, in Smarna? A red haze swirled before Gavril's eyes. He swayed on his feet. Pride alone had kept him standing to face his captors, and he was not sure how long he could sustain the effort.

Lukan caught hold of him and steadied him, both hands resting on his shoulders.

"So who is this young man, Lukan?" asked the woman, coming forward.

"You know his mother well, Minister. This is Elysia Andar's son, Gavril."

"Then why is he chained like a prisoner?"

"Iovan?" Lukan turned to Iovan Korneli, smiling. "Would you like to explain to Minister Vashteli why Gavril is in chains?"

"Because," Iovan said, scowling, "we were ordered to round up anyone found on the beaches. And we found him—his clothes wringing wet—as if he'd just swam ashore from one of the sinking ships."

"I see." Minister Vashteli gazed searchingly at Gavril. "Gavril Andar, can you explain why you were found in such suspicious circumstances?"

It was time for the truth. "I came to help you."

One of the minister's elegantly plucked brows quirked in a look of surprise. "To help us?"

"You?" burst out Iovan, his voice hot with scorn.

"I have a . . . weapon," Gavril said, choosing his words with care. "A lethal weapon. Yesterday I unleashed it on the Tielens in the bay. But in using it, I almost drowned. If Raïsa had not found me . . ."

"Tell us about this weapon," said Minister Vashteli, her eyes fixed on his. "Is it some kind of explosive device? Those who watched from the citadel were half-blinded by the brightness."

"And what of this dark-winged creature?" said Iovan. "Many witnesses insist they saw a winged creature sweep across the bay just before the attack on the Tielen fleet. How do you explain that?"

Gavril closed his eyes a moment. He was still so depleted by the effects of Baltzar's clumsy surgery that he feared he might blab too much and give himself away. Even the use of the word "weapon" now seemed ill-judged; Iovan, for one, would not let the matter rest.

"Why did you not confer with us first?" said Minister Vashteli. "We could have stood together as allies against the Tielens."

"And from where exactly did you launch this weapon?" broke in Iovan. "From the sea or the land? Is it some kind of fire-rocket?"

Gavril was losing patience with Iovan's constant goading. "Isn't it enough that I came to your aid? Does it matter where I launched the attack? The Tielens are gone!"

Minister Vashteli exchanged a long look with Lukan. Then she nodded. "You are free to go home, Gavril Andar. Please send my regards to your mother; she has supported us wholeheartedly throughout this ordeal."

"You'd better call in at my house first," Lukan said, flashing Gavril a conspiratorial smile. "For a bath and a change of clothes."

Free to go home. Those four simple words meant so much. Not home to an empty villa, but home to his mother, his paints, and his own bed. And was it too much to hope that Kiukiu might have accompanied Elysia to Smarna and was waiting for him even now?

As he turned to follow Lukan from the council chamber, the minister came up to him, touching him lightly on the shoulder. "And thank you. On behalf of us all. You saved us."

"This time, maybe," Gavril said, managing a wry smile.

Elysia looked down in puzzlement at the note that had just been delivered into her hands. It read:

> I've found him and he will be with you very soon. But this is to warn you, dear Elysia, to be prepared for what you will see. He has suffered much at the hands of his captors. Try not to be too upset, for his sake.
>
> Your loving friend, R.L.

Elysia clutched the letter tightly.

"Thank you, dear friend, for the warning," she whispered. Then she hurried back inside the house, calling out, "Palmyre! Gavril's coming!"

Suddenly she was all in a tizzy, ideas skittering through her head like windblown petals. What should she do first? Check that there was clean, lavender-scented linen on his bed and that the room was well-aired, with garden flowers spilling from a bowl on the windowsill? Or should she lay out some clothes for him—for all his clothes were still here, freshly laundered and pressed, waiting, against all hope, for his return.

"Is the kettle on? He may want tea." She almost collided with Palmyre in the hall; she seemed to be on a similar route. "Or maybe he may just want to be alone for a while, to rest—"

"Elysia," Palmyre said, patting her hand reassuringly, "it will be all right."

"And I won't weep when I see him; I mustn't weep. It won't do any good to either of us if I do—" Elysia broke off, hearing the sound of hooves and carriage wheels on the gravel drive. She clutched at Palmyre's hand. "Is that—?"

Palmyre seemed speechless with excitement.

"Look at us," Elysia said, breaking into laughter. "A couple of silly women, too flustered to go to the door to greet him! What will he think?" And she ran to fling open the front door, hurrying out into the drive, just as the door of the barouche opened and Gavril stepped down.

She stared a moment, shocked to see his shaven head, his gaunt face, and sunken eyes. Then, joy and relief overwhelmed all other feelings and she rushed to embrace him. But although he hugged her back, she could sense a change in him, a wariness, and something else that she could not yet define—something darker, more ominous.

What have they done to you in that terrible prison, child? her heart cried out. But all she did was wind her arm around him and lead him toward the open door where Palmyre stood, so overcome with emotion that she could only nod speechlessly and smile.

As they reached the doorway, Elysia glanced back over her shoulder to see Lukan waiting, watching from inside the barouche.

Thank you. Her lips framed the words as she inclined her head gratefully to him. *Thank you, dear friend.*

Footsteps on the landing. Keys jangling in the lock of his cell. Skar's lean face in the lanternlight, eyes chill in their lack of expression, as he bent over him—

Gavril woke with a start. He was breathing fast, pulse racing, terrified that Skar had come to take him back to Director Baltzar and his razor-sharp scalpels. And then he heard it. The sound of the sea, but not the crash of the storm tides raging against the rocks below Arnskammar. This was the gentle, reassuring wash of summer tides lapping against the pale sands of Vermeille Bay. The sound that had lulled him to sleep in childhood and whispered through his dreams.

He lay back, staring at the half-open window, the gauze curtains drifting a little with the night breeze off the bay. The faint scent of jasmine wafted in from the terrace below.

No, he was not dreaming. He was here in his own bed, in the Villa Andara. After months of enduring the deprivations of Baltzar's asylum, he was no longer a number to be maltreated and experimented upon. He was Gavril again.

He let his fingers run over the clean linen of the sheets. Crisp, clean sheets, scented with lavender from the villa gardens. He had forgotten how good it was to enjoy this simple comfort.

At peace, he drifted off to sleep, and did not wake again until morning.

Elysia tapped on Gavril's bedroom door and went in, carrying a cup of chamomile tea, a plate with fresh-baked rolls, and Palmyre's apricot and almond conserve. The windows were wide-open and the curtains billowed and flapped in the morning breeze. Her son stood on the balcony, gazing out across the blue bay.

"Breakfast, Gavril," she called.

He looked back over his shoulder. "Thank you."

She set down the cup and plate and went out to join him. For a while they stood side by side in silence. Then he said, still gazing out to sea, "Don't be surprised if there are strands of blue in my hair when it regrows."

She nodded. So it was true.

"I guessed as much." She wanted to ask him so many questions: What really happened to you? Who inflicted these terrible injuries? Yet she knew she must let him tell her in his own time, in his own way.

"If it hadn't come back to me when it did, I would have died." His voice was distant, his eyes still rested on the misty horizon. "Its first act of compassion. Who would have thought it possible?"

"It rescued you?"

He turned to face her. The sight of his scarred head still made her stomach lurch, but she must not let him see her distress, for fear it might break his courage.

"I still don't know how it knew. But it came back and healed me. Now I begin to wonder. Are we destined to be one until I die?"

She saw the shadow-glitter in his eyes, as she had seen it in Volkh's eyes too. And she felt bleak despair chill her heart. He had come back to her. But he was no longer her son; he was Drakhaoul. And she, better than anyone, knew that doomed his chances for any hope of true happiness.

Then, smitten with guilt at such thoughts, she reached out and folded her arms around her daemon-possessed son, hugging him tight.

"Drink your tea before it goes cold," she whispered.

CHAPTER 23

Kiukiu rubbed her eyes. She was standing beside the Magus, high up on the windswept top of a steep, rocky hill. Far below, a broad green river wound through the center of a great city: a city full of spires and towers and the rising smoke from innumerable chimneys. She had never seen so many houses crammed together before—or so many ships crowding the river.

"Where are we?" she asked in amazement.

"That is Tielborg, capital city of Tielen," said Linnaius.

"But why have you brought me here?" She was still sleepy, her mind not yet fully awake.

"Look behind you."

She turned and saw a ruin dominating the crown of the hill. A great hall of ancient stone, its broken walls towered above them, guarded by weatherworn statues of tall warriors, helmed for battle. The Magus beckoned her toward it. The sun was sinking westward, gilding the ancient stones with a rich, warm light. But as she came closer, she saw only the lengthening shadows cast by the giant warriors.

Gazing up as they passed underneath the arched gateway, she noticed that the worn stone had once been painted, and that little traces of blue and ochre still remained. Now she saw the stern-faced warriors were winged, each wing-feather carved with exquisite artistry.

"Heavenly Guardians?" she murmured. And then she found herself in a courtyard, where another unexpected sight awaited. Tielen soldiers lounged around, their horses cropping the grass growing up between the cracked flagstones. On seeing the Magus, the soldiers straightened up and a young officer came to meet them, saluting with alacrity.

"Lieutenant Vassian at your service, Magus. His imperial highness awaits you in the inner court. I am under orders to conduct you to him straightaway."

"Where *are* we?" whispered Kiukiu as the lieutenant led them farther into the ruin. The daylight was dimming and she felt a sudden chill envelop her. "It feels like a tomb." She hugged her gusly tightly to her, as if it could ward off evil spirits.

Lieutenant Vassian brought them into a vaulted inner chamber as high as the nave of the monastery church in Kerjhenezh. Their footsteps echoed hollowly in the gloom. Torches had been lit and placed in links around the walls, and by their flickering light she caught glimpses of worn carvings and warlike friezes that depicted battles from long ago. Armed horsemen trampled the broken bodies of their enemies underfoot, hacking and stabbing in a frenzy of slaughter. Kiukiu averted her eyes. The place reeked of spilled blood and carnage.

"Magus Linnaius is here," announced the lieutenant, standing to attention so stiffly Kiukiu feared the shining buttons on his uniform would pop off.

A tall, broad-shouldered man walked toward them out of the shadows. The instant she glimpsed his burned face, she knew him.

"P-Prince Eugene?" she stammered.

"Emperor Eugene," prompted Linnaius, "and you must not speak unless spoken to. When you reply, you must call the Emperor 'your imperial highness.'"

So you're the one who's caused us so much heartache. She fumbled a curtsy. *You're the one who took Lord Gavril from us and made the* druzhina *your slaves.* Yet when she looked into his eyes, she could not help but feel sorry for him. His features, once handsome, had been ruined by the extensive scarring where he had been seared by Drakhaon's Fire. And she glimpsed what he strove to hide from others, the shadow of the constant pain, darkening his clear, incisive gaze.

"So you're Kiukirilya, the Spirit Singer," the Emperor said.

Suddenly she realized she was standing before the Emperor of all New Rossiya with her hair mussed, wearing her old, creased washday dress. Embarrassment overwhelmed her. What must he think?

"I'd like you to help me find the answer to a question." He was still speaking to her and she was now in such a muddle she could hardly hear the words. Should she reply? What was it she was supposed to call him, 'your high imperialness?' No, no, that couldn't be right. . . .

"Well, Kiukirilya?" The Magus was prompting her again. "Can you do it?"

"Do what?" she said helplessly. She had spent her life in service, always doing as she was bidden and being beaten if she made a mistake. She was not yet used to being asked.

"Summon the spirit of the Emperor Artamon, to answer his highness's question."

She stared at the Magus, dumbstruck.

"We are standing in his mausoleum now. His sarcophagus lies in the chamber below."

Kiukiu felt her skin crawl. Had they any idea of the risks of such a venture? This was not just any spirit; it was powerful and ancient.

"Remember our arrangement," Linnaius said quietly. She hated him in that moment for reminding her. They held Gavril, and they knew she would do anything to see him again.

"Don't keep his imperial highness waiting," Linnaius whispered.

Had they no idea of the careful preparation required for such a summoning? Did they expect her just to wave her hands and conjure a spirit out of the air?

"I'll need something that belonged to the Emperor. A lock of hair, or nail parings would work even better."

Eugene glanced at the Magus. "What do we have, Linnaius?"

"Let's go down into the burial chamber."

Lieutenant Vassian clicked his fingers and two of the guardsmen took the torches from the wall to light their way.

The Emperor set off at a brisk pace, but Kiukiu hung back, reluctant to descend into the subterranean darkness of the burial chamber. Back home with Malusha, her spirit-summonings had been simple affairs: Piotr from the village inn wanting to ask his grandmother her secret ingredient when brewing *kvass,* or poor Yelena needing to say a second farewell to her littlest daughter, dead at only five years from the winter sickness. They had been affecting ceremonies, with many tears shed, but they were healing tears, and the relatives had gone away at peace with themselves afterward. And the spirits were gentle and benevolent, though more than a little confused at finding themselves in a cottage filled with roosting snow owls.

As she crept down the dusty stone stairs, she felt the air get colder and mustier. It smelled old, stale, and unwholesome.

In the center of the chamber stood a stone plinth; on the plinth was a massive stone sarcophagus, sculpted to represent the Emperor's body lying in state. At his feet lay curled a hound. Once, like the warrior guardians outside, the likeness had been covered in bright paint and gold leaf. Now only the faintest traces remained, outlining a stern carved face with long, curling stone locks and beard.

Kiukiu looked on the rigid face and shivered, feeling again that dark dread.

"Open the tomb," said Emperor Eugene.

The guardsmen took a crowbar and began to lever the heavy stone lid off the base. The yellow torchflames flickered in a sudden draft. One guardsman paused, glancing around uneasily.

Is there something else in here? A sentinel, set here by Artamon's magi to guard his body?

Kiukiu took out her gusly and began to tune it. The flames flickered again and almost went out. One of the guardsmen swore under his breath.

"Linnaius, we haven't come here to listen to a recital of folk music," she heard the Emperor say impatiently. "Are you sure this is the right girl?"

The guardsmen were grunting and sweating with their efforts. Then suddenly the sarcophagus lid slid open.

The torches went out as if someone had doused them with water. Kiukiu heard the guardsmen fumbling with tinders and cursing in the dark. She struck a first flurry of notes and the echoing sound of the gusly strings filled the burial chamber.

She could sense the sentinel now, close at hand. She struck another flurry of notes to force it to reveal itself.

She finally saw it, limned in pale ghoulfire, crouched at the foot of the sarcophagus like the faithful hound ready to spring. Malusha had told her of tomb sentinels, but this was the first she had ever seen. And now it knew she could see it, for it turned its face toward her, snarling.

"There you are!" she breathed. She had trapped it just in time. And she knew now exactly what it was. A bodyguard, slain in the Emperor's tomb to guard his master's body. His bones must lie somewhere in this vault: unburied, unmourned. The trapped spirit had forgotten all but its eternal mission: to protect the tomb. But the snarling skull of a face, the clutching, clawing fingers, still held the power to instill paralyzing fear—and maybe much worse.

Her fingers were shaking as she began to play the Sending Song, so much so that she missed a note, marring the perfection of the ancient ritual.

The sentinel snatched its chance. Freed from the gusly's hold, it let out a shriek and sprang straight toward the Emperor, hooked nails clawing, jaws opened wide to breathe a pestilential miasma in his face.

"Stop!" Kiukiu struck the holding chord again, with as much force as she could muster.

The sentinel froze in midleap.

This time she knew the others could see it. The Emperor stood his ground, staring with extraordinary sangfroid at the decayed ghoul-face so close to his own.

Her fingers found the deep, slow notes of the Sending Song and the taut form slowly relaxed.

"Go," she whispered. "Your task is done. You are free."

The sentinel's pale form shimmered, then swiftly began to fade until, like wisping candlesmoke, it drifted away.

Linnaius clicked his fingers and a little flame blossomed like a golden rose in the darkness. By its light, Kiukiu saw the guardsmen—white-faced and evidently shaken by what they had glimpsed.

"Man the entrance to the chamber," the Emperor ordered. "No one is to disturb us. Understood?"

They seemed only too glad to be given the excuse to leave, almost tripping over each other in their haste to reach the stairway.

"Now, Kiukirilya," the Emperor said, wiping his brow with a handkerchief. "Let's get this over with." He behaved so calmly, but now she could see he was as rattled as his men. And, in truth, if she dared to admit it to herself, she was too. But this had to be done.

She forced herself to approach the dais and climbed up beside the gaping stone tomb. She peered inside, half-fearing that a second sentinel-ghoul would come shrieking out and breathe its mephitic grave-stench in her face.

In the uncertain mage-light, she saw a mummified corpse, partially fallen to dust, the withered skin like parchment, with the bones protruding through. The grave clothes, once fine linens embroidered with purple and gold thread, had all but rotted away. She could smell a faint odor of old tomb-spices, bitter salts, and resins. And—oh horror—there was what she had foolishly asked for, the last long grey strands of dry hair clinging to the skull.

Closing her eyes and wincing with revulsion, she reached in and with shaking fingers pulled out a lock of the dead Emperor's hair.

"Forgive me," she said. Grave robbery was not her usual practice. Already she could hear Malusha scolding her for breaking the ages-old code of the Guslyars. She sat down at the foot of the sarcophagus, her gusly across her knees. She was trembling. She prayed the fragile strands of hair would not crumble to dust before she could call their owner back to the vault.

Just this one summoning, she told herself, and then they will be satisfied.

"You must not look into the spirit's eyes," she said, staring directly at the Emperor. "Whatever the spirit may say, no matter how persuasive it may be, never look into its eyes."

"Why?" asked the Emperor bluntly.

Kiukiu answered, equally bluntly, "Spirits cannot resist the desire to become flesh again. It will try to possess you."

"How could we prevent such a thing, were it to try?" asked the Magus.

"You must burn the hair. The spirit will be forced to return to the Ways Beyond."

"I doubt such a precaution will be necessary," said Eugene. He sounded so confident. Had he no idea of the seductive power of summoned spirits? Or the weakness of mere mortals in the face of such persuasions?

She placed the lock of hair before her on the dusty flagstones and sat back to begin the Summoning Song.

*   *   *

Kiukiu closed her eyes as she played the long, slow notes, sending her consciousness far out from the burial vault into the burnished gold of the sunset. As she played, she made herself repeat aloud the names of the note patterns, a repetitive litany:

"Twilight. Starlight. Midnight. Memory."

Each resonant pitch carried her farther onward, drifting from the pale light of dusk toward the starless darkness . . . and beyond.

And then she saw him. Tall, broad-shouldered as Eugene himself, he was gliding toward her through the eternal dusk as though pulled by an irresistible force. It had to be Artamon.

"Come with me, Lord Artamon," she said.

"Memory. Midnight. Starlight . . ." She must keep playing, each note in its right place or the pattern binding the spirit would fail and it would break free.

She opened her eyes. Mist was rising from the ground of the vault.

A man appeared, half-hidden in the fog—a tall, hawk-nosed man with a thick mane of oak-brown hair. She caught a glimpse of dark, troubled eyes staring at her, but hastily averted her gaze.

"Necromancy," muttered Emperor Eugene. "Or some outrageous piece of fairground trickery. Whichever, it's damnably convincing."

"Why have you summoned me? You cannot hold me long against my will, Guslyar."

"Forgive me," Kiukiu whispered again. She could feel the strength of the spirit struggling to be free. She must hold it bound in the chains of her Summoning Song and not let it loose. But it would take all her strength and skill to do it.

"Speak to it, highness," urged Linnaius.

Eugene squared his shoulders. He addressed the apparition.

"Are you Artamon the Great?"

"That was my name when I was alive."

"You had a son, Prince Volkhar. He gave you a ruby."

"That ruby was cursed." Artamon's deep voice reverberated through the vault, heavy with grief and sorrow. *"It was a daemon-stone. It brought strife and ruin to my empire. It was used to unleash terrible daemons into the world, daemon-warriors that possessed my beloved sons and turned them against one another."*

"A daemon-stone?" repeated Eugene.

"It contained powers, powers strong enough to open a gate between the worlds. When I held the gem in my hands, I could feel the

power burning in its bloodred heart. It was the most beautiful jewel I had ever possessed." Artamon's strong voice began to falter. *"But I vowed that it should never be used to cause such devastation again. And so I had my jewelers divide it. Three craftsmen died, burned by its fire, until my mages laid such strong wards upon it that the division was achieved."*

"So you—not your sons—ordered the stone to be divided?"

"My sons?" Artamon's voice echoed. *"They were no longer my sons. They looked like daemon-lords; they fought like daemon-lords. In their madness, they were too powerful for me to control. Only Serzhei of Azhkendir had the courage to confront them. And he died, battling my youngest boy. So Volkhar was lost to me forever."*

Kiukiu was concentrating hard on keeping Artamon bound by the droning notes of the Summoning Song, within the drifting mists where the world and that of the Ways Beyond mingled. She glanced up and saw Eugene move closer to the tomb and the tall spirit. Had he forgotten her warning?

"But how did it happen? How were your sons—all your sons—possessed by daemons?"

She could tell from the urgency of Eugene's voice that he burned to know the answer.

"And who are you that you dare ask me, Emperor of all Rossiya, such a question?"

Eugene smiled. "I am Eugene, Emperor of New Rossiya."

Artamon fell silent. His spirit-form wavered. The temperature was dropping fast and Kiukiu's fingertips ached with cold.

"We're losing him, Kiukirilya." Linnaius's voice muttered warningly.

"They took the ruby from me. Their intent was to unlock the ancient gateway to the realm of daemons and send the spirit that possessed Volkhar back. But the temptation to seek power of their own was too strong, and when the gate was opened, they too were possessed."

"And where is this gateway?" Eugene's voice trembled now with excitement.

"Far from here, on an island sacred to the Serpent God, Nagar. My boy, my Volkhar, forswore his faith in the One God and became one of the priests of Nagar. Such was the strength of his new faith that he even took the Serpent God's name, calling himself Nagarian."

Nagarian? Kiukiu forced herself to keep playing, though her arms and back were stiff from holding the heavy gusly. Did that mean Lord Gavril was descended from the Great Artamon?

"Come closer, Eugene. There are other secrets still I could impart. But they are not for the ears of common servants. Let me whisper them to you, alone."

The chill in the tomb had begun to numb Kiukiu's mind as well as her fingers. She heard the spirit's seductive offer but did not at once realize what it intended. She looked up and saw Eugene walking into the swirling mists, directly toward Artamon. She saw the spirit lean forward, arms opening as though to embrace him.

And she had warned him!

"No!" she cried, breaking off in midpattern. The broken notes hung as if frozen on the cold air, jagged as icicles.

The spirit froze too, arms raised to draw Eugene close.

"Don't look into his eyes!"

Artamon turned toward her. Cold fire blazed from his eyes, a fury of rage and blatant desire. She dug her heels into the floor, determined not to give way.

"He is mine. I shall be Emperor again. I shall take back my empire."

She faced the spirit, eyes still downcast, avoiding the silver fire of his gaze.

"Your time in this world is past, Lord Artamon. Let him go. I command you—*let him go!*"

"You dare to cross me, Guslyar? Look in my eyes, if you dare. You are not strong enough to withstand my will."

"Magus!" Kiukiu cried out, forcing all her strength into her voice. "Burn the hair!"

Linnaius snatched up the ancient lock of hair. The spirit turned toward him, its face twisted with hatred. The Magus's little golden flame bloomed in the darkness, flaring blue as the hair sizzled to ashes and a foul smell of burning tainted the vault.

The spirit let out a rasping shriek that seared Kiukiu's ears. It wavered to and fro, as though the Magus's flame was fast consuming its energy. It dwindled, shrinking until—with one last gasping shudder—it faded into the tomb. The golden mage-light went out and there was only darkness.

The Magus relit the torches.

Eugene still stood as though rooted to the ground. Kiukiu's heart was pounding as she set down the gusly.

"Is—is he—"

And then the Emperor let out a shout of triumph.

"Extraordinary!" He punched the air with his fist. "Quite extraordinary."

So he was unharmed. Kiukiu slithered slowly down the side of the tomb, huddling at the foot of the sarcophagus. She was shivering with relief, her strength utterly spent.

"Lieutenant Vassian. In here," called the Emperor.

Guardsmen came down the stairs into the vault. She heard the Emperor instructing them to replace the stone lid on the sarcophagus. She was so weary she could not move.

"Thank you, Kiukirilya."

She looked up dazedly and saw the Emperor standing over her, his eyes bright with exhilaration.

"Lieutenant Vassian, have you a flask of aquavit?"

"Here."

The lieutenant knelt beside her and put a small silver flask into her hands. Slowly she raised it to her lips and took a mouthful, coughing as the strong spirits stung the back of her throat.

"Let the vault be sealed. I shall send antiquaries from the university to restore the tomb." Eugene's voice seemed to be coming from farther and farther off. "Until then, let no one else disturb the first Emperor's rest."

Had they forgotten her? Did they mean to seal her in the vault as well? She tried to get to her feet to follow, but sank back, exhausted.

Don't leave me here in the dark with the dead.

"Come, miss. It's time to go."

Kiukiu felt a strong arm around her shoulders, raising her to her feet. She looked up into the face of Lieutenant Vassian. It was a good-hearted face, she thought, an honest face.

"My gusly," she said. She bent to pick it up. It seemed to weigh as much as an anvil.

"Let me carry that for you," he said.

She placed it in his arms and followed him, one dragging step after another, out of the unwholesome air of the burial vault, up toward the fresh night air and the light of the spring stars.

*　　*　　*

"You will awake now."

Kiukiu opened her eyes. She had been so deeply asleep that she did not know where she was for a moment. But when she saw Kaspar Linnaius, when she felt the swift onrushing throb of the sky craft, she remembered.

"I didn't mean to fall asleep—"

"We are approaching Arnskammar."

So they were close. She was choked with excitement. She would see Lord Gavril at last, after all these long months apart. Only now did she begin to feel apprehensive. He would be changed; that was for certain. No one could live a prisoner's life and not be. But she was strong; she was prepared. She loved him. Surely love would be enough to see them through the difficulties that lay ahead?

On the distant horizon she saw high cliffs, craggy and sharp. Rocks protruded out of the heaving sea. The waters had turned a dark, metallic color except where they foamed white as they smashed against the iron-brown stone of the cliffs.

"The prison? Where is the prison?" She gazed out, shading her eyes.

They were scudding faster now, rainclouds close behind them.

"There." Linnaius pointed toward the farthest cliff. He brought them low over the water so that the prison's looming towers, rising up out of the cliff itself, were silhouetted against the pale, rain-filled sky.

She let out a little cry. The tower on the farthest, most precipitate edge of the cliffs was half-blown away, a jagged shell surrounded by shattered debris.

"What is it?"

"Look!" She stabbed her finger at the prison. "What's happened here? That tower is in ruins!"

"Let's take a closer look." Linnaius guided the craft closer, speeding past the formidable walls of the prison.

She was kneeling up now, frowning intently at the brown, sea-stained walls towering above them. Spray fountained into the air from the wild waves below. Cormorants, black-winged and predatory, hunched on the lower rocks, oblivious of the sea's assault on their perch.

"Has the prison been attacked?" Her voice was hardly audible above the roar of the waves. "Has there been a battle?"

Linnaius brought the craft about, scanning the ground below for a suitable landing place. "I have a bad feeling about this."

"What do you mean?"

But the Magus did not answer. All his attention was focused on landing the sky craft.

"This is most—ahem—awkward." The director of the prison seemed embarrassed by their arrival. "I sent a full report to the Emperor about the unfortunate affair involving Twenty-One."

"Twenty-One?" Kiukiu echoed angrily. "Do you mean Lord Gavril? Doesn't he have a name anymore?"

"I've been abroad, Director Baltzar," Linnaius said. "It may be that your communication has not been forwarded to me."

"Then"—the director kept rubbing his palms together nervously—"I'm afraid your journey has been a wasted one. There was a storm, you see, and the tower in which Twenty-One was confined was struck by lightning. We searched the rubble—but—"

"Oh no," Kiukiu said softly. "It can't be."

"The top of the tower disintegrated. Part fell into the sea below, the rest landed in the courtyard. It was completely destroyed."

Kiukiu stared at him. She had heard the words but was not sure she understood them. "Completely destroyed?"

"No trace has been found of a body."

Struck by lightning? Kiukiu could not even bear to think of it. And yet her mind began to produce images, horrible images of raging fire and crumbling stone.

"You're saying the prisoner is dead?" Linnaius persisted.

Director Baltzar gave a little, helpless shrug of the shoulders. "No one could have survived a fall from such a height into the sea. The rocks . . ."

Linnaius turned to Kiukiu. "I'm sorry," he said. "I had not anticipated such an outcome to our journey. Shall we go?"

All she could see was the Magus's pale eyes; everything else around her had dwindled to shadows. She felt cold now, and numb.

"Wait." She could hardly speak. "Let me at least see the place where he—where—"

"Family?" Director Baltzar mouthed the word and Linnaius nodded. At once the director's manner altered; his tone of voice became unctuous in its solicitude. "But of course. And I would have handed over the deceased's personal effects to you, only everything was destroyed in the storm."

What did she care about personal effects? She could only think of Lord Gavril.

"Just take me there."

Director Baltzar led them out into the inner courtyard. A dank passageway led to a locked grille and then another gloomy courtyard hemmed in by grim, water-stained walls. Warders with clanking keys unlocked gate after gate to let them pass along a dark tunnel into the heart of the asylum.

And then they came out on the edge of the cliff, wind-buffeted, with the broken walls the only barrier between them and the raging sea beneath.

Kiukiu gazed at the piles of rubble lying at the base of the ruined tower.

"How?" she cried over the roar of the wind. "How can you be dead, Gavril, and I not know?"

Linnaius saw Kiukiu suddenly start out toward the rubble, moving with swift determination. For a second he feared she was about to throw herself over the edge of the cliff. But she just stood there, her back to him, gazing down at the pounding sea.

"Well?" he said, trying to sound kindly.

He saw her draw her sleeve over her face, as though dashing away tears. There was something in the way she wept for her dead lord, silently and with her face averted, that touched even his cold heart. Rain began to fall—a light patter at first, and then, as darker clouds swept in swiftly over the headland, the drops spattered down in earnest.

"Kiukirilya," he said. "You'll catch cold out here. Let's take shelter."

"Very well." Her voice was devoid of emotion.

Director Baltzar took them back to his office. Linnaius watched Kiukiu all the way. At one time, hearing a distant voice crying out from one of the high tower cells, she stopped in the rain-swept courtyard, raising her head to listen. "Poor wretches," she said in the same emotionless tone. "Better to be dead than imprisoned here for life."

*   *   *

The sky above Arnskammar had darkened to the color of lead. Kiukiu trailed slowly after the Magus through the falling rain, one dragging step after another. She was soaked to the skin and she didn't care.

Gavril was dead.

She had touched the lightning-blasted stones. She had stood on the edge of the cliff where the tower had crumbled into the sea. So why didn't she believe what they told her? Why, in her heart, did she feel he was still alive?

Stupid girl! Raindrops mingled with the tears running unchecked down her cheeks. No mortal man could have survived such a blast. And even if Gavril had somehow been thrown free, he would have been dashed to pieces on the rocks far below, his bloodied and broken body washed away by the tide.

"Back to Azhkendir?" Linnaius said. Rain ran down his thin nose; a drop was hanging on the tip.

"It can't be true," she said, as obstinate as a child. "It just can't be."

"How can you be sure?" he asked.

Suddenly she understood what he meant. "Oh no," she whispered. "I can't do it. Don't make me. Don't . . ."

He shrugged. "Who else is there who can confirm—once and for all—that Gavril Nagarian is dead?"

She said nothing, remembering her grandmother's teaching: "*The newly dead are very difficult to trace. There is always chaos and confusion. Many refuse to accept that they have passed beyond the bournes of this world. Others, with unfinished business here, strive to return by any means possible.*"

This would be the hardest task she had ever undertaken, searching for her lover's spirit.

Tears choked her; tears of bitter anger.

I'll sing him back, she vowed fiercely. *I'll sing his spirit back into another body.*

But whose body would she choose? Semyon? The young lieutenant who had treated her so chivalrously at the mausoleum? The Emperor Eugene? And where would their spirits go? Wouldn't it be a kind of murder, to force an alien spirit into their unwilling bodies? Wouldn't it send them mad?

Now she remembered Lord Jaromir lurching toward her, possessed by his father's spirit-wraith. She saw again the incipient madness in his golden eyes.

"No!" she sobbed aloud. "No, not that."

Besides, she could still feel Gavril's arms around her. She could still see the warmth in his blue eyes when he smiled at her, still hear his voice saying her name. How could she dare to think she could recreate that intimacy using a stranger's body?

"We must go." The Magus touched her arm.

"No. Not yet." She shook his hand away.

"Surely you can perform your ritual anywhere? Does it have to be here, where Lord Gavril died?" There was a slight hint of tetchiness in his voice.

"I have nothing of his to perform a summoning, so it must be here," she cried, her voice raw. It was true. She had not one single token of love, no lock of hair or ring to remember him by. Just his last promise, when they had parted on the snowy moorlands. *I will come for you.*

Now it was never to be. Instead she was going to have to wander the eternal vasts of the Ways Beyond, searching for her dead lover.

"If it must be here, then here it must be," said the Magus. "But come sit in the sky craft; at least it's dry."

"The sky craft?" Kiukiu gazed around, seeing only boulders and scrubby bushes, bowed over by the sea wind.

The Magus moved his bony hands with extraordinary rapidity, like Sosia whisking a linen cloth from a dining table. There lay the craft, no longer concealed by his clever artifice, and inside it her gusly. As she lifted the instrument onto her lap, it felt as heavy as if it were made of lead. The strings would not stay in tune. She moved slowly as though in a dream. Everything took too much effort.

This was the hardest task she had ever attempted. Her fingers began to pluck the strings; the slow, sad notes began to issue from her throat as though someone else were singing them.

Where shall I look?

She was singing herself into the trance, letting each pitch resonate through her whole body until her spirit broke free and began to drift away. . . .

And if I find him, will he even know me? Kiukiu passed through ragged festoons and swags of dark mist. She had set all her thoughts on Gavril, not knowing where this would take her in the Ways Beyond. And now she found herself in a vast hall, filled with a crowd of milling, aimless souls, all wandering about, lost and confused.

A distraught woman rushed up to her, crying out, "There you are at last, Linna, I've been searching for you for so long—"

Kiukiu saw the look of bitter disappointment as the woman realized she was not the one she was searching for.

Almost instantly a little boy stretched out his arms to her imploringly. "Where's my mother? I can't find her. Help me."

Kiukiu steeled herself to ignore the harrowing pleas and walked on, scanning the hall in vain. How could she ever track Gavril down in this chaos? She halted, closing her eyes, willing his image into her mind, keeping all her thoughts fixed on him and him alone. When she opened her eyes again, the others had faded and were nothing now but whispering shadows. She passed on through the echoing vaults of the hall, trying to block out the whisper-voices of the newly dead. And all the time, the pain in her heart burned like a brand. Her feet dragged. For when she found him here, as find him she must, she would know for sure that her life had lost all meaning.

She had no idea how long she had been wandering onward through the gloomy vastness of the hall when she found herself facing a tall portico. Shreds of mist fluttered and flapped like gauze curtains across the opening.

"Where *are* you, Gavril?" she cried. "Why can't I find you?"

"Well?" asked a soft voice. Rain glistened on the rocks and slowly dripped from the stunted branches of a sea pine overhead.

Kaspar Linnaius was regarding her inquiringly with his cloud-pale eyes.

She shivered. "No," she said. Her mind was still filled with the pleading voices of the newly dead. "There were so many, so very many . . ."

He nodded. "Perhaps your trance was not deep enough to take you where he has gone."

She glared at him. "Are you suggesting I'm not skilled enough to find him?" But he had spoken the truth and she resented it; she had never undertaken such a search before. "What do you know of such things?"

"You must not abandon your search so easily. You must go further in."

She opened her mouth to make another retort but realized that he was right. She must try again. If only to say one last farewell. . . .

Kaspar Linnaius stood looking down at Kiukiu. Her voice, so strong at first, was fading slowly to a whisper as her fingers ceased to pluck the strings of the gusly. Such potent music. Even he, who understood little of the crude and dangerous magic of the Azhkendi shamans, sensed its energy and power.

Her voice died, her head drooped forward, and her fingers rested loosely on the metal strings. She was out of her body now, lost in the singing-trance. He must act now and swiftly.

Her grandmother's influence was far too strong in Azhkendir; here, at least, he could work his glamour on her without fear of interference.

He drew from inside his robe an alchymist's crystal glass, fashioned like a teardrop. The wavering daylight, penetrating the thin, high clouds, spun a swirl of rainbows in the heart of the glass.

It was this forbidden use of his art—soul-stealing—that had brought about the closure of the Thaumaturgical College in Francia and the inquisition and deaths of his fellow mages. The Guslyars of Azhkendir talked with the spirits of the dead, but the Francian magi had learned how to imprison the souls of the living.

He leaned closer to Kiukiu, listening to the gentle, regular rhythm of her breathing, raising the soul-glass toward her lips.

"Now," he whispered, "now you are mine, Kiukirilya."

CHAPTER 24

Pavel Velemir tried to shift into a position that would ease the crippling stiffness in his back and legs. His captors had somehow contrived to chain him so that he could hardly move. Kneeling was difficult and standing impossible, except in a ludicrously stooped position.

He let a slow sigh escape his lips.

He had known it would not be easy to be accepted as one of the Smarnan rebels. But he had not planned on being chained up in the Old Citadel with other Tielen prisoners who, one by one, were being taken out into the courtyard to be shot. Now, of the few who remained, one sat white-faced in a dazed stupor, another mumbled prayers over and over under his breath, and a third was so terrified that fear had loosened his bowels with the inevitable disagreeable results.

Poor devils.

As the day wore on, the heat and the smell grew more and more offensive. Even though the citadel walls were at least a foot thick, the Tielens had blasted so many holes in them that they let in the fierce midday sun. Pavel leaned back against the shrapnel-pitted stone and closed his eyes. He had planned on using the "Disgraced at the Winter Palace" story from the Mirom Journal as his alibi, but now he realized that the rebels had been so caught up with their own troubles, his exploits in Mirom would be of no significance to them whatsoever. He would have to think fast if he was to escape the firing squad.

What would you have done in my place, Uncle Feodor?

And then he heard a girl's voice, passionate and young, raised in argument with the guards.

"You were wrong about Gavril Andar, Iovan! How many more mistakes are you going to make?"

"My conscience is clear."

The rebel girl with the short-cropped hair. He had seen her giving a cup of water to a sick prisoner. She, at least, showed some compassion. What was her name . . . Raïsa? Was she his salvation?

Iovan appeared in the doorway, carbine in hand. He came straight up to Pavel. "Get up." He prodded Pavel with the end of his carbine barrel.

Pavel tried to stand, but the shackles pulled him back down to his knees.

"This one isn't in Tielen uniform. Why did you arrest him?" asked a strong, resonant voice.

"Lukan!" cried Raïsa, hurrying to the newcomer's side.

Pavel looked up and saw another man looking down at him. He was strong-featured, sunburned, with a wild head of silvered black hair. The others, even Iovan, deferred to him, so he must be one of the leaders.

"What is your name?" Lukan asked him.

"Pavel Velemir."

"They tell me you come from Muscobar." Lukan's face swam in and out of focus. "What are you doing in Smarna?"

"I came to join you."

"I see." Lukan glanced at Iovan. "And why should we trust you? You could be a spy."

"Why?" Pavel said. "Because I am a fugitive from the Emperor's tyranny."

"You?" burst out Iovan, his voice sour with scorn.

"Because I was working in the diplomatic service before I was publicly disgraced. Because I know things that you cannot possibly know about the plans of Eugene and his ministers."

Lukan glanced at Iovan again. Pavel saw uncertainty in the look that passed between them.

"He's bluffing," said Iovan.

"But what if he's telling the truth?" Raïsa cried. "What if he really has come from Muscobar to help us?"

"And what if he's a Tielen double agent? Eugene's spies are every-where. And—remember, Raïsa?—we shoot spies."

"Do something, Lukan!" Raïsa pleaded, ignoring her brother.

Lukan's forehead was still furrowed, the expression in his dark eyes wary.

"Bring him to the council chamber. Let him make his case to the other Wardens of the Citadel."

Iovan put finger and thumb to his lips and let out a piercing whis-tle. Two of the militia, who had been lounging around smoking to-bacco, hastily put down their pipes and came over.

"Prisoner to the council chamber," Iovan ordered. "Now."

Three men and a woman sat at a long table in the blast-damaged chamber. A shaft of golden afternoon sun, sparkling with dust motes, shone down from a ragged hole in the roof. It dazzled Pavel so that he could only make out the shadowy outlines of his inquisitors.

Lukan crossed the wide chamber swiftly and leaned down to con-fer with the wardens.

"Bring the man calling himself Pavel Velemir before us," said the woman at the table.

Iovan tugged hard on the chain around Pavel's ankles; Pavel stag-gered, almost losing his balance, then lurched forward to stand be-fore the wardens.

"We are the elected Wardens of the Citadel." The woman spoke briskly. "My name is Nina Vashteli, Minister of Justice in Vermeille. You claim to bring us intelligence of the New Rossiyan government—"

"Ready—aim—*fire!*"

A fusillade of shots rang out from the courtyard below.

Nina Vashteli gave Pavel a sharp, appraising look.

"We show no mercy to our enemies—especially spies."

Pavel closed his eyes a moment, remembering his fellow prisoners. *Those poor wretches. They'll never get to see Tielen again, now.*

"Can you prove your identity?" Minister Vashteli asked.

"No," he said. "But I spent many childhood summers here with my mother Xenia at the Villa Sapara. Some of the servants there might re-member me."

Lukan whispered in Minister Vashteli's ear.

"We'll send to the Villa Sapara for some of the staff, to verify your story," the minister said. "Raïsa Korneli, would you go? Take my barouche."

"Thank you." Raïsa shot a triumphant look at her brother as she hurried from the chamber.

"I've attended receptions at the Villa Sapara," the minister went on. "So has Professor Lukan."

Lukan nodded; he was gazing searchingly at Pavel now, as though trying to identify some familiar feature. "We've both met Lady Xenia and her son. You certainly resemble him. But we must be sure you're not an impostor."

"Wait a moment, here!" Iovan strode up to the table. "If this is Pavel Velemir, what has become of that uncle of his? Didn't he go over to Eugene of Tielen's side? That same Eugene who is enforcing his imperial tyranny on us today?" He turned around to Pavel, eyes narrowed. "Just where do your allegiances lie?"

Another volley of shots cracked out from the courtyard below. More summary executions by firing squad. Pavel clenched his fists. It could soon be his turn—and he could think of no explanation that would satisfy his inquisitors.

"My allegiances," he said, affecting a careless tone, "such as they were, lay with Muscobar. I worked in the diplomatic service for the Orlovs. But when Eugene deposed Grand Duke Aleksei, I was swiftly removed from my post and it was given to a Tielen civil servant."

"No great tragedy," said Iovan under his breath.

"And as for my uncle"—Pavel let a tinge of discontent color his voice—"his estates should have come to me. I was his only surviving heir. But Eugene humiliated me in front of the court and gave them to one of his favorites—Roskovski, the turncoat who betrayed his own people by swearing allegiance to a Tielen—" He made his voice crack as if in suppressed anger.

"So you would have stayed at the Emperor's court if he had awarded you your uncle's estates?" asked Minister Vashteli in the coolest of tones.

She was not going to be easily swayed; Pavel decided he must play his trump card if he was to walk out of the chamber a free man.

He lowered his voice. "There was another reason."

"And that was—?"

"Astasia Orlova."

"The Empress?" Nina Vashteli raised one perfectly plucked brow.

"She was not always Empress. And there was once an . . . understanding between us." It was, in part, true. And how could the insinuation hurt Astasia now? "We used to meet in secret at the soirées at the Villa Orlova."

"You're asking us to believe that you—a poor, low-ranking diplomat from Muscobar—and Altessa Astasia Orlova—" jeered Iovan.

"I would rather die than dishonor her reputation!" Pavel said hotly. "But neither can I bear to see her married to that Tielen dictator."

Minister Vashteli was conferring with the other inquisitors.

"So what can you offer Smarna, Pavel Velemir?" she asked.

"Secrets, Madame Minister. I learned much from my uncle about the workings of the Tielen war machine and the Emperor."

"We can get as much from questioning the prisoners," put in Iovan sourly.

"Give me an example." She propped her chin on her hands and stared at him, pointedly ignoring Iovan.

"Were you aware," said Pavel, "that Eugene and his armies use a highly sophisticated communication device? And that—if you were to return to my lodgings—you would find one such concealed there, that I have stolen from the palace? One which enables me to listen in to their conversations?"

"Whoever heard such rubbish!" exploded Iovan. "Sophisticated, my ass!"

Pavel found himself taking a certain pleasure in goading the irascible Iovan to these outbursts. And he sensed that Nina Vashteli was intrigued by his revelation and growing increasingly irritated by Iovan.

"Find the device and shoot the spy," went on Iovan. "How do we know he's not using it to feed information on us straight back to Tielen?"

The council chamber doors opened and a small, plump woman was brought in.

"What's this all about?" she demanded loudly. "I want an explanation—dragging me away from my housework without so much as a please or a—" And then she saw Pavel. One hand flew to her mouth.

As a little boy he had called her Chadi after the cornbread she used to make for him. She had been his mother's cook and housekeeper at the Villa Sapara for as long as he could remember.

"Mama Chadi," he said, his voice genuinely trembling with relief.

"Master Pavel?" She came forward haltingly, one cautious step at a time. "Look at you, all grown-up—" She reached out, tears sparkling in her eyes. "Give your old Chadi a hug; there's a good boy!"

He would have run to her and hugged her then and there if his chains had not tugged him back.

"I'm sorry to intrude on such a touching reunion," broke in Iovan sarcastically, "but this could all be playacting, specially arranged for our benefit."

"Can you make a positive identification?" asked the minister, ignoring him.

"Beg your pardon, Madame?" Chadi said blankly.

"Who is this man?"

"Well you should know, Madame Minister; you've been up to the villa on enough occasions!" Chadi stared at her indignantly. "It's only my special boy, Pavel Velemir, Lady Xenia's son."

Minister Vashteli rose to her feet.

"Accept our apologies, Pavel Velemir. We had to be sure, you understand."

"Will you be coming back to the villa, Master Pavel?" Chadi asked. "I'll need to send word ahead. The furniture's all covered up with dust sheets. . . ."

"You're not going to let him just walk out of here?" burst out Iovan.

Minister Vashteli turned to stare at Iovan. "Are you questioning my judgment, Iovan?" she asked in a voice of ice. "If we'd listened to you, an innocent man would have been executed."

Iovan glared at her but did not answer back.

"Lukan, can you arrange some food for our guest? And transport to the villa? He looks in need of a good meal and some clean clothes." Minister Vashteli walked briskly up to Pavel. "We would like to see this communication device of yours. I suspect we can put it to good use."

"It's in my luggage. Several of your loyal rebels relieved me of it when I was arrested."

"Iovan, see to it. Bring the luggage here. We shall convene again in a few hours. And then, Pavel Velemir, you will show us how to operate your device."

As soon as his chains were removed, Pavel hobbled straight to

Mama Chadi and let himself be hugged, kissed, and properly fussed over. It was a small price to pay, he reckoned, for his life.

The blue waters of the bay slowly darkened to indigo in the balmy twilight. Elysia and Gavril stood on the villa balcony watching the new moon rise over the sea.

The sea looked so calm . . . and yet, if Gavril closed his eyes, he could still see burning ships and hear the anguished cries of drowning men. He could still feel the daemonic rage that had made him attack the Tielen fleet until his strength failed and he crashed into the waves.

"I've held them off for a little while," he said. "But I know Eugene. He'll retaliate."

"When will this end?" Elysia said. She sounded weary and heartsore. "Is there no hope of compromise, Gavril? There's been so much destruction already."

"I don't know, Mother." It was a question that he could hardly bear to contemplate.

"She came back, Gavril," Elysia said. "Kiukiu came back to the kastel looking for you."

Kiukiu. How he longed to see her. And yet his heart ached at the thought of what he must tell her.

"She's a strong-minded young woman. She was ready to set out to find you, without money, without papers."

He almost smiled at the thought. Yes, that was just the way she was: stubborn, determined, against all the odds. "But what will she say when she sees me as I am now?"

"She'll just be glad that you're free, my dear. As I am." Elysia placed a hand gently on his shoulder. "Go back to Azhkendir. She's waiting for you."

His mother still had the same gift for reassuring him as she had when he was a boy. From the calm, steady way she spoke, he almost began to believe that he could soon be free to follow his heart.

"I'll go, then. Just as soon as I've made certain there's no immediate threat from Eugene."

It was evening by the time Pavel returned to the citadel, no longer limping and in chains, but washed, shaved, and in fresh clothes. There were armed Smarnans everywhere, many of them young, all carrying looted Tielen carbines. They seemed in ebullient good spirits, swaggering about, flushed with cheap wine and victory. But as he passed through the first courtyard he couldn't help noticing a cart covered with a bloodstained tarpaulin. From underneath, hands and naked feet protruded.

They had shown their Tielen prisoners no mercy. He felt a dry, sick feeling at the back of his throat. These men had been shot without a trial; they had not been accorded even the most basic of rights. Eugene would not take kindly to this barbaric treatment of his soldiers. There would be reprisals.

He was shown into the council chamber with much more civility than before. Nina Vashteli, Lukan, and the two older ministers were conferring earnestly around an open box on the table. And he couldn't resist smiling at their evident confusion.

"Now you can settle our dispute," Minister Vashteli said a little tartly. "Is this your communication device? Or some kind of *objet d'art*?"

"I suppose you could call it both," Pavel said. He had taken a calculated risk in revealing one of the secrets of the Emperor's intelligence network to the Smarnans. He hoped it would not end in his execution by one side or the other. He lifted the crystal out of its protective wrappings and placed it on the table.

"What does it do?" asked one of the elder ministers, scratching his head bemusedly.

"It will enable you to speak to one of the Emperor's staff."

"In Tielen?" Lukan said. "Or in Mirom?"

"Wherever the device has been tuned to be received. This one, a diplomatic Vox, is tuned directly to the imperial office. Others are used by the navy and army out in the field."

"So I could address the Emperor's diplomatic staff with this?" said Minister Vashteli. "Not some petty clerk in an obscure bureau?"

"They'll be a little surprised that they're being contacted from Smarna, not Francia . . . but yes."

Nina Vashteli looked up. Her expression was grimly resolute. "Bring in the hostage," she ordered the guards on the door.

Hostage? Pavel turned to see a portly, broad-shouldered man enter between two armed guards. His uniform coat, though tattered and stained with dirt and dried blood, showed the colors of the New Rossiyan Empire.

"This is an outrage!" he bellowed. "I demand my rights. I demand—"

"Governor Armfeld, you are about to speak to one of the Emperor's staff. You will inform him that Smarna is no longer part of Eugene's empire."

"I will do no such thing," blustered Armfeld, his face turning a choleric red. "I—"

"You will tell him that unless all empire forces are withdrawn from Smarna within thirty-six hours, we will shoot you and any other Tielen prisoners."

"But that—that goes against the treaty!"

"Pavel?" Minister Vashteli turned to him. "Would you be so good as to make your device work for us?"

Pavel lifted off the thick glass dome and listened carefully; to his relief he could hear a faint crackling buzz emanating from the sparkling crystal. It had survived the rigors of the journey from Mirom intact.

"What's that? A Vox Aethyria?" spluttered Armfeld. "How the devil did you get your hands on one of those? It can't be mine; your vandals smashed it when they ransacked my quarters—"

"*Good evening, Lutèce.*" A distant voice issued, distorted yet audible. "*What is your information?*"

To his satisfaction, Pavel saw the consternation on the faces of the Smarnans. If this didn't convince them, then—

"Lutèce?" Armfeld cried.

"This is the Smarnan council in Colchise," Pavel said into the device, speaking slowly and carefully. "We have Governor Armfeld here."

"*Armfeld?*" There was no mistaking the surprise in the reaction. "*Proceed.*"

The guards brought Armfeld over to the Vox Aethyria. Pavel saw the governor sigh, his shoulders sagging as he realized he had no choice but to do as he was bidden.

"Armfeld here. The rebels have taken the citadel and shot most of my men," Armfeld mumbled into the device. "They'll shoot me too if all imperial troops are not withdrawn in thirty-six hours."

"*Could you clarify that last point?*" came back the distant response.

"They're going to execute me! Good God, man, isn't that clear enough? Can't you get me out of here?" As Armfeld's voice rose hysterically, the guards pulled him away from the table.

"You've missed one vital point, Governor," said Nina Vashteli. She approached the device and bent low to speak into it with ice-clear diction. "This is Nina Vashteli, Minister of Justice for Smarna. Smarna is no longer a part of the New Rossiyan Empire. Any attempt to invade our country will be regarded as an act of war. We have powerful allies across the sea, and will not hesitate to call them to our defense if necessary."

She rose and looked at Pavel, her eyes shrewd and cold.

"And now we wait for the Emperor's response."

"If you like, Madame Minister," said Pavel in his easiest, most reasonable voice, "I can monitor the Vox Aethyria. I know how to operate it—and it's not as if I've anything else to do tonight."

The minister glanced at her fellow counselors for approval.

"We'd better supply a pot of our strongest coffee to keep you awake," Lukan said, laughing. "You could be in for a long wait."

Eugene was at dinner with his ministers in the Amber Dining Room when the communiqué from the Smarnan rebels was received.

He had Chancellor Maltheus read it aloud to the assembled company.

" 'We have powerful allies across the sea and will not hesitate to call them to our defense if necessary.' "

Maltheus lowered the paper and looked expectantly at Eugene. There was silence in the dining room now, as his ministers glanced uneasily at one another.

"Powerful allies?" said one. "They're bluffing, surely."

Eugene was pushing a crumb of cheese around his plate with one finger. He had lost his appetite.

"Emperor?" Maltheus prompted.

"Smarna's allies? Well, we have our suspicions," he said. Did the Vashteli woman mean Gavril Nagarian? And if so, why did she couch her threat in such ambiguous terms? "We must check with our agents in Allegonde, Tourmalise, and Francia. Has any unusual massing of troops or ships been observed?"

"So you take this threat seriously, highness?" asked the Minister of Finance. "Our coffers have taken quite a hit with the sinking of the

Southern Fleet. And, of course, all the expense of the coronation. And the new uniforms for the Imperial Household Cavalry, not to mention the considerable sum in pensions that will have to be paid out to the war widows . . ."

Money. It always came down to money.

"Yes, yes, I hear you." Eugene had no need to be reminded. But he was damned if he was going to be dictated to by some motley collection of rebels and students. "But how will it look to the rest of the world if we concede? No. Smarna is still part of New Rossiya."

"Could we not enter into negotiations?" ventured another minister timidly.

Eugene's fist hit the polished tabletop, making the plates and glasses rattle. "I will not negotiate with revolutionaries."

"So our reply to Smarna—"

"General Froding and his troops are even now making their way south from the borders. Let the Smarnans work out our reply for themselves."

"A toast," said Maltheus hastily, raising his glass. "A toast to Froding and his brave men."

"Victory to Froding's Light Infantry!" The ministers clinked glasses and drank.

Eugene sent Maltheus a grateful glance over the rim of his glass. In spite of the careless bravado of his reply, he felt unsure for the first time in his military career.

Doubting my own judgment? I must be getting old.

Pavel Velemir poured himself a third cup of coffee. But after one sip, he grimaced and set the cup down; it had gone cold. It was past midnight and there had still been no response from Tielen to the Smarnans' defiant message.

He was weary and beginning to regret his offer to stand by the Vox Aethyria. There was a comfortable bed awaiting him in the Villa Sapara. He had begun the day in chains, under threat of imminent execution. If it had not been for Mama Chadi . . .

He stood up and paced the council chamber a couple of times, stopping to stare up at the starry night sky through one of the jagged holes in the roof.

He could hear the sound of drunken singing drifting up from the taverns outside. The Smarnans were celebrating their victory. Celebrating far too soon. He knew all too well what the Emperor's response would be. Eugene's troops would be back. And when they least expected them.

He rubbed his tired eyes, blinking to try to keep them open.

"Well, Pavel Velemir?"

He turned around, startled, to see Nina Vashteli. The minister was dressed in a gown of dark green brocade and she wore emerald feathers in her neatly arranged hair; she must have been out to dinner.

"No answer from Tielen, Minister," he said with a regretful smile.

"You didn't expect one, did you?" she said, peeling off her long satin gloves, finger by finger.

"Frankly, no."

"Neither did I. Tell me, Pavel, does your device send messages to places other than Tielen?"

"Not yet, Madame Minister."

"A pity. It would be useful to communicate directly with our allies. We will just have to rely on more traditional methods."

"Allies?" Pavel, tired as he was, remembered the direct threat she had made to Eugene. Had the council already summoned help from overseas? It might not be so easy to find out who had secretly allied themselves with Smarna without giving himself away.

"How long do you think we can hold out against Eugene's troops? Tell me truthfully." Her dark eyes fixed on his; he felt uncomfortable, as if he were being tested.

"If he attacks by land and sea? It would depend on how close his forces are to the border. He overran Azhkendir in a matter of days."

The strains of singing came swelling up from outside again; to Pavel's ears it sounded much like a rousing marching song.

She sighed. "How can I convince these hotheads to be patient, to wait for support? Their blood is up. I hope to God that our request for assistance will get through before Eugene's armies come marching across the mountains."

It is a dream and yet not a dream. Gavril slowly rises through layers of sleep to find himself enmeshed in a dark cloud shot through with jewel-bright lights that shiver through him like little lightning bolts. It is as if he has been drawn deep into the daemon's consciousness.

"*Can I trust you?*" whispers the Drakhaoul. "*Can I really trust you, Gavril Nagarian?"* Every emotion is a shimmer of vivid color. For now Gavril can feel the daemon's doubt and desire, a deep desire for something long unobtainable; the colors flicker from a pale, uncertain violet to a deep, rich crimson.

"You talk of trust. Yet you told me you would die if we were separated. I believed you dead, Drakhaoul; so why are you still alive?"

Another shimmer of colors, changing from the dark thunder blue of anger to softer, more conciliatory hues.

"I found another who needed me."

"You took another host? I thought you could only meld with those of Nagarian blood." Had the daemon not been entirely truthful with him?

"This one also has the blood of Artamon's sons in his veins. But then I heard you calling to me. Your need was greater. And so I returned to you."

"Did this new fusion not work so well, then?" Gavril is curious, wondering who this other host, this far-distant blood relative might be.

"You had to want me to be part of you once more, Gavril."

"And I would have died if you had not come when you did." He cannot hide the truth from the Drakhaoul: He feels more grateful for his life and his freedom than mere words can express.

"There is a journey I must undertake. But I cannot do it without your help. And you are not strong enough yet . . ."

"A journey? Where do you want to go?"

When it speaks again, its voice is deep-hued with longing. *"I want to find a way home."*

Gavril wandered around his room, picking up his possessions and putting them down again. Here were his poetry books and the abstruse volumes of philosophy Lukan had given him when he was a student. And here were his paints and pastels, all neatly tidied away. Next to them lay his brushes, from the slender squirrel hair he used for picking out the finest details to the big, rough-bristled ones used for applying large quantities of oil paint for the background of a portrait. Each brush had been carefully cleaned and wrapped in cloth. Elysia had obviously been busy since she returned from Azhkendir.

Azhkendir. He sat down on the bed. All this time he had been so obsessed with his own struggle to survive that he had put Azhkendir out of his mind. He had even chosen to revert to using his Smarnan name: Andar.

Soon he would have to face his responsibilities. But it was one thing to help liberate Smarna, and quite another to try to put things to rights in Azhkendir. Would his *druzhina* even want him back? In their eyes, he had betrayed their trust. He had denied them the chance to die gloriously, defending their lord.

He needed time to come to terms with what had been done to him. Healing time. He knew that somewhere, deep inside, he was still damaged. The Drakhaoul had mended the wounds inflicted by Director Baltzar—had even miraculously repaired most of the botched surgery done to his brain. But he still felt *wrong*.

His easel stood in a corner, an empty canvas propped on it, already prepared for use. He walked past it a number of times. The blank canvas mocked him. Could he still paint? Or had Baltzar's scalpel destroyed his gift?

"Gavril!"

He heard Elysia calling his name from the hall. Reluctantly, he opened his bedroom door.

"Minister Vashteli is here to see you."

"Palmyre has just made some barley water . . ."

"Nothing for me, thank you, Elysia," Nina Vashteli said as Gavril entered the salon. She looked directly at him. "There have been reports coming in since yesterday of large numbers of dead fish washed up on the shore. Dead gulls too."

He saw Elysia's hands tremble violently, spilling the barley water she had been pouring for herself.

"Can you explain this, Gavril Andar?"

He could remember little of the attack now, save the utter exhilaration as the power tore from his body in one terrifying burst of brilliant light. There had been smoke afterward . . . yet as far as he could recall, the sea breeze had gusted it away from land, toward the Tielen fleet and beyond.

"Gavril?" said Elysia. He could hear consternation in her voice. He had not thought of the damage it could do to the very people he was trying to save. And no one in Smarna, except Elysia, was protected against the deadly aftereffects of Drakhaon's Fire.

"Well?" Nina Vashteli said, her voice stern. "Is this your doing? Is this anything to do with the weapon you used to defeat the Tielens?"

For a moment Gavril could only stand there dumbly, his mind whirling with unspeakable possibilities.

"Gavril?" said Elysia again, more gently this time.

"The beach could be polluted," he said at last. "Let no one go there until I can be sure it is safe."

"Polluted with what, precisely?"

"Minister." Gavril moved closer to her. "Have there been any reports of sickness among those who were on the citadel ramparts yesterday?"

Nina Vashteli gave him a searching look. But all she said was, "I take it you have seen these aftereffects before?"

Gavril lowered his eyes.

"And I also take it that you know how to treat them?"

How could he reply to that? The only protection against Drakhaon's Fire that he knew of was the ritual bloodbond. Was it possible it could also work as a remedy?

"Well, Gavril Andar?"

"I might. But I can't guarantee it will work."

Gavril hurried out into the villa gardens and followed the winding path down to the beach. Now the soft scents of pink tamarisk and lilac were nothing but a torment, reminding him of what he had done. The last part of the path was rocky, overgrown by burgeoning weeds and mean-toothed brambles that caught and clawed at his legs as he ran. He reached the sands and stared out to sea, shading his eyes as he scanned for fishing boats in the bay. But even as he looked at the glittering blue water and the pale gold of the sands, another landscape kept superimposing itself: a stark, empty, grey desolation. The Arkhel Waste in Azhkendir, blasted with Drakhaon's Fire by his father Volkh.

He set out across the damp sands, making toward the citadel. Here, not far from the path that led up to the Villa Orlova, was where he had swooped down on the Tielen troops and seared them all to oblivion in his fury. And in spite of the lapping tide that had risen and fallen several times since his attack, he could plainly see the ash clogging the sands, the residue of charred bone and melted metal, the last remains of Eugene's invasion force. The cinders would have washed into the bay, polluting the waters for miles around.

He sank slowly to his knees in the sand.

"Damn you, Eugene," he said, his voice choked with bitterness. "Look what you've driven me to now."

CHAPTER 25

Eugene shut the door to his study and leaned his back against the paneled wood as if to keep the disorder that reigned outside from bursting in.

"Never again," he muttered. "Never again."

The corridors were filled with servants, all running to and fro in confusion. Hammering and sawing could be heard in every room. It was as noisy as if they were rebuilding the whole palace. There was nowhere to hide from the din.

"All this for one Dievona's Night Ball? Why did I ever agree? . . ."

He had ridden back to Swanholm from Artamon's Mausoleum, buzzing with plans for a journey to find Ty Nagar. And in his excitement, he had forgotten all about the ball.

On his desk lay a letter; it was from Malherbe, the celebrated landscape gardener from Allegonde, who had been working on a special commission in the grounds.

> . . . and I most humbly invite your imperial highness to inspect the works, now at last complete . . .

Anything was preferable to enduring this cacophony. Eugene went to the stables and was soon on horseback again.

Outside on the lawns, the Imperial Household Cavalry had been pressed into helping erect the giant marquees. *At least their campaign experience means the job will be done efficiently,* Eugene reflected, watching the guardsmen—uniform jackets discarded, shirtsleeves rolled up—pulling and tugging at ropes in the warmth of the spring sun.

Sunlight glittered on the green waters of the lake. Eugene turned Cinnamor's head toward the deer park and rode off along the gravel path to inspect the new works.

He had learned that to preserve his sanity there were times when it was necessary to put the worries of state aside. And he had built Swanholm as a retreat for just such occasions.

Soon Eugene heard the gentle sound of wind chimes borne on the breeze. Dismounting, he led Cinnamor down into a little grassy dell, sheltered from view.

As a birthday surprise for Karila, he had commissioned a Khitari dragon pavilion from Malherbe. He had imported stone dragons, one for each of the four corners, and another smaller one to top the roof. Inside the pavilion, the walls were hung with green and blue Khitari silks to complement the glossy black lacquer furniture exquisitely painted in gold and scarlet. He hoped it would provide the princess with her own private retreat from the rigors of court life in the palace.

As an extra delight, he had created a private menagerie for her. Fluting birds with colorful feathers and bright golden eyes hopped about a gilded aviary built in the same exotic style as the pavilion. Little bells hung from every corner and chimed sweetly in the breeze. A pair of tiny deer, no higher than his knee, came to nuzzle against his leg, gazing expectantly at him with their mild, dark eyes. He reached into his pocket and held out some oats garnered from the stables on the palm of his hand for them to nibble, feeling the brush of their quick, rough tongues on his skin.

Karila would fall in love with this secret little kingdom he had created for her. He couldn't wait for her to recover her strength so he could bring her here and watch the expression on her face as the dell revealed its treasures.

Why did the sweet air and green valley of Swanholm always put him into a good humor, whereas the Winter Palace in Mirom induced nothing but feelings of tension?

Grooms came running out to greet him as he rode back into the stables. Eugene jumped down from Cinnamor's back and patted her flank affectionately before handing over the reins. He was exhilarated by the fine weather and by the sheer pleasure of riding. He walked away from the stables, pulling off his riding gloves, finger by finger. He was planning on taking a bath—a good hot steam—followed by an invigorating plunge into the ice-cold pool. But he had not even reached the main stair before Gustave appeared. He seemed uncharacteristically agitated.

"You have a visitor, highness."

"The visitor can wait, Gustave." Damn it, what was the point in being Emperor of all New Rossiya, if he couldn't take a bath when he wished?

"It's the Francian ambassador, highness. He says it's extremely urgent."

Eugene let out a snort of exasperation. "Well, if it's that urgent, damn protocol! He'll have to put up with me as I am: hot, sweaty, and in need of a bath!"

"I took the precaution of showing him into the Willow Room, highness," Gustave said in a low voice, "rather than the Malachite Room with your father's favorite painting."

" 'The Defeat of the Francian Fleet'?" Eugene said loudly. "Why so sensitive, Gustave? Our nations are on the best of terms now. I'm sure the ambassador won't be offended by a reminder of his country's past disappointments."

Gustave, wincing at Eugene's deliberate jibe, opened the door to the Willow Room and announced, "His Imperial Highness."

The Willow Room was one of Eugene's favorite rooms in the whole palace; the walls were hung with Khitari brocades woven with a pattern of willow leaves in the subtlest shades of silver-grey and green. The willow green had been picked up in the buttoned silk upholstery of the chairs and the elegant fringes of the swagged curtains.

Fabien d'Abrissard stood gazing out of the window at the newly planted Water Garden.

"Ah, Ambassador." Eugene strode in briskly. "The matter is urgent, I understand?"

Abrissard turned and bowed formally but with no great reverence. He was dressed in an immaculately tailored black coat with a dazzlingly white starched shirt beneath; his sole concession to ornamentation was the dark blue ribbon and medallion of the Francian Order of the Golden Salamander. His impeccable appearance only served to remind Eugene how hot and disheveled he was.

"There is, I understand, one named Kaspar Linnaius here at Swanholm?"

"Magus Linnaius is one of the most respected members of my household, Ambassador." All Eugene's instincts warned him that Abrissard's seemingly innocuous question was the prelude to some far more complicated negotiation.

"Are you aware that he is a wanted man in Francia, highness? I have here a warrant for his extradition."

Eugene had taken a dislike to Abrissard at their very first meeting in Mirom, and now the ambassador's haughty tone irritated him even more. "I regret to inform you that your journey here has been in vain. Kaspar Linnaius is away from Swanholm at present. And I have no idea when he will return."

"You're protecting a dangerous man, highness. Are you aware that he is accused of the most heinous of crimes—heresy and soul-stealing?"

"I'm aware that he is one of the most brilliant scientific minds of our age." Eugene could feel his sense of irritation growing. "Your religious courts sought to stifle that genius, Abrissard. I like to think that Tielen is more enlightened. We encourage our scientists to develop their ideas."

"Perhaps I have not spoken plainly enough in this matter," Abrissard said stiffly. "King Enguerrand does not request Linnaius's extradition; he demands it on behalf of the Holy Commanderie."

"Demands?" Eugene was not accustomed to being spoken to so bluntly.

"The king suspects you have never been fully furnished with details of the heretical crimes Linnaius committed in Francia." Abrissard drew a folded paper from his jacket and handed it to Eugene.

Eugene's first instinct was to tear the paper to pieces in front of the ambassador and let them drop to the fine parquet floor. But he resisted the temptation, glancing briefly at the long list of indictments. Then he looked again at Abrissard and smiled.

"Linnaius's researches have taken him far from Tielen and I have not the slightest idea when he will return. Ask anyone from my household here and they will confirm what I have told you."

Fabien d'Abrissard stared at him, his face a mask of disdain. "The king will not be pleased to hear this news. He had hoped that Tielen and Francia might achieve a better understanding by cooperating in this endeavor. But if Tielen continues to protect this criminal, Francia will be obliged to take matters into its own hands."

So this is the crux of the matter, thought Eugene. A threat.

"Let me remind you, Ambassador," he said in his softest, most silken tones, "that Tielen has always replied in the strongest possible terms to interventions from Francia—and will do so again, if need be. Good-day."

Abrissard stood speechless a moment. Then he gave a curt little bow and withdrew.

Eugene waited until the doors to the Willow Room had closed, then looked down again at the list of crimes attributed to Kaspar Linnaius:

Heresy. Necromancy. Pyromancy. Alchymy . . .

He must warn the Magus to be on his guard. But he had no idea why Enguerrand of Francia had chosen this moment to demand his extradition.

"Gustave!" he called.

"Ambassador d'Abrissard has just left, highness," Gustave said as he appeared. "He declined any offers of refreshment. He seemed in quite a hurry."

"Get me our embassy in Francia," Eugene said, making for his study.

"But your bath, highness—"

"I need to know what's going on at the court of King Enguerrand. Something has changed, Gustave, and we were not made fully aware of it. No matter how insignificant it might seem, I want to be kept informed. Day or night."

"Right away!" Gustave hurried away down the corridor.

Still smarting from Fabien d'Abrissard's insolent manner, Eugene stopped at a window and gazed out into the park. He could just see the ambassador's coach and horses as they climbed the winding road, making toward the gilded gates.

What did Enguerrand of Francia really want with Kaspar Linnaius? Was all this talk of heresy just a front? Had word of Linnaius's genius with weaponry spread beyond the borders of New Rossiya?

And . . . most strange of all, why had Abrissard not once mentioned Smarna?

"Don't worry, old friend," Eugene murmured to the absent Magus, "I won't let them have you."

Karila held out her hands, palms full of little seeds for her tiny golden-eyed finches to feed upon. Eugene watched her rapt face, eyes wide with surprise and delight as the little birds came hopping down from their perches in the aviary and alighted on her hands, pecking with rapid darting movements.

She began to giggle. "Their beaks tickle!" Others fluttered over her head, their wings whirring softly.

Her delight was infectious. He had come down to the menagerie in a stormy mood, still smarting from his latest defeats in Smarna. The sound of her laughter had driven away the clouds of ill temper. She was so happy in this garden paradise he had created for her.

She gazed up at him, still smiling.

"I can imagine I've traveled all the way to Khitari here. You're a magician, Papa!"

He smiled back. "One day you shall travel to Khitari with me. When you're stronger."

"Is it true, Papa? That the children make kites out of paper, in the shape of dragons? And they fly them on a special dragon day?"

"All true. And if you would like to fly a dragon kite, I can send to Khitari for one, especially for you." But he would have to fly it for her, he thought sadly, looking at the thinness of her arms. With her crooked little body, she would not have the strength to control one of the magnificent scarlet and gold kites.

"I'd like to play with some Khitari children. I'd like them to teach me how to fly a kite. And to tell me all about dragons . . ." She gave a little sigh. Her face was suddenly blank and sad.

"What is it, Kari?"

"Best of all I'd like a friend, Papa. Someone to talk to, to play with. Someone eight years old too."

"I shall have Lovisa arrange it. There must be many noble children your age—"

She put one hand on his. "A real friend, Papa. Not someone who has been told to be nice to me because I am your daughter."

He felt a pang of sympathy. It was a hard fact to come to terms with, one he had been forced to learn very early in childhood: Royal children were different. He went down on one knee, still holding her hand, and looked directly into her eyes. "Kari, real friendship is very hard to find when you are born a princess. Or a prince. But one day you will find a companion, someone who values you for your true worth and not your title or your riches. I promise you that."

He felt something nudge his leg; surprised, he turned and saw one of the little Khitari deer staring at him with liquid brown eyes.

Karila started to giggle again. "Look, Papa, it wants you to stroke it!"

He let his hand run over the softness of its smooth spotted flank and it nuzzled its head up against his arm. It seemed utterly unafraid.

"I shall call you Pippi," Karila said, putting out her hand too. "Here, Pippi." The little deer was startled by her sudden movement and bolted away to join the others. Karila eagerly started out after it, but in her haste she lost her balance and tripped, falling headlong onto the damp grass.

All the little deer scattered.

Eugene went to help his daughter up but she thrust him away.

"I can manage!" Her voice was taut with hurt pride.

Clumsily, awkwardly, she struggled to her feet again. Her pretty blue-striped dress was green with grass stains. Watching her made his heart ache. She was brave, his little crippled daughter, and she was proud. And he would have given anything in the whole world to make her twisted body straight again.

He felt her hand slip into his.

"Let's go back now, Papa."

Somewhere in the palace, musicians began tuning up. Reedy squeaks were punctuated by low brass groanings, more akin to the sounds of some great beast in pain than musical notes. Eugene groaned too as he read the latest dispatches, putting his hands to his head. How could he think coherently amid this racket?

Gustave had marked the last communiqué with a secret cypher meaning "of special significance." It was a transcript of a message sent by Vox Aethyria from one of his agents in Francia:

Royal naval regatta off coast of Fenez-Tyr. King Enguerrand
present on royal barge. Many newly built men-o'-war and frigates.

Were his instincts right? Was Francia arming itself for some new military initiative? Was New Rossiya under threat of attack? This did not fit the picture his agents had built up of the pious Enguerrand, who preferred to spend his days in prayer and good works.

Enguerrand would never dare attack us. He's too busy with his clerics and his Commanderie inquisitions to look beyond his own borders.

There came a tap at his door.

"Enter."

He looked up and saw to his astonishment that his visitor was Kaspar Linnaius. The Magus must have just returned from his travels, for he rarely came inside the palace; it was their custom for Eugene to visit him in his laboratory, where no one could overhear their conversations. So this unexpected visit must mean he had urgent news.

He raised his voice in case anyone was listening. "So you've come to discuss the fireworks for the ball, Linnaius? I hope you've prepared some surprises for us this year."

"Oh I think your highness will not be disappointed." Linnaius glanced warily around the study. "I'll just take a few precautions," he said softly. He moved from the threshold to the windows, scattering grains of colorless dust on the polished floorboards as he walked, enclosing them both in a circle. Then he drew a tiny bone whistle from his robes and breathed into it until it emitted an unpleasant, high-pitched hiss. The dust granules began to vibrate in sympathy with the whistle's ear-grating note, then they slowly rose into the air, encompassing Linnaius and Eugene in a subtly shimmering canopy, almost invisible to the naked eye.

"What is that dust? What does it do?"

"Imagine, if you will, the equivalent of shadowsilk in sound, highness. Anyone passing by your study would catch nothing of our conversation but an inaudible murmur."

"You never cease to amaze me, Linnaius. And what will you call this new invention of yours?"

" 'Whisperdust' seems appropriate . . . but a better title may yet present itself. Now we may talk without fear of being overheard."

"Our agent in Smarna has confirmed it. Gavril Nagarian is very much alive. Alive and waiting to lure me into another confrontation. God knows how, he seemed a broken man back in Muscobar." And suddenly he found himself saying what, until now, he had not put into words. "Why did I spare his life? I should have sent him to his death on the scaffold."

"And why *did* you spare his life?" asked Linnaius slyly.

Eugene sighed; the old man knew him better than he knew himself.

"I wanted to learn his secrets. And now he is free and more powerful than before."

"Powerful, maybe, but you have Artamon's Tears. And I believe I have finally located the lost land they call Ty Nagar."

Eugene felt a dark thrill of excitement. "Then what's to stop us? We shall leave tonight—"

"We can be in Ty Nagar in a matter of hours, highness. Oh—and in case you still require her services, I have brought Kiukirilya." Linnaius loosened his outer robe, revealing a thick golden chain around his neck. Suspended from the chain hung a delicate, jewellike glass in the shape of a lotus flower.

"Her spirit?" Eugene's voice dropped to a whisper. "Trapped in there? How is that possible?"

"It is a trap that can only be sprung when the spirit leaves the body, highness. A shaman is always vulnerable to such snares."

"And the body?" Eugene was fascinated in spite of himself. "Doesn't it decay without the spirit to animate it?"

"She lies in a deep sleep. The longer she lies asleep, the harder it will be to reunite body and spirit."

"She'll die?" The shaman girl's spirit burned blue as a peerless spring sky; leaning closer, Eugene caught shimmers of pale iridescent colors against the blue, like drifts of mist. "Then perhaps you'd better wake her. She's too useful to us."

"I believe you have another official duty to be fulfilled first." Linnaius gestured toward the window. "And I have to check that my artificers have prepared the fireworks display exactly as I instructed."

Until then, Eugene had been so intent on the Magus's news that he had not noticed how effectively the whisperdust had screened out the cacophony created by his busy household.

"The ball." He let out a groan. Just when his elusive goal seemed a little more attainable, there was this farce of a ball to endure. But he had promised Karila he would be there. He could not let her down again. And then there was Astasia . . .

"As soon as the Dievona Bonfires are lit, then."

"And your alibi?"

Damn it all, must he think up an alibi as well? Of course, now that he was Emperor, he could not just ride off hunting; he had to tell a hundred officials and more. And yet, a solitary hunting trip seemed as good an alibi as any other. . . .

"Leave it to me."

"Very good." Linnaius bowed.

Eugene saw him raise his hand to collapse the canopy of whisper-dust. "Wait!" he said, remembering. There was one more matter of some urgency left to discuss. "Linnaius, does the name Fabien d'Abrissard mean anything to you?"

The Magus slowly shook his head. "A Francian name. No, I recall no one called d'Abrissard."

"He is the new Francian ambassador. It seems that King Enguerrand is most eager that I hand you over to his inquisitors. In fact, the word used was 'demands.' " All the while he was speaking, Eugene was watching Linnaius closely to see how he reacted. But Linnaius showed little reaction, other than to quirk one wispy white brow.

"And how did your imperial highness answer?"

Eugene found himself smiling. "How do you think, Magus? An emperor does not take kindly to such terms as 'demand' or 'insist.' " He leaned toward the Magus, earnest now. "I have never asked what caused you to flee Francia. I have not the slightest interest in what happened before you came to Tielen. But Abrissard is not a man to take no for an answer. They mean to hunt you down, old friend. I will protect you in every way I can, but please take care. They are out for your blood."

The Emperor's warning still tolling in his head, Kaspar Linnaius went out onto the terrace to supervize the installation of his fireworks. In his grey robes, he passed all but unnoticed among the harassed servants who were now hurrying to and fro with trays of clinking wine glasses and baskets of silver cutlery.

Fabien d'Abrissard. The name meant nothing to him. And as far as he knew, the Francian courts had ensured that no one among his fellow magisters at the Thaumaturgical College had survived the purge—not even the students. One devout order in particular, the Commanderie, had devoted itself to the cause with great zeal. Their leader claimed to be divinely inspired in his quest to rid the world of daemonic influences. He was even said to be able to summon angels.

Linnaius was continuing on toward his rooms when he heard music and laughter issuing from an open window. Glancing inside, he saw the Empress Astasia at the fortepiano, accompanying a young woman singer. Her voice, when she began the interrupted phrase again, was golden and glorious. It stirred echoes deep within him of some unfamiliar feeling, long buried. He knew he should not linger here, he had work to do . . . and yet he could not tear himself away.

He stood there until the Empress lost control of the keyboard part and broke off, laughing helplessly. The singer sang on for a bar or two and then joined in the laughter, leaning on the fortepiano to support herself. And then the Empress caught sight of him on the terrace outside.

"Hush," she said, wiping tears of laughter from her eyes, "we have an audience."

The singer glanced around. Such blue eyes; the intense blue of a cloudless summer sky . . . Linnaius felt a shiver run through him. What was he doing, a man of his age, allowing himself to be distracted by a young woman? He made an effort to collect himself and bowed to the Empress.

"Beautiful music, ladies," he said. "I must congratulate you." And he turned away, hastily directing his steps toward the West Wing and his laboratory.

Astasia watched from the Music Room window until the Magus had disappeared around the corner of the palace.

"There is no privacy to be had in Swanholm," she said. She no longer felt like laughing.

"Tell me, highness," said Celestine, "who is that ancient scholar we saw just now?"

Astasia pulled a grimace. "The Magus? His name is Kaspar Linnaius. He's a scientist, I believe, though he has an official court title like 'Royal Artificier' or some such."

"He looks at least a hundred years old!" said Celestine with a mischievous laugh.

"I confess he gives me the shivers. It's his eyes: so lifeless, so cold . . ."

"And he resides here at Swanholm?"

"He has his own laboratory in a wing of the palace. The Emperor had it built especially for him."

"The Emperor is such a generous patron to the arts and sciences."

Yes, Astasia thought, *I suppose he is, whatever other faults he may have. My husband encourages those with talents to make the most of their gifts, even if he doesn't appreciate or understand them himself. Perhaps he will dance with me at the ball. . . .*

Kaspar Linnaius made certain that the invisible wards protecting his laboratory were doubly secure before he entered his rooms.

Abrissard . . .

He took down a red-bound ledger and checked the list of names inscribed on its age-stained pages. There was no mention of a Fabien d'Abrissard in this dossier recording the movements of his few surviving enemies in Francia, painstakingly compiled over the years from Eugene's sources abroad. Surely the Commanderie would not dare to strike at him here in Tielen, under the Emperor's protection? And yet . . . had he risked too much in performing the forbidden rite of soul-stealing?

The Magus unlocked the door to his bedchamber.

There she lay, on his simple bed, the Guslyar Kiukirilya—or at least her body, for her life-spirit was trapped in the crystal soul-glass he wore on a chain close to his heart. How pale her skin had become, almost translucent.

He bent a little closer to his prisoner, to ensure that she still breathed. Yes, there was the faintest sound of respiration.

A strand of wheat-fair hair had strayed loose from her braids; he stretched out to brush it off her forehead. And the fact that she did not even stir as his fingertips touched her brow set his troubled mind at rest. She, at least, was no threat.

He padded softly from the room, securing the door with a simple lock ward that would respond only to his voice. Then he unrolled the chart he had been working on, based on his studies of Zakhar Nagarian's books and Serzhei of Azhkendir's hidden star chart.

It was a map of the seas and lands that lay far to the south, beyond the shores of Djihan-Djihar. An archipelago had been charted by Tielen explorers on a perilous journey in search of new lands to colonize, early in Prince Karl's reign. Volcanoes dominated the islands of the archipelago, and the partial eruption of one of the smaller cones had sunk one of the ships and sent the others scurrying away. But not before the explorers had noted the existence of ruins on several islands, that hinted at some past great civilization.

"It has to be Ty Nagar," he muttered.

*   *   *

Karila was dreaming. . . .

The priests from the Sacred Island stand on the shore, tall, lean, their shaven heads gleaming in the sun. They are wearing robes of white and each has the emblem of the god painted on his forehead and shoulder in dark red dye: a winged serpent.

"Tell your children we bring gifts; gifts from the Sacred Isle."

The people of the village gather in twos and threes; the men have left their fishing and their net-mending, the women their hearths.

"Gifts?" She is curious in spite of herself. Other children creep out from their hiding places as one of the priests spreads a woven cloth on the sand and places on it honey cakes, strings of beads, and little painted animals fired from clay. A bird catches her eye: Its colors are as fresh and bright as her fire-feather. She cannot stop herself; she has to have it for herself. As her fingers close around her treasure, her mother arrives, carrying her little brother.

"Tilua? Come away!"

"Look," she says, proud and happy to show her mother the beautiful toy. But her mother stares at it as if it were a poisonous snake.

"Put it back—quick, now!" she hisses.

One of the priests blocks her way. He is old and hunched, like her grandfather. "Show me what you have chosen, little one." He takes her hand and gently uncurls her clenched fingers. When he sees the firebird, he holds it aloft with a shout of triumph.

Now the priests move toward her. She gazes up at them as they slowly encircle her, and feels herself begin to shake with fear.

"It is an honor, Tilua. Nagar has chosen you to serve him."

She begins to cry. "I don't want to be chosen." She doesn't want to go with these horrible men. She doesn't want to leave her mother. She clings to her. "Don't make me go!" Her little brother starts to cry too.

"You must go, Tilua. The god has chosen you."

"But I want to stay here."

"If Nagar is angry, he will make the fire-mountain spit out flame and rocks; the sea will boil and wash away your village." The oldest priest kneels beside her and points to the distant trace of drifting grey smoke on the horizon. "You don't want to make the god angry, do you, Tilua?"

"Don't make me . . ."

"Whatever is the matter, Princess?" Marta, in nightgown, her hair in curling papers, held up the night-light. "Crying out like that in your sleep, you'll wake the whole palace!"

Karila blinked away the tears that had filled her eyes. The sunlight in her dream had been so bright, so hot . . .

"Don't make me go. Go where?" Marta set the night-light on the bedside table and felt Karila's forehead. "Are you cooking up another fever?"

"I don't know," Karila said. Her heart was still brimming with a fear and grief that was so vivid it felt as if it were her own. How could a mere dream cause her so much pain?

"Tilua," she whispered.

CHAPTER 26

"Am I dead?" Kiukiu wondered. If so, this was unlike any part of the Ways Beyond she had ever experienced before. It was cold here—the kind of cold that slowly numbs the consciousness until a dull stupor overcomes the senses. It felt as if she had been encased in ice, ice so opaque she could not see through it to what lay beyond.

"Could I be up in the Kharzhgylls? Trapped in an ice cave?" Had Magus Linnaius imprisoned her in ice and left her to die? Had she become no more than a nuisance to him and Emperor Eugene? Had she seen and heard too much in the mausoleum to be allowed to live? She had certainly understood that Lord Gavril was a direct descendant of Artamon the Great. And didn't that mean he had as much a right, if not more, to the throne of New Rossiya as Eugene?

And then she remembered.

Gavril was dead.

The shimmering ice dulled, darkened until it was black as obsidian. Black as her grief, as the pain in her broken heart.

Odd . . .

What kind of ice could change color to match her moods, her emotions?

I must be dreaming. . . .

Time must have passed, but she had no idea whether it was minutes, hours, days. She was still lying, as before, encased in ice. But how could it be ice? Surely she would have frozen to death by now. Unless—

"A coffin? A glass coffin?" Panic began to rise, clouding her thoughts. "Did they think I was dead? And yet I'm still alive? Buried alive?" She tried to beat her fists against the imprisoning glass and found she was powerless to move. She seemed to be paralyzed from head to foot.

"Help me. *Help!*" she called with all her strength, but as much as she strained, no sound issued from her mouth.

This is one of those horrible smothering dawn dreams. Any moment now, I'll wake up.

But she didn't.

As they approached his rooms, the Magus suddenly stopped, one hand raised. He glanced all around, sniffing like one of Eugene's hunting hounds, as though scenting the air.

"What is it?" Eugene had never seen him so agitated before.

"Someone has tried to break into my laboratory." Linnaius, hand still raised, appeared to be testing certain invisible seals and wards that should respond only to his command. "It seems they were unsuccessful."

"Do you have any idea who?"

Linnaius slowly shook his head.

"First Abrissard, now this. I will set a guard on this stair, day and night."

"My wards have worked perfectly well—"

"Your research is of vital importance to the empire. This is a matter of national security."

Linnaius gave a little shrug and opened the door. But in spite of his protestations, Eugene observed him checking outside one more time, his wispy brows furrowed in a puzzled frown.

The Magus had assembled an elaborate construction of pipes, filters, and alembics. A small refining furnace burned brightly in one corner. The air smelled hot and dry, with the slightest hint of some chymical taint that made Eugene's eyes smart.

"The Drakhaon may have unwittingly given you what you seek, highness," said Linnaius obliquely. "Nils Lindgren has made a vital discovery in Azhkendir."

"Mineral deposits? Yes, I am aware of his mining activities." Eugene wiped the perspiration from his brow. "How can you stand to work in this infernal heat, Linnaius?"

"At my age, when the blood thins, one is glad of a little extra warmth." Linnaius picked up a glass dish containing some dark granules and handed it to Eugene. "Has your highness ever seen any mineral deposits like these?"

"This looks much like common garden soil," said Eugene impatiently. He was not in the mood to indulge the Magus and his latest experiments; there were weightier matters to attend to.

"Hold it to the light, highness."

Eugene lifted the dish until the daylight from the window shone directly onto its contents. Only then did he detect a faint bluish glitter emanating from the earth. "It's very pretty, but—"

"Indulge me a moment, highness." Linnaius picked up a second dish, which he set down on an empty laboratory table. Eugene squinted to see what this dish contained. It seemed to be but a few grains of a dark powder.

"Now, please hold this protective visor to cover your face. And stand well back."

The metal visor contained a thick ochre-tinted strip of glass to look through. Eugene held it up and watched Linnaius light a little fuse that led to the dish. As Linnaius hurried out of the way, there came a flash of blinding light and a rending sound that bruised Eugene's ears. The whole contents of the laboratory trembled and one or two glass phials shattered.

"Impressive," said Eugene, his ears still ringing.

Linnaius opened a window and began to fan bluish smoke out into the air.

"So what goes into this new type of gunpowder you've developed?"

"I've merely refined the latest earth samples from Azhkendir that Captain Lindgren gave me."

"Azhkendi soil?" Eugene went to look at the dish; there was nothing left of it but a charred stain on the top of the table.

"From the escarpment at Kastel Drakhaon."

"Where my men died."

"Burned by Drakhaon's Fire."

"And you're saying that Drakhaon's Fire has caused the soil to crystallize into this lethally explosive powder?"

"And the Azhkendi have no idea of its potential." Linnaius seemed thoroughly pleased with himself; he kept rubbing his thin hands together.

"Even so . . ." Eugene felt a strange reluctance to approve the development of this potentially powerful weapon. Many men had died, their bodies vaporized by the infernal heat of the Drakhaon's lethal breath. There had been no trace of his beloved Jaromir's body after the conflagration. And this dark crystalline deposit had been dug from the escarpment. It seemed, in some way, like the violation of a grave, disturbing the mortal remains of the fallen.

And then he sighed. There was the security of the empire to consider now. He must put personal feelings aside and give his permission for Linnaius to start a series of experiments.

"Very well. I'll make sure Captain Lindgren puts all his efforts into mining the escarpment."

"Not just the escarpment, highness. Remember the Arkhel Waste, the site of Lord Stavyor's kastel and estate?" Linnaius's eyes gleamed with unconcealed greed. "Azhkendir must be rich in these crystal deposits indeed."

They have made her bathe in a deep stone bath, in water scented with flower oil and sprinkled with flower petals. Her hair hangs in wet tendrils about her shoulders. They have dressed her in a clean white robe. They have painted the mark of the god on her forehead.

She can hear the insistent beat of the gong-drums again, the deepest notes thrumming like the pulsing of a heart. Her own heart begins to pound in rhythm with the drumbeats.

One of the priests approaches her with a bowl.

"Drink," he says, smiling. "It will do you good."

She sniffs the dark liquid cautiously; it smells sweet, like crushed fruit. The priest nods encouragingly. She takes a sip and then another; it tastes good; it makes her feel happy and very peaceful.

The pounding of the gong-drums grows louder. She can hear the priests chanting now, a deep, sonorous drone.

"Come with me," says the priest, beckoning. When she stands, she feels dizzy and light-headed; when she starts to walk, it seems as if she is floating over the ground.

"Where are we going?" she asks, holding back.

The priest reaches out and takes her hand in his. "You are honored, Tilua. You are going to meet Nagar."

Nagar, the devourer of children. She shrinks back, trying to jerk her hand from his. But now he grips it tightly and pulls her along. She cannot escape.

"No, no," she cries out.

The air is hazy with incense smoke as he pulls her onward, past the musicians beating the gong-drums, past ranks of chanting white-robed priests, up steep wide steps, up until she stands beneath a great archway. A winged serpent of stone snorts clouds of smoke at her from the top of the arch through flared nostrils and fanged jaws so lifelike that, for a moment, she cannot breathe for fear.

And then she forgets her fear as the two priests bring out a young man, supporting him between them. His legs drag awkwardly beneath him, as though they have been broken and not mended right. His skin is pale, his hair golden-brown—and as he turns his head to look curiously at her, she sees that his eyes are blue as the sky. Who can he be, this stranger? And what do the priests intend to do with him—or with her?

"Nagar, accept this child."

As the incense smoke swirls and clears, she sees a slab of stone beneath the archway. On the slab of stone lies a metal bowl and beside it, a curved knife of black, polished stone.

The priests move swiftly. They lift her and place her, struggling wildly, on the stone slab. The gong-drums din louder.

"No!" she screams. "I want to go home!"

The blue-eyed stranger cries out in some strange tongue she does not understand. He lurches forward, arms outstretched, as if trying to stop the priests, falling to his knees beneath the archway.

The priest who held her hand lifts the black-bladed knife.

"You are blessed, Tilua," he says, smiling. The knife gleams like lightning in the smoke and sunlight as it descends.

She opens her mouth to cry aloud her terror and rage. But the jagged lightning slices into her throat—and her voice is silenced.

I want to live. I want my life. I want—

A crimson light washes over her vision, staining everything red, then dwindles to a single point of flame.

The world begins to fall apart. A rushing sound, like diving into deep, chill water, fills her ears. The priest's face, the beating of the drums, the bright daylight, all are fading fast. Only the archway remains, looming over her, vast and dark. And a single point of red light still burns at its heart. It draws her in and she cannot resist.

And then she sees it. Its luminous body glittering blue like a star, it comes hurtling toward her through the whirling darkness.

Toward her, right through her, and as it passes through she feels it drain her of her life force, leaving nothing but a shadow, a sad, keening little ghost . . .

"Wake up. Wake *up*, Karila!" Someone was shaking her, insistently calling her name. And she jerked awake with a cry, sitting up, staring around her in utter terror. Marta was bending over her, holding an oil lamp. Then relief overwhelmed her and she clung tightly to Marta as if she would never let go.

"Not another nightmare," said Marta. "There now, it was only a silly dream." She patted Karila soothingly. "Heavens, child, you're soaked through. We must get you into a dry nightgown. What can be giving you these bad dreams?" She tugged the damp garment over Karila's head, hurting her ears. "What have you been reading? Is it that book of old legends Duchess Greta gave you? It's not suitable for a child your age."

Karila badly wanted to unburden herself of her dreams. But she knew Marta would dismiss her fears and blame the toasted cheese she had eaten for her supper. Yet as Marta buttoned her clean nightgown up to the neck, she could still feel little shivers of terror.

"Screaming out like that, waking the whole palace," Marta went on, briskly tucking her back into bed. "What will people say?"

"Don't take the lamp away," Karila begged. "Don't leave me in the dark." She wanted Marta to stay. She wanted light and familiar, comforting things. Most of all, she wanted her father. "Can't you fetch Papa?"

"Great heavens, no, you can't disturb your father's sleep! I'll leave the lamp. Just settle down now and think of your little pets in the menagerie. That'll give you pleasant dreams."

Karila huddled under the sheets, her heart still pattering wildly.

"Think of Pippi," she whispered, trying to imagine playing with her favorite deer, with its soft coat and delicate legs. But the terrors of her nightmare kept invading her thoughts, driving away the comforting images.

And the luminous spirit-creature in the darkness beyond the archway—she knew it now.

"Drakhaoul," she whispered into the pillow. "Tilua's Drakhaoul. *My* Drakhaoul."

"Die. You must die, Tilua, so that the dragon can live."

Astasia hesitated in the antechamber to Karila's bedroom. She had come to read a bedtime story—but from what she could hear, it sounded as if Kari was reading a story, a violent and unsuitable story, out loud to herself.

She crept a little closer and peered around the door.

Karila knelt on the floor beside her bed, with dolls lying around her.

"No, no, I don't want to die!" Kari cried in a high, frightened voice, making one of her dolls, a raven-haired porcelain beauty, tremble as though begging for her life.

"The Serpent God is going to devour you!" This was said in a deep growl as she made the doll in her right hand advance menacingly on the other.

Astasia watched from the doorway, wondering what bizarre ritual Karila was enacting. And then she saw Kari take a silver fruit knife and attack the raven-haired doll, stabbing it again and again, making little cries and screams as she did so, until the stuffing began to come out and the porcelain head was nearly severed. Then the child daubed red paint over the doll's broken body.

Appalled, Astasia could watch no longer. "Whatever are you doing, Kari?"

Karila looked up at her and said matter-of-factly, "It's not real blood. Tilua bled real blood till she died. This is only paint."

Astasia knelt down beside her and picked up the broken doll, shuddering as she did so. She had heard of dark witchcraft rites that involved such acts. Surely Karila had no malicious intent?

"Why did you hurt your doll, Kari?"

"It's only a doll; it can't be hurt," Karila said, taking it back.

"What's her name?"

"Tilua." Karila absently stroked the dark hair on the broken doll's head.

"That's a pretty name." Astasia cast around in her memory,

wondering if there could be a Tilua in Karila's life who had wronged her so cruelly as to provoke this violent revenge.

Marta came in, carrying a tray with a cup of warm cinnamon milk and a plate of biscuits. When she saw what Karila had done, she set the tray down with a bang.

"You'll have no dolls left if you carry on like this, Princess. And no one will buy you new ones, just for you to break them."

Karila appeared not to hear what Marta had said.

"Would you like me to read you a story, Karila?" Astasia reached for the gold-tooled book, searching for a calming, reassuring tale with a happy ending.

"More stories, highness? Is that wise?" said Marta. "Exciting an overactive imagination just before bedtime? I think we've had quite enough, thank you."

Astasia closed the book with a snap. Another snub from Marta. Though she had to admit that Marta looked harassed and tired, with dark circles under her eyes.

"Has the princess been suffering from restless nights?" she asked in what she hoped would sound like a sympathetic tone.

Marta raised her eyes heavenward. "We haven't had an unbroken night in weeks! I've told Doctor Amandel, but he just dismisses it. I've asked him for a sleep draft to calm her down. He says it's unnecessary."

"Would you like me to stay with her tonight?" Astasia offered. "So that you can get some rest?"

Marta glanced at her suspiciously.

"I'd be happy to. She is my stepdaughter, after all."

"I'd like that, Tasia," said Karila, letting the broken doll drop.

"I'll be in the chamber next door if you need me," said Marta. But something in her manner had altered; Astasia even detected a softening of the sharp, defensive tone she usually adopted in their exchanges.

As Karila snuggled under the sheets, she suddenly looked at Astasia and said, "I feel safe with you here, Tasia."

"No stories, Marta said," Astasia whispered in a conspiratorial tone, "but shall I tell you about some of the games I used to play with my brother Andrei when we were your age?"

"A brother," Karila said with a wistful sigh. "I'd like a brother to play with."

"Oh brothers can be very annoying! Once Andrei tied my hair to the back of the chair when I wasn't paying attention, so that when I tried to get up, the chair came too."

Karila let out a little giggle, which she smothered with her hand. "We mustn't disturb Marta!" she whispered. "What did you do?"

"I waited to pay him back," said Astasia. "I sewed up the bottoms of his cadet uniform's breeches and the cuffs of his shirt, just before he had to go to the Military Academy for the first time. He was furious! And late."

"I'd like to have seen him hopping about, trying to put his foot through," said Karila, breaking into laughter. Her laughter was infectious and Astasia found herself joining in, glad to see Karila looking less anxious.

"Tell me more about you and Andrei!" demanded Karila.

"Not tonight, Kari." Astasia bent forward and kissed her. "But I will place my own special ward around your bed so that you can sleep soundly." She twitched her fingers twice at each corner of the swan bed. "There," she said, settling herself in the chair beside the fire. "Now you're safe."

Astasia had almost dozed off in front of the dying fire when she thought she heard a door click open. Taking up the lamp, she went over to the swan bed, only to see it was empty, the covers thrown back. Yet the bedchamber door was shut.

Karila must have left by the secret passage.

Where can she have gone all alone at this late hour?

Astasia felt along the wall until she found the catch in the paneling that Karila had shown her once before. The concealed door slid open, letting a draft into the bedchamber that set the lamp flame flickering.

Astasia was not as adept at navigating the secret passages in the palace as Karila. She gathered her skirts in one hand and squeezed through the little doorway. But her only consolation was that Karila would make slow progress because of her twisted body.

Soon she spotted a pale little figure in the drafty darkness ahead. Astasia hastened onward just as Karila opened another doorway and disappeared from her view.

"Wait for me, Kari!" she called. The doorway opened into an inner courtyard lit by lanterns; Astasia emerged into the starry night to see Karila limping away from her. "No wonder the child is always ill, if she's wandering outside late at night," she muttered as she hurried after her. "Is she going to her menagerie, to feed her little deer?" And then she stopped abruptly, seeing where Karila was going. "Or to the Magus? Is he working some spell on her?"

"Halt! Who goes there!"

Astasia heard a sentry bark out a warning. Karila had turned left, before the archway that led to the Magus's laboratory. Catching up at last, she came upon an extraordinary sight. Karila stood, blinking confusedly in the torchlight, on the steps that led down to the Palace Treasury. Massive doors of timber and iron were guarded day and night by four sentries. And there was Karila, confronted by these tall, broad-shouldered soldiers.

"Kari!" Astasia reached her and knelt to put her arms around her. "What are you doing here?" Karila looked at her blankly from eyes that were opaque as shadow in the torchlight. She must have been walking in her sleep.

"Imperial highness!" The sentries saluted her.

"Where am I?" Karila seemed to be still half-asleep.

"Outside, catching your death of cold. Come with me." Astasia took hold of her hand firmly and led her back toward the nearest entrance to the palace.

"Your daughter has been sleepwalking, Eugene." Astasia sat down opposite Eugene at the little table in their private morning room. "Our daughter," she corrected herself.

"What's that?" Eugene was drinking coffee as he read the morning's dispatches; he seemed preoccupied and was obviously not listening to what she said.

"I'm worried about her," said Astasia. "She's been having nightmares. She's playing violent, horrible games with her dolls. And the servants have heard her talking to an imaginary friend. I think she's lonely; she needs friends."

"Children play strange games," said Eugene, glancing up a moment as he turned over a page. "And it's hard to choose friends for her. She can't join in their games and it makes her sad."

"Even so, there must be some nice, quiet little girls among the courtiers' children," persisted Astasia.

Eugene set down his coffee cup and picked up his papers. He

looked as if he was mulling over important matters of state and her interruption was disturbing his train of thought. "How long have these episodes been going on now?"

"Marta thinks they began the night before the coronation. Just after—"

"The night of the beacon." Now she had caught his attention. "She had just disembarked." He leaned over and kissed the top of her head, almost absentmindedly. "I'll consult the Magus. He must know some way to put a stop to bad dreams."

"Kiukirilya," said the Magus.

"Surely a Spirit Singer can only work with the spirits of the dead?" Eugene stared down at Kiukiu's body, fascinated that, while her breast rose and fell gently as though she were asleep, there was no other sign of life.

"Precisely so," said Linnaius. "Your daughter may be possessed. And until the spirit that has possessed her is exorcised, the princess will continue to wander the night like a revenant, endangering her health."

"You know I do not hold with any of this talk of spirits." Eugene clasped his hands behind his back and began to pace the Magus's room. It went against everything he believed in. After what had occurred in Artamon's Mausoleum, he had vowed there would be no more summonings. And now, Linnaius was suggesting Karila should be subjected to some barbaric Azhkendi rite . . . But if Kiukirilya's arts could ease Astasia's mind and stop Karila from wandering the palace at night, then perhaps spirit-singing might work where Doctor Amandel's physic had failed.

"Shall I restore her soul to her body?" asked Linnaius, carefully lifting the soul-glass on its chain from around his neck.

"Yes," said Eugene, curious to watch this forbidden procedure. "Do it, Linnaius."

The Magus unstoppered the crystal phial and set it against the girl's lips. He breathed words in a tongue Eugene had never heard before.

And as Eugene watched, the translucent shimmer in the phial slowly poured out, melting into Kiukirilya's mouth until the phial was empty.

"And now?" Eugene whispered, bending close, searching for signs of life.

Linnaius brushed the girl's closed lids once, twice, thrice with his index finger.

Gold-lashed lids fluttered a little. Kiukirilya muttered, shifted a little on the couch, but did not wake.

"Has it worked?" Eugene did not want to find they had a living corpse to dispose of.

"It may take some while for her to wake. I shall keep watch and inform you of any progress."

The girl was courageous; she had extraordinary talents and she had served him well.

He did not want her damaged by Linnaius's dark arts.

CHAPTER 27

Fire cones simmer in the ash-grey sky. A distant ominous rumble trembles through the air. The burning sands shift beneath Gavril's bare feet and the dark sea sizzles with heat.

He senses he is not alone. He turns and sees a tall winged figure, wild-haired, clothed in shadow, hovering behind him. Eyes glitter in the smoky air, lightning-blue.

It is like looking in a mirror at his own reflection.

"Drakhaoul."

"I have another name, Gavril. A secret name that must not be spoken aloud on earth—except by the one closest to my soul." The dry voice, so familiar now, has taken on a new, more intimate tone. "Maybe the time has come to tell you my true name."

"Then tell me."

"My name is Khezef."

"Khezef," repeats Gavril. The name has an ancient, forbidden ring to it; it is resonant with hidden meanings. This is a kind of ritual, he understands now, the exchanging of names. "Why have you brought me back here? Why is it always here?"

"Because this is the Serpent Gate. The gateway between this world and the Ways Beyond."

Gavril raises his eyes and sees in the lurid glare that they are standing beneath the stone arch carved with twisting serpents—the one he has painted in Arnskammar. The daemon gateway that has haunted his dreams.

"And because you are the one, Gavril Nagarian, who will release me and my kin from this world."

"Is that really what you want?" Gavril is not certain he has understood the daemon completely.

"Look carefully at the Serpent Gate. What do you see?"

Now that Gavril stands so close to the great gate, he sees that the coils of the twisting serpents are wrapped around broken bodies, taut, distorted with agony, faces frozen in screams of perpetual anguish. Torn wing-shafts protrude from dislocated shoulders. Whoever sculpted the images must have worked from life to achieve such a realistic depiction of the tortured souls—

"No," whispers Khezef, "look again."

"They look just like you." Gavril's voice fades as he realizes the full horror of what he is looking at. "They are just like you!"

"When Serzhei called upon the Heavenly Guardians to destroy us, this is where he bound my kindred in stone." A look of fierce sorrow gleams in the Drakhaoul's star-blue eyes. "So that they might forever gaze upon the gateway to our home, yet never pass through and know again the joy of freedom."

Another rumble shakes the ground beneath Gavril's feet.

"If the volcano erupts once more, the gate will fall and we will be trapped here for all eternity."

Gavril sees a strange look soften the fierce gleam of his daemon's eyes. He remembers he has glimpsed that look once before when he lay helpless in Arnskammar, dying, and the one called Khezef came to his aid.

"How? How can I release you?"

"Nagar's Eye. The ruby your ancestor Volkhar stole from Ty Nagar. Only that ruby will open the gate. Find the Eye and open the gate, Gavril. Then, I promise you, you will be free. . . ."

Gavril opened his eyes. It was dawn and a blackbird in the villa gardens was fluting outside his window. The fiery volcanic light still bathed his vision. Even his crisp white linen sheets seemed tinged with that baleful glow. And the Drakhaoul's promises wreathed around his mind, as softly insistent as the blackbird's song.

"Find my ancestor's ruby? But where do I start? My father left no jewels to me."

And then he remembered his mother's portrait of Lord Volkh,

painted here in the Villa Andara. In that portrait his father was wearing a magnificent ruby, crimson as vintage wine, about his neck. Where was that ruby now? Hadn't she mentioned something about leaving it at Swanholm?

He found Elysia drinking her morning tea on the sunny balcony, cupping the delicate tea bowl in both hands. She smiled at him.

"What a beautiful morning," she said, taking in a deep breath of air. "Can you smell my white lilacs? I look forward to that scent every year."

"That ruby in the portrait, Mother," he said. "You said you left it behind at Swanholm?"

She started, spilling a little of her tea. "Oh, Gavril. Whatever made you think of the ruby now? Is it really so important?"

"Was it at Swanholm? Think, Mother!"

She glanced up at him and he saw that she was blushing.

"It was made into a necklace, Gavril. And earrings. Count Velemir asked his jeweler to do it for me. Why do you ask?"

Earrings. And a necklace. It could take weeks, maybe months to track them down. He needed the rubies now.

Pavel walked out onto the balcony of the Villa Sapara. The morning sky was the intense blue that promises great heat at midday. He stretched and gazed up at the cloudless sky, feeling the sun's warmth on his skin. It felt good to be alive.

Yesterday he had come close to death, far too close. He could not afford to be so careless again.

He sniffed, smelling the steam from hot, fresh-brewed coffee as Mama Chadi appeared, carrying a laden tray.

"Here's your breakfast, Master Pavel." She set the tray down and beamed at him.

"Thank you." He smiled back. He sat down at the little ironwork table and poured coffee, strong and black, into one of his mother's gilded porcelain cups. He was just stirring in a second spoonful of sugar when he heard voices.

"He's at breakfast." Mama Chadi sounded flustered. "If you'd be so good as to wait till he's finished—"

"Good morning!"

He looked around and saw Raïsa Korneli. Dressed in a simple

white linen shirt and riding breeches, with the morning sun glinting in her short-cropped auburn hair, she looked deliciously ambivalent, neither girl nor boy.

"I'm so sorry, Master Pavel, but this young person insisted," puffed Mama Chadi.

"It's all right," he said, rising. "Good morning, Raïsa. Would you care for some coffee?"

"I'll fetch another cup." Mama Chadi shuffled back indoors.

"What a wonderful view!" Raïsa went to the balcony balustrade and leaned over, gazing at the bay far below, the sea breeze ruffling her hair. "When all this is over, would you let me come up here and make some sketches? The quality of the light is remarkable."

"So you're an artist?"

She laughed. "I wouldn't make that claim. I'm studying philosophy at the university with Professor Lukan. Painting is only a hobby."

Mama Chadi shuffled back with a second porcelain cup and saucer.

"Cream? Sugar?" he asked, pouring coffee.

"Lots—of both!" She stirred the sugared coffee vigorously and drank it down in two gulps.

Pavel watched her, captivated. She was refreshingly different from the well-bred young Francian women he had been obliged to associate with in the last year—a free spirit, unfettered by the constraints of polite society.

"I owe you my life," he said. "If you hadn't spoken up for me, I'd be dead."

She shrugged his thanks aside. "My brother shoots first and asks questions after. I try to reason with him. What's the point in destroying our allies as well as our enemies? Besides . . ." All the vivacity faded from her eyes. "Our younger brother Miran is still fighting for his life in Colchise. The Tielens shot him outside the citadel. He's a boy, only seventeen years old."

He wanted to say something to console her. But looking into her stricken face, he saw that she was fighting back tears, and an ill-timed sympathetic word might break her courage.

"Better to keep busy!" she said, forcing a laugh. "There's plenty to be done."

"If there's any way I can help—"

"You didn't think this was merely a social call, did you?" She laughed again, more easily this time. "I've come to bring you to the university. We've had news. A Tielen raiding party's sneaked in over the border from Muscobar."

"Ah." Pavel rose. "So our morning idyll is over."

"I'd love to see the rest of the villa some time," Raïsa said as he led her inside under the wisteria-laden arch framing the door, sniffing in its sweet, mauve-pea perfume appreciatively.

"It needs love and attention," said Pavel, saddened to see how the sunlight revealed the threadbare patches in the heavy brocades of lilac and rose, and the spots of mold darkening the rose-leaf cornices. "My mother has neglected it since my father's death. Lack of funds, I'm afraid."

"I love this salon." Raïsa spun around, arms outstretched. "You could hold dances in here."

Was she as free with all the men she encountered? In truth, he couldn't tell if she was openly flirting with him. All he knew was that he was enjoying this encounter, wondering where it might lead . . .

"Where's Pavel Velemir?" demanded a loud voice in the hallway. "Take me to him."

Raïsa winced. "Iovan," she mouthed at Pavel.

"You can't just barge your way in uninvited," they heard Mama Chadi protest. "You wait out here till I see if the master is free to receive you."

Pavel threw open the double doors to see Mama Chadi jabbing a broom, bristles to the fore, in Iovan's face.

"It's all right, Mama Chadi," Pavel said. "You can let him in."

"Not till he mends his manners," muttered Mama Chadi, lowering the broom.

Iovan pushed past her, face red with annoyance. "And what are you doing here, Raïsa?"

"Waiting for you," she replied coolly. "So, what's the latest news from Ormalo?"

"An incursion. Over the border with Muscobar."

"How many?" Pavel asked.

Iovan swore. "We don't know. They've taken Ormalo. And now there are reports from Koshara. Looks like the Tielens are coming at us from all sides."

"Eugene doesn't know the meaning of the word 'defeat,' " Pavel said with a wry grimace.

"No one said it would be easy." Iovan scowled at him. "But we know the terrain. Up in the foothills, we can pick 'em off a few at a time."

"Listen to you, city boy!" Raïsa let out a derisive whistle. "Since when have you become such an expert on the northern strongholds? You've never been farther than Colchise in your entire life."

Iovan ignored the taunt. "So, are you with us, Pavel Velemir? Let's see where your allegiances really lie."

Iovan's unrelenting hostility was beginning to grate on Pavel's nerves.

"Give me five minutes to saddle my horse. Meet me outside in the drive."

"Wait." Raïsa caught hold of Pavel's arm. He felt the warmth of her fingers through his shirt. "Why don't we go fetch Gavril Andar too?"

The name sent a little shiver of anticipation through Pavel's body. Eugene's nemesis, the deposed Drakhaon of Azhkendir. He could not believe his luck.

"That one's trouble," grumbled Iovan. "He goes missing for months on end, then shows up with some mystery weapon and wipes out the opposition."

"I wasn't asking your opinion, Iovan," Raïsa said sharply. "I don't ask where he's been or what he's done. I only know he saved us."

"Given the alchymical firepower of Eugene's forces, we need all the help we can get," said Pavel, and was rewarded with another scowl from Iovan.

"The meeting place is outside the Ormalo Gate in Colchise. One hour's time. Bring your own water and rations." Iovan opened the front door. "But travel light. We intend to move fast. Come on, Raïsa."

Raïsa paused, gazing questioningly at Pavel.

"I'll see you at the Ormalo Gate, then," he said. "In an hour."

He watched them untie their horses from the rail at the front of the house and ride down the lime-lined drive toward the upper cliff road and the Villa Andara.

All he had to do to fulfill his mission for Eugene was to make some excuse to use the Vox Aethyria and whisper the rebels' plans to Gustave. Then he would take the first ship out of Vermeille and . . . disappear.

The sun caught burnished lights in her hair as she parted from her brother. Suddenly she looked back over her shoulder and waved to him.

And all of a sudden he knew with terrible, ironic certainty that he cared for her. There was something about her carefree manner that had caught his heart. If he betrayed Gavril Andar, he would also betray Raïsa Korneli. It must be possible to stay with the rebels, yet keep Eugene's agents satisfied with little hints that promised more than they delivered.

He caught himself smiling. Uncle Feodor would have been proud of him.

Raïsa had heard Lukan talk of Elysia's famous soirées at the Villa Andara. She had glimpsed it from the sands far below—another white stucco seaside villa, half-hidden by maritime pines. But now she felt suddenly nervous as she knocked at the door.

A smiling housekeeper showed her into the salon.

"Please excuse the disarray, Miss Korneli," she said, "but we were searched by the Tielens and we're still repairing the damage."

Raïsa gazed around. This salon had none of the faded grandeur of the Villa Sapara; the walls were painted in shades of linen and raw silk. But the paintings that hung on this plain backdrop were filled with color and light. Landscapes, imbued with the rich earthy hues of the Smarnan countryside; and blue seascapes, so watery you could almost dip your finger in them . . . She knew Elysia Andar was famed for her portraiture, yet these canvases showed another less well-known side of her gift.

"My mother calls these her 'little daubs,' but I think they're her finest work."

Raïsa started. She had been so absorbed in Elysia's paintings that she had not heard anyone come in.

"I startled you." Gavril Andar stood in the doorway. "I'm sorry. What can I do for you, Miss Korneli?"

He looked haggard. His shadowed eyes had a strange glitter to them, as if he were suffering from fever.

"Are you well, Maistre Andar?" she asked, concerned to see him still looking so ill. Was this a wasted journey?

"I've felt better." His mouth twisted into a gaunt smile. "It'll take a while to recover from the Emperor's hospitality."

So he had a personal score to settle with the Tielens as well. What had he endured to make him loose such a terrible weapon on his enemies? There was a brooding silence about him that made her imagine they must have made him suffer all manner of atrocities.

"I've come to ask for your help. The Tielens have taken Ormalo. They're sneaking in over the Muscobar border. Now they're in Koshara."

"Eugene is a stubborn man," Gavril Andar said tersely. "He won't accept defeat."

"That's what Pavel said."

"Pavel? Who is Pavel?"

"Pavel Velemir. He's another fugitive from the Emperor's injustice."

"Velemir?" Gavril repeated slowly. The name seemed to mean something to him.

"You know him?"

"No."

And yet it seemed to her she saw a haunted look darken his eyes. There was much, she guessed, he had not told them.

"There are so few of us," she said haltingly, "and so many of them. We need your help."

He did not reply. Instead he walked slowly to the windows and gazed down at the bay. "Were you there?" he asked. "When I attacked the Tielen fleet? Were you in the citadel?"

"Yes," she said, not understanding where this was leading. "I was on the ramparts. I saw the flash of light; I saw the ships explode."

He turned around, staring at her with feverish intensity. "And have you, or any of those who fought beside you, fallen sick?"

"No, not as far as I—"

"You didn't breathe in any of the smoke that drifted inshore?"

"Why? Is it harmful?"

Again, no reply. Instead he drew in a deep breath and said, "I'll come with you to reconnoiter, not to fight. I think I understand Eugene's tactics. And I think I know what game he's playing. He's trying to lure me out into the open."

"Why you? Because of your secret weapon?"

"I'll need a horse. My Merani is—" he stopped, checking himself, "is not in Smarna."

She looked at him, overwhelmed with curiosity. Everything he said, these little slips and half-finished sentences, only added to the enigma.

"Meet me at the Ormalo Gate, then. In half an hour. I'll have a horse for you. You can take my brother Miran's."

He accompanied her out into the hall. A painting hung near the front door, a double portrait, very naturally posed, of a man and a woman. The woman was sitting on a daisy-filled lawn, reading, and the man was leaning over her shoulder. It was an intimate portrayal, simply yet masterfully done. She had not noticed it before, but now she saw with a little shock that the man was Rafael Lukan and the woman he was leaning so affectionately close to was Elysia Andar.

"Oh!" she said. She knew—of course, who didn't?—that Lukan and Elysia had been lovers. But this painting offered proof of the strength of their relationship. Her cheeks flaming, she tried to cover her reaction with a question. "Who painted this?"

"I did." Gavril Andar was frowning at the picture as if he was not at all pleased with it. "I don't know why my mother has hung it in the hall. It's an early piece, done for my first year examination."

"I think it's charming." Raïsa spoke from the heart. Subject matter aside, the painting was very accomplished for an early piece. "It's so fresh, so full of spring air and light—" She broke off. "You're as talented as your mother. You should be painting, not fighting."

And then, seeing the desolation in his eyes, she realized she had touched on a sensitive issue. "Listen to me, babbling on without thinking. I didn't mean—"

"No," he said. "You're right. I should be painting."

When she went to untether Luciole, she found that someone, perhaps the housekeeper, had thoughtfully provided a trough of water. As she rode away, she caught herself glancing back at the Villa Andara, shivering in spite of the day's warmth. There were mysteries there—and they were all hidden in the darkness haunting Gavril Andar's fever-bright eyes.

Gavril stood at an upstairs window and watched Raïsa Korneli ride off toward Colchise.

Had he given anything away? His shoulders were stiff with tension, his fingers were still clenched tight with the effort of controlling himself. And when, without thinking, he had said Merani's name, he had seen a sudden, vivid image of Kastel Drakhaon and the stables: young Ivar and Movsar playing each other at knuckle stones in an empty stall, jumping up with red faces when he appeared, running to saddle up coal-black Merani . . .

My druzhina.

Elysia had told him a little of the indignities the *druzhina* had been forced to undergo, chained together like slaves, made to labor long hours on meager rations, excavating deep underground for minerals to feed the Emperor's munitions factories.

My faithful bodyguard—and I've abandoned you. The ache was almost too hard to bear.

"Who was that, Gavril?" Elysia appeared in *deshabille,* wet hair wound up in a towel, Djihari-fashion.

"Raïsa Korneli. The Tielens have come back—over the northern border this time."

He saw her face fall. "And they want you to go fight them? Gavril, no. You've done enough. You've exhausted yourself. Let the militia handle this one."

"Mother, you know the militia is no match for the Tielens."

She caught hold of his hand and turned it over, looking at the nails.

"Look," she said, raising them to the light. A faint taint of blue had already begun to show. "Think of what you've done to the bay. Think of—"

"I know!" Angrily he drew his hand away. He didn't want a lecture; he was only too aware of the risks of using his powers again. "I'm going anyway," he said.

"Well, then. You have to do what you feel is right," she said. Yet there was no criticism in her voice, only regret. "But take care, Gavril." She reached out and briefly stroked his forehead; there was not enough hair yet to smooth back into place.

He flinched at her touch.

Don't treat me as a child, Mother. I've done things you can't begin to imagine—even in your worst nightmares.

It was already hot and Gavril was glad he had worn his old, broad-brimmed straw hat to shade his head. As he walked up over the brow of the hill, he saw the Smarnan forces massing outside the Ormalo Gate. Forces? Ninety or so of the Colchise militia on foot, another hundred or so of the national guard—and a ragbag assortment of eager students, volunteers, and other hangers-on, all ill-equipped with ancient muskets and hunting pistols. Three hundred at best, he reckoned. More than his *druzhina,* and armed with some basic firepower, but still no match for Eugene's troops.

He spotted Raïsa toward the front of the motley column, her rich auburn hair catching the light of the midday sun. She was in conversation with a tall, fair-haired young man. *One of the students?* he wondered.

She caught sight of him and beckoned him to join her. As he approached, the young man turned, shading his eyes against the midday sun.

"Gavril, this is Pavel Velemir; you remember I told you about him."

Feodor Velemir spins around to face him, his eyes wide, crazed with wonder and fear. And then . . .

Gavril blinked. This Velemir was young, about his own age. The name could just be a coincidence. Maybe Velemir is a common surname in Muscobar. . . .

On the third day out from Colchise, the northern road began to climb, and the coastal plain gave way to the foothills of the far-distant ridge of mountains, the Larani Range, which acted as a natural border between Smarna and southern Muscobar.

They were called mountains, but to Gavril they were nothing compared to the terrifying splendors of the snow-capped Kharzhgylls in Azhkendir, looming up out of the Arkhel Waste. At this time of year there was only the slightest dusting of snow on the highest peak, Mount Diktra.

There had been little intelligence as to the movements of the Tielen invaders; there were rumors, odd sightings, but no verifiable evidence. Gavril had even begun to wonder if the earlier reports were nothing but Tielen propaganda, designed to lure them away from Colchise in order to retake the citadel.

These thoughts troubled him the most. Because that was what he would have attempted in Eugene's place. And he knew that Eugene had worked that plan on him before, at Narvazh in Azhkendir.

Gavril rode alongside Raïsa near the head of the column, with Pavel on her other side. The young Muscobite had engaged Raïsa in conversation and was telling her entertaining anecdotes about life in the embassy in Francia. Gavril half-heard snippets about the ambassador's lapdog—an overindulged pug who was apt to disgrace himself at soirées—and the ambassador's younger daughter and her ill-advised affair with her music-master. He heard Raïsa laughing, both delighted and shocked by Pavel's tales of embassy indiscretions. And he found himself wishing he could chatter away so lightheartedly. He was poor company, he knew it. And this morning, as the heat increased, so did the black ache in his head—the last lingering legacy of Baltzar's operation. Had he expected too much of himself too soon? Perhaps he should have allowed himself several days' rest at the Villa Andara to recuperate. . . .

"Are you all right, Gavril?"

He glanced up, grimacing as the sunlight sent a stab of pain through his head. Raïsa was regarding him with concern.

"There's an inn up ahead. You could stop and rest."

"Do I look that bad?" he said, forcing a smile.

"You're not fully recovered from your wounds. I saw the scars, re-member? I've brought powdered willow bark and feverfew. I could mix you a draft to ease the pain."

Her concern for his well-being took him by surprise. He was just about to reply when he spotted a small whirl of dust on the horizon, coming toward them.

"Riders!" yelled Iovan. "Take cover!"

The Smarnans rode around in confusion; one or two of the horses reared and threw their riders to the ground.

"Far too late," Gavril heard Pavel Velemir murmur.

"Where are our scouts?" Gavril scanned the road ahead. "Is no one up ahead?" Bogatyr Askold would have bawled Iovan out for such negligence, he thought wryly.

"Amateurs," Pavel Velemir said with a little confidential smile.

"It's all right," Iovan shouted, "they're friends."

"Just as well," Pavel said, "for we'd all be shot to pieces by now if they were Tielens."

Gavril nodded. He had no reason to trust Pavel Velemir and yet he couldn't help feeling a certain affinity with the young Muscobite. "So you're a soldier?" he asked.

"Seven long years in the Muscobar Military Academy." A lock of fair hair flopped into his eyes and he flicked it away carelessly. "I es-caped into the diplomatic service. But you never forget what they drill into you."

Iovan was conferring with the riders up ahead. Gavril uncorked his water bottle and took a mouthful, swilling it around before swallowing. All his instincts told him that he was the only effective defense the little column had against the Tielens.

He saw Raïsa ride up to her brother, her face flushed with excitement as she joined in the council of war. To her, this rebellion was an act of desperate heroism—a glorious stand against the tyranny of a foreign despot. She was fighting for her wounded brother, fighting for her country—

She saw the glory. She did not see her own death—or that of her fellow students.

"The Tielens have taken Koshara," Iovan said. "And now they've fanned out into the foothills."

"What about the Larani Gorge?" one of the students asked. "We could lie in wait for them up there."

"Who knows if they'll come that way?"

"If we split up, we stand a better chance of taking them by surprise," said Pavel.

Iovan frowned at him.

"Pavel's right," Raïsa said.

"What do *you* think, Gavril Andar?" Iovan said bullishly.

"I agree with Pavel." Gavril stared Iovan straight in the eyes, challenging him to counter the suggestion. "We need intelligence out in the villages, outriders to keep us informed of the Tielens' movements."

"As you're so keen on scouting ahead, perhaps you'd care to go reconnoiter?" Iovan's voice rang with scorn and resentment.

It was the chance Gavril had been hoping for, the excuse to separate himself from the others and assess the situation from the air.

"And you, Pavel Velemir, why don't you keep him company? Rejoin us at Anisieli by nightfall."

Gavril only just restrained himself from swearing aloud.

Pavel Velemir smiled in reply—a disarming smile, open and friendly. But Gavril could not bring himself to smile back.

They rode along without speaking, Gavril leading the way. He was following a stony track that, if his memory served him, wound past remote farms and hamlets, well away from the road.

Anger still simmered deep inside and he knew he must use all his self-control to contain it. Iovan had come close to goading him too far—and he was not sure how much self-control he had left in his current condition. And why, of all the rebels, had Iovan singled out Pavel Velemir to go along with him? He narrowed his eyes at the sun-baked countryside, seeing shadows from the past. He could hear Elysia's voice, telling him about her doomed visit to Swanholm.

"Feodor Velemir duped me, Gavril. He was so charming and so earnest that I truly believed he had your best interests at heart. But to die such a horrible death—" She had covered her eyes with her fingers, as though trying to blot out the memory of what she had seen.

"I thought—I thought he meant to harm you." The words had come out slowly, painfully, as he relived the moment. *"How was I to know? I couldn't take the risk."*

"Is Anisieli far?" Pavel asked suddenly.

Gavril started. He had been so absorbed in his memories, he had forgotten about their mission. "At the foot of the gorge. We should get there before sunset."

Pavel Velemir took out a slender eyeglass and extended it, surveying the distant hills. "They won't risk breaking cover in open country like this. They'll have hidden themselves away."

Gavril gazed at him guardedly. "That's a useful little contrivance."

"It was my Uncle Feodor's," Pavel said, offering it to Gavril. "It's about all I inherited from him. Most of his possessions were looted when the rebels sacked the Winter Palace."

Uncle Feodor's. Gavril took the cylindrical tube and raised it to one eye, handling it as if it were red-hot. There were workers toiling away, tending the vines on the sunny slopes higher up. But there was no sign of the Tielens.

He doesn't know that I'm the one who killed his uncle.

"Excellent magnification," he said curtly, handing it back. "But I'd be surprised if the Tielens have penetrated this far into Smarna in so short a time, unless they've developed wings."

"At least up here we're spared Field Marshal Iovan's tetchy little tirades." Pavel grinned at Gavril, another friendly, open grin.

That smile awoke something buried deep within Gavril's damaged mind—the memory of what it felt like to have friends, to share a joke, to be easy in someone else's company . . . But because of the terrible thing he had done, he could never be Pavel's friend. He was Drakhaon. And since a Drakhaon was not as other men, he must live apart, gifted and cursed by his dragon-daemon.

* * *

Gavril turned Capriole's head away from the vineyards with their neat rows of fresh green vines, and rode up toward the higher, rougher pasture land. It had not rained in many days and everything was powdered in a fine reddish dust from the rich earth.

He had not traveled this route in some years. When he was fourteen or fifteen years old, Elysia and Lukan had taken a house on a wine-growing estate. All that hot summer they had played at living the country life: He and Lukan had gone fishing in the weed-choked little river that irrigated the vineyards and Elysia had painted, wandering off through the fields with her sketchbook, easel, and parasol. The sound of the cicadas whirring noisily in the trees brought back something of those lazy, carefree days. He could feel the cool mud squelching between his toes as he waded barefoot through the stony river shallows. And he remembered the luscious taste of the new grapes, bursting juicily sweet and sharp in his mouth. . . .

Maybe out here he could find the solitude that would help him start to paint again.

As Capriole jogged on upward, he saw himself in the overgrown garden at the vineyard house, brush in hand and canvas in front of him, putting the finishing touches to a portrait whose subject sat in the shade of the old olive tree, smiling at him, her fair hair catching glints of amber and gold from the dappled sunlight. . . .

Kiukiu?

"*How* much farther to Anisieli?" asked Pavel.

"Not far." Gavril, startled out of his daydream, answered him brusquely. "Two or three miles, no more." He glanced back over his shoulder. The empty hillside shimmered in the heat of the late afternoon sun. Cicadas and birds chirped; flies droned. "Let's give the horses a rest."

On the brow of the hill, a clump of chestnuts promised some welcome shade. Gavril dismounted and tied Capriole on a long tether so that she could graze on the short grass beneath the trees. Then he walked to the farthest side of the hilltop and gazed out over the next valley, wanting to be alone with his thoughts.

There was no denying it. He had caught himself daydreaming about Kiukiu. Painting Kiukiu, he corrected himself. And an aching feeling of longing swept over him like a drowning wave. As soon as they flushed out Eugene's troops, he would leave the rebels to finish the job, and set off for Azhkendir.

Pavel offered him his flask. "Watered wine?"

Gavril's head throbbed at the thought. "No. I have a headache from the sun."

He sat down and took out his water bottle, drinking a long draft to relieve the dryness of his mouth and throat.

"She's quite something, that Korneli girl," Pavel said idly. "Worth a hundred of those insipid convent-educated girls in Mirom. I'd like to see some of them cut their hair and go riding bareback in their brother's borrowed clothes!"

Gavril stared at him from under close-drawn brows. He had been so long in solitary confinement in the Iron Tower that he had almost forgotten how to participate in this kind of idle, companionable conversation.

"Of course, in Mirom, such bold behavior would ruin her chances in society. 'By all means, make her your mistress,' my mother would say, 'but she's utterly unsuitable as a bride.' "

"And do you intend to follow your mother's advice?"

"I heard a rumor that she has eyes only for Rafael Lukan."

"Lukan?"

"He's old enough to be her father, but some girls prefer older men." Pavel lay back on the dry grass, gazing up at the sky. "My Uncle Feodor could vouch for that. He was always having to extricate himself from some intrigue with the Grand Duchess's ladies-in-waiting. Means you and I have to work twice as hard to impress—"

Gavril heard the distant crack and rattle of carbine fire, far-off but unmistakeable. He was on his feet in an instant, listening intently. "What's that?"

"Gunfire." Pavel leaped up.

"Sounds as if the Tielens have reached Anisieli before us."

Had the Tielens been shadowing Iovan and his men all this time? Or had they just run into a raiding party by chance? Whatever the circumstances, Gavril didn't rate the rebels' chances too highly. And Raïsa would be caught in the ambush.

"Come on." Pavel hurried toward the horses.

Gavril hung back, torn. If he rode with Pavel, he would never reach the rebels in time to help.

"Ahh!" He clutched his head with both hands, half-acting, half in earnest. He dropped to his knees, doubling up as if in pain.

"What's wrong?" Pavel was in the saddle already.

"You go ahead. I'll—catch up."

"You look dreadful."

"Head wound. It'll pass. Just go!"

The sound of shots came again, echoing through the green valley.

Pavel hesitated another second, then kicked his heels into his horse's glossy flanks. Gavril opened one eye and saw him ride down the other side of the hill.

"Drakhaoul," he muttered as he got to his feet, "can you hear me? They need us."

Even now he might be too late to save them. He cast aside his water bottle and hat and ran toward the edge, leaping up into the air, arms spread wide.

"Khezef!" he cried. *"Now!"*

The air whirled about him, dark as a tornado. He felt a tremor go twisting through his whole body.

"I hear you!"

Wings burst from his daemon-altered body, wrenching his shoulders and arms until he felt they would be torn from their sockets. Flight, as he powered upward, was utter agony, working every strained sinew and muscle till they burned.

And then it became sheer ecstasy as he forgot the physical pain and skimmed into the blue of the summer sky, riding the air currents, swooping down over the hill he and Capriole had toiled up in the heat, with the cool wind behind him.

The crack of carbines rose from far below. He spotted little puffs of white smoke first—and then a sight far worse. The rebel column was surrounded. He smelled blood, and the horribly familiar acrid stink of Linnaius's alchymical gunpowder.

There were at least a hundred Tielens in the raiding party, and from the air, he knew instantly that they had sprung their ambush with military precision. He could see bodies on the road, horses and men. Some were trying to crawl away; others had adopted defensive positions in a ditch.

Raïsa. Where was Raïsa?

He circled high above, searching for a glimpse of her bright hair, dreading to see her slender body lying sprawled among the dead.

Then he saw her. She was crouched behind an upturned munitions cart, frantically ramming shot into her pistols.

"Fire!" a Tielen voice yelled, and another round of mortar shells exploded among the fleeing rebels.

"Get down, Raïsa!" he cried out. Buffeted by the rush of burning air as shrapnel burst in the air, he turned, readying himself to strike back.

Had she survived that last blast? Smoke billowed across the road. The upturned cart was on fire; it had taken a direct hit.

Rage burned through his whole body. If they had killed her—

His powers were still not fully restored after Vermeille Bay. But in the heat and smoke of the melee, no one had noticed him overhead. He had that advantage, at least.

The Tielens had positioned their mortars behind a dry stone wall, all that remained of a shepherd's summer hut.

The Drakhaon narrowed his eyes. *Take out the artillery.*

As he dove down, the air rushing past him, his Drakhaon-body snaking through the sky, he felt nothing but the fierce, exultant joy of battle.

Blue fire seared the row of mortars. Smoke filled the air.

Splinters of stone exploded as the wall collapsed. The blast blew him off course; he slewed around in midair, shadow-wings beating a hot, dry wind toward the fleeing Tielens.

From below he heard screams of fear.

A Tielen trumpeter blew a ragged retreat. A few soldiers, their uniforms besmirched and tattered, staggered away.

"Let them go." Already he knew he had overstretched his resources; he felt weak and dizzy, his power spent. "Let them tell the Emperor what they saw. Much good it will do him . . ."

The wing-beats came more slowly now, each one a juddering effort that wracked his whole body. He began to spiral downward, searching for a place to land where no one would see him.

He alighted on a grassy hillside, screened from the road by tall hornbeams, thudding onto his knees and hands as the glamour faded from his body, leaving him a shuddering, defenseless man again, his clothes all torn to tatters.

"Why am I still so weak, Drakhaoul?" he whispered, toppling slowly forward onto his face in the coarse grass.

"You are weak because you refuse to replenish yourself," came

back the hoarse, smoke-voiced reply. *"If you don't find nourishment soon, you will lose the power to sustain me."*

"Must . . . be some other way." Gavril dug his nails deep into the coarse grass as the first surge of nausea washed through his depleted body.

"You were dying when I rescued you. Even I cannot save you this time. You must feed—or die."

"No . . ." Gavril mouthed the denial, his lips pressing into the grass.

"It's a good thing you brought a change of clothes."

Gavril opened his eyes and saw Pavel Velemir standing over him, holding his pack.

"Here." Pavel threw the pack down beside him. "You'd better put these on."

Damn. Pavel Velemir was the last person in all Smarna he wanted to find him in this condition. He tried to push himself up but fell down again.

"Water . . ."

"You're in pretty poor shape, aren't you?" Pavel squatted down beside him and held his water bottle to his lips. The acid taste of the watered wine made Gavril choke—but after he had swallowed a mouthful or two, his head felt less muzzy and he sat up, reaching for his clothes.

"So what happened?"

Was that an ironic question? Gavril, wearily trying to fasten his breeches, looked quizzically at Pavel.

"How about—I was caught in the blast of a Tielen mortar and my clothes were all blown to ribbons."

"It might have to do," Pavel said. "They're in such confusion, they'll probably believe you."

"But you don't." Had Pavel guessed everything? How much had he seen? And what had he been told of his uncle's death? The official version might be quite different from the facts; the Tielen clerks might have found it impossible to write that "Feodor Velemir was burned to death by a dragon-daemon."

"I only know what I saw. Perhaps I'm suffering from heatstroke. Do you always lose your clothes when this happens? I see you haven't brought a spare pair of boots."

Now that Gavril had recovered a little, he realized Pavel must have gone back to fetch his horse.

"I'll ride on to Anisieli. Someone will sell me a pair of boots there." Bare feet were the least of his worries.

"What you did back there was pretty impressive." Pavel grinned at him. "Those Tielens were obviously under orders to blast us off the road. They must have had quite a surprise when you came swooping down from the hillside!"

"And our side? Casualties?" Gavril forced himself to ask the question he had been dreading.

"More than a few." Pavel's pleasant expression grew grave.

"Raïsa?"

"A nasty gash on the head. It'll leave a scar. But she's alive—and swearing at her brother. I take that as a good sign."

Raïsa was alive. Gavril felt the pain troubling his heart slowly melt away. He had saved her. So it had not been in vain, then, his reckless attack.

And then he remembered Pavel Velemir.

"Please, say nothing. If there are any questions to be answered, I'll answer them my own way."

"Don't worry." Pavel offered him his hand, pulling him to his feet and steadying him. "I value my life too much. I wouldn't do anything to offend such a powerful dragon-lord."

Dragon-lord. In spite of his weariness, Gavril found himself grinning back at Pavel. It had such an absurdly chivalrous ring to it.

The ragged rebel column limped into Anisieli as the sun was setting. Dusklight, violet-hued, seeped down through the steep rocks of the gorge behind. The people of Anisieli cheered and waved the Smarnan flag from upstairs windows as they entered the town, but, as Pavel said to Gavril, there wasn't much to cheer about.

They had left behind a scene of carnage. Predatory mountain crows were already circling above the broken bodies, even as they piled their own dead onto the one remaining cart.

Iovan, left arm tied up in a blood-soaked scarf, was still directing operations. By now his voice was hoarse and cracked as he gave his orders. He said nothing to Gavril, but he cast him a suspicious, sidelong glance.

They met up with Raïsa at the gates into Anisieli. Her forehead was bound in a makeshift, bloodstained bandage, but she still managed to smile as she came toward them, flinging an arm around each of their shoulders.

"My brave boys," she said, hugging them. She was crying, but she didn't seem to care. Pavel kissed her on each cheek, then full on the mouth.

Gavril breathed in the delicious scent emanating from her body.

Blood. Fresh, warm, innocent blood.

Dizzy with hunger, he pulled away.

The river ran through the center of Anisieli, cold and fresh from the gorge. The tavern owner had set tables out on the cobbled riverside and lit lanterns to welcome them. The mayor of Anisieli appeared and made a long-winded but heartfelt speech, thanking them for defeating the Tielen invaders and offering free food and lodgings for the night.

A doctor was found to attend to the wounded. Tavern girls came out with bottles of the rich, red local wine and baskets of fresh-baked cornbread. There would be lamb stewed with green plums and tarragon, to follow, they promised.

Gavril was not hungry. The smell of the lamb stew wafting from the tavern kitchen only made his stomach gripe. He sat at the mayor's table opposite Pavel and Raïsa, wondering how long he could stay in their company before the inevitable aftereffects of using his powers set in.

The rich wine soon loosened the tongues of the rebels and the noisy recounting of the afternoon's ambush made Gavril's head ache.

"One moment the Tielens had us surrounded—mortar fire everywhere, and clouds of that evil smoke they use to confuse the enemy." Raïsa was describing the battle, with wild and vivid hand gestures. The wine had brought color back to her pale cheeks. "And then the sky went dark—and their mortar battery exploded. Boom! My ears are still ringing. When we went to check—and God, that was a gruesome sight—there was little left. They'd blown themselves up."

"Not quite accurate," Pavel said. "It was Gavril's work."

Gavril set down his wine and stared hard at Pavel.

Don't betray my secret if you value your life, Velemir.

"Your work, Gavril? But how?" Raïsa asked.

"It's not the first time I've done this," he said as obscurely as he could. "It was just a case of igniting their explosives."

"Rusta says he saw something in the sky. Dark, winged, flying down from the mountains."

"Rusta must have suffered a bad blow to the head," Gavril said with a dry smile.

"He's not been so well since he was caught in the blast. Says he breathed in some of the smoke after the explosion. But then, we all did."

They had all breathed in the smoke from his virulent burst of Drakhaon's Fire, and none of them were protected. If they were not to fall sick and die, he must act to save them.

He stared down at the crimson wine in his mug. Stallion's Blood, they called it in these parts, fermented from a robust dark grape grown on the southern slopes beyond the gorge. The taste was strong enough to mask what he was about to add to it.

He left the table and went around the side of the tavern, carrying his mug with him. There, beside a stinking privy, he gritted his teeth and made a quick slash in his wrist, letting the daemon-purple blood sizzle, drop by drop, into his wine.

"What are you doing?" the Drakhaoul hissed. *"You have barely enough blood to sustain you. You can't afford to lose anymore."*

"This," Gavril said, wincing as he pressed his sleeve cuff to the raw edges of the cut, "is necessary."

It was dark now, and from somewhere high in the wooded slopes of the gorge beyond, he heard the distant call of an owl floating down on the warm night air. As he had hoped, the tavern girls were refilling the wine jugs from a big oak barrel near the kitchen. It was just a matter of slipping some of the wine from his blood-tainted mug into each jug.

He stood, leaning against the tavern doorframe, watching the girls take the healing wine to the rebels, watching until all had refilled their glasses and drunk.

Suddenly it seemed as if the air around him was sucked dry. A wave of intolerable heat rippled through his whole body. Gasping, he buckled, grasping at the wall for support. Glitters of light flashed before his eyes, tiny darts of amethyst and sapphire that pierced his aching head like needles.

"Drakhaoul," he whispered. "What's . . . happening to me?"

"Our . . . synthesis . . . is failing. . . ."

"Failing?" Another wave of heat surged through his body, leaving his head pounding, his stomach seized with burning cramps.

One of the tavern girls came out, carrying a big pot of lamb stew. The greasy smell of the meat made him feel even more ill.

"Are you all right, sir?"

He heard her set down the pot and come closer, one tentative step at a time. And through the surging nausea, he caught a new, enticing scent—fresh and sweet—that, as she knelt beside him, he knew issued from her.

"You look really poorly." He felt cool fingers brush his cheek. "You're burning hot! Shall I send for a doctor?"

"Water . . ." Though even as he said the word, he knew it was not water that he needed.

"I'll go get some."

"No. Wait." He reached out and caught hold of her hand. "Stay with me."

"B-but—"

He raised his head to look at her. Through the swirls of smoke that hazed his vision, he saw a black-haired young girl with skin the ripe brown sheen of hazelnuts. "You're very pretty. What's your name?"

"My name's Gulvardi." A blush darkened her cheeks. "I'm new here at the tavern." Even her warm breath smelled deliciously sweet.

A sudden flurry of lascivious images whirled through his mind. Desire burned through his whole body, enflamed his brain. He wanted her.

"Then take her."

"No," Gavril whispered.

"You fought the Tielens today, didn't you? That was so brave." Her eyes, dark as sloes, gazed at him, brimming with admiration.

Gavril doubled up again, clutching his arms about himself, trying to hold the pain in. And then the pain and the desire merged. He would lure her away from watching eyes, to some dark and lonely place where no one would hear her cries for help.

"Maybe—a breath of fresh air—will restore me." He tried to straighten up. Who was speaking now, Gavril or the Drakhaoul? He no longer knew. He had lost control. "Help me, Gulvardi."

"Here. Take my arm."

He leaned against her as she guided him down the steps toward the sound of the rushing river. Every hesitant step they took away from the tavern led him closer to the achievement of his desire.

Ahead loomed the dark trunks of pines on the gorge edge. There would be hollows between the gnarled roots, soft with dry pine needles.

"Do you feel better out here?" Gulvardi said.

"A little."

The desire was almost unbearable, the cramping hunger a torment—the last desperate need of a man dying of famine. But he must not make his move. Not yet, not until he was sure they were well out of sight of the tavern.

The rising moon, a slender paring, touched the rushing river water far below with flickers of silver.

"Look," she said. "The moonlight's so beautiful."

"But not as beautiful as you." Gavril heard the trite words issue from his mouth as he reached for her, crushing her to him. "Kiss me, Gulvardi."

His lips touched hers.

"No." She resisted a little, twisting away. "Someone will see—"

He could feel the softness of her nut-brown breasts beneath the blouse—poor-quality linen that ripped open so easily beneath his questing fingers.

He pulled her closer, forcing his mouth against hers. He heard her give a little cry—and tasted blood on her lips.

The taste—warm, salt-sweet—sent him into a frenzy. He nuzzled his face against her throat, her breasts, licking, biting, sucking . . .

"No!" Gulvardi fought him, squirming and kicking, all sharp knees and elbows. She was screaming at him now, but all he could hear was the pulsing of the warm blood in her veins. All he knew was his own need to take in as much of that red, salty sweetness as he could to soothe the burning agony inside.

"Gulvardi?" Someone was calling her name.

The dark smoke-haze melted away and his sight cleared. A thin taper of moonlight illumined the scene.

He was kneeling in the soft carpet of pine needles and sandy soil. In front of him crouched a bloodstained girl, half-naked, her clothes torn, her moonlit eyes wide and terrified.

"Are you—are you all right?" he asked dazedly.

She began to edge away, shuffling backward, one arm outstretched to keep him from her. "M-monster!" she whispered. "Keep away!"

She turned and began to run, stumbling through the trees.

"Wait!"

The river shimmered far below.

"Keep away from me, monster!"

"The river—be careful—"

His warning cry came too late. In her headlong dash to escape him, she tripped—and fell from sight over the edge onto the jagged rocks far below.

"Oh no. No." He leaned out over the rushing river, trying in vain to see where she had fallen, but seeing only the silvered water, fast-flowing over its stony bed.

"Let her go. She's served her purpose."

"Gulvardi!" he shouted, his voice echoing around the rocky walls of the gorge.

There was no reply. How could she have survived a fall from such a height?

And then he began to cry, tears of grief and shame for the girl he had just destroyed; useless tears for himself, damned as he was now to perdition. She had called him a monster. And she was right. From the darkest shadows of his mind, a creature had been loosed: a ravening beast whose obscene hunger would not be denied.

CHAPTER 28

Shifting patterns of dappled light filtered through breeze-stirred leaves, moving across Gavril's face as he opened his eyes. He lay staring up at the tree branches above him, hearing the faint rustle of the wind and the distant splash of fast-flowing water.

Where am I?

He sat up and found he had been lying on a bed of dried fallen leaves, moss, and twigs; his clothes were covered in grime. From the position of the sun overhead it must be nearly midday.

The sound of rushing water told him there was a stream or river nearby. He got to his feet, brushing the woodland debris from his clothes and hair. When he moved, he found his back and legs were stiff from sleeping on roots and hard earth.

What am I doing out here?

He went toward the sound of the water, out of the dappled shade, and found himself on the banks of a mountain river. Up above him, on either side, towered the steep walls of a gorge, overhung with bushes and glossy ivies. The water rushed past, tumbling over massive boulders and eddying around smaller stones.

And as he leaned over the rushing river, he suddenly saw the image of a bloodstained girl, half-naked, her clothes torn, her moonlit eyes wide and terrified.

"Gulvardi." He remembered her name, and dear God, now he began to remember the terrible things he had done to her.

He sank to his knees, overwhelmed with self-loathing. All he could see was the terror distorting her face as she ran from him. All he could hear was her voice, screaming out to him to stop.

"I *am* a monster." He covered his face with his shaking hands. "I attacked her. I—I did worse—"

"*You were dying,*" whispered the Drakhaoul. "*You took what you needed to survive.*"

Only once before had he been driven to drink innocent blood—and then it had been willingly offered. Kiukiu's self-sacrifice had saved his life. But this time the Drakhaoul had driven him to attack a helpless stranger.

"How can I live with myself, knowing what I've done?" He looked down at his clothes, seeing now that what he had taken for earth stains was dried blood. Gulvardi's blood. "And now she's fallen to her death, and all because I hadn't the self-control to, to—"

"*Her blood healed you.*"

Gavril heard at last what the daemon was telling him and knew it to be true. He had not felt so well in many months. His sight was clear, there was no throbbing in his skull, and no constant pain cramping his stomach. But that was little consolation for the shame and guilt that burned to the core of his soul.

"But how can I go back and pretend that nothing happened, knowing what I have done?"

"*You will go back. And you will live with that knowledge. Because you must.*"

"First my fleet. My *Rogned* sunk. Now Froding and his brave men seared to ashes—" Eugene could hardly contain his fury. He looked up from the latest communication from Smarna and saw Gustave watching him warily. He had even retreated a step or two, as if fearful of his master's temper.

"Is this Gavril Nagarian's revenge?" Eugene dropped his voice. He felt as if New Rossiya were a castle of sand crumbling under the assault of a fast-flooding tide. A tide that could rapidly sweep him and all he had fought for away.

"The council is awaiting you, highness."

"He's gone. Vanished." Raïsa came back down the mountain path, arms open wide in a gesture of bewilderment. "We've searched everywhere." She seemed utterly desolate at the thought.

Flown away, Pavel thought, unable to refrain from grinning.

"Pavel, you don't think he's lying hurt somewhere, do you?" She caught hold of him, her eyes wide with worry. "That head wound of his wasn't properly healed. . . ."

Ironic that she was touching him, her hand on his arm, yet all her thoughts were about Gavril Andar. Don't waste your affections on him, Raïsa, he wanted to tell her. A man like Gavril Andar could break your heart.

"And your wound?" he said tenderly.

"Just a scratch. Almost healed." But she was pale beneath the golden sheen the sun had burned into her skin.

Iovan came swaggering up to them. He looked pleased with himself.

"No sign of Tielens. No sign of Muscobites either. We've been talking to a couple of shepherds in the high pastures up beyond Anisieli. They said they saw soldiers making for the border."

"A strategic retreat? Or just regrouping, waiting for reinforcements?"

"We must send word to Colchise," Raïsa said.

Gavril climbed a winding path that led up through twisted tree roots and humid, fly-infested forest to the top of the gorge. After an hour's walking he found himself on a high, scrubland plain with a clear view to the north of the hazy outline of Mount Diktra. A buzzard skimmed overhead, letting out a desolate cry. There was no sign of the rebels up here, or the Tielens.

If he was to find them, there was no alternative but to take to the air, like the buzzard.

Eugene glowered at the assembled ministers of the Rossiyan council. He did not like what they had come to tell him. And they had chosen Chancellor Maltheus to deliver their ultimatum.

"We judge the situation in Smarna to be critical, imperial highness. It is the council's opinion that we cannot afford to lose any more men. I fear we have no alternative but to withdraw and discuss terms."

"Withdraw?" Eugene thundered. "You mean capitulate?"

"My terminology was perhaps a little vague—"

"Lose Smarna?" Had they never studied history? "If we give in, all we have gained will be lost. Azhkendir will rise up. Then Khitari."

"But the men are becoming demoralized, highness."

"*My* men, demoralized?" Eugene could hardly believe what he was hearing. "I will travel to Smarna and lead them myself. I've been out of the field for too long."

"Is that advisable in the current situation? Now that you are Emperor, there are other considerations—"

"Could we not at least offer to talk terms with the Smarnan council?" ventured the Minister of Foreign Affairs.

"I will not be dictated to by a rabble of students and anarchists!"

"A rabble who possess a secret weapon vastly superior to anything the Magus has been able to devise," said Chancellor Maltheus, gazing levelly at Eugene.

"The Magus and Captain Lindgren are working even now on a new type of powder," Eugene said, not rising to Maltheus's challenge.

"Time and money, highness; it all comes down to time and money. Money to support widows and fatherless children; the time it will take to develop and produce this new gunpowder. I advocate a strategic withdrawal—"

"And is it strategic for Tielen, Chancellor, to leave the Smarnan waters unprotected?" Eugene, both hands on the table, leaned toward Maltheus.

"We have nothing to fear at present from other nations," said Maltheus, not even blinking under Eugene's fierce gaze.

"Can we be so sure of that? What about this Francian 'naval regatta'? Since when did Enguerrand take such a passionate interest in his fleet? Do we have any new intelligence?"

"Let me see . . ." Maltheus shuffled through the pile of dispatches on the table in front of him. "Enguerrand embarking on pilgrimage to the holy sites in Djihan-Djihar, accompanied by members of the Francian Commanderie."

" 'A pilgrimage'?" Eugene fell silent, his mind working on the information. Djihan-Djihar lay to the far south of Smarna. "And how many ships has he taken for this pilgrimage?"

"We have no further details yet."

"Enguerrand is by all accounts a very devout man," put in the Minister of Foreign Affairs.

Eugene did not respond. He could sense all his ministers watching him warily, bracing themselves to withstand his next outburst.

You've bested me and my men again, Gavril Nagarian.

"A withdrawal it is, then," he said. "But only to regroup."

"We haven't much left on the Smarnan borders to regroup, highness."

Eugene left the council chamber, silent with fury. There was no other course of action left to him. He sent a message containing a single word to Linnaius: *Tonight.*

The Drakhaon flew over the gorge on long, slow wing-beats, drifting on the currents. Now that he was airborne again, he felt the guilt and shame melt away. Up here, floating so high above Smarna, he felt detached, free of the cares that obsessed him. He could be one with the sunlit blue of the sky.

When he finally caught sight of the rebel column, marching away from Anisieli, their tattered standard fluttering in the afternoon breeze, he shadowed them a while, trying to guess where they would make camp for the night.

The column was considerably shorter than when they had set out from the citadel. It looked, from the air, as if they had lost almost a third of their number in the Tielen ambush.

He spied Raïsa, her head still bandaged, riding beside Pavel; Capriole was on a leading rein behind Luciole. And at the sight of her, even so far below, he felt the stirring again of that dark flame of hunger.

Now I can never allow myself to be alone with her. Now I can never trust myself with any woman again.

"Don't you remember, Gavril Nagarian? You are Drakhaon. You can do as you please."

"What am I doing here?" Kiukiu rubbed her sleep-crusted eyes; she felt as if she had slept in too long and was not yet wholly awake. She gazed around her, suddenly suspicious. This didn't look like a prison. She was lying on a comfortable feather mattress covered in sheets of the finest linen. She felt the linen between finger and thumb, remembering the countless sheets she had laundered and ironed at Kastel Drakhaon. She sniffed it, scenting the faintest sharp hint of lavender. She was certain they did not give prisoners lavender-scented sheets.

Unless the Magus has housed me in the prison governor's house?

She pushed back the sheets and left the bed to gaze out of the wide-paned window.

"What is this place?" she whispered. She saw tall buildings all around, beautiful buildings of the palest honeyed stone, decorated with elegant carvings. And beyond the buildings she could see green lawns and formal gardens with bobble-headed trees stretching to the horizon, where fountains sprayed great jets of sparkling water high into the air.

"It's so . . . grand. It can't be Arnskammar."

As she watched, mouth open, she saw guards marching in a neat column to a steady drumbeat across the courtyard below, carbines on their shoulders. Their uniforms, grey and purple, were similar to those of the regiment stationed at Kastel Drakhaon. They seemed to be performing some changing of the guard ceremony involving much saluting.

"Arnskammar is by the sea. I don't see any sea. So where—"

She went to the door and tried the handle. It was locked. She knocked, she called, but no one answered.

"It seems that I'm the prisoner." A fluttery, panicky feeling had begun in her chest. "Now, Kiukiu, don't get all flustered." She sat down on the bed again and forced herself to breathe more slowly. "There has to be a reason I'm here, locked up. For my own safety, maybe?"

But in the back of her mind she kept hearing Malusha's voice warning her of the Magus's trickery.

The room was simply furnished, the paneling painted in a delicate shade of ivory outlined in duck-egg blue. The window and bed hangings were of a cream brocade, fringed with gold and blue. The soft tapestry rug beneath her feet and the china ewer bore the same design of two gilded swans, beak to beak, making a heart with the curve of their necks.

Now she noticed that a tray had been placed on the other side of the bed; she lifted the silver cover and saw a plate of fruit, cheese, and little sugared almond cakes.

Her stomach was empty. She must have been asleep for some time, for, judging by the sun, it was approaching noon. Her hand crept out; she nibbled at an almond cake. It was delicious. She ate another, and another. Just as she was eating the last cake, she heard soft footsteps outside. Guiltily wiping the crumbs and sugar from her lips, she jumped up as the locked door opened.

"You're awake, Kiukirilya. Good." Pale eyes gleamed in the Magus's lined face.

"Kaspar Linnaius," she gasped, recovering. "I should have known this was your doing. Where am I? And why am I here?"

"This is the Emperor's palace. It's called Swanholm."

"I'm in a palace?"

"If there was one wish I could grant for you, what would it be?"

Kiukiu heard the question and found herself drowning in a wave of longing for what could not be.

"There is only one thing I want," she said quietly, "and that is beyond your powers to give me."

"Think carefully. I cannot bring him back to life, true. But is there nothing else? A comfortable house with land for your grandmother? A friend on whose behalf I could petition the Emperor?"

He was tempting her. Why?

"Think of Kastel Drakhaon, Kiukirilya."

She could not help but fall under the suggestive spell of his words; she saw Semyon limping along in chains, horribly thin, his ribs showing like a skeleton's beneath his skin. She saw the half-healed scars of the overseer's whip scoring Gorian's back. And she knew what Lord Gavril would have wanted her to ask.

"The *druzhina*. Free the *druzhina*."

"And if the Emperor agrees to free the *druzhina,* will you agree to use your skills one more time?"

"No more summonings," she said, shuddering at the memory.

"This will not involve a summoning. This is, I suspect, a simple case of possession."

"*Simple?*" He could have no idea of the risks involved. But for Semyon's sake alone, she would do it.

"The Emperor will reward you generously if you cure his daughter."

"The little princess?" Kiukiu began to wish she had not agreed so rashly. What would the Emperor do to her if she failed?

Kiukiu hugged her gusly tightly, holding it like a shield between her and this unfamiliar world that was the Palace of Swanholm. She glimpsed maidservants in neat grey dresses, silently disappearing into doorways as they approached. The palace was so light and clean. And she knew, better than most, how much painstaking work had gone into polishing the floorboards and cleaning the great window-panes till they sparkled; she could smell the beeswax.

Tall guardsmen stood outside the gilded door to the princess's apartments.

"We are not to be disturbed," said the Magus.

Inside, Kiukiu saw a comfortable sitting room with a fire burning in the grate. Chairs and a couch in a pretty sprigged brocade of blue and pale yellow had been placed close to the fire, but the room was empty. Close by someone was coughing; a high, painful, repetitive rasp.

"Put down your instrument, Kiukiu."

Kiukiu gratefully placed the heavy gusly on the table next to a little slate with chalks and open books. A half-sewn sampler was stretched across a frame, with colored wools hanging down. The princess must have been at her lessons.

An inner door opened and a little girl in a blue gown appeared. She spoke to Linnaius in Tielen.

"This is Kiukirilya, a Spirit Singer, Princess," said Linnaius in the common tongue.

As Princess Karila came toward her, Kiukiu saw how badly twisted her body was; she only managed to walk with a strange lurching gait. But as she bobbed a curtsy to the princess, she could not sense any evidence of spirit possession at all.

"Is that a zither, Kiukirilya?" asked the princess.

"It's called a gusly, highness."

"I'm learning the fortepiano, but my music-master is very strict and makes me practice boring scales."

"Practice is important if you want to play well," Kiukiu said guiltily, aware that she had been neglecting her instrument.

"Can I try?" One hand crept out toward the strings and plucked a few notes. "Ow. The strings bite!"

"You have to wear these little metal hooks to protect your fingers until your nails grow strong and hard." Kiukiu slipped the plectra onto her fingertips for the princess to see and struck a playful volley of notes, light and fast and bright as shooting stars.

"You're so clever!" cried Karila. "It's sky music. Flying music!"

Kiukiu was unused to playing to an appreciative audience; she was about to delight the princess with more of her improvisation when she heard Linnaius clearing his throat. Glancing up, she saw him pointing sternly to the clock.

"Sit down, please, highness," she said, suppressing a little sigh.

Kiukiu began to play a Sending Song to try to charm out any elusive spirit that might be haunting the princess.

"I don't like this tune," said Karila, kicking her heels against the couch. "It's too slow and sad."

Kiukiu tried to ignore the princess's complaints and played on, weaving a mist of dark notes until the firelight dwindled to a distant dull glimmer.

"Why are we here?" Karila's voice came clearly through the darkness. "What is this place?"

If there was another spirit inhabiting the princess's body, then it had concealed itself with great skill.

"*Show yourself,*" Kiukiu commanded. "*I am here to help you.*"

Suddenly the dark mists melted away, revealing a great expanse of azure water.

"The sea!" cried Karila happily. A long, white shore stretched into the distance.

And then the children came clustering about them, the children Kiukiu had seen in her vision in Kastel Drakhaon, the poor, dead children with their dark, imploring eyes and their terrible wounds.

"Who are you?" Kiukiu said, backing away.

And now, as she looked at Princess Karila, she saw another child standing beside her, half in shadow; a girl with dark hair and dark eyes.

"We are the children of the Serpent God," said the girl. "We died to bring the Drakhaouls from the Realm of Shadows."

"This is Tilua," said Karila.

"Help us," said another child, a boy, stretching out his hands to her.

"But what do you want?"

"We want to go home."

"I'll take you, then. I'll sing you all home."

"We can't go home. Our blood is mingled with the blood of the Drakhaoulim. We are part of them—and they are part of us," said Tilua. "We are their children."

"Grandma," whispered Kiukiu to Malusha, so far away in Azhkendir, "I don't know what to do. There's so many of them." This was much more complicated than she had imagined. She needed time to think. "Come, Karila," she commanded. "Come with me."

"But I want to stay and play," said Karila, her hand entwining with Tilua's. "I'm free here, Kiukirilya. I can run and not fall over."

Kiukiu shivered. The light was fading fast. And she could see shadows creeping toward them across the white sand. "But it's not where you're meant to be, Princess." She grabbed hold of Karila's other hand and tugged. "We must go." This place was not what it seemed to be at all; she could sense it now.

Clouds overhead darkened the white sand to a dull, dusty grey. And a wind began to whine, whipping up the dunes. The azure sea vanished beneath drifting mounds of sand, even as she stared at it, horrified.

She knew this place. And she must get Karila out as swiftly as possible.

She turned to see the portal she had sung for them shrinking fast.

"Now!" she cried, tugging again. And she shoved Karila, with Tilua still clinging to her hand, through the portal just as it closed, leaving her beating her hands on empty air.

"Why won't Kiukirilya wake up, Linnaius?" asked Karila, her eyes wide with alarm. "Why is she staring like that?"

"I think she is unwell," said Linnaius. His mind raced, trying to invent a plausible reason for what had happened. "Some people suffer from this unfortunate affliction: the falling sickness. Let me ring for help."

He saw Karila gently touch the Guslyar girl's face. And the fact that there was no response from Kiukirilya, not even the slightest twitch or blink, confirmed what he feared the most. She was lost in the dark spirit-world of the dead that the Azhkendi shamans navigated at their peril. "Crude, dangerous magic," he muttered under his breath. Now what was he going to do with her?

"You rang, highness?" A little red-cheeked maid appeared, bobbing a curtsy. And then she caught a glimpse of Kiukiu lying on the couch and let out a squeak of alarm.

"Our Azhkendi musician has been taken ill," Linnaius said, steering her toward the door, away from the couch. "Please fetch two strong men to help carry her back to her room. I will call Doctor Amandel to attend to her."

As two footmen lifted Kiukiu up and a third followed, carrying the gusly, Linnaius said pointedly, "Let's take the servants' stair. We don't want to excite vulgar comments." Perhaps in the confusion of preparations and the many musicians milling about in the palace, no one would pay particular attention to one more, seemingly the worse for drink. . . .

Karila came up to him as he bowed to her, and touched his arm. "She wanted to take the children home, Linnaius. But they can't go home. Not without the Drakhaouls."

The Drakhaon scouted the surrounding area: hills, woods, and valleys. There was no sign of the Tielens at all this morning. Those that could escape must have made a hasty retreat into Muscobar.

Thirsty now after flying in the sunlight all day, he searched for water. He caught the rushing sound of fast-falling water; a waterfall tumbled down the rocky hillside, the spray glinting with little rainbows. He drank from the icy mountain cascade and then followed the course of the clear-flowing stream until it brought him to a lake.

Wading birds moved among the reeds; tufted goldeneyes dived and preened on the still water. There was no sound but the whisper of the breeze in the reeds and the burbling cries of the waterfowl.

He walked beside the lake, listening to the quiet and relishing the calm. Damselflies darted low across the surface. One settled on a reed and he crouched down to try to get a better look at its jeweled body.

He started back, catching sight of the face that bent toward the glassy sheen of the lake. His stunted hair had completely regrown, hiding the scars left by Baltzar's scalpel.

"Had you forgotten? You needed blood, innocent blood to restore your human face."

Now he remembered the terrible pleasure he had taken in Gulvardi's body, her screams, her struggles. He remembered the sweet taste of her flesh, her living blood as she writhed and arched beneath him. But whose pleasure did he recall, his own, or that of the daemon that drove him to ravish an innocent stranger?

And why, when that soft, persuasive voice whispered of innocent blood, did he suddenly think of Raïsa? Why did he find himself overwhelmed with images of her: the way the sunlight caught copper strands in her boyish hair, the open-necked man's shirt, all the more intriguing for the occasional glimpse it afforded of small, firm breasts, brown nipples dark beneath the whiteness of the crumpled linen . . .

Suddenly he was unbearably hot, his whole body burning with the unquenchable hunger of his daemon-blood. He sat down beside the lake and let his face sink into his hands. Despair overcame him, dark as a stormcloud.

I daren't go near her. I can't control this gnawing bloodlust any longer. I can't go back.

CHAPTER 29

Askold raised his hand to wipe the sweat and grime from his eyes. "Did you feel that, lads?"

The oppressive darkness of the mineshaft was lit only by the dimmest of flames, well-encased in lantern glass to prevent any risk of explosion. The *druzhina* were at work underground in Captain Lindgren's mine, excavating another new shaft into the hillside. Wooden props, hewn from the great forest pines in Kerjhenezh, held up the low roof. Yet even here, deep below the surface, Askold had felt the pull of the blood oath, the bond that tied him to his master, the Drakhaon.

"I felt it!" cried a young voice, full of hope—and was rewarded with a crack of a whip and a curse from the supervising Tielen soldier.

"Keep it down, Semyon," Askold said, shuffling slowly forward, shackles clanking, with another barrowful of dully-glittering earth to be wheeled outside for sieving.

"But how can it be?" grunted Barsuk. "How can it be Lord Gavril?"

"Search me," Askold said. "All I know is that's our Drakhaon."

"Lord Gavril?" Gorian spat.

"You watch your tongue, Gorian," advised Barsuk. "Remember what happened to Michailo."

"Wherever he may be, he hasn't forgotten us," Semyon said loyally. "And it was stronger than last time. He's getting closer."

"No talking!" The Tielen overseer cracked his whip again. "You're here to work."

"Work?" Gorian hawked and spat again. "How can we work on the pigswill they give out? They feed their horses better."

It was no more than the truth. They were so weak from the meager rations, they could hardly last to the end of their shift.

"Are you deaf? I said no more talking!" The whip came down hard on Gorian's back. Instinctively he lashed out, striking the Tielen, knocking him to the dirt floor. He straddled the fallen officer, eyes burning with hatred.

"No, Gorian!" Askold cried, too late.

"We're men, like you. We deserve better!"

As the Tielen struggled to get up, Gorian landed a kick in his side, with as much force as his shackled ankles would permit.

"Stop, Gorian. That's an order!"

As the Tielen rolled over, retching, more soldiers came hurrying down the low passageway, alerted by the shouting.

Askold cursed under his breath.

"You damned fool, Gorian. See what you've done?"

"That one—attacked me—" gasped out the Tielen. In seconds, the others had grabbed hold of Gorian by the arms and pinned him to the wall.

"I'm not taking any more Tielen orders!" cried Gorian. "I'm not cleaning out any more Tielen latrines! Let them shovel their own shit. If I can't live like a warrior, then I'll die like a warrior!"

Barsuk let out a great roar and swung his shovel at the Tielens. One turned, catching the blow on the side of the head. His skull was split open; he toppled, blood spurting.

"They'll execute you for this, Barsuk!" Askold tried to restrain him, but Barsuk threw him off.

"We're dead men, anyway, Askold," he said, dealing another Tielen a ringing blow in the face with the shovel. "Let's give 'em something to write a song about!"

"Riot! Riot in the mine!" cried one of the Tielens, blowing a whistle in short, frantic bursts.

"Put down your shovels or we shoot," ordered another, striking a tinder to light his fuse.

"Go on, shoot," sneered Gorian. "Shoot and be done with it."

"No—" cried Askold, foreseeing the danger too late. He leaped forward to try to knock the carbine from the soldier's hands, but his shackles tripped him.

The gun went off—and though the shot went wide, missing Gorian, it pierced one of the open barrels.

There was a blinding flash of light and then all went black as the props fell and the roof caved in.

Gavril lay back in the shade of ancient olive trees, staring up at the blue sky through twisted branches sparsely sprinkled with grey-green leaves. In this lonely grove high up in the foothills, he could rest without fear of being discovered.

He had just drifted into sleep when he heard the far distant sound of voices crying out to him. Starting awake, he felt a sudden deep ache in his wrist, where once his *druzhina* had sealed their bond of eternal fealty to him, touching their lips to his welling blood.

"My *druzhina*. They need me!"

It was a call he could no longer ignore. He had fought the urge to return to Azhkendir, fearing to see again the looks of betrayal and contempt in the faces of his enslaved men. He did not need to be reminded that he had failed them; he had agonized over his failure night after dark night in Arnskammar. Now he knew he had delayed too long. This was a desperate, fading cry for help. Even now he might not reach Kastel Drakhaon in time.

"Can we make Azhkendir?" he asked Khezef.

"Your will is mine, Gavril Nagarian."

Gavril rose high above the foothills and headed for the Larani Mountains. As he flew, he scanned the land beneath for signs of soldiers. But he saw none; for whatever reason, Eugene had withdrawn his troops from the Smarnan side of the border. It could well be a ruse, but it could also mean that the Emperor had agreed to negotiations.

Agreeing to negotiations? That didn't sound like Eugene of Tielen. It was most likely he was massing his troops beyond the mountains, making ready for another assault when the Smarnans least expected it.

But as he winged on northward, passing over the rocky crags and grey-sheened glaciers of Mount Diktra, crossing into Muscobar, he saw no sign of army encampments, only a thin straggle of a column, winding its way dejectedly down a steep mountain path, with heavy cannons drawn by mules. Had he inflicted more damage on Eugene's forces than he first imagined? The idea brought a sense of grim satisfaction.

And then he was flying over the green pastures and birch forests of

Muscobar, over peasants toiling in the fields, goading teams of oxen to plough. Muscobar, with its fertile plains and many rivers, looked so much more prosperous than rugged Azhkendir. He saw villages and towns, well-stocked farms with orchards and monasteries whose gilded onion domes glinted in the slow-sinking sun.

He must make Kastel Drakhaon before night fell.

Nils Lindgren leaned over his plan of the mine, desperately searching for a shaft or air vent that could be dug out to provide an alternative escape route. If they tried to blast their way through the collapsed entrance, they only risked killing more men. And the rockfall at the entrance was so heavy it would take hours of digging to clear it.

"If you please, Captain," said a nervous voice.

"What is it now?" He looked around to see Ilsi, the tart-tempered little maidservant, standing behind him. She was biting her lip.

"There are old tunnels beneath the kastel. Secret passages. If you could run a new tunnel between one of the kastel passages and the mine—"

"Where are these secret passages?"

"Under the East Wing."

"Which fell down in the bombardment." This was leading nowhere.

"Was that our fault? I thought your engineers had ways of finding tunnels and wells," she said.

"We don't have time to run a survey. The men will die for lack of air!" he said more angrily than he intended.

"Well pardon me for trying to help!" Ilsi flounced away, head held high.

Lindgren put his hands to his head in utter frustration. He was an engineer, skilled at his work. And he enjoyed it as long as it involved calculations, plans, and excavating. But this collapse deep within the mine was a disaster. His men were trapped. The *druzhina* were trapped. And what was worse was that his engineering would probably be blamed for the accident.

"Lord Stoyan is here," announced his adjutant from the doorway.

Lindgren half-turned, not believing what he was hearing. The Governor of Azhkendir at Kastel Drakhaon? Without any advance warning? It must be a coincidence. A horrible coincidence.

Boris Stoyan strode in.

"Lindgren!" he shouted in his great voice. "We've come to see how the restoration's progressing."

"We?" echoed Lindgren weakly.

"Good-day to you, Captain Lindgren." A woman had appeared at Lord Stoyan's side: a handsome woman with red hair and langorous green eyes. Behind her came a maidservant, carrying a wide-eyed baby. "I heard that a trunk containing my personal possessions had been found. So I thought I'd come to collect it when the last snows had melted from the moors."

"I-I'm not sure I've had the pleasure—" he stammered.

She left Lord Stoyan's side and came up to him, her hand held out. "Lilias Arbelian, wife to the late Lord Jaromir Arkhel," she said, smiling at him. "This is Stavyomir, our son. He will rule Azhkendir when he comes of age."

Lindgren took the proffered hand and briefly brushed it with his lips. Her perfume was exotically sweet and strong; it reminded him how long it was since he had been in society, how long he had been dealing with trenches, props, earth-moving. He wondered if he had any polite conversation left.

And then he became aware of a little huddle of kastel servants skulking outside the half-open door. All the maids were there, staring. He opened his mouth to send them away, then realized they might be his salvation.

"Sosia," he called sternly.

The kastel housekeeper came in, eyes downcast, deliberately not looking at the visitors.

"Sosia, would you fetch our visitors some refreshment?"

"If that's what you want, Captain." From her disapproving expression, he saw that the visitors were as unwelcome to her as to him. As she passed Lilias Arbelian, she said distinctly, "I wonder you have the nerve to show your face here."

Lilias slipped her hand through Lord Stoyan's arm. "Dear Boris, the kastel staff are lacking in manners. Perhaps you could ask the captain to have them disciplined?"

"Where are all your men, Captain?" Lord Stoyan asked. "The place looks remarkably quiet."

The governor had missed nothing.

"We have—a situation over at the mine. Nothing we can't bring under control," he added hastily. "In time."

"Situation?" Lord Stoyan stared at him under thick, dark brows. "A rockfall? D'you want me to send in some of my own men to help?"

"That would be—yes, thank you." Lindgren was desperate to get back to the mine; every minute counted, where men's lives were at risk.

Sosia reappeared with a bottle of Tielen aquavit and a pot of mint tea on a tray, which she placed on the little table near the fire.

"Mint tea?" Lilias said disdainfully. "Don't you have any real tea? From Khitari?"

"If you'd care to bring us some," Sosia said sourly. "We've had to make do as best we can here. My pantry was blown to pieces in the bombardment—oh but you wouldn't know that, would you, as you'd gone running off into the hills with Michailo."

"We'll be staying the night. The baby's tired."

"Sosia, make the necessary preparations for our guests." Lindgren grabbed his plans and hurried away.

Gavril had forgotten how long the sun stayed in the sky in the far north during spring and early summer.

He had left Azhkendir as the first snowdrops were piercing the snow. He returned now to a land he hardly recognized—to moorlands bright with gorse, the moss starred with tiny white flowers, the cloudberry and lingonberry bushes in bloom.

He had no need to look for landmarks to navigate by; the pulsing of the scar on his wrist grew stronger, as did the confusion of voices in his mind as he neared Kastel Drakhaon.

There lay the vast, wild forest of Kerjhenezh, stretching on toward the distant mountains. And there was the Kalika Tower, rising up into the pale sky where the evening star glittered, even though the sun had still not set.

At the sight of Kastel Drakhaon, Gavril felt a sudden rush of emotion. He had escaped the Iron Tower, but he was not unscathed. He was not the same man who had left in a prison carriage with barred windows, his mind filled with fear and despair. He was even less the naïve young painter who had come to Kastel Drakhaon with Kostya on a cold autumn evening so many months ago. He had been abused and experimented on by Eugene's torturers in Arnskammar. And he had killed for prey.

Fluttering from every remaining tower in the evening breeze were the flags of Eugene's army, the standards of New Rossiya. His first instinct was to rip them all down. And then he sensed cries again, much fainter than before. They were dying.

He had a duty to save his *druzhina*.

But where were they? Circling high above the kastel, he noticed now the extensive excavations on the escarpment—the pulleys, the carts, all the trappings of some kind of mineworks. And from the Tielens' frantic activity below—the digging and shouting—he guessed that this was the heart of the problem.

His *druzhina* must be trapped underground.

Nils Lindgren threw down his shovel and wiped his damp forehead on his sleeve.

"It's no use," he said. "We'll never reach them. Too much earth has come down."

All around him, his men leaned on their spades and stared at him, their faces smeared with earth and sweat, their eyes dull with exhaustion.

"We can't just leave them to suffocate to death," said one of his men.

"For all we know, they're dead already," said another.

"I can assure you that some are still alive," said a voice from outside the mine entrance.

Lindgren looked up.

A man stood there in the twilight, a man unlike any other he had ever seen. A mane of untamed black hair hung about his shoulders and his eyes gleamed in the torchlight, unnaturally blue and bright. He looked like some wild spirit from the forest.

"Who are you?" Lindgren demanded. "And what's your interest in this matter?"

"I have come to help you," said the stranger. "You're wasting your time digging here."

"And do you have a better suggestion?" jeered one of the Tielens.

The stranger turned, beckoning. "Come with me, Captain Lindgren."

How did the stranger know his name? Lindgren picked up his

shovel and set out after him. The Tielens and Lord Stoyan's men followed, bringing torches.

"Where are you taking us?" Lindgren called, for the stranger was moving fast and purposefully.

"To the summerhouse," he called back over his shoulder.

Lindgren had noticed the ramshackle summerhouse, covered in a tangle of rose briars, but never paid it much attention. Was this man mad, or was this something to do with the secret passages Ilsi had mentioned? He certainly seemed to know his way about the kastel as she led them into the neglected garden.

Inside the summerhouse, the stranger knelt down on the rotting boards. "There is a trapdoor here that leads down into one of the kastel passages. There's another at the old watchtower up on the forest road. If these tunnels are still secure, we can use them to go back down beneath the kastel, toward the escarpment."

"We?" Lindgren echoed warily. This could be a trap, plotted by the *druzhina*, to lead him and his men into an ambush. Their bodies could lie in the tunnels for weeks and no one would know. . . .

"You'll need me to show you the way," said the stranger, his blue eyes glinting in the gloom. He let himself down into the tunnel, gripping hold of the rim of the open trapdoor until he could drop into the dank darkness beneath. "Hurry," he called, his tone urgent. "They've not got much time."

Lindgren looked at his men, shrugged, and followed the stranger down into the tunnel. The others came after, handing down lanterns, picks, and shovels.

The tunnel was hardly high enough for a man to stand upright, but as they moved farther along, it slowly opened up until they came out into the dilapidated ruins of a great hall. Lindgren could not help noticing that the stranger's skin gave off a faint glimmer, almost phosphorescent, in the darkness. It must be a trick of the light on his tired eyes.

The stranger moved swiftly ahead of them, counting shadowed doorways that led off the hall. He stopped at the fourth. "This one," he muttered, more to himself than to Lindgren. "Yes, it must be this one."

This tunnel stank of mold and the walls were moist; air vents, overgrown with moss and lichen, let in the occasional draft of damp night air.

"Quiet!" The stranger stopped suddenly, holding up his hand for silence. He put one hand to his forehead, as though concentrating on some sound no one else had detected. He looked around at Lindgren.

"They're in there." He pointed at the wall. "Open a tunnel here. We may yet get to them in time."

Had he heard a faint call for help? Or a desperate tapping? But there was something so authoritative in his voice and manner that every man did as he was ordered. Lindgren took a pick and began to swing it at the bricks, sending mortar and chippings flying.

"Can't you work any faster?" cried the stranger. He began to tear at the earth with his bare hands. "There's hardly any air left. They'll suffocate."

And then he stopped, breathing hard. "Stand back," he said. His blue eyes blazed warning. Lindgren took a stumbling step or two down the passage. This was no ordinary man; he knew it now for sure. "Stand farther back!"

He saw the stranger raise one hand, fingers extended toward the rock. Little flickers of brilliant blue began to crackle between his fingertips. And then a blinding burst of fire shot the length of his arm and pierced solid earth and rock, splitting them apart. A hole appeared. Faint cries and groans could now be heard, coming from the fetid darkness beyond.

Lindgren stared at the stranger. He knew him now. When they had last met, he had been New Rossiya's prisoner.

"Drakhaon," he whispered.

"Come, Lindgren," said Gavril Nagarian, clambering through the hole he had blasted, "they're through here."

A young man lay close to the hole, white-faced and filthy, his fingers bleeding; he had been trying to claw his way out.

Gavril knelt down beside him, checking for a pulse. At his touch, the young man's eyelids flickered open and Gavril recognized the emaciated face of Semyon beneath the dirt and sweat.

"Lord Drakhaon," he whispered, "I said . . . you'd come for us."

Gavril felt his throat tighten. "Hold on, Semyon," he said, placing his hand on his shoulder. "This one's alive!" he called. "Get him out, fast!"

But the Tielens were busy with their own casualties and seemed not to have heard him. Gavril slipped his arms beneath Semyon's thin frame and tried to lift him. Only then did he see the shackles that bound him to the other prisoners.

A terrible anger burned through Gavril's brain. He knew only too well what it was to be shackled. He could not bear to think his *druzhina* had been forced to endure this indignity. He looked at the Tielen soldiers through narrowed eyes. The blue fire began to crackle at his fingertips again.

"Lord Gavril," came another faint voice. Distracted, he looked up and saw Askold, hollow-eyed and barely recognizable beneath several weeks' growth of matted beard. "Gorian's here. Out cold. And Barsuk doesn't look too good."

Gavril concentrated the energy at his fingertips on the shackles. Metal sizzled and the dim light in the cramped shaft turned a lurid blue as one by one, he burned through the links.

"Here. You take the boy's head, I'll take his legs." It was Lindgren, offering to help him carry Semyon out into the passageway.

The anger still simmered, but there were too many men to be brought out to give vent to it. As Gavril went back into the shaft for Askold, he sensed a faint but distinct tremor in the escarpment above.

"Captain!"

Lindgren turned around.

"Hear that? Get your men out. Now."

Gavril pulled Askold's arm about his shoulder and half-carried him out; Lindgren followed close behind, dragging Gorian by the legs. The Tielens came after as the rumbling grew louder.

"It's all coming down!"

They dragged or carried the casualties into the passageway as rock and earth thundered down into the shaft behind them.

For a moment as they retreated, Gavril feared that the ancient kastel brickwork would not be strong enough to withstand the force of the earthfall and that they would all be crushed. But the rumbling subsided and the dustclouds slowly settled.

Gavril gave Lindgren a long shrewd look. They were filthy—Tielens and Azhkendi alike—but together they had brought fifteen men out alive from the collapsed shaft.

"They were good builders, our forebears; they built to last," said Askold, coughing up a mouthful of dust and slapping the brickwork.

Gavril stood in the darkened garden, staring up at the lit windows in the kastel. He wanted to go in. He wanted news. But he was still a fugitive.

Elysia had told him Kiukiu was here at the kastel, but there was no sign of her. Perhaps, weary of waiting on the Tielens, she had gone back to Malusha. There was no way to know without risking discovery, though he sensed Nils Lindgren would not order his arrest tonight, nor begrudge him the shelter of his own kastel.

He went into the kitchen in search of Sosia. He could smell mulled ale: the scent of cloves and ginger reminded him of cold winter evenings in the kastel. Ilsi was busy ladling out ale. When she saw him, she let out a little cry and dropped the ladle in the pan.

"Drakhaon?"

He placed one finger over his lips. "Where's Sosia?"

"Ilsi? Where's that mulled ale for the men?" Sosia appeared, carrying an empty tray. Ilsi pointed with the dripping ladle, which she had fished out of the pan.

"My lord." Sosia stared. "So it's true what the men are saying."

"Sosia." Gavril felt suddenly weary; the spicy smell of the ale was not so pleasing now. "Sosia, where's Kiukiu?"

Sosia put down her tray. He saw in the lamplight that her face was more lined, more drawn than he remembered; she had aged in the last months.

"We don't know where she is," she said. "We had a visitor some weeks back. An old man who came to see the captain on the Emperor's business. He went up to your father's study, my lord. He asked to see Kiukiu. An hour or so later, Ivar saw them go off up the lane together. Then they . . . disappeared. Since then, not a word."

Gavril heard Sosia's news with growing apprehension. "An old man? Did anyone catch his name?"

"I asked Captain Lindgren. He said he was 'not at liberty to divulge such information'—you know how punctilious these Tielens can be. But Ilsi thought she heard him address the old man as 'Magus.' "

"Kaspar Linnaius has taken Kiukiu?" Now he remembered the Magus using his dark arts to probe his mind when he was imprisoned in Arnskammar. He felt deathly cold at the thought. What had Linnaius learned? Why had he taken her? And how did he plan to use her?

"Kiukiu," he whispered, choking on her name. "I didn't mean to put you in danger. He was just too strong for me. . . ."

"Danger?" echoed Sosia. "What danger do you mean, my lord?"

"I must go to her." Gavril hurried out of the warm kitchen and into the garden. He had first seen the Magus at Swanholm; that must be where he had taken Kiukiu, to the laboratory Elysia had told him about.

He stopped in the stableyard, his head spinning. Little specks of colored light swarmed across his vision. If only he had not expended so much of his strength on the flight here. That last burst of flame he had used to blast through the blocked tunnel had left him drained.

He pushed himself on toward the garden. He could rest in the summerhouse and then set out for Swanholm.

Halfway toward the summerhouse, his knees began to tremble. He stumbled.

"You are too weak to make it to Tielen."

Figures moved across a lit window in the kastel. For a moment he stared, wondering if Captain Lindgren had brought his wife and child here from Tielen.

Suddenly he felt feverishly hot. Hands clutched to his belly, he doubled up and dropped to the ground. His skin burned. Not the clean burn of the sun or wind, but a terrible itching as if it had blistered up and was slowly peeling away. His throat was parched again, his mouth and tongue dry as sandpaper.

"No," he whispered, "I can't kill again."

His brain conjured fevered images: he was not possessed by this shadow-creature at all; he was sick, his body corrupted by some virulent disease . . .

And then he caught a faint fragrance wafting from the lit window.

Fresh scent of a child's translucent flesh, the blood pulsing just below the pale skin, deliciously clean and untainted . . .

"Why not just take what you need where you find it? You are still Drakhaon. Who will dare stop you?"

Dysis crooned a lullaby as she gently placed little Stavyomir back in his cradle. The drowsy baby began to protest, but then, too sleepy to resist, he relaxed into sleep. She stood, one hand rocking the cradle, waiting for the moment when she could steal away and continue with her chores.

A flicker of movement at the window made her glance up.

"Who's there?"

The heavy brocade drapes had not been drawn quite to. The wind gusted in the chimney and a thin draft whispered about her ankles. It must have been a stray rose branch lashed against the panes by the wind. She went across to pull the curtains closed, to block out the draft. And then she saw the eyes. Drakhaoul eyes. A gleam of gold and electric blue, cruel and bright as lightning.

She froze.

Someone—something—was crouched on the sill, watching her. Waiting.

Suddenly the creature hurled itself at the glass. The window shattered in a shower of shards as it crashed onto the floor.

Dysis screamed and ran toward the cradle.

All the lamps went out. Curtains flapped and fluttered. It seemed as if the creature's body gave off a faint glimmer, a shiver of phosphorescent blue against the turbulent darkness. Dysis half-saw, half-sensed the intruder rise to his feet.

"Help!" Her voice seemed so feeble. "Help me!"

It was moving toward her. Toward the baby.

She placed herself between him and the cradle.

"You shan't touch him." She heard her voice, thin and shrill with terror, defying the creature to come any closer—and despised herself for her weakness.

Somewhere far away it seemed she heard other voices outside, people running, fists pounding at the door.

"Can't—control—any—longer—" Words came from the creature's throat: hoarse, strangled words. Talons clawed out toward her. The darkness was scored with bright slashes, red as blood, white as pain.

"If not—him—then—*you*."

Caught in its claws, she felt herself drawn helplessly into its dark embrace, felt a breath hot and dry as flame sear her skin, then the graze of burning lips and tongue against her throat. Kissing, licking, sucking . . .

"No," she said faintly. "No . . ."

Drakhaoul eyes blazed blue in the darkness. Glittering wings enfolded her. She was flying; she was soaring up into the night sky . . .

Blue of thunder-flame, blue of angelfire, blue of dying stars.

The door burst open and Tielen soldiers came tumbling in. Torchlight illuminated the room—and the shadow-creature crouched at her feet, its lips wet with blood. Her blood.

"The baby," Dysis whispered, sinking to the floor. "Save the baby . . ."

Even as the soldiers threw themselves on it, the shadow-creature tore itself free and hurled itself through the broken window, disappearing into the night.

Gouts of red dripped across Gavril's sight. All he could see was a woman's face, white as snow, distorted by pain and fear. A white mask slashed with stains of scarlet.

He looked down at his hands. There was blood on the dark blue curve of the claw-nails. And a strange, metallic sweetness in his mouth. Had he done this terrible thing?

He felt sick with self-loathing. How could he have struck out so viciously again?

He could hear the Tielens blundering through the gardens, searching for the intruder. He turned his back on Kastel Drakhaon and made his way through the darkened forest to the ruined watchtower. There he sat down, hugging his knees, rocking to and fro in misery.

"Make it stop, Khezef," he cried aloud, his voice more the howl of a forest beast than a man. "Please make it stop!"

CHAPTER 30

"Never trust a wind-mage," muttered Malusha as she buckled the harness around Harim's shaggy-coated body, "for they're as fickle as a spring gale, blowing this way and that."

Harim patiently allowed himself to be led to the cart. It was a fine spring day, with fresh gusts of wind sending little white clouds dancing across a pure blue sky. The air tasted of green buds and sweet spring rain.

"First he whisks my granddaughter away on the Emperor's business." Malusha stopped. "And where is she, my Kiukiu? You miss her too, don't you, Harim? I know she used to give you apples sneaked from the winter store when I wasn't looking." She gave a sigh. She had not worried at first when Kiukiu failed to return, but now as the days stretched to weeks, she began to wonder if some harm might have befallen her. "I should never have let her go with that Kaspar Linnaius."

And then there had been the dream last night. She had woken in the darkest hour, certain that lightning had shivered across the moorlands. Yet when she had opened the shutter, the night was calm and still, with not even the faintest tremor of distant thunder.

Since then she had been troubled by an indefinable feeling of unease.

"And what of the promise that Magus made to me? I ask you, Harim, what's more important to a Spirit Singer than her duty to her House?"

Harim gave a little snort and nuzzled her shoulder.

"There's an Arkhel baby to be named. Little Lord Stavyomir." She chuckled to herself. "That I should live to see this day—an heir to the House of Arkhel."

Malusha climbed slowly, rheumatically, up into the cart, easing herself down onto the wooden seat beside the little pots of honey and dried herbs she planned to sell or trade in the city.

"Take care of the place for me while I'm away, my lords and ladies," she called to the owls. "And now, Harim—let's be off to Azhgorod."

"Papers? What papers?" Malusha turned to the red-faced young soldier on the Southgate, arms folded. "I never needed papers in Lord Stavyor's time. What does an old woman like me need with papers? I'd just lose 'em."

"Now then, Grandma—"

"Don't you 'grandma' me, young man! Do I look dangerous to you? Just let me through and we won't say another word about it."

"Is there anyone in the city who could vouch for you?"

A little queue was building up at the gate; mutterings could be heard from the others waiting to enter the city. A farmer shouted out, "Just let the old woman in, lad, and be done with it. I'll vouch for her."

The soldier shifted uneasily from foot to foot. Another came out to whisper in his ear. Both were scarcely older than boys and their uniform jackets looked several sizes too big.

"You're allowed in, just this once," he said. "But next time you have to stop to have official papers made up for you."

"What's the Tielen army coming to—cradle-snatching?" called the farmer. "You lads should still be at school, not ordering your elders and betters around."

Malusha didn't stop to hear the reply; she shook Harim's reins and the cart rattled under the archway and into the city.

Several hours later, and after many fruitless inquiries, she found herself perplexed. No one seemed to know the name Stavyomir Arkhel. Had Linnaius spun her the tale to get her away from her granddaughter?

She sold the honey and the herbs in the marketplace and listened to the chatter around her, hoping for clues. What had Kiukiu said the mother's name was? The "nasty piece of work" she had warned her of? Was it Lilias?

Malusha stopped at the stall of a Khitari tea merchant and sampled a bowl or two of tea: first green, then black scented with jasmine petals. Tea from Khitari was an expensive luxury; if she waited long enough, some servant from a big house was certain to come by. As she waited, she treated herself to a scoop of jasmine tea, which cost her the money she'd earned from the sale of three pots of honey.

Sure enough, a well-dressed serving woman approached and asked for a jar of green tea. Malusha's eyes widened at such extravagance.

"I'm looking for someone called Lilias," she said.

The woman turned to gaze at her with an expression of disdain.

"That is a name my mistress has forbidden to be spoken in the house."

Malusha was intrigued. "Why so?"

"It's none of your business." The serving woman took up her jar of tea and walked off.

"She's Lady Stoyan's maid. Haven't you heard?" called out a woman from the linen stall. "Lilias Arbelian has become Lord Stoyan's mistress."

"Arbelian?" Malusha was confused. "The Lilias I'm looking for is called 'Arkhel.' She has a little son."

"Lilias Arbelian has a baby son."

"Then maybe she's the one. Where can I find her?"

"At Lord Stoyan's mansion, across from the cathedral."

Malusha was tired now; her feet ached with tramping over uneven cobblestones and her skirts were dirtied with mud. Yet she was determined to do what she had come to do, so she set off toward the tall, black spires of the cathedral.

When she came out into the square, the first thing she noticed was the guard of Tielen soldiers around Lord Stoyan's mansion.

"Don't ask for my papers, I haven't got any," she said before the soldier could ask. "I just want to pay a visit to Lilias Arbelian and her baby."

The soldier looked at her. "I'm under orders not to admit anyone without papers."

"I just want to see the baby."

"He's not here. Lord Stoyan has taken Lady Lilias and the baby away for a few days."

"Away?" Malusha repeated. "How can they be away when I've come across the moors to see them? When will they be back?"

The soldier shrugged.

"I'll wait, then." But even as she turned away, disappointed, she knew she would not wait; she wanted to return home.

The bells of Saint Sergius began to clang, each iron-tongued note making her head throb. The constant noise and bustle of Azhgorod were bewildering and exhausting after the lonely quiet of the moor-lands.

"I'll find you, little Lord Stavyomir. And you'll get your proper Arkhel naming ceremony, like your father Jaromir and his father Stavyor before him, whatever your mother says. It just won't be today."

The advance guard of the Smarnan rebels reached the grassy hill overlooking Colchise and Vermeille Bay beyond. Iovan elected him-self to ride ahead to report to the council. No one contested his deci-sion; all were tired, and glad of a chance to sprawl on the grass, smoke tobacco, and do nothing for a while.

Pavel dismounted, leaving his horse to crop the short turf, and gazed down at the Old Citadel. Raïsa joined him.

"Look," she said, "the Smarnan standard is still flying."

The ragged standard, bloodstained and shot through by Tielen bullets, fluttered defiantly above the broken battlements.

"I hope there will be better news of Miran," she said quietly.

But Pavel had caught sight of something on the far horizon. "Are those sails?" He pulled out his little spyglass to get a clearer look.

Raïsa shaded her eyes against the setting sun. "Too many ships for a fishing fleet."

Pavel twisted the lens, trying to read the colors flying on the mast of the foremost ship.

"Francia?" he said. "The Francian fleet, off Smarna?"

"Let me see!" Raïsa grabbed the glass from him, putting it to her eye. She let out a soft whistle. "There's so many of them. What are they doing out there? Where are they headed?"

"*We have powerful allies . . .*" Nina Vashteli had told the Emperor, and Pavel had thought she was calling his bluff. Now, looking at this vast fleet, he felt overwhelmed by a sense of impending disaster. Did Eugene have any idea that King Enguerrand had entered the field?

The stakes had been raised. Smarna had become the pawn in a greater game between two powerful rivals.

When he agreed to become Eugene's agent in Smarna, the Emperor had given him no specific instructions except to infiltrate the rebels' camp and extract as much information as he could. *"Exactly how you act on that information, I leave to your discretion."*

It was time to act.

"We must go to the citadel," he said, hurrying toward his horse.

"I'll come with you!" Raïsa's eyes burned with excitement, and he hated himself for what he was about to do. Part of him, the better part, yearned to break the promise he had made to the Emperor. He didn't want to risk her seeing him betraying her cause. For she would see it as a betrayal. She wouldn't listen to his reasons. She wouldn't want to hear that life as part of the enlightened New Rossiyan Empire would be infinitely preferable to the code of conduct that Enguerrand and his fanatical clerics would impose.

"Leave this to me, Raïsa." He put his hands on her shoulders. "Go home and see how Miran is."

"But, Pavel—"

He climbed up into the saddle and urged his horse down the winding hill road.

"The Francian fleet?" Nina Vashteli smiled at Pavel. Her hair was sleekly swept up, she was wearing kohl around her eyes and her lips were glossily red with rouge. "Yes, the council has granted permission for them to carry out a naval exercise in the bay. It seems the waters off Fenez-Tyr are too stormy at this time of year."

The Vox Aethyria bloomed, a flower of crystal in the somber light.

"In late spring?" Pavel said. It didn't seem too convincing an excuse. He tried to stop glancing at the Vox Aethyria, wondering when he might engineer an opportunity to send a warning to the Emperor. "So, in spite of the retreat of the invasion force, there's still been no response to your message from the Emperor?"

"No," she said coldly.

"And Governor Armfeld?"

"Governor? We do not recognize anyone as governor here, Pavel. Armfeld is still our prisoner."

"You do realize, Madame Minister," Pavel said in earnest now, "that the enmity between Francia and Tielen goes back many centuries? And in inviting the Francian fleet to defend your shores, you may have set fire to a powder trail that will end in the destruction of all our countries?"

"We have acted in the best interests of Smarna. I suggest you return to the Villa Sapara and enjoy one of Mama Chadi's good meals, Pavel. You can relax now for a little while."

Iovan came in. "You're wanted to authorize permits for the Francian crewmen to come ashore, Madame Minister."

"Very well." She followed Iovan out of the chamber. Pavel glanced again at the Vox Aethyria. He had been dismissed by Nina Vashteli, told his services were not required. It would only take a minute to transmit a message to Tielen. . . .

He moved silently to the Vox and, activating the connection, began to whisper into it, not daring to raise his voice. "Francian fleet off Southern Smarna—"

He felt the cold muzzle of a pistol pressed into the back of his neck.

"I knew it," said Iovan Korneli. "I was right all along. You *are* a spy."

As soon as she was sure she was alone, Astasia opened the little calendar she had hidden inside her novel and counted.

"Surely not," she whispered and counted again. All the upset of traveling to and fro from country to country must have upset her monthly cycle. Her mother Sofia had assured her that all the women in the family were slow to conceive. She knew so little about such matters. And for the first time, she found herself wishing Mama was here. But Mama was far away, at their country estate at Erinaskoe in Muscobar.

Someone tapped at the door; hastily, Astasia slipped the calendar back inside the novel and pretended to read.

"Come in."

"Here are the masks, imperial highness, that you requested. And the perukes."

Astasia looked up to see that the Countess Lovisa had—uninvited—decided to supervise the choosing of her costume for the masked ball. Nadezhda hovered, making helpless little signs of apology to Astasia behind the countess's back.

Astasia slowly closed the novel, replacing her silk-tasseled book-mark with care.

"Thank you, countess," she said with her best attempt at a gracious smile. "You may leave us now. I'm sure you have many demands on your time."

"But nothing is more important to me than attending upon your imperial highness," said Countess Lovisa with an equally gracious smile.

"But helping me try on a dress or two is surely more appropriate for a lady's maid."

"I only wanted to be sure of your imperial highness's final choice of costume so that I could ensure no one else was impertinent enough to copy it."

She's suspicious. But why? Has she been spying on me?

"Nadezhda is very clever with her needle. She can always swiftly transform my costume with a ribbon or a feather if anyone dares to be so impertinent."

Nadezhda bobbed a cheeky little curtsy, acknowledging the com-pliment. But Countess Lovisa did not move. Astasia tried to think up an urgent errand that only the countess could accomplish.

Nadezhda began to open boxes and lift out their contents from rustling layers of tissue paper.

"Oh dear, highness, there's been a mix-up here," she said, winking at Astasia out of the countess's line of sight. "This is Princess Karila's costume."

"Countess, would you be so good as to take the princess's costume to her rooms?" Astasia said with her sweetest smile. "You know the Emperor has allowed only the closest family members to visit Karila until she is fully recovered."

"What—now?" Pale blue eyes looked at her coolly.

"What better time?" Astasia replied, equally cool.

"I've packed it up for you, countess." Nadezhda retied the ribbons in a bow and passed the blue and white striped box to the countess with another little bob of a curtsy.

The countess withdrew without another word. The stiffness of her back and the haughty tilt of her chin told Astasia that she was of-fended at being asked to run an errand.

As the door closed behind her, Astasia let out a pent-up sigh.

"Quick, Nadezhda, run and fetch Demoiselle de Joyeuse. I'll bolt the door. That way when Countess High-and-Mighty returns, I'll be warned in time."

While Nadezhda was away, Astasia examined some of the costumes her maid had laid out. They were all created from the most delicious fabrics: gauzes, silks, muslins, and brocades, dyed in subtle shades.

She could not resist holding up one and then another against herself and looking in the mirror: first, a water-nymph's robes in floating silver gauze and net over blue watered silk; next, a sylph in the palest shades of white, grey, and tender pink. Or this exotic temple-dancer's costume from the deserts of Djihan-Djihar, dyed the colors of the setting sun: orange, crimson, and violet deepening into indigo, all spangled with gold. Oh yes, this was the one. She just had to try it on . . .

There came a scratch at the door and she hurried to unbolt it, holding it open to let Nadezhda and Celestine in, then hastily securing it again.

They stared at her.

"Does it suit me?" she asked, spinning around on bare feet, so that the tiny little bells sewn into the fabric tinkled.

"Pantaloons?" Nadezhda said. "On a lady? On the Empress? Isn't that rather immodest, highness? What would your mother say?"

"You look wonderful!" cried Celestine. "And look—there's a headdress, and the mask has a veil. No one would ever guess . . ."

Immodest. Astasia's excitement was abruptly tempered. If Celestine and she were to succeed in their little plan, it would be important not to draw too much attention to herself.

"There was a shepherdess's costume," she said with a sigh. "Pretty in an insipid way: panniers, puffed sleeves. It came with one of those Francian powdered wigs with a single long curl trailing over one shoulder."

Nadezhda helped her out of the temple-dancer's costume and she gazed at it regretfully as Nadezhda laid it back on the bed. "The colors were so gorgeous. . . ."

Nadezhda began to lace her into the shepherdess's costume.

"Ow! Must you pull quite so tight?"

"Someone's been eating too many sugared almonds," Nadezhda said severely. "I'm going to have to leave the last hooks undone."

"You must have given the costumiers the wrong measurements." Astasia looked down at herself, trying to see the extra inches

Nadezhda had so rudely drawn her attention to. Had she been eating too many sweets? If anything, she had lost her appetite. Certain foods made her feel quite queasy.

"And you've filled out since we left Mirom," added Nadezhda.

Astasia looked at her reflection in the mirror. The tight-laced bodice and daringly low-cut neck of the pale blue shepherdess's gown had forced her little breasts upward, making them look plumper than before, the veins blue against the creamy pallor of her skin. The constrictions of the bodice certainly made them feel more tender and swollen. Then there were the calculations she had made with her calendar. Surely she couldn't be with child so soon?

"It's just the cut of this dress," she said defensively. "And why is the bodice less immodest than my lovely Djihari pantaloons?"

"Now the wig." Nadezhda sat her down and, deftly sweeping her mistress's long dark hair into a chignon, eased the soft white curls into place.

"I look like a sheep," Astasia complained, looking at herself critically in the mirror. "Baaa . . ."

"You look charming," said Celestine. "All you need now is a crook with a pale blue bow and some blue-ribboned shoes."

"And a mask." Astasia took the gilded mask from Nadezhda and put it on. "Stand next to me, Celestine."

The singer obeyed.

"We are a good match in stature. I think this costume will suit our needs very well."

Celestine nodded. "Then Jagu will come as a shepherd. What a pastoral trio we will make."

"Nadezhda," Astasia said. "You remember what we agreed?"

"You leave it to me, highness." Nadezhda bobbed another little curtsy. "I'll go whisper your requests to the costumier now. We could do with a more generous size for you anyway." And before Astasia could protest, she unbolted the door and darted off, still laughing mischievously.

Astasia made sure the door was firmly bolted. Then she handed a gilded mask identical to her own to the singer.

"Can Nadezhda be trusted?"

"Oh yes," Astasia said earnestly, "she's utterly loyal to me. She's more like a sister than a maidservant."

Celestine put on the mask and Astasia tied the golden ribbons firmly behind her ears to stop it slipping. Then they checked their reflections in the mirror, masked faces close together.

"Perfect," said Astasia. "Who would guess? We look like identical twins."

"Did you know, highness," said Celestine, taking off the gilded mask, "that Kaspar Linnaius, whom we saw earlier, is no ordinary scientist?"

"I had some notion, yes," Astasia said, looking at herself critically in the mirror as she tried to tuck in stray dark strands that kept escaping from under her wig. "I know that he has placed certain wards on the palace and its grounds to protect us from harm."

"But were you also aware," and Celestine's voice, normally so clear and lighthearted, dropped to a low whisper, "of his other talents? Or that his title, 'Magus,' is not a fanciful conceit? He is a wind-mage, able to bend the winds to his will."

"I had no idea." A year ago Astasia would have dismissed Celestine's statement as absurd. But the last few months had shown her that there were darker forces at work in the world than she had ever imagined.

"In the conflict between Francia and Tielen, your husband's father, Prince Karl, won a decisive victory over my countrymen in a sea battle off the Saltyk Peninsula. At the height of the battle, a terrible storm broke and many of the Francian fleet were blown onto the rocks."

Astasia stared at Celestine. The conversation had suddenly become too intense for her liking. She wanted to steer it back to lighter topics before someone overheard and reported back to Eugene.

"The seas around the Saltyk Peninsula can be treacherously unpredictable," she said, taking off the heavy wig and replacing it on its stand, "even in the best of weather."

"And Prince Karl was Kaspar Linnaius's patron."

"I don't think we should be talking of this, Celestine. . . ."

But Celestine continued, seemingly unconcerned about her warning. "Your brother's ship, the *Sirin*, went down in a storm that blew up out of nowhere. On a calm, moonlit night."

There came a loud rap on the door. Someone rattled the door handle.

"Imperial highness!" It was Countess Lovisa's voice. "Why is your door bolted?"

"To keep you out," muttered Astasia. The door handle rattled again, louder this time. Annoyed, she hastily loosened one of her laces until the bodice slipped off one shoulder. She would shame Lovisa in the one way she suspected would hurt the well-bred count- ess the most: a breach of etiquette.

"Please open the door for the countess," she said loudly. As Celestine let Lovasia in, keeping out of sight, Astasia half-turned, her shoulder and one breast exposed. She let out a loud cry of feigned embarrassment, crossing her arms over her nakedness.

"But wait until I've put on my *peignoir!*"

"Highness—I'm so sorry—" The countess froze in the doorway and then retreated, slamming the door shut.

"Did she see me behind the door, do you think?" asked Celestine, her blue eyes wide with apprehension.

"I don't think she did. But you can't stay here," Astasia said to Celestine, hastily putting on her ivory silk peignoir. It was time to risk revealing one of Swanholm's most well-guarded secrets, yet she felt she could trust Celestine de Joyeuse not to abuse the privilege. She beckoned her to the fireplace. Reaching out, she touched the marble acanthus leaf on the right and heard the grating of hidden machinery as a panel slowly slid into the wall.

"Ah," said Celestine, her look of apprehension changing to one of amazement. "A secret passageway."

"Once inside, take twenty-one steps to your right. That brings you to a little stair." Astasia's voice dropped to a conspiratorial whisper. "Go down until you feel fresh air from a grating on your face. There's a handle directly below the grating. Turn it to your right as far as it will go. It opens into the shrubbery near the Orangery—but be careful there is no one about to see you."

"With so many people around for the ball, I shall simply melt into the crowd." Celestine bent low to enter the secret passage.

"Nadezhda will bring the costumes to your room."

"And the next time we meet, sweet shepherdess . . ."

"You will introduce me to a certain shepherd."

"Are you dressed yet, highness?" called a voice from the corridor.

Astasia gave a little groan. "Lovisa is back. Go. And don't forget— twenty-one steps to the right."

She touched the acanthus leaf again and the panel slid to, hiding Celestine in the dark of the secret passageway.

Andrei, she whispered in her heart as she went to unbolt the door, *can it be true that Linnaius sent the storm to sink your ship? Because if so . . . was it my husband Eugene who gave the order?*

She had opened the door and was staring into the ice-blue eyes of Lovisa when the terrible implications struck her. Suddenly she felt hot and dizzy. Too late, she grasped at the doorframe to keep herself from falling. As she tumbled forward into the countess's arms, she heard the countess cry out in alarm, "Help, here! The Empress has fainted!"

CHAPTER 31

Astasia lay listlessly on the ivory silk-canopied bed with the shutters drawn. Nadezhda had placed a little cloth impregnated with lavender water on her forehead, but the strong scent made her feel queasy again, so she threw it to the other end of the bedchamber as soon as Nadezhda tiptoed away.

"I never faint," she murmured.

"It's just a headache," Countess Lovisa had pronounced briskly. "A touch of the megrims. She'll be over it soon."

Even though the shutters were drawn against the bright daylight, they did not prevent the racket of the preparations for the ball from penetrating the bedchamber: the shouts of guardsmen tugging on the marquee ropes and the endless dull thuds as they hammered stakes into the grass.

"Eugene's beautiful lawns will be quite ruined. . . ." She closed her eyes again, wishing all the noise would fade away and leave her in peace. But sleep eluded her as one thought kept going around and around in her brain like a horribly repetitive refrain.

Did you do it, Eugene? Did you order the sinking of the Sirin?

If it were true . . .

"No," she whispered, "not Eugene."

Why did this revelation have to come now, just as she realized she was carrying his child? And why did it hurt so much? Was it a simple feeling of betrayal? Or was it that, in spite of their differences, she had begun to love him . . . just a little?

Such a devious and ignoble act was difficult to reconcile with the man she had come to know more intimately than any other.

Now she remembered Eugene's determination to ensure all the children of Muscobar would be properly fed and educated. She remembered how passionately he had spoken of his plans for the empire. And she remembered how he had kissed her the night they were married. . . .

Of course, Celestine could be wrong. It was even possible she had been sent to poison her mind against her husband. But then there was the fact that Andrei was alive, against all the odds.

I must get better before the ball. I can't miss this chance to see Andrei; I can't.

Until now she had not allowed herself to think how much this reunion meant to her. But lying here sick in this unfamiliar bed, so far from her own country, she felt helpless tears of homesickness begin to leak from her eyes. She missed Mama and Papa. She missed Varvara and Svetlana, her closest friends. She even missed Eupraxia and her constant chiding.

"Poor Tasia," said a soft little voice.

Astasia opened her eyes and saw a golden-haired child standing at her bedside.

"Kari?" she said, startled.

"I'm sorry you're ill," said Karila. "It's horrid to be ill, isn't it? I was ill on my birthday."

"I know," Astasia said, wiping away her tears with her fingertips. "And I'm sorry we were late for your party—"

"I don't really remember my party," Karila said, "so it doesn't matter. Have you seen my costume for the ball?"

"No . . ." The ball. Astasia closed her eyes again at the thought.

"It's very pretty. It's the Swan Princess. It's white satin with soft feathers around the hem and the neck. They tickle, so I hope I won't sneeze and make my swan mask fall off."

Astasia could not stop herself from smiling.

"That's better," Karila said. "Now you don't look so sad."

"Does Marta know you're here?"

"Of course not! I came through the secret passageways."

"But if she comes back and finds you're gone—"

"I've been made to stay in my rooms for too long. I was bored."

"At least you came to see me, little Kari. I've lain here all these hours, and not once has your father appeared or even inquired after my health. Too busy, I suppose, with affairs of state and the ball . . ."

"It's good to rest. It's good for the baby," Karila said.

Astasia raised her head.

"Baby? What baby?"

"My little stepbrother," Karila said in matter-of-fact tones.

Astasia caught hold of Karila's hand and pulled her closer.

"Kari, what nonsense are you talking?"

Karila stretched out her other hand and let it rest gently on Astasia's stomach.

"This baby," she said, smiling.

"But how—" Astasia let go of Karila's hand.

"What will you call him? Will it have to be Karl after my grandfather? I don't like the name; it's too short."

"Kari, *how did you know*?" If Karila had guessed, then who else might have come to the same conclusion?

"And when he's old enough, I'll let him visit my menagerie and feed the deer. Have you seen my little deer? They come from Khitari, Papa says, and they live on the steppes, eating lichen . . ." Karila prattled on, quite oblivious of the impact of her revelation.

Astasia sat up and swung her legs off the bed.

"Karila," she said, "you must say nothing of the baby to anyone. It must be our secret."

"Not even to Papa?"

"Papa . . ." Astasia hesitated, desperately trying to think of a reason to convince the child. She did not want Karila babbling the news about before she had told Eugene herself. And Celestine's disclosure had thrown all thoughts of telling Eugene into disarray. "I haven't told Papa. I'm keeping it as a special surprise." She placed one finger over her lips. Karila imitated her, nodding and smiling.

"Our secret. Like my menagerie. Have you seen my dragon pavilion?"

"Not yet." Astasia could not concentrate on what Karila was saying.

"If you stand at this window, you can just see the Khitari dragon on top of the pavilion with the little bells . . ."

And if what Celestine told me is true? . . .

*   *   *

The shadows were lengthening on the parterres and golden evening light glimmered on the still, dark lake. Eugene, making a short tour of the preparations for the ball, noticed that little clouds of midges were rising over the water.

"We will need citronella flares burning near the lake, to keep our guests from being eaten alive," he said to the Master of Ceremonies, who was accompanying him. An assistant was busy scribbling down in a ledger what still needed to be done.

A woman was coming toward them past the white marquees; Eugene recognized her by her upright, stately bearing and the proud tilt of her chin.

"You asked to see me, imperial highness?" Countess Lovisa curtsied low to Eugene.

The Master of Ceremonies discreetly withdrew.

"Walk with me, Lovisa. I hear the first roses are in bud in the rose garden."

"Delightful," Lovisa said, accepting his arm.

They strolled in silence through the slowly darkening garden toward the walled rose garden. A blackbird began to sing from the top of the old stone wall, its piercing notes fluting questioningly into the dusk. From farther away, another answered.

"I'm glad we preserved a wall or two of my father's hunting lodge," Eugene said as they entered the rose garden, "though I'm not sure he would have approved of the use we put it to."

"This will be such a pleasant place to stroll or to sit in during high summer." Lovisa sniffed the evening air appreciatively. "Was it your inspiration, Eugene, to plant lavender beds beneath the roses? So charming."

"My head gardener's idea, so I can take no credit for it, I fear." Eugene stopped a moment, checking to see if they were alone. From here, he was confident that the high walls would protect them from prying eyes or ears. He turned to the countess, determined to learn the truth. "So what is this sickness of Astasia's? Is it real or feigned?"

"It seems to be nothing more than a touch of the megrims. Genuine, I believe. She has been acting rather dizzily these last few days."

"Can we be sure it's not the first symptom of some more serious affliction?" Margret's death had brutally brought home to Eugene the fragility of human life. It had led him to endow the new school of the science of medicine at Tielborg University, in the hope that the researches there would prevent such tragedies occurring in the future. "Should I send Doctor Amandel to her?"

Lovisa smiled. "I really think there's no need, Eugene. We women learn to endure these minor discomforts."

Eugene let out a suppressed sigh. He lifted a cream and blush rosebud and stroked it pensively between finger and thumb. "I went ahead with all this frippery just to please her. Because she loves to dance. Given the situation in Smarna, I should have canceled the whole damned affair. God knows, I can ill spare the time at the moment— and now she's sick." He tugged a little too hard at the rosebud and it snapped off.

"I'm certain she'll be well enough by tomorrow," remarked the countess dryly.

"And must I wear some foolish costume? You know how I hate dressing up, Lovisa."

"I have organized a disguise that will in no way harm your dignity."

Was it a trick of the fading light or was she smiling at him? He had known Lovisa since they were children, and she still perplexed him: one moment icy calm, the next mysteriously alluring.

"What will Astasia be wearing?"

"Some flimsy little shepherdess costume in blue. In my opinion, the bodice is cut far too low. I will persuade her to drape a scarf over the décolletage."

Eugene was silent a moment. Then he moved nearer to Lovisa, bending his head close to hers so that no one else could possibly hear what he said. "Are you certain, Lovisa?"

"Not entirely," she said coolly. "And as to who, and the circumstances, I still have no firm evidence."

"And you believe he will make an appearance at the ball?"

"She and the Francian singer are plotting some kind of charade together." Lovisa gave a haughty little cough. "A child could see through their little plot."

Lovisa's opinions were not improving his mood. At first he had not entertained the slightest suspicion that Astasia was capable of deceiving him. He had even begun to believe that she felt some kind of affection toward him. Now, as dusk shadows crept through the garden

and the servants began to light the candles within the palace, he felt
as though the dark of night had seeped into his heart.

He slowly opened his clenched fist, and the crushed petals of the
rosebud fell to the path.

"Oh look, Tasia, there's Papa."

Astasia had been standing at the tall windows, wistfully gazing out
over the parklands, darkly gilded by the setting sun.

"Wh-where?" she asked dazedly.

"Down there in the rose garden."

Astasia looked to where Karila was pointing and saw a tall figure,
unmistakably Eugene, head inclined, close, far too close to—

She stared.

"Lovisa?" she whispered. She could not see the countess's face from
here, but that erect carriage, those white-blond curls so immaculately
dressed in a chignon, that elegant silver-grey and rose gown . . .

So close. Close enough to be kissing, his mouth brushing the curls
by her delicate little earlobe, the nape of her neck . . .

"Cousin Lovisa!" said Karila happily.

"Oh," said Astasia, her voice soft, shocked. "Oh." She tried to
look away, but found she could not, some cruel impulse forcing her
to watch what she had no wish to see. But the secret lovers had
moved apart from each other, aware perhaps that they could be seen
from the palace. This brief moment of intimacy she had glimpsed,
was it a prelude to some later nocturnal assignation? Or was it evidence of a long-standing liaison?

Was she perhaps the only person in all of Swanholm to be unaware
that Lovisa was her husband's mistress?

Andrei Orlov gazed in amazement at the prospect below them.
There, in the dusk, lay the Palace of Swanholm, its gardens, parklands, and lake all lit by strings of jewel-colored lanterns, so that the
whole valley glowed.

"It's magnificent." So this was Astasia's new home. Even at this
first glance, he could see the palace was far more elegant than the old
Winter Palace in Mirom. He was already excited at the prospect of
seeing Astasia again after so long; impersonating Celestine's accompanist Jagu only increased that excitement.

A magnificent stucco gatehouse with elaborate gilded ironwork grilles lay ahead. Guards were stopping each carriage as it arrived and checking the gilt-edged invitations and papers of each guest individually. They held lanterns and torches so that they could scrutinize each new arrival in a good light.

A lieutenant in the Imperial Household Cavalry approached and all the guards stood stiffly to attention, returning his salute.

"At ease, at ease . . ."

There was something familiar about the lieutenant's voice and bearing. Andrei shrank back into the shadows as the officer popped his head in the open carriage window.

"Good evening to you, Demoiselle de Joyeuse!"

It was Valery Vassian, Andrei's boyhood friend. What the devil was he doing here in Swanholm, in a Tielen uniform?

"Just a simple shepherdess and her swain," Celestine said sweetly, smiling at Lieutenant Vassian.

For God's sake, don't ask me to remove my mask or wig, Valery! Andrei had begun to sweat under his disguise.

"Jagu and I make quite a fetchingly pastoral pair, don't you agree?"

"You would look fetching in any costume, demoiselle."

The dazzle of her smile worked its magic; they were waved through and their carriage began the long winding descent toward the palace.

Andrei let out a quiet whistle. "That was too close." What was Valery Vassian doing in Eugene's imperial bodyguard? Was he here to protect Astasia?

Andrei's fingers began to tap out an insistent repetitive rhythm on the side of the carriage as they rattled down the wide graveled drive. His whole body was taut with nerves. He had been out of society for so long that the sight of so many people gathered together made him feel jittery. He still walked with a slight limp; suppose someone noticed? This illicit meeting with Astasia meant everything to him. Nothing must jeopardize it.

Music drifted in; by the lakeside, a wind-band was playing in a torchlit pavilion, the high notes of the flutes and hautbois carrying on the darkening air. And though the melodies were familiar old dance tunes, they seemed to Andrei to exude a strangely sinister quality that matched his jangled nerves.

Celestine leaned across and placed her hand on his, her touch soft yet reassuring.

"Don't worry," she said, gazing earnestly into his eyes. "You will see your sister. And very soon."

The carriage stopped and a masked flunky opened the door. Andrei got down first, awkwardly; his mended legs were still stiff and unpredictable. Then he offered his hand to Celestine.

All around them, guests were descending from carriages, sporting a bizarre assortment of masks: from simple velvet or silk dominos to painted plaster, cleverly molded to cover the whole face. Andrei saw slant-eyed, powder-white Khitari actors' masks, and grotesque blue and scarlet temple thunder-gods from lands far beyond the eastern mountains. Some guests wore jeweled bird masks with beaks and curling feathers; others furry animal snouts of fox, bear, and lion.

"We look very ordinary," he said in Celestine's ear as they joined the queue of guests.

"Exactly," she said. "Who will take notice of such a boringly pastoral pair alongside all these exotic creations? Now don't forget. Your cue is the fanfare announcing the start of the fireworks. Your sister knows that is the moment we will change places. The rest . . . is up to you."

*   *   *

Francian fleet off Southern Smarna—

Eugene raised his eyes from the paper to see Gustave staring back at him tensely.

"Where's the rest of the message?"

"We think our operative was interrupted. The transmission was terminated abruptly. Then the connection went dead."

"Pavel," Eugene murmured. If the Smarnan rebels had caught Pavel Velemir, he would be tried and shot as a spy, but not before being subjected to a lengthy and painful interrogation. He remembered the young man's charm—and the frayed cuffs on his shirts. Pavel had shown such promise; and if he had been discovered, there was nothing Eugene could do to rescue him.

"Is this the same fleet that was taking Enguerrand on his pilgrimage to Djihan-Djihar?" A feeling of anxiety gripped his stomach. Had he and his ministers misread the Smarnan conflict? Was a small uprising about to escalate into full-scale war?

Outside in the gardens a little orchestra began to play a lively gavotte. There came a tap at the locked door.

"Imperial highness?" It was his valet, ready to dress him for the ball.

"One moment." Eugene grimaced at Gustave. "The ball! How can I dance and joke and play the good host with the situation in Smarna out of control?"

Astasia had managed to smile her way through the formal reception. From time to time the temptation to scan the crowd of guests for a glimpse of Celestine and Andrei grew too great and she found herself glancing around, almost forgetting what she was saying to Countess this or Counsellor that.

When Fredrik, the majordomo, came to whisper to her that the ball was to start, she was almost glad that she could calm her nerves with dancing.

Eugene, evidently uncomfortable in his heavy costume, stood waiting for her at the head of the great marble staircase that led into the ballroom. As she placed her hand on his, she could tell that his mind was elsewhere; behind the mask, his eyes looked at her, through her.

"What's wrong?" she whispered as the guests thronged into the ballroom.

"Nothing that need concern you tonight, Astasia."

"Your concerns are my concerns too," she said sharply, hurt that he had spoken to her as if to a child. But before he could reply, a dazzling fanfare rang out and the Master of Ceremonies announced, "The Emperor and Empress of New Rossiya!" and they were obliged to walk down the staircase to the applause of the assembled guests, smiling and nodding.

"And now the Emperor and Empress will start our Dievona Ball."

The musicians began to play. Astasia stood on the empty dance floor staring at Eugene.

"We are expected to dance together," she whispered, feeling herself blushing beneath her mask.

"You know I have no skill at dancing," he replied brusquely.

For a moment she felt sorry for him. She placed one hand on his shoulder and slipped the other into his unburned hand and gently nudged his foot with her own. "Just walk it through," she said in his ear, "one step at a time. Leave the counting to me."

She could sense from the tension in his body that he was furious at being made to undergo this indignity. Slowly they moved off and the Master of Ceremonies began to applaud. Soon other dancers joined them and Eugene relaxed his grip on her hand, leading her to the side of the ballroom.

She glanced up at him, her feelings even more confused. For a moment on the dance floor, she had forgotten Celestine's revelation, had forgotten Lovisa, had just let herself relax against him and felt . . . *safe*.

Now she found herself wishing that Andrei would tell her Celestine was mistaken and his ship had been dashed on the rocks by a genuine storm, not one whistled up by Kaspar Linnaius.

Eugene glowered at the bobbing sea of masked dancers who had invaded his palace. The riotous colors of their costumes offended his restrained tastes.

I should be on my way to Ty Nagar. Every minute spent here is another acre of Smarna lost to the empire.

His costume, organized by Lovisa, was considerably less dignified than she had promised. Whose fancy had it been to dress him as Artamon the Great? The robes were heavy and hot; the purple, turquoise, and gold brocades were far too ostentatious, and the gilt on the paste crown and mask were beginning to flake off as he perspired.

And the dance music was too insipid for his liking; these tedious, simpering little tunes, sighed out on violins and chalumeaux, lacked the vigor of martial music. They were probably Francian!

Young noblewomen of the court, dressed as wood-sylphs, with little sequinned wings attached to their gauze skirts and silk flowers in their unbound hair, ran past, giggling. Eugene sternly averted his gaze; their thin costumes were far too revealing, showing more than a tantalizing glimpse of unbound breasts.

No wife or daughter of mine . . .

He glanced at Astasia, who was dancing with Chancellor Maltheus now. Maltheus had come as a wild boar; his mask sported bristles and curling tusks. For a man of his bulk, he was a more than passable dancer and was partnering Astasia with skill.

More skill than I was capable of in the opening dance. Eugene had merely led his wife once around the dance floor to start the ball; he had not even attempted to perform a step or two.

"Papa, why do you look so unhappy?" Karila touched his arm. "This is such a lovely ball." Her face, beneath the swan mask with its black and gold beak, was radiant.

Chastened at his show of ill humor, he bent down and picked her up in his arms so that she could see better. At least the night's revels had made Kari happy.

"Astasia dances beautifully, doesn't she?"

He heard such wistfulness in her voice. He looked at Astasia. She was transformed when she danced: graceful in her movements, wild, free. He glimpsed something that he knew she withheld from him when they were together, something she could only express when unconstrained by duty or court etiquette. And poor, lame Karila could only dream of moving with such grace and freedom.

"Yes," he said, hugging her close, "she does dance beautifully. But dancing isn't everything, Kari."

"Why aren't you dancing with her?"

"Me?" The directness of her question took him by surprise. "Because I have two left feet on a dance floor, Kari, and I would only embarrass your new mama with my clumsiness."

She gave a little sigh of sympathy, which he felt resonate through his own body as well. And at that moment, the dance came to a close. The dancers broke into noisy chatter as they left the polished floor and the musicians changed their music sheets, indulging in a little tuning. Eugene winced; he could endure the whine and crash of exploding mortars in battle, but the wailing of catgut violin strings sliding in and out of pitch set his teeth on edge.

Astasia approached with Chancellor Maltheus; both looked a little out of breath and Maltheus was fanning himself with one hand.

"The Empress dances exquisitely," he said, puffing. "Oh it's no good, highness, I shall have to take off this boar's head; whatever made me agree to wear such a hot, hairy mask?"

Instantly a servant appeared with a tray of refreshing drinks: fruit punch, lemonade, and sparkling wine, both white and delicate pink.

"Wine, Astasia?" Eugene took a tall fluted glass, remembering that she was fond of this sparkling rosé he had imported from Francia for the occasion, and handed it to her.

"No, thank you," she said—rather brusquely, he thought. "Lemonade is more to my taste tonight." Her manner was distinctly chilly toward him; he supposed it must be because of his poor performance in the opening dance.

Brilliant fanfares rang out from the terraces. And at the same moment, the darkening sky lit with showers of gold and silver explosions.

"The fireworks!" cried Karila, clapping her hands in an ecstasy of excitement. "The fireworks have begun!"

Astasia's heart was pattering so fast with anticipation and fear that she could not speak. This was the moment. As the imperial party moved toward the terrace, she spotted Celestine behind one of the pale marble pillars. It was almost too easy, in the mêlée, to slip behind the next pillar just as Celestine slid into her place behind Eugene.

Astasia felt a hand on her shoulder. She turned—and saw dark eyes gazing into hers from behind a gilded mask.

"Andrei?" she whispered. For a moment, the candleflames of the chandeliers overhead merged to a blur and she feared she would faint. Outside, rockets whizzed and screamed as starbursts of color lit up the dark gardens.

"We'll get a better view down here." Her shepherd guided her down the steps, moving away from the terrace. Everyone was watching the fireworks; no one would notice a shepherd and shepherdess slipping out into the night.

"The Orangery," Astasia said, making swiftly for the graceful white-painted pavilion. Inside, the air was perfumed with the sugar-sweet scent of orange blossom and the earthier aroma of leaf mold and mulch. It was dark enough under the glossy-leaved trees, but Astasia led Andrei to an arbor at the heart of the Orangery, where no one could glimpse them when the fireworks lit up the night sky.

"Is it really you?" she said in their home tongue, breathless now with nerves.

He took off the gilded mask and powdered wig. Dark curls, tousled from confinement beneath the wig, sprang up. Dark eyes gazed at her from a face that was far leaner than she remembered, all the boyish contours honed away.

"Andrei," she said again and threw her arms around him, clutching him tightly. "It is you!" She was laughing and crying and she didn't care; she was just unspeakably happy that he was alive.

After a while he put his hands on her shoulders and held her at arm's length, looking into her eyes as if trying to read her thoughts. She saw his cheeks were wet with tears too; he was weeping unashamedly, her big, strong brother who never cried.

"Don't," she said, reaching up to gently wipe the wetness away with the tip of one finger.

"How long have we got?" he asked, his voice unsteady.

"The finale of the display is to be the illumination of the lake with the emblems of the five countries of New Rossiya."

"So short a time."

"Stay, Andrei." She caught hold of his hand, clutching it between her own. "Eugene will welcome you at court. For my sake, he'll welcome you—"

Andrei shook his head. "I can't, Tasia. Not now that I know what I have to do." A dazzling cascade of silver stars erupted overhead, outlining the orange branches in stark shadow. "His work, I suppose?"

"Kaspar Linnaius?"

"Celestine told you?"

"But I still can't believe it to be true. How can a man, a mere man, control the winds? How can he send storms where he wants them to go?"

"Your husband has built his empire using the occult arts to defeat his enemies." Another brilliant cascade, white as cherry blossom, lit up the Orangery. "Better he still believes me dead."

"And what of Mama and Papa?" Astasia felt her lower lip trembling; she bit it to stop herself from weeping. "Papa is a broken man, Andrei. He has never recovered from the news. And Mama . . ."

She saw him swallow hard. "Believe me, I'd like nothing better than to see them, Tasia. But I've been advised that it's too soon."

"Advised? By whom?"

"I'm going to Francia for a while, to the court of King Enguerrand. I have information that they need to make use of."

"Information?" Astasia drew away from him. Suddenly she felt she was treading dangerous ground. Could she trust this new, reborn Andrei? "About Tielen?"

"Don't worry, little sister; I'm not here to spy on you."

She looked at him, wary now. Had she been unwise to agree to this meeting?

"The information is to do with my miraculous recovery. It's too long a story for now, but I was a mess, Tasia—nearly every bone in my body broken in the wreck." As a flight of rockets burst overhead into swooping, shrilling phoenixes, trailing fire, he drew down the silken hose, revealing the scars still seaming his mended legs.

Astasia looked away, overcome with guilt.

"I'm sorry, Andrei," she whispered. "I'm so, so sorry. They searched for you, you know? They searched for weeks until the riots began in Mirom. Then the search was abandoned."

White light, diamond-bright, began to suffuse the gardens and the Orangery. Fanfares brayed out again. Astasia glanced over Andrei's shoulder and saw that the finale of the fireworks had begun. One by one, heraldic panels began to burn beyond the lake: a giant silver swan for Tielen, a two-headed sea eagle for Muscobar, the fiery phoenix of Khitari, the green-scaled tail of the Smarnan merman, and the brilliant blue dragon of Azhkendir.

"It's nearly over," she said, clinging to him in sudden panic. "Must we say farewell so soon?"

"We mustn't be seen together." Andrei hastily pulled on the white powdered wig; she stood on tiptoe to help him adjust it. "Tasia," he said, kissing her forehead, "take care. Once Celestine and I are gone, who will be here to look out for you?"

His words frightened her. "What do you mean? What do you know?"

"Come away with me. There's a ship in Haeven harbor bound for Francia, the *Melusine*. She sails tomorrow on the evening tide."

"Run away?" The suggestion shocked her. "But how can I leave my husband, Andrei?"

"If you change your mind, meet me at the harbor."

The fresh colors of the heraldic shields faded as another, darker glow began to illumine the lake, bathing the waters and gardens, even the pale stone of the palace in its deep, crimson glow. Kettle drums beat a thunderous roll and trumpets blared. This was what Eugene enjoyed best: the music of war. Transfixed, Astasia clutched hold of Andrei's hand.

"Artamon's Tears," she said softly. "The Ruby of Rossiya . . ." It was only another of Linnaius's artifices, she knew, but for one horrible moment it looked to her as if the palace and all the guests were drowning in a sea of blood.

She felt Andrei's warm grip loosen on her hand—and, as the red light of the fireworks died, she found she was alone in the Orangery.

CHAPTER 32

The martial music swelled to a triumphant climax as the brilliant red fireworks turned the lake waters from black to crimson.

Eugene stared, amazed. It was as if Linnaius's artistry had recreated the fiery column that had lit the sky the night the five rubies, Artamon's Tears, had been reunited.

"Only the Emperor's tears will unlock the gate."

He had lingered too long; it was time he was on his way to Ty Nagar.

The military bands broke into the Tielen national anthem. And Eugene was obliged to stand at attention, hand raised to acknowledge this loyal salute until the last strains of the anthem died away.

The guests broke into spontaneous applause. Karila clapped too, her little hands batting hard against each other in enthusiasm.

Eugene turned to Astasia who stood demurely beside him. After the fireworks came the old ceremony of jumping the bonfires, after which amorous couples disappeared into the shrubberies.

"I have urgent business. Can you and Maltheus preside over the lighting of the bonfires?"

Astasia bowed her head in assent. She seemed very subdued; all her earlier exuberance had faded. Should he ask what was troubling her? He tentatively put out one hand to touch her shoulder—and caught sight of an elegant milkmaid hastening toward him from the gardens, waving a fan. He knew it was Lovisa, because she had not troubled to hide the color of her ice-pale hair. Damn it, what did she want now? Astasia was at his side; she had been there all evening, so there had been no opportunity for dalliance as far as he was aware.

"Excuse me, ladies." He went out onto the terrace toward the wide steps to meet her.

Astasia waited until the last glow of the fireworks died. From the path, she could see Eugene's tall figure on the terrace, Celestine at his side in her identical blue costume, Karila between them.

How odd, she thought. *It's like looking at myself from outside. . . .*
And then she halted. Karila was sure to sense it wasn't her!

She hurried on through the darkness, darting between the strolling guests, desperate now to reach the terrace before Karila blurted out the truth. She could just imagine that clear voice declaring, "You're not my stepmama. Who are you and what have you done with her?"

And now Eugene was coming down the steps, making straight toward her! Had he seen her? Would he grab hold of her and demand an explanation in front of all the guests? She shrank behind a pilaster bearing a stone basket overspilling with ivies and crimson peonies, praying her deception had not been discovered.

Eugene was halfway down the steps when someone coughed politely behind him.

"What now?" Eugene cried. Gustave stood there, as plain in his sober secretary's jacket as a sparrow among Karila's exotic birds, holding out a silver tray on which lay a folded paper.

"News from Azhkendir," he said in his most formal voice.
Eugene faltered, torn between Lovisa's frantic signaling and reading the contents of the letter. He snatched up the letter and started toward her, stopping under the light of a flambeau to read what was written:

> Lord Gavril has returned.
> Nils Lindgren, Captain.

"Ah!" said Eugene aloud. He held the paper to the torchflame until it flared up, then collapsed to ash.

Astasia tapped Celestine lightly on the shoulder. In a matter of seconds, the switch was effected and Astasia, heart still fluttering like a trapped bird in her breast, took her place again beside Karila. The little girl was happily licking the icing off a marchpane swan. Astasia smiled and nodded at her stepdaughter.

Please don't blurt anything out, Kari.

But when the swan was half-nibbled away, Karila lost interest and the swan dropped from her sticky fingers. Astasia had never been so glad to see Marta appear to take the child away to bed.

Karila began to protest. "But I want to see the bonfires, Marta."

"You need your sleep," said Marta severely. "You can see them from your bedroom window. Say good-night to the Empress."

" 'Night, Tasia . . ."

A little string orchestra struck up on the terrace; to Astasia's dismay, she recognized the yearning strains of "White Nights," her favorite waltz. The violins soared, the melody throbbing out across the dark gardens, high and intense.

Homesickness suddenly flooded through her. She had been so happy to see Andrei. But now that he was gone, she felt even more bereft, knowing that her marriage had divided them, sending him far away to Francia.

And where was Eugene? It was most uncivil of him to leave his empress standing on her own, without an escort, among all these strangers.

Through her tears, she stared down into the darkening gardens. Bright flames sprang up as the servants lit the first Dievona Bonfire, illuminating the parterres. There was Eugene—and he was deep in intimate conversation with a tall, elegant woman.

"Lovisa!" she muttered, clenching her fists till her nails dug into her palms.

"I haven't time for this now, Lovisa," Eugene said quietly. "You should be protecting my wife." He looked up to the terrace and saw Astasia standing on her own. A little pang of guilt—an unfamiliar sensation—unsettled him. "Why is no one with her? I want her guarded at all times, especially in this crowd."

"Can you be sure that woman is your wife?" Lovisa asked coolly. "I tell you, I saw two identical shepherdesses in blue on the terrace a moment ago. I signaled to you, but you were distracted by Gustave."

"And for all I know, there are three milkmaids dressed as you are here tonight, maybe four." Eugene was impatient to escape the festivities. This was no time for dancing or singing.

Lord Gavril has returned.

For all he knew, Gavril Nagarian was already winging his way here to Swanholm to take his final revenge. The security of New Rossiya was at stake—and he must act quickly or lose his hold over the empire.

The guests had grabbed torches and were gathering around the bonfires for the ancient ceremony. Florets of flame flickered and danced in the dark gardens, like fireflies. Servants moved among the guests, offering steaming glasses of hot punch to keep out the night's chill. A lone singer burst into the time-old Dievona Night chant and soon many voices joined in, raising a raucous, full-throated paean to the ancient gods of spring. As the flames died down to smoldering ashes, the boldest (or most inebriated) of the youngsters would leap the bonfire, hand-in-hand, to ensure fertility and good fortune in the coming year.

He realized that Lovisa had been talking to him while his thoughts raced to Vermeille and far beyond.

"All I'm saying is, I lost sight of her for some minutes."

"Yes, yes." Eugene had no more time for the countess's excuses and vague insinuations. He had to find Linnaius.

"And then I glimpsed them together. In the Orangery. He was kissing her."

"Saw whom?" Eugene had only half-heard what she said.

"The Empress. Or a woman who was wearing the same costume. With a man."

Now he heard her clearly. She was insinuating that she had seen Astasia in a compromising situation in the Orangery. His heart went cold. But all he said was, "Can you be sure, Lovisa?"

"Well, no, Eugene, but—"

"Watch her. And report to me again only when you have firm evidence." He strode briskly away before she could say any more. He did not have time to deal with this now.

The strength of the singing startled Astasia. She leaned on the balustrade, listening to the voices singing in some old Tielen dialect she couldn't understand. The bonfire chant had a raw, pagan quality, as if it had been sung under the bright spring stars for years without number since the dawn of the world.

A sweet, alcoholic smell, flavored with cinnamon and cloves, wafted under her nose. One of the servants was offering her a silver-handled glass of some steaming beverage.

"Hot Dievona punch, imperial highness?"

Hastily, she waved him away. The smell made her dizzy and nauseous and she grasped at the smooth-polished stone of the balustrade for support.

Why do I weep one moment and feel faint the next? I was never that kind of silly moping girl! And then she remembered. Her hands instinctively crept to cover her stomach.

His child. Our child.

Great cheers arose from the onlookers around the bonfire. They were jumping over the dampened flames, young men and their girls, hand-in-hand, shouting with exhilaration as they leaped into the spark-dusted air.

I'd like to run, to leap high over the bonfire . . . but whose hand would be clasped around mine? Eugene's?

She saw him now, striding purposefully up the gardens from his rendezvous with Lovisa.

Is it true, Eugene? Did you order Linnaius to sink my brother's ship, and all of Muscobar's hopes with it?

He took the steps two at a time, as vigorously as a young man.

"I'm going hunting, Astasia."

"Very well." She looked back at him coldly through the eyeholes of her mask. If hunting was his alibi for spending time with his mistress, then she must play along with his little game for the sake of propriety.

I'm carrying his heir and he doesn't even know it. Nor shall he! It's obvious that his secret affairs are of far greater importance.

"Come," Celestine whispered in Andrei's ear, "now's our moment; everyone's busy around the bonfires."

But Andrei stood staring at the flames. He did not want to leave his sister all alone in this foreign court. His heart, so light and happy at the start of the ball at the thought of seeing her, now ached with despair.

"What pressures did they put on you to marry him, Tasia?" he murmured. "What happened in those long months when I was dead?"

As in a dream, he saw men and women catch hands and leap the bonfires, transient as flickering shadows against the fiery brightness.

"Come on!" Celestine tapped his shoulder. "It's too dangerous to stay. Someone might start asking questions. . . ."

"What would be the harm?" he said slowly, still staring into the flames, mesmerized by their brilliance. "Tasia needs me, Celestine. If all you've told me is true about Eugene—"

"Oh no," said Celestine firmly. "*No!* Imagine what a difficult situation that would be. It's not yet time for you to come out of the shadows. Though that time will come, Andrei. Have faith in me."

She spoke with such authority that he gazed at her in astonishment.

"Who *are* you, Celestine?"

"One who has your best interests at heart," she said lightly. "And now we really must be on our way."

They reached the gravel drive where the coaches were drawn up, waiting; little stableboys ran to and fro collecting the fresh manure left by the horses. Celestine moved swiftly, searching in the darkness for their coach. But in the darkness, they all looked very much alike, the family crests painted on the doors difficult to distinguish on the ill-lit drive. Andrei followed slowly, unable to disguise his limp any longer; he had stood too long and was badly in need of a rest.

"Can I help you?"

Andrei hung back; he recognized the voice too well. It was Valery Vassian; ever the gentleman, he had approached Celestine, lantern in hand.

"I seem to have mislaid my coach and driver, Lieutenant."

Andrei heard Celestine, adept at charming anyone she met, working her magic on Valery. He lingered in the shadows, listening, longing to speak to his old friend, yet not daring to reveal his identity. In a few minutes, the coach was found.

"Lieutenant, how can I thank you? I could have been searching till dawn and not found my driver in this crowd. . . ."

"My pleasure, demoiselle. I'm honored to have been of service."

Andrei smiled, hearing Valery's gallant reply; it seemed that Vassian had not lost any of his old-fashioned courtesy in the Emperor's service.

He started out toward the coach. The ache in his legs made him clumsy. He reached for the door to pull himself up onto the first step, and his left leg buckled beneath him. To his embarrassment, he fell back onto the gravel. His wig came off, and the mask slipped awry. Before he could right himself, someone caught hold of him and steadied him.

He knew, without looking, that it was Valery. Eyes lowered, cheeks smarting with shame, he tried to avert his face.

"Andrei?" Valery whispered his name. "Andrei—is it you?"

Andrei turned, Valery's arm still supporting him. "Don't give me away, Valery, I beg you. For Astasia's sake."

"But—they said you were dead!" Valery's dark eyes were wide with surprise.

"Valery, I *am* dead." Andrei gripped Valery's arm tightly. "Do you understand?"

Vassian nodded. He seemed stunned.

"Listen," Andrei said, aware that other guests were approaching, "I want you to do something for me." He leaned forward, his head close to Valery's. "Look out for my sister. She's so alone here in Tielen. And vulnerable."

Vassian nodded again. "Count on me. But what—"

"Time to leave," Celestine called warningly from the coach.

Andrei squeezed Valery's arm gratefully. "Later." He turned and hoisted himself up into the coach.

Vassian closed the door and saluted them. "I hope you've had a pleasant evening," he called loudly. "I wish you a safe journey."

As the coach driver guided the horses away from the palace, Andrei saw Valery still standing to attention, watching them.

"That was unfortunate. Can he be trusted?" Celestine said. There was a hard, merciless gleam in her eyes that Andrei had never seen before. "If not, an accident could be arranged . . ."

"That won't be necessary." He spoke with equal conviction. "I'd trust Valery with my life."

"Very well. I need a sound alibi. And Lieutenant Vassian has just seen me leave the palace in my coach." Celestine rapped on the coach roof with her fan. "Stop a moment, driver!" She opened the door and climbed lightly down onto the gravel drive.

"Where are you going?" Andrei asked, bemused. "I thought—"

"There's one more thing I must attend to. Wait for me at the lodge gate. Drive on, coachman!"

Astasia raised her mask to wipe the tears from her eyes. She was vexed with herself for crying, even more vexed for caring enough about her husband's indifference to cry at all.

"Imperial highness."

She turned and saw Valery Vassian. There he stood in his New Rossiyan uniform, his brown eyes filled with kindly concern, the sole familiar face in this crowd of strangers.

"Speak to me in our home tongue, Valery," she said.

He bowed. "Your highness looks tired. Your highness's brother has asked me to look after you in his absence."

Startled, she gazed up at him.

"Don't worry; I am sworn to secrecy," he said gallantly.

All of a sudden she felt exhausted. She was not sure if she had the strength to cross the terrace and reenter the palace. A strong arm to lean on was all she wished for.

"I *am* tired," she said. He offered her his arm and gratefully she slipped her hand through. As they walked slowly away from the lantern-lit gardens, she said, "Thank you, Valery."

She felt ashamed now when she remembered how she used to tease him for his clumsiness, how his face had turned a deep red at her unkind words.

"You know," he said fervently, "I would do anything for you. You have only to ask."

"Anything, Valery?" The *Melusine,* Andrei had said, in the harbor at Haeven. "Even if it meant deserting your duty here at the palace?"

A gaudily dressed pantaloon was bending over a bay tree, being noisily sick into its white-painted wooden tub. Kaspar Linnaius passed hastily by. These Tielens were too fond of their alcohol. They drank to excess, as if they might never see wine or aquavit again. Before the night was over, many of the guests would have to be carried to their carriages, insensible with drink. But long before then, he and Eugene would be far from Swanholm.

"Good evening, Magus."

Linnaius started. A masked, snow-wigged young woman in a pale blue shepherdess's costume had appeared out of the darkness. She was standing in the archway that led into his courtyard. Could it be the Empress? Astasia had been wearing a costume very like this one. And the woman's voice, though light and young, was tinged with a foreign accent.

"I have been waiting for you, Magus."

He slowed, wondering what possible reason the Empress could have for coming to see him here, alone, so late at night. Faint strains of dance music still drifted from the gardens, mingled with raucous bursts of cheering.

She lifted one hand to her gilded mask and untied the ribbons. Eyes of an angelic blue gazed at him; he recognized the young singer with the glorious voice he had seen earlier with the Empress Astasia.

"You have me at a disadvantage—" he began, stuttering a little.

"Let me introduce myself." She peeled off the white wig, shaking loose her golden hair. "My professional name is Celestine de Joyeuse. But Joyeuse is the name of my singing-master, the man who adopted me, a poor orphan in a convent school."

"This is all very interesting, demoiselle, but—"

"My real name is Celestine de Maunoir."

Linnaius felt a dull shudder of pain in his breast at the sound of that name. "Maunoir's child?" he repeated. "Impossible. You are too young."

"I was just five years old when the Commanderie took my father. That was twenty-one years ago."

Linnaius twitched his finger and thumb, making the lanternlight brighter so that he could see her face more clearly.

"But—my dear child—"

"I am no child, Kaspar Linnaius. After they burned my father at the stake for heresy, I was forced to grow up all too fast."

Had she come for money? Or revenge? How much did she know? He could not tell from looking into her clear blue eyes. All he knew was that this conversation was wasting valuable time and that Eugene was waiting for him. And it was not prudent to keep an emperor waiting.

"This is fascinating, my dear. Let us arrange a tête-à-tête for tomorrow and I will tell you everything I know about your father."

"I sail for Allegonde tomorrow."

She seemed determined to speak to him. Which was unfortunate, as he would now be obliged to work some glamour upon her. It was difficult enough trying to keep Kiukirilya hidden without having to deal with this spectre from his past.

He moved closer, gazing deep into her eyes.

"Yes, I see the likeness now; your eyes are the same color as his," he murmured. Her will was strong, and he could sense considerable resistance to his attempt to enthrall her mind. He slid his hand into the deep inner pocket of his robe, where he kept a few granules of sleepdust.

"And don't try your mage trickery on me," she said. "I took precautions to protect myself. . . ." Her voice began to trail away as the little shimmering cloud drifted down around her and she slowly sank to the ground, insensible.

Linnaius went for help and almost bumped into a tall young lieutenant striding purposefully back toward the palace.

"There's a young woman lying in my courtyard; I think she may have taken a little too much punch tonight."

The lieutenant followed him.

"Why, it's Demoiselle de Joyeuse," he said, kneeling down beside her. "I'll take her back to her coach; the queue to the gate is moving very slowly."

He gathered the young woman up in his arms and carried her off toward the drive.

Linnaius watched him, leaning for support against the wall. He could still feel the dull, heavy pain around his heart and his breathing had not yet steadied.

Maunoir's daughter. What did she really want with him? And was she the one who had attempted to break the wards on his rooms? Still, by the time she awoke tomorrow, he would be far away.

The palace clock chimed midnight; there was no time for such conjecture now. He was late for his meeting with the Emperor.

Eugene cast his mask and wig down on the floor and shrugged off the heavy purple robes. His valet discreetly whisked them out of sight and, used to Eugene's habits, filled a washing bowl with fresh cold water.

"Gustave—I'm going hunting," Eugene called, plunging his face and hands into the bowl. After being burned by Drakhaon's Fire, he could rarely bear hot water on his face and preferred the rough shock of the cold. Besides, it reminded him of being on campaign. No luxuries, just the bare essentials a man needed to live.

"Hunting?" Gustave handed him a towel to dry himself, as the valet reappeared with a *robe de chambre*. "Shall I call the Master of the Hunt to make arrangements?"

"No, Gustave, I've had enough arrangements. I'm going alone."

Gustave raised his eyebrows. "But, highness, is it wise, in view of the Francian fleet—?"

Eugene shot him a severe look.

"Not that I meant to imply in any way that your highness is incapable of looking after himself. It's just that, should any emergency occur—"

"The Chancellor and the council will deal with it. What can happen in a day's hunting?"

"Smarna?" ventured Gustave.

"When I return from my hunting," Eugene said, unable to hide the exultation in his voice, "Smarna will no longer be a poisoned thorn in New Rossiya's side."

The nail-studded door to the Rossiyan treasury creaked slowly open, the sound echoing around the bare stone vault. Even as the Magus held high a lantern to illuminate the darkness, Eugene made out a dull red glow emanating from its deepest recess.

"The Tears, Linnaius. The Tears are glowing."

He hurried ahead into the vault. The Magus followed, having first set a ward around the threshold to prevent them from being disturbed.

The imperial crown rested on a cushion of crimson silk in its crystal cabinet. As Eugene approached, he saw that the rubies glowed with a more intense radiance.

"The Tears of Artamon," he said softly. "Here is our key, Linnaius, the key to unlock the Serpent Gate." He released the intricate cypher-lock Paer Paersson had devised to protect his handiwork. Only one other living person knew the cypher, and that was Chancellor Maltheus. The crystal door swung slowly open and Eugene reached inside to take out his crown.

Linnaius produced a thin-bladed scalpel and began to prize apart the delicate golden clasps that secured each ruby in place.

"It seems a crime to ruin Paer Paersson's artistry," said Eugene.

"He and his craftsmen labored long and hard to perfect these settings."

"And he will be just as delighted to repair it for you, highness." Linnaius placed the rubies, one by one, in a finely wrought golden clasp, cleverly partitioned to hold the stones close to one another.

"I feel like a thief in my own treasure vault," Eugene confessed, "sneaking in at dead of night . . ."

"My concern, highness, is that the energy of these stones has slowly leaked away since they were divided centuries ago."

"Ssh. Listen."

A faint sound had begun, deep as the drone of a nest of bees.

"They may not still contain enough power to open the Serpent Gate," said Linnaius, placing the final stone beside its peers.

A column of fiery light sprang out, like a swift arrow loosed from a bow, piercing the roof of the vault.

"But they will show us the way to Ty Nagar." Eugene gazed at the glowing rubies. He passed a hand over them and felt a shock of energy tremble through his fingers.

The bonfires burned brightly, and the skirling of the wild music made Karila's heart sing. Why should she have to go to bed when all the other guests were still enjoying themselves?

Marta kept a firm hold on her hand as they walked across the ballroom. Servants were clearing away the debris from supper: the smeared crystal dishes that had held elaborate cream-topped desserts, the delicate glasses stained with dregs of wine, the greasy chicken, guinea fowl, and duck carcasses, stripped clean of meat.

"Couldn't we just stay for a few minutes more?" Karila begged, lagging behind so that Marta had to tug her along. "Please, Marta? I won't be able to sleep with all the music playing in the gardens."

"You'll catch cold in that flimsy costume," said Marta severely.

And then Karila saw Lieutenant Petter at the far entrance to the ballroom. She knew Marta saw him too, for her governess faltered in her determined pace. Karila had seen Marta behave strangely whenever they encountered the good-looking lieutenant, blushing and stammering over the most simple of greetings.

The lieutenant was coming straight toward them; Marta slowed down. He saluted them both, smiling. He was in uniform, not a costume, Karila noted.

"Still on duty, Lieutenant?" Marta said.

"No, I've just been relieved," he said. *What a warm smile he has*, Karila thought. "And just in time to see the bonfires. Shall I escort you, ladies?"

"Well—" began Marta.

Karila seized her opportunity. "Yes please, Lieutenant!"

"But her highness is supposed to be in bed—"

"*Please*, Marta." Karila used her most endearing voice.

"Just five minutes, then, no more." Marta slipped her hand through the lieutenant's arm.

The night air felt chillier now and a sharp little breeze had begun to tease the flames, whisking glowing sparks high in the air like clouds of fireflies. The smoke, carried on the breeze, irritated Karila's throat and made her eyes sting. She tried to swallow down a cough, knowing Marta would march her straight back indoors at the slightest wheeze. But Marta only had eyes for Lieutenant Petter. They were gazing at each other, the firelight bright on their faces. The wild fiddle music and the singing and stamping grew louder as they approached the roaring flames. Were they going to jump? Karila was almost sick with excitement at the idea.

Close to the flames, Karila could see that the fire had been constructed so that it would do no more than singe the heels of those brave enough to jump across. Slow-burning coals lined the firepit, with just enough pine logs above to burn with crackling and orange-blue flames.

The smoke made her throat sore and she coughed, trying to smother the sound with her hand.

"Ready, Marta?" Lieutenant Petter grasped her hand in his. She lifted her skirts with her other hand. They were going to do it! Karila clapped enthusiastically with the other watchers as the fiddlers scraped, releasing a raw, soaring melody, full of grindingly dissonant double-stops.

Marta and the lieutenant paused a moment. Then he shouted, "Now!" and they ran forward, leaping high, the flames licking at their heels.

A rousing cheer greeted their landing and through the red-flame shadows Karila saw them lean closer to each other . . . and kiss.

A strange yearning overcame her as she stood alone beneath the star-dusted sky. The fiddle music whirled on, and the dancers leaped, dark silhouettes against the brightness of the bonfire. But she felt as if a spear of crimson light had pierced her heart. She took in a breath— and felt the pain again, as sharp as death.

The dancers were receding, the music growing fainter and fainter, the firelit gardens were dissolving into dark mists . . .

CHAPTER 33

Red light, crimson as a winter sunset, bathed Gavril's fevered dreams.

"*Nagar's Eye,*" the Drakhaoul's voice whispered. "*I can sense it.*"

Gavril opened his eyes. He had fallen asleep in the ruined watchtower above the kastel. The stars were bright in the black sky overhead. But his vision was still stained with the bloodred light that had tinged his dreams.

"*Someone seeks to open the Serpent Gate!*" There was a new urgency in the Drakhaoul's voice.

"What are you saying?" Gavril was not yet fully awake.

"*We must go now.*"

"Now? But how can I leave Azhkendir now?"

"*Your druzhina are out of danger.*"

"And how can you be so sure that it's Nagar's Eye you can sense? It could be a trap."

"*It could be. But can you deny me this one chance of freedom? The first since the Gate was sealed and the Eye stolen?*"

Gavril heard the desperate yearning in the daemon's voice. It had rescued him from a living death in Arnskammar and healed him. How could he deny Khezef his one chance of release?

The coach jogged on, carrying Andrei toward the port at Haeven and passage to a new life in Francia. Celestine, her head resting on a silken cushion, was still in a doze.

Although he had been up all night, Andrei could not sleep. He could think only of leaving Astasia behind. Marriage to Eugene had altered her more than he had imagined; in spite of her pleasure at seeing him, she had seemed dispirited and unhappy. He was half of a mind to order the coach to turn around and go back for her.

It was nearly dawn. Suddenly the grey skies turned red as a fiery light streaked across the horizon.

"What's that? A comet?" cried Andrei, leaning out of the coach window.

"That's no comet." Celestine was awake now, gazing intently at the skies. "That's not a natural phenomenon, Andrei. That light could augur the end of the world."

He turned to her, thinking she was jesting, but saw from her expression that she was in deadly earnest.

Astasia woke to the smell of fresh-brewed coffee. The smell, usually one of the small pleasures that brightened her mornings, made her feel horribly queasy.

"Good morning!" said Nadezhda chirpily, bringing a cup to her bedside table.

"Take it away!" snapped Astasia, burying her face in the pillows.

"A little too much fruit punch at the ball?" said Nadezhda, doing as she was bidden. "Or is there some other reason, dear altessa?"

Astasia stayed where she was, face hidden in the soft silk pillows.

"All right, then, keep it a secret; although I've already a fair idea when we can expect the happy event. It would be about nine months from last—"

"Ssh, Nadezhda!" Astasia sat up and threw a pillow at her. "Nobody knows."

"I guessed as much." Nadezhda neatly caught the pillow. "I just wasn't sure *you* knew. And once the Emperor hears of the happy event, the bells will be ringing in all the steeples between here and Mirom."

"Oh, Nadezhda." All the unhappiness Astasia had been holding in suddenly threatened to burst out. She put one hand to her mouth, trying not to sob. "This isn't how I'd imagined it would be. Not at all. I feel so—*lonely* here. If it weren't for you and Celestine—"

"Don't take on so," Nadezhda said.

"I even miss Eupraxia. Dear, fussy old Eupraxia." At the thought of her governess, Astasia felt the tears brim over. "I'm not ready to have a baby, Nadezhda, I'm too young."

"It's a little late to be crying over it now." Nadezhda handed her a lacy handkerchief. "There's nothing you can do." Mischievously, she held the pillow beneath her breasts, arching her back, mimicking a pregnant belly.

"Oh!" Astasia cried, outraged. "I should have you beaten for insolence!"

"So when were you thinking of telling his imperial highness? Don't you think he deserves to be told?"

"Where is his imperial highness? I don't see him here. He's gone hunting." Astasia had not forgotten her humiliation at the ball last night. "He does as he pleases." Eugene had paid far more attention to Countess Lovisa than to her. She was still smarting. "For all I know, he's . . ." She could not bring herself to say it aloud. *With his mistress Lovisa.* Her eyes filled with tears again. "He doesn't talk to me, Nadezhda."

"He's the Emperor," said Nadezhda with a shrug.

"How can I stay here?" Astasia whispered. "Among strangers? I want to go home to Mirom."

Nadezhda came and sat beside her on the bed. She put her arms around her and gave her a hug. It was an utterly improper thing for a servant to do, but Astasia did not care. She clung to Nadezhda.

"I feel so alone," she whispered.

The sky craft sped through the dawn, borne on a soft southern wind that Linnaius had conjured. Following the slender beaconlight, the Magus steered the craft far away from the cooler shores of Tielen toward the burning sands of Djihan-Djihar.

A shiver of anger went through Eugene as he remembered Astasia's secret assignation at the ball. Was she playing him for a fool? It was behavior that seemed at odds with her usual conduct. He had thought her charming and naïve, a little unsophisticated, maybe, but all the more endearing for that. But all these qualities had attracted many admirers—and an unscrupulous suitor could so easily play on her naïvety.

Unless Lovisa was mistaken. Unless she had another motive in smirching Astasia's reputation—

No. He had chosen Lovisa as Astasia's secret bodyguard because she was unassailable in matters of virtue and loyalty. Perhaps he should have let Astasia in on the secret? And yet he had judged she would be safer not knowing who was watching out for her. Had his judgment been flawed, not trusting Astasia with the knowledge? Perhaps he had treated her too much as a child—and in doing so, had driven her to seek out more sympathetic company. And that thought alone made his heart ache with bitter regret. For it was too late now to change matters; what was done, was done.

He sat back, holding the velvet pouch that contained the Tears of Artamon. Little tingles of energy pulsed through his fingers from time to time, as though the power in the rubies could not be contained within either the golden casing or the velvet pile. And the farther south they flew, the stronger the pulsing became.

"We must be on the right course," he shouted to Linnaius above the crackle of the wind in the leather sail. "The rubies are reacting like lodestones."

Linnaius nodded. He was recording their progress on a chart, checking the faint beacon against both the fast-fading stars overhead and the rising sun.

"It's time," he said. "Time to bind them more securely together."

Eugene took out a length of slender golden wire Linnaius had given him. He began to wind the wire around the rubies until they made one single stone again.

Each tremor of energy provoked a sympathetic surge of excitement in Eugene as he worked. This journey into the unknown was the most daring venture he had ever undertaken. It contradicted every rational thought. It went against every one of the enlightened principles by which he had lived his life. And he no longer cared.

The wind blew more gently now and it was a warm, moist wind, bringing faint wafts of unfamiliar smells: rich, ripe, and spicy. And with the warm wind came heat. Eugene undid his jacket buttons and reached for the water flask.

The Azure Ocean far below them had turned a deep tropical blue. Shoals of little islands appeared, their shores white with fine sand.

Linnaius began to sniff the air. "Do you smell that, highness?"

Eugene pulled a face. "That abominable stink? It smells like the pits of hell."

"Volcanic fumes. We must be approaching the archipelago."

Linnaius brought the craft about while Eugene scanned the horizon for any sign of volcanic activity. He spotted a faint trace of smoke, like fine ribbons of gauze darkening the brilliant blue of the sky.

"There!" Even as he pointed, he heard the rubies begin to buzz as though they were alive. "That must be Ty Nagar!" He could not conceal the throb of anticipation in his voice.

As they sped closer, he saw the jagged volcanic cone rising out of the gauzy haze.

"Any signs of human habitation?" He looked down at the ocean. There was not a single ship to be seen, unlike the busy waterways around Tielen.

"Hold tight," Linnaius cried. "We've hit crosswinds."

The craft slewed suddenly to one side, then dropped like a stone. They went hurtling down toward the ocean. Eugene's ears ached with the change in pressure; he gripped the flimsy side of the craft with one hand, the other clutching the precious rubies tight. If he was thrown into the sea, the rubies could sink to the fathomless deep and never be gathered together again—

"For God's sake, Linnaius!"

They careered along the tops of the waves, spattered by flecks of spray, Linnaius steering erratically as he whistled in vain for a fresh wind to carry them.

"I can't control her, highness—"

Eugene grabbed the rudder from him and, one-handed, steadied the craft.

Ahead he could see the volcano's dark peak looming up out of the ocean, hazed by drifts of pale smoke. The foul smell of the vapors tainted the fresh salty tang of the ocean air. He thought for a moment that he could detect the faintest orange glow of fire around the rim of the cone . . . and then the billowing vapors again fogged his vision.

"What a magnificent sight," he murmured. "What grandeur. What fearsome destructive power."

Now the shoreline was visible, the sands as grey as cinders, with lush, dense vegetation behind, the leaves oozing moisture.

Linnaius brought the craft bumping down across the sands until it skidded to a halt and Eugene relaxed his grip on the rudder. His hands were sweating. His cramped limbs still felt the juddering of the craft, even though they had landed.

Heat hung in the heavy air. It was as if he had stepped into the steam room at Swanholm. He shrugged off his jacket and rolled up his shirtsleeves; the linen already felt damp.

Birds, bright-feathered and raucous, darted about the liana-festooned trees. "Now to find this Serpent Gate." Eugene wiped the back of his hand across his forehead. It came away glossy with sweat.

He took the rubies from the velvet pouch and held them aloft. The droning pulse grew louder; he could feel the jewels vibrating faster, stronger . . . The slender column of fiery light intensified, burning so brightly that even in the light of the merciless sun, its flame could clearly be seen.

"And it points deep into the heart of the jungle." Eugene gazed at the thick-tangled vegetation, perplexed. "It could take a couple of days to hack our way through. Damn it all, Linnaius, why didn't we think of this?"

"I've come prepared," Linnaius said, removing a phial from his robes. It contained grains that glittered a dull blue in the sunlight.

"Is that the new firedust from Azhkendir?"

"The same." Following the beacon's path, Linnaius began to scatter a trail of grains from the phial into the jungle.

The busy chatter of tree creatures began high overhead; Eugene spotted little monkeys with dark eyes staring at them from the overhanging branches. How Karila would love to have a pair of the pretty little creatures with their curlicue tails and white ruffs of fur!

Karila. He had set out on this journey without even bidding her farewell. If he perished here, so far from home, how would she remember her negligent father? Would she ever forgive him for abandoning her?

Why am I thinking such morbid thoughts? When I've opened the Serpent Gate, I'll be invincible.

Linnaius emerged from the undergrowth.

"I advise a strategic retreat," he said, making for the sky craft. He lit a firestick and tossed it toward the little trail of glittering grains. Eugene crouched down behind the sky craft.

There was a deafening explosion. The sky turned white and the shore beneath them trembled. They were flung forward onto ash-covered sand. Although Eugene had shut his eyes, the light scored blinding brightness through his closed lids. When he opened his eyes again, he could hardly see.

"In God's name, Linnaius, that stuff is dangerous!" He sat up, the rubies clutched in one hand, brushing sand from his clothes. His ears still jangled with the force of the blast. "You could have blown us both to pieces. You could have destroyed the Gate—"

As the drifting grey smoke slowly cleared, Eugene saw that a path had been blasted right into the heart of the jungle. Blackened tree stumps were all that remained of a grove of trees. An eerie silence had fallen. The pretty monkeys were gone, incinerated, he guessed, along with the bright-feathered birds. But ahead he could distinguish the remains of great stone buildings, all fallen to ruin and covered with centuries' growth of creepers and vines.

"Look." The ruby beacon pointed to the ruins.

"These must be the temples to the Serpent God Nagar," Linnaius said.

They crunched across the carbonized remains of trees, feeling the heat through the soles of their boots. Here and there little tongues of fire still licked at the charred branches. The choking smell of burning caught at the back of Eugene's throat. His dazzled eyes watered, yet still he followed the bloodred beacon emanating from the stones in his hands. And then he felt the stones begin to judder, straining at the metal casing that bound them, as if they were striving to burst free.

Looming up out of the far-distant trees, he saw it. Untouched by Linnaius's blast, it still towered above the fallen temples at the top of a stone stairway. And it was just as Gavril Nagarian had painted it: an archway of writhing winged serpents, carved out of grey, volcanic rock, dominated by the terrible blind head of Nagar himself, fanged jaws gaping wide as if to swallow whole his human sacrifices.

Eugene halted. He had conversed with the spirit of Artamon and he had crossed the ocean by sky craft, but nothing could have prepared him for this, the culmination of his plans and dreams.

Linnaius was gazing up at the Gate in awed silence.

"This must be the sacrificial stair," he murmured, "leading up to the gateway through which the priests sent their victims as sacrifices to Nagar. Until the day they summoned one of his daemons into this world—"

"It's high," Eugene said, standing beneath the archway and assessing the best way to climb it. "How ironic if I came all this way, then fell to my death before I had accomplished my goal and replaced the Eye?" He slung the velvet pouch around his neck and grasped hold of one of the stone tails, testing for a foothold.

"Take care, I beg you, highness!" cried Linnaius.

"I've always enjoyed rock climbing." Eugene, sweating in the heavy humidity, clung tightly to a snarling serpent-head and pulled himself farther up. "I used to go bird-nesting when I was a boy—"

His foot suddenly slipped off a scaly head and he dangled from his fingers, his breath coming fast. The volcanic fumes were making him a little dizzy. The rubies, swinging to and fro in the velvet bag, burned hot against his chest.

Closer to, the daemon-serpents stared at him with a terrible malevolence. He managed to get his feet firmly back under him, but as he climbed on, he began to think he could hear voices whispering slanderous obscenities. They hissed that Astasia had been unfaithful to him; that Linnaius was in the pay of the King Enguerrand; that Gavril Nagarian had declared himself rightful emperor in his absence . . . And from far away, he heard a rumbling that juddered up through the ground, making the ancient archway shiver.

"Highness!" Linnaius called, far below. He sounded agitated. "Make haste, I beg you!"

Eugene reached the top. He straddled the arch, face-to-face with the giant head of the Serpent God. He needed both hands to free the rubies from the velvet bag. Good balance was essential. The empty eye socket was filled with dirt and lichen; he scraped it away before leaning forward and lifting the pulsating stones, still bound together with golden wire. Slowly, and with painstaking care, he inserted them in the hole.

Nothing happened. The rubies glowed, reddening the ancient grey stone.

"Come down, highness!" cried Linnaius. There was such urgency in his voice that Eugene obeyed. Climbing down was less easy than climbing up. He scraped his hands on the daemon-serpents' spines and scales; he bruised his legs against the wing shafts and carved claws. He jumped the last few feet, landing heavily on the cracked stone of the sacrificial stair.

Nagar's carved daemon-face glared balefully at them from one glowing eye of flame. Still nothing happened.

"I've failed." Eugene sat down on the cracked stones and wiped his dripping face on his sleeve. "So there was only enough energy left in the stones to light our way here, but not enough to open the Gate."

He was too hot, too exhausted by the climb to feel any disappointment yet. "Maybe it's all for the best. Maybe it's wiser not to meddle in—"

"Wait." Linnaius held up one hand. "What's that sound?"

Eugene could feel the rumble of vibrations through the weathered stone. He stood up. "An earthquake? Or is the volcano about to blow?"

It was growing darker. Smoky fog began to issue from Nagar's maw, billowing out until the archway was filled with swirling darkness. And in that darkness, the red eye burned ever more intensely, a daemon's eye, fixing its unblinking gaze upon them.

The earth shook with such violence that Eugene was thrown to the ground.

An intense light suffused the cloudy smoke, as luminously bright as Drakhaon's Fire and growing stronger—as though some unimaginable power was fast approaching. A roaring gust, as though of some elemental force, whipped the mists to a whirlwind of spinning dust.

One of the stone dragon-daemons on the Gate had begun to move, to uncurl itself from the tangle of twisted, contorted bodies. Grey stone shimmered and bloomed with iridescent color.

Eugene pushed himself up onto his knees.

It was alive.

He saw it stretch the scales of its glittering body. Wild tatters of flowing hair, gold and copper and malachite green, streamed down its back. He glimpsed its great, hooked wings as it furled them behind its back. Powerful wings. Drakhaoul wings.

And now it turned its dazzling gaze on him. Wide, slanted eyes stared into his, fierce and cruel. It was a summons he was powerless to disobey.

He rose to his feet, began to move toward the glittering creature. He opened his arms wide, as if to embrace his daemon-shadow. But it was like walking into thick smoke; all was dark and confusion.

A fluttering sensation began deep in Eugene's mind. He clutched hold of his head with both hands.

"Help—me—" Eugene could hardly enunciate the words. The fluttering had become a spinning spiral of light. Sick with the pain, he pitched forward onto the weed-covered ground.

"Dra—Drakhaoul—" he whispered—and lost consciousness.

CHAPTER 34

Eugene lay on the worn sacrificial stone. It was as if he were gripped in the coils of some terrifying nightmare. He wanted to call out to the Magus to come to his aid, but his whole body was paralyzed, even his tongue. Time had stopped.

"I know you now, mortal. You are powerful." A voice that smoldered with heat, whispered in Eugene's brain. *"You are Emperor. And yet you bear scars, inflicted by one of my kin."*

"Heal me," Eugene managed at last to stammer out the words. "Make me whole again."

"You are a warrior, Eugene. Your instinct is to fight me. But if I am to heal you, you must surrender your will to mine."

The daemon-spirit knew him better than he knew himself. The instant it had entered his body, he had begun to resist it. Now he struggled to overmaster his own stubborn nature, to let the Drakhaoul take control.

A haze of heat burned around him, shot through with dazzling sparks of green and gold. The heat passed through his whole body like a cresting wave of golden flame. It felt as if every inch of skin were being seared away. He writhed in agony, sure he would be utterly consumed in its cleansing blaze. And then the dazzle died away and his sight gradually returned.

Slowly he raised his burned hand and gazed at it, turning it this way and that. The skin was smooth, unblemished, and the stiff pain that had accompanied every smallest movement had gone.

He gave a shout. "Look. Look at that!"

He sat up and put one hand tentatively to his face. His skin felt cool, soft, renewed. He moved his fingers up to his scalp, still feeling for scars. Not one remained.

"You've done it!" For months he had dreaded catching sight of himself in mirrors, windows, water. Now he longed to gaze at his reflection and see himself renewed.

"Highness." He had forgotten all about Kaspar Linnaius until the old man came hesitantly toward him. "You—you have been restored." It was the first time he remembered seeing the Magus at a loss for words.

Eugene stretched out his healed hand. "And this is all thanks to your dedication, my friend."

Linnaius tentatively took Eugene's outstretched hand in his own and pressed it. "Your highness honors me," he said quietly.

Eugene felt a tremor of warning go through his whole body.

"One of my kindred is coming. I can sense him."

"What do you mean?"

"The Son of the Serpent. The one who burned you."

"Gavril Nagarian, coming here?" Eugene was not prepared for this encounter so soon.

"You restored Nagar's Eye. It calls to him; it draws him back."

"If it's Gavril Nagarian, there is unfinished business between us." Eugene got to his feet. He could feel the daemon's strength pulsing through his veins. "And we shall be ready for him this time."

The barren sides of the volcano rose up from the jungle, dominating the island, hazing the clear sky with wisps of smoke.

Gavril gazed down at Ty Nagar. It lay below them, just as he had seen it in his dreams, gleaned from his grandfather's memories.

"Is this where he died?" he asked. "Zakhar Nagarian?"

They had flown for many hours without stopping and he was tired. His body ached now with the strain of staying in the air so long.

"He died here."

"Why didn't you save his life?"

"The mountain of fire spilled over. I tried to save him. The air was full of choking fog and ash. Then came the heat. It was a furnace, too much for a human body to withstand. He burned—and I fled."

Gavril looked down at the volcano. It looked quiet enough—but he had read how unpredictable they could be. He had no wish to repeat his grandfather's fate.

"Is there fresh water here?" His throat was so dry, he could hardly speak.

"I will take you to a clean spring."

And then Gavril felt a tingle of shock go through him.

"My brother is free and he is bound to another human." Khezef hissed. *"Now it begins again."*

"Another human?" Was it possible that Eugene's obsessive desire had driven him to such a desperate measure? Hadn't he heeded his warnings? He had come to Ty Nagar in the hope that this would be their final parting, that Khezef would return at last to his own world.

Now he began to realize that this could not be their final parting. For if Eugene had become Drakhaoul, he would be forced to persuade Khezef to stay. How else could he defend his people?

"Water, first," he said. With his thirst quenched, his mind would be clearer, quicker to plan a strategy. But as they flew lower over the ocean, approaching the island shore, Gavril could sense Khezef's growing agitation.

"There," Eugene breathed, shading his eyes against the glare of the sun. "There he is at last. Gavril Nagarian."

The creature flying slowly toward them might have been a great seabird, were it not for the smoky glitter that emanated from its wings. And suddenly it seemed to Eugene that everything he had striven for was about to come to fruition here on Ty Nagar.

"He's tired," he said, "and we have the advantage of surprise."

"Our fusion is new, unproven. It could fail."

Eugene's mind felt clean, pared of every extraneous thought. All that mattered now was the duel to come. It was time for Gavril Nagarian to pay for the damage he had wrought on Eugene's troops, his fleet, his pride.

"You won't fail me, Drakhaoul!" he cried.

"Highness, wait, I beg you." Kaspar Linnaius came stumbling after Eugene. The merciless heat and the poisonous fumes were slowing him down, reminding him of his age and frailty. But Eugene either did not hear him or was not to be stopped, for he walked on toward the shore without once turning back. Linnaius reached the edge of the burned trees in time to see Eugene raise his arms wide to the sea.

A shudder ran through the Emperor's body as a dark spiral of daemon-smoke enveloped him. Then Linnaius watched, speechless, as great shadow-wings unfurled from the Emperor's back, and out of the smoke emerged a creature of terrifying beauty: a daemon-dragon with scales that shimmered jade-green, malachite, and gold in the sunlight.

You have found the power you desired, imperial highness. But you've paid a high enough price for it. And then, as he watched the green Drakhaon take to the air in a rush of wings that stirred up the ashy sand, Linnaius found himself wondering fearfully, "And now, where will it end?"

It was like a mirror image—his mirror image—winging straight toward them in a shimmer of smoke.

But the daemon-eyes that burned through the smoke, staring at him with naked hatred, were green as malachite. And Eugene's eyes had been blue as the wintry skies over Tielen.

Gavril hesitated, hovering over the waves. Was this Eugene? And what did he intend?

A bolt of green fire seared the tip of his left wing. The malachite-green Drakhaon was on the attack.

"Gavril Nagarian! Do you know me now?"

"Eugene!" he cried back.

"The last time you attacked me, you had the advantage. Now we are evenly matched."

If only he'd taken time to rest a little, to find that spring and quench his thirst. Tired and thirsty, he knew that the Drakhaon Eugene could easily defeat him.

"Eugene, listen to me." His voice rang out over the whisper of the waves, hoarse with emotion. "Don't do this to yourself, to your people—to those you love most dearly!"

"You have bested me once too often, Nagarian." The Drakhaon Eugene snaked around in the sky, gaining height. "Now we fight on equal terms."

Shaft after shaft of green fire rained down on Gavril. Pain burned bright as he lost control of one wing and went plunging toward the waves. Struggling to right himself, he came about, concentrating all his energy on keeping in the air. And then he heard Khezef cry out, *"Belberith, my brother! Don't you know me?"*

"Brother? What manner of brother leaves his own kin imprisoned in agony for years without number?"

"I've not come to fight you, Eugene!" Gavril cried. "I've come to end it. To send my Drakhaoul back through the Serpent Gate."

The Drakhaon Eugene breathed another shimmering blast of green fire from its flared nostrils. Gavril swiveled, darting low beneath the sheet of green flame. Even as he winged away, he could feel the intense heat. The waves below him sizzled. Another blast like that could finish him.

"We must fight back. Brother or no, Khezef, we have to defend ourselves." Gavril forced himself onward, trying to control the ragged rhythm of his wing-strokes. He could sense Eugene close behind, could feel the hot wind from his beating wings, the heat of his breath. One more searing blast from those flaring nostrils would send him down in flames. He would die, burning in agony, and not even Khezef could save him.

"You may not survive the next blast, Gavril. Belberith is powerful; even more powerful than I."

"And now you run from me, Khezef, coward that you are."

Gavril felt a surge of sadness overwhelm him. He could no longer distinguish between his own emotions and Khezef's.

"I don't want to fight you. I want us to be free!"

As if in answer, Eugene slewed around and snarled fire. The blast hit Gavril and sent him hurtling back over the waves. He tried to twist, to rise above its destructive power. But instead he fell into the sea. And before he could lift himself from the water, he saw Eugene bearing down on him, his Drakhaon eyes blazing bright with the ecstasy of the fight.

"Eugene!" he shouted again and sent an answering burst of blue fire straight toward those triumphant green eyes.

Eugene was too close to avoid his counterattack. He jerked as the bolt of fire struck home. For a moment, Gavril thought he too would tumble into the sea—but then he righted himself and with slow, strong wing-beats began to rise again.

Rocked to and fro by the tide, Gavril strove to find the energy to take to the air once more. He struggled out of the water, the pain in his burned shoulder making him catch his breath with every wing-stroke.

Above him, the sky darkened as the great winged form of the Drakhaon Eugene hovered overhead, those malachite eyes gazing down at him, triumphant and cruel.

"This," he said, "is for my fleet. For Froding and his Light Infantry. For Jaromir." He breathed down fire again.

Flames scorched Gavril's skin. Tainted smoke smirched his vision, and he fell.

"*Forgive me,*" Khezef whispered. Their fusion faded and Gavril felt his daemon-form melt away as he hit the water.

"Is he gone, Linnaius?" cried Eugene. He had seen Gavril Nagarian fall from the sky into the sea a second time. There was no sign of his enemy, in human or Drakhaon form.

"This time," Linnaius said in a trembling voice, tottering toward him, "I believe he is finally gone."

Even so, Gavril Nagarian had cheated him of the coup de grâce. Even at the end of this bitter and protracted duel, he had not allowed him to relish his final victory. Why had he not finished him in one final burst of fire, and seen him writhe and burn, as he himself had burned on the escarpment outside Kastel Drakhaon? He was still possessed of this daemon-fueled rage; still obsessed with the driving impulse to destroy anything that stood in his way.

The sinister rumbling began again. The ground began to shake.

Other influences were at work here.

"Linnaius," Eugene cried, "the volcano! Climb up on my back and I'll carry you to safety."

"I fear I could not cling on for long enough to reach land, highness," said Linnaius. He looked very pale around the lips. "I will follow in my sky craft."

Black clouds had come swiftly rolling up, hiding the sun.

"A storm?"

"Not of my making," said Linnaius, shivering. "We should be on our way."

Eugene took to the air again and hovered close to the Serpent Gate, until Nagar's Eye bathed him and the twisted, tortured stone-daemons in its bloodied light. Beyond the Gate he could see nothing but a turbulence of wind and shadow. He reached out for the Tears of Artamon, to prize them out with his talons. Then he tossed them down to the Magus.

"Keep them safe for me, Linnaius, till we get back to Swanholm."

"I will guard them with my life," replied the Magus.

Then the Drakhaon Eugene turned his head to the north and with slow, powerful wing-strokes began the long flight across the Azure Ocean toward the cooler shores of distant New Rossiya.

CHAPTER 35

Kiukiu wandered on over the dunes, lost in the Realm of Shadows.

"I mustn't give up," she said to herself. "I know I can find my way back to the way I came in." A whirlwind came twisting across the arid plain, a dark spiral of swirling shadows. She raised a hand to her eyes, trying to keep out the dust and grit.

To her horror she saw agonized, distorted faces in the spiral, heard distant cries, high and inhuman as the shriek of the merciless wind. And it was coming straight toward her.

She began to run, her feet slipping in the dry grey sands, trying to find a place to shelter. But whichever way she turned, the whirlwind seemed to follow her. And now it was gaining on her. It would sweep her up and she would never find her way back. . . .

She could hear the roar of the fast-approaching funnel; she could feel the pull that would suck her up and spit her out far away from her only way home. She threw herself to the ground, burrowing into the sand with both hands like an animal.

The whirlwind passed on across the plain, and she came up blinking from her burrow, spitting out grains of sand.

And then she saw a luminous glimmer of gold and blue through the blowing dust. Those brilliant colors, so bright in this dull place . . .

She began to stagger toward it, one hand outstretched. The dust clouds parted a moment and she saw the Drakhaoul in all its shimmering daemon-splendor—and borne in its powerful arms was Lord Gavril.

"Gavril!" she screamed, trying to make herself heard above the shriek of the wind. "Gavril, I'm here! Can't you hear me? It's Kiukiu!"

He lifted his head, almost as if he had heard her. But the howl of the winds was so loud that her voice was drowned. And as she stumbled on toward them, she saw the Drakhaoul winging away into the distance.

"No!" she cried. "Don't leave me!" Another whirlwind was spinning fast toward her. Why couldn't they see her? *"Gavril!"* She tripped in the sand and fell. The deafening drone of the whirlwind bore down on her. This time there was no escape. She was sucked into the spiral and borne fast and far away over the bleak plain.

"Gavril, I'm here! Can't you hear me? It's Kiukiu! Don't leave me. . . ."

"Kiukiu?" He can hear her distantly calling to him through a roar of wind and dust. "Where are you?"

"Wake up, Gavril Nagarian." The repeated command inside his skull brought Gavril back to his senses. He was lying on his back on the volcanic sand of Ty Nagar, washed up by the receding tide. *"Wake up!"*

He spat out a mouthful of seawater and tried to roll over. Pain shot down his shoulder and arm, ending in an agony of fire. He began to realize he had been badly injured in the battle with Eugene. *"But still alive,"* said Khezef wryly.

"Are you sure?" he murmured in a charred voice.

"Belberith has gone."

"And with him, Eugene." Gavril wanted nothing but to crawl back into the sea and lose himself in its cold depths. "I failed. I failed to stop him."

"This time, maybe. But your world is changing. It's started. Already."

Overhead the sky had gone dark, as if a storm was on its way. A cold, dry wind tossed the branches this way and that. He had heard a wind like that when he was drowning . . . and the Drakhaoul had brought him back to this world. That was when he heard her calling to him.

"Kiukiu," he said. The Magus had been here with Eugene; Gavril had glimpsed him far below, watching their duel. Where was he now, damn him? Had he gone too, well-satisfied with the evil deed he had helped his master commit? "We must go back to find her. Must go to Swanholm. Before Linnaius gets back."

The sky grew darker.

"Is it night?" Gavril slowly dragged himself up the shore.

"Not yet."

"Then what? . . ." He raised his head and found he was staring through the blasted trees directly at the Serpent Gate. The darkness was seeping from the Gate itself, from Nagar's gaping jaws. The red eye no longer shone like a beacon. But on either side of the arch he became aware of a ripple of movement. Grey stone had melted to translucent color. Daemon-eyes glimmered in the darkness: scarlet, gold, and violet. Each distorted form was slowly uncurling from its rigid position beneath Nagar's outswept wings.

"Khezef, what's happening?"

"Eugene opened the Serpent Gate. He set them free."

Gavril heard the words but did not fully understand.

"But—you told me the Gate was the way home. You told me, you told my grandfather: *'Find the Eye, open the Gate and then, I promise you, you will be free.'* " Had Khezef been deceiving him?

"The Gate leads back to the Realm of Shadows, our eternal prison."

"So it was never your way home?" All the time Gavril was speaking, he was watching the Drakhaouls unfurl transparent wings, stretch slender arms, taloned hands. Colors swirled through their limbs like oil spilled in water. They were possessed of a deadly beauty; he could sense the raw power that emanated from them.

Suddenly all three rose from the stone arch and swept toward Gavril, enveloping him in a swirling cloud, fiery colors and emotions mingled, so brilliant and intense that he nearly fainted.

"My brothers," he heard Khezef cry. *"Araziel. Nilaihah. Adramelech."*

"Brothers?" Gavril echoed. The daemons circled his head once more and then swept away across the sea like a whirlwind.

"We were banished from our true home long, long ago. I do not know if we can ever find our way back."

"But—but you told me you cannot survive for long in our world on your own."

"It is true. Now they must find human hosts."

"Khezef—you lied to me." He felt betrayed. "You told me it would be our final parting. That I would be free—and so would you."

"Don't you understand, Gavril Nagarian? Any kind of existence is preferable to the Realm of Shadows. We are creatures of light. The Realm of Shadows is torment, a living death to us. Now that the Gate has been breached, others will follow."

Gavril sank down, hands clasped to his head. "What have you done, Eugene?" he murmured. "What have you unleashed on us all?"

And then, in the depths of his mind, he thought he caught a last, faint cry: *"Gavril . . . don't leave me. . . ."*

He could do nothing now to stop Khezef's brothers. But he could use Khezef's strength to help him find Kiukiu. Damn it all, he would *force* Khezef to help him.

"Swanholm," he said. "We must make Swanholm."

Celestine de Maunoir stood outside Kaspar Linnaius's rooms, her hands raised, testing. The Magus's wards had repelled her every time she had tried to break them before, sending unpleasant shocks through her hand and arm that lingered for hours afterward. But this time, armed with the only keepsake her father had left her, his grimoire, which he had hidden in the mattress of her little bed the night he was arrested, she had found an incantation, "To Break Down Mysterious Barricades." She murmured the words three times, knocking on the invisible door in the initiate's fashion.

No one had challenged her. All the servants were busy clearing up after the ball. Many of the household were wandering dazedly around as if still in a drunken stupor. But then, she was well-known here as the Empress's intimate companion. Why should they wonder what she was doing?

Although she saw nothing alter, she felt the air ripple as though an invisible curtain had been drawn back. And when she raised her gloved hand to open the door, she met no resistance. The gloves were another precaution; Linnaius was almost certain to have left some trace of alchymical poison on the handles to snare the unwary.

The door swung inward. She went in, muttering the incantation again, just for good measure. And then she let out a cry of surprise.

"Well?" said Jagu, who had been waiting at the foot of the stairs. "Come and see."

A young woman lay on the bed, still as death, her skin pale, her eyes open and staring, as if at some horror only she could see.

"Is she dead?" Jagu asked. "If so, we have more than enough evidence against him."

Celestine knelt and held a glass to her lips. "Look," she said, showing him the blurring made by the slightest trace of breath. "She's alive." She touched the young woman's shoulder. She shook her. "Wake up!" she cried. The young woman made no response at all.

"Alive, yet not alive," said Jagu. "He's stolen her soul."

"What has he been using her for, I wonder?" Celestine said with a shudder of disgust.

"Is this hers, do you think?" Jagu pointed to a painted wooden zither that lay on the table. He plucked a few notes, which resounded with a strange metallic timbre. "It doesn't look like the kind of instrument a Magus would play. It's too crude, too unrefined. And it needs tuning," he added dryly.

Celestine rose. "We have much to do. He could return at any minute. Is the carriage ready?"

"Are we just going to leave her here like this?"

"We must travel fast," said Celestine, "and she would only prove a burden. She must have family close by; let them care for her."

The Drakhaon Eugene flew over the red deserts of Djihan-Djihar, making for the coast. Ahead lay Smarna and the cooler shores of his empire. His veins pulsed with daemonic power. His whole body was filled with energy and light. He felt invincible.

He had drawn the Smarnan rebels' teeth. Or, more precisely, he had beaten Gavril Nagarian into submission. Now Smarna had no daemonic powers to defend it, and the rebels would be hunted down one by one and tried for their crimes. Pavel Velemir must have compiled a sizeable dossier on the ringleaders by now.

He still relished the moment he had swooped down on Gavril Nagarian and seared him with Belberith's virulent green fire, sending him crashing into the sea. The sky duel was the most exhilarating battle he had ever fought.

That just left the unannounced presence of the Francian fleet off Smarna. And what better way to determine their purpose than from the air? If there were just a few ships escorting their king on his pilgrimage to the ancient holy sites and temples, then New Rossiya had nothing to fear. But if the ships numbered more than a dozen . . .

The waters beneath him were a softer green now that he had left Djihan-Djihar far behind, no longer the intense, hot blue of the distant Azure Ocean. And the rocky outline of the distant shore, with little bays and inlets, must be Smarna.

"But what are all those ships?"

White sails billowed from a forest of masts. And on each mast flew the flag of Francia, a golden salamander on a white background.

"Enguerrand!" he hissed.

He circled high overhead, counting the ships in the bay beneath. There were two dozen men-o'-war, bristling with cannons and at least another dozen frigates. At the center of the formation was the royal flagship, flying the black and gold pennant of the Commanderie. They outnumbered his Southern Fleet by four to one.

"And if Gavril Nagarian hadn't sunk half my warships in this very bay . . ." He began to descend, seeing the shadow of his great wings darkening the water. Fire filled his mind, fire and destruction. He could take out the royal flagship and set the sails alight on the men-o'-war.

"Drakhaoul," he cried aloud, concentrating his sights on Enguerrand's ship.

"No." Belberith's voice whispered. *"You do not have enough strength for another attack."*

"Not enough strength?" Eugene had thought the Drakhaouls invincible, their power inexhaustible.

"You have barely enough strength to reach your home without replenishing yourself." Was that a tinge of mockery in the daemon's words? *"You must conserve what little energy we have left between us. If you attack these ships, you will fall into the sea and drown."*

Even as Belberith spoke, Eugene realized he was right; his wings were beating more slowly and his sight was less clear, as though a sea mist had hazed his vision. And now he could feel his own heart laboring in his breast to keep himself aloft.

And for the first time since he fused with the Drakhaoul Belberith, he remembered Gavril Nagarian's warning, spoken back in the prison cell in Mirom.

"It winds itself into your will, your consciousness, until you no longer know who is in control."

Who is in control now? Is it me—or Belberith?

CHAPTER 36

The sky craft flew on above the clouds. The Magus lay slumped inside, one hand feebly guiding the rudder. He felt ill and old. The journey to Ty Nagar had left him depleted of strength. He desperately needed to take some of his precious elixir of youth . . . but the little phial was in his laboratory at Swanholm and he was still too far from Tielen.

He must have breathed in some of the deadly drifting smoke from the Drakhaouls' battle. Why else would he feel so weak?

At last he landed in a grove of parkland trees at Swanholm and began to make his way toward the palace, stopping frequently to rest and catch his breath, leaning against a tree or slumping down on one of the benches.

He was within sight of the palace when he was forced to sit down again on a garden seat of wrought ironwork at the edge of the formal gardens. Closing his eyes, he took in a few shallow breaths, trying to calm his juddering heart. The sun seemed so bright, and the riotous colors of the flowers in the beds and tubs so intense they made his eyes ache.

"You don't look very well. Can I help you?"

Linnaius slowly raised his head, squinting in the bright sunlight. A young man, pale-faced and garbed in black, was bending over him. Linnaius didn't recognize him, though from his sober attire he guessed he was either a lawyer or a cleric.

"I'm just a little . . . fatigued." He forced himself to his feet, clinging to the side of the seat.

"Here, let me take your arm." The young man steadied him. "Are you going into the palace?"

Frustrated by his own weakness, Linnaius nodded his agreement. He was ashamed to have to lean on the young man's arm, and yet he knew he would never make his rooms without assistance. They set off at a slow pace toward the stables, and it was only as they passed under the archway that Linnaius began to wonder why they were going this way.

"Just a little farther now," said the young man easily.

A black coach stood in the stable courtyard, horses in harness, ready to leave. The coach door opened and a young woman descended.

"Good-day, Kaspar Linnaius," she said. "We have been waiting for you."

He recognized with a sinking feeling the golden hair and blue eyes of Celestine de Maunoir. At the same time, the young man's grip on his arm tightened.

"What do you want with me?" he demanded—and heard, to his shame, a quiver of fear in his voice.

"Just to take a ride in this coach together," she said. "It's a lovely day for a ride, isn't it?"

"I will not be taken anywhere against my own will—" began Linnaius.

"Please don't make a fuss," said the young man in tones of quiet menace, "or we will be obliged to compel you by other, less pleasant means."

"At least let me bring a few possessions—" If only he could reach his rooms, there were powders and potions there he could use to defend himself against his abductors.

As if in reply, he felt the young man press the muzzle of a pistol against his neck. "Into the coach," he whispered. "Now."

Astasia and Andrei stood side by side on the quay at Haeven. The skies had turned dark and stormclouds were racing across the Straits. Astasia shivered and pulled her cloak closer about her.

"You don't think anyone has recognized me?" she asked Andrei anxiously. She was certain that her escape would be discovered and the Imperial Household Cavalry dispatched to bring her back.

Every moment that passed on Tielen soil made her more apprehensive.

"Let's wait for them on board," Andrei said, squeezing her hand. "I can't think what has detained them. They said they'd be here so that we could sail on the evening tide."

"Look!" squeaked Nadezhda, pointing out to sea. She seemed to have lost her voice. "What *is* that?"

"Oh dear God," Astasia said faintly. "It's coming straight for us."

Speeding over the waves came what seemed at first a waterspout—a wild, dark spiral of cloud, wind, and water. Yet as Astasia stared, she thought she detected a shimmer of blue within the fast-moving cloud. Were those eyes? And were those great wings of shadow, powerfully beating?

"It's a Drakhaoul," she said in a hoarse whisper. But surely it was not Gavril Nagarian she sensed bearing down on them; how could it be? Hadn't he been locked away for life in the prison at Arnskammar?

And just as she was certain it was making straight for her, it veered away from the port and headed inland, following the path of the river.

She glanced at Andrei and saw that he had been utterly transfixed by the sight, one hand clutched to his head. His eyes rolled, unfocused.

"Andrei? Andrei, what is it?" She gripped hold of his arm, afraid he was going to fall into a fit. "Nadezhda, do we have any brandy?"

Nadezhda shook her head, speechless.

Andrei slowly began to form words. But they seemed like gibberish, or some foreign tongue she had never encountered before. And each word made her skin crawl, though she had no idea why.

"Khezef," he said. "Belberith. Araziel. Nilaihah. *Adramelech!*" Then he turned to her and said in urgent tones, "They are coming. Get on board the ship, Tasia, quick."

"I won't go without you," she said, still holding on to him, not knowing who "they" were, only that she had never seen him so possessed before.

With a cry, he pulled free of her grip and went stumbling off along the quay toward the long jetty that stretched out into the open sea.

*   *   *

Gavril flew onward until he saw the great park and the pale stone buildings of Swanholm. The first time he had flown here to rescue Elysia there had been no time to hide his Drakhaoul form. But today he could not risk causing so great a disturbance. He dipped down into a grove of trees and began to walk through the grounds toward the palace. It looked as if there had been a celebration here, for men were at work in the park dismantling marquees and servants were sweeping and cleaning. With any luck, no one would even stop to ask who he was; he could always pretend he was helping load one of the great carts that had come rolling up to be piled with tent posts and bales of canvas.

"Drakhaoul."

His heart racing, he turned and saw a little girl staring up at him with eyes as blue as the sea that washed Ty Nagar's shores.

"H-how do you know?" he stammered.

"I am the Drakhaoul's child," she said. "I sensed you were coming."

"Then help me, Drakhaoul's child." He was desperate now; he didn't know who she was, but he sensed she would not refuse. "I'm looking for the Magus."

"Follow me." It was a command. She started out, making for an inner courtyard and only now did he see from her limp that she was badly crippled.

She pointed to an archway. "Up there. But he's gone. You won't find him."

"Princess Karila, where are you? Are you outside without your cloak?"

"I'm here, Marta!" she called.

"Princess Karila?" Gavril echoed. Eugene's daughter? And yet she had called herself Drakhaoul's child.

"Come back for me," she said, reaching up to touch his hand, yet he knew it was not to him that she spoke.

"*When the time is right, then I will come for you,*" he heard Khezef answer.

A woman in a dark blue dress appeared in the courtyard; Gavril shrank back into the archway as she led the princess away, scolding her for forgetting her cloak.

He had wasted enough time. He went up the stairs and saw the door to the Magus's rooms was ajar. Someone had been here before him.

Pushing open the door, he checked inside. The place had been ransacked; books lay everywhere. He went in, treading on broken-backed spines, torn pages, broken glass.

And then he saw the inner door half-open. A woman was lying on the bed, her golden hair glinting in the sunlight that filtered in through the window.

"Kiukiu?" he said, astonished.

She lay as though dead, her eyes staring into the distance with an expression of horror and disbelief. Beside her lay her gusly.

He put out a shaking hand to touch her face and found it was still warm. He checked for a pulse in her limp wrist and felt the faintest beat beneath the skin.

"So they made you work for them," he murmured, "and now you're lost in the Ways Beyond . . . and I have no idea how to get you back." He touched the soft tendrils of her hair and saw that there were many threads of white among the gold. She was aging. If her spirit did not return to her body soon . . .

He lifted her, cradling her head and shoulders against him, noticing how heavy they felt.

"Come back, Kiukiu," he murmured, kissing her. "Come back to me."

When she still did not stir at the sound of his voice or the touch of his lips, he carried her out of the Magus's rooms and on, up the stairs, making for the door to the roof.

It would be a long flight back to Azhkendir, and a hard one, with her in his arms. But there was only one person he knew who had the skills and the experience to bring her back.

Malusha dozed fitfully in front of the embers of the fire.

"Grandma . . . Grandma, help me. . . ." She hears Kiukiu calling to her from very far away, her voice faint and desperate.

"Kiukiu? Where are you, child?" she calls back. "Just give me a sign, a hint, and I'll find you!"

Dust blows in her face, dry and stinging. She raises her hands to cover her eyes. All she can see is an endless, dreary landscape, stretching on to forever—a place of lost hope, lost dreams, of despair.

"No, not here! Anywhere but here—"

An insistent tapping at the window woke her.

"Kiukiu?" she cried out. "Is that you?"

There was no reply. She wrapped her shawl around her and went to open the shutters, peering into the night.

Lady Iceflower was hunched on the sill, her snowy feathers gleaming in the darkness.

"My lady, why can't you use the hole in the roof like the others?"

The owl sidled along the sill and gave her a little nip.

"So there's still no sign of my girl?"

The owl hopped inside and allowed Malusha to stroke her sleek head feathers. Malusha sighed and pulled the shutters to.

"She's been gone too long with that cursed wind-mage. I warned her, Iceflower, but would she listen to me? No, her head's too full of that Nagarian boy, and no good will come of it." Malusha shuffled over to the dying fire and began to rake it, tossing on handfuls of pine needles to revive the flames.

"Was the hunting good, my lady?"

Lady Iceflower gave a few convulsive coughs and spat out a bony pellet onto the cottage floor. Malusha inspected it. "Mice, again? Well, it keeps them out of my stores. . . ." She put water to heat and settled back in her chair. "I can't sleep, my lady, for worrying about her." The owl jumped up and perched beside her companionably.

And then Malusha sat up, listening intently. It felt as if a shadow had passed over the cottage, jarring her nerves, stirring up dark memories. Iceflower gave a cry of alarm and flapped her white wings.

"D'you feel that, my lady? That's a Drakhaoul. And winging low overhead."

A man's voice cried outside, "Malusha! Let us in, for God's sake!"

Malusha picked up a walking stick from beside the fire and went to open the door. In the gloom of a starless night, she saw a glimmer of bright eyes, daemon-blue.

"You keep your distance, Gavril Nagarian."

"I've brought Kiukiu," he gasped. "But she sorely needs your help."

"Kiukiu?" Malusha hastily muttered the words to break the protection spell around the cottage and Gavril staggered inside, carrying her granddaughter.

"Put her down on the settle," Malusha commanded, "and stand back."

He collapsed to his hands and knees, heaving in great breaths of air, and she realized he was little threat to her right now.

"And what have they done to you, my poor girl?" she crooned, kneeling beside Kiukiu and running her fingertips down her cheek. "Look at these grey hairs. You're aging; your life force is slipping away. Where are you? And why can't you get back?"

"She was in the Magus's rooms," said Gavril Nagarian, still wheezing. He looked as if he'd been in a fight. "Her gusly was there, but it was too heavy to bring."

He'd risked much to bring Kiukiu home, she allowed grudgingly. He deserved a cup of her medicinal herbal tea, if nothing more. The water was boiling; Malusha put a generous pinch of her special tea in a bowl and some healing herbs in another. "I'm going to look for her." She poured on hot water, inhaling the fragrant narcotic fumes as the dream-herbs began to infuse. "You drink this when it's cooled a little," she said to Gavril. "It'll ease your wounds and your weariness."

He took the bowl from her, nodding his thanks.

"No good ever comes of troubling the dead for their secrets; what's buried should stay buried. If we hadn't agreed to disturb Serzhei—" She stopped, hearing again Kiukiu's voice calling to her from far, far away. She saw the dust storms blowing across the bleak plain. "That's it! Eugene wasn't satisfied with what he learned and he wanted more. They always want more. And if she's trapped in the Realm of Shadows . . ."

This would call for the most perilous of the shaman's arts.

"Lady Iceflower," she said in commanding tones. "I'll need your help. If we don't move fast, she'll be trapped there forever."

Kiukiu crouched, whimpering in the shade of a grey dune of sand and ash, her hands over her head. She no longer had any idea where she was. And then she thought she saw a speck of white in the gloom. She looked up, wondering if she were hallucinating.

A snow-white owl was flitting through the winds and clouds of dust.

Iceflower? And then she cried the name aloud, "Iceflower!"

At first she feared the owl had not heard her above the roar of the winds. She frantically waved her arms, jumping up and down in the blowing dust.

And then a familiar voice said, "Didn't I warn you not to come to this place?"

Lady Iceflower alighted on her outstretched arm and stared at her with golden eyes. But the voice that spoke to her was Malusha's.

"Grandma?" said Kiukiu tearfully. "How did you know to find me here?"

"I heard you crying out for help. Lucky my lady here was able to assist me. Hurry now; we have to get you back to the way you came in. You've been out of your body too long. You're beginning to fade."

The owl flapped off into the gloom, Kiukiu trailing wearily after.

"Keep up!" cried Malusha, her voice sharp as Lady Iceflower's cry.

"But it's so far, and I'm so tired, Grandma . . ."

Iceflower fluttered down and nipped Kiukiu sharply.

"That's to keep you awake, child! And don't give in to despair. Once you give in to despair here, you're lost to me forever. Think of something. Keep your mind active. What was the last thing you remember seeing?"

Kiukiu tried to think as she trudged onward.

Daemon-glimmer of blue-and-gold eyes in the darkness . . .

"Gavril," she said softly. "I called out to him, but he couldn't hear me."

"I told you that boy was nothing but trouble."

"But he was here, I saw him," protested Kiukiu.

"That's it, child, keep remembering," urged Malusha in Iceflower's shrill owl-voice. "The more you remember, the closer we come . . ."

As she spoke, the clouds of dust and sand began to die down, like veils of mist slowly melting in the morning sun. The winds abated a little. A shadowed archway could be seen beyond the blowing dust.

"Go on, Kiukiu, you're nearly there," cried Malusha, flapping on like a pale ghost toward the Gate.

"I'm nearly there," Kiukiu repeated. Her strength was failing. Each shuffling step took so much energy . . . "Must I go alone?"

"We cannot come with you, child; we must go back the way we came."

"Take care, Grandma. Make it back home safely. And thank you. Thank you for rescuing me—"

"*Go, Kiukirilya!*" cried Malusha. Iceflower gave her a nudge toward the Gate.

Kiukiu stumbled forward and plunged into the shadows beneath the Gate.

*   *   *

Eugene had been thinking like a Drakhaon, and now, as he approached his palace, he began to think like a man again. If he swooped down on Swanholm in full magnificent Drakhaon form, he would terrify and alienate his whole court. His own men would fire on him, thinking the palace was under attack.

No; he must reappear as a man. He had told Gustave he was going hunting; well, now he had returned. And when Gustave asked, "Was the hunting good?" he would reply, "Magnificent! The best day I've had in years."

There was a grove of birch trees within the deer park, which would afford shade and cover. Eugene circled lower and lower, sending a herd of startled roe deer galloping for cover.

He landed in a cloud of dust and stones. For a moment he lay motionless, at full length in the rough grass, arms widespread, as though still flying. Then, his head singing with the rush of the wind, he pushed himself to his knees and then to his feet.

His clothes were in tatters. He had lost his shoes. He wasn't sure how he would explain this to any courtiers he encountered on the way back to the palace.

He set off, barefooted, across the park. He kept looking down at his hand, at the healed skin—and then touching his face and scalp, feeling the smoothness again and again, just to make sure it was not a dream. There was a strange tint of green coloring his fingernails, so that in the sunlight they glinted like emeralds.

As he walked on, he began to become aware of how weary he felt. And thirsty. Suddenly he felt as if his throat and mouth were filled with burning cinders. The need to find refreshment drove him stumbling onward.

"Water." He whispered the word aloud.

Then he spotted the Dievona Fountain on the edge of the park. Deer often drank there, but right now he didn't care if he shared a water trough with his horses in the stables. He had to have water to quench this burning thirst.

He plunged his head and shoulders into the wide basin of the fountain, gulping down great mouthfuls, not caring that it was dirtied by birds and animals. Above him, Dievona the Huntress gazed proudly down on his palace below.

Dripping wet, he rose from the fountain and set out down the path that led from the trees toward the formal gardens, but still the thirst burned on. He stopped, leaning against a fluted ornamental pillar, gripped suddenly by violent pains in his stomach.

I shouldn't have drunk from the fountain. . . .

Yet if the water was bad, surely it was too soon for it to take effect?

He straightened up and kept walking. It must be hunger. He could not remember the last time he had eaten. At the ball supper, probably.

Everywhere in the gardens, the last traces of the ball were being cleaned up. The marquees were gone. The ruts and holes in his lawns had not, but somehow it all seemed very unimportant now.

"Imperial highness?" A servant gasped out his name, bowing low as he passed by. Gardeners dropped their rakes and brooms to stare; maidservants gave little shocked cries.

Was he in such a state? He lurched on, aware that the gravel was grazing his bare feet and the griping pain in his stomach was growing worse. Could he make the shelter of the palace before he disgraced himself?

He staggered up the wide steps toward the terrace where he had stood with Karila and Astasia to watch the fireworks. Maids were busy in the dining hall; when they saw him, they scattered.

What is wrong? Do I really look so terrifying?

And then he came face-to-face with his reflection in one of the full-length gilt-framed mirrors.

A daemon with long locks of green and gold-streaked hair stared back at him through strangely striated, slanted malachite eyes.

"What's this?" he demanded, horrified. "What have you done to me, Belberith?"

"*You have used much of my power,*" whispered Beleberith, "*and the more you use, the more you will resemble me.*"

"You must restore my human face." How could he explain away his daemonic appearance to his terrified household? "And swiftly!"

He sensed a flicker of dry laughter deep within him.

"*Your human face will be swiftly restored if you satisfy the thirst.*" Was Belberith mocking him? "*Your thirst for innocent blood.*"

"Papa," said a clear, high voice. He saw in the reflection that Karila had entered the hall and was hurrying joyfully to welcome him, arms open wide. "You're home!"

*   *   *

"Kari," said Eugene, backing away. "Kari, don't come too close."

A sweet and delicious odor, fresh and enticing, wafted toward him. The gripping pains in his stomach intensified. He winced, doubling up.

"Papa?" Karila came closer. She was wearing a plain white gown, with her hair unbound about her shoulders. That delicious scent that overwhelmed his senses was coming from her. It was her blood he could smell, sweeter than the strongest wine.

Why not just take what I want where I find it? Who will dare stop me? I am Drakhaon, after all!

"No!" he cried. "Keep back, Kari! Keep away from me!"

"Unnatural lusts and desires . . ." whispered Gavril Nagarian's voice in his memory.

She stared up at him, transfixed. "You—you've become Drakhaoul."

Fresh scent of a child's translucent flesh, the blood pulsing just below the pale skin, deliciously clean and untainted . . .

"My own child," he muttered. "Not my own child. Don't make me—"

He turned suddenly and ran, making for the gardens, not caring whom he crashed into as he ran, driven by the need to get as far away from Karila as he could before Belberith's terrible hunger made him attack her.

Kiukiu stirred. Her eyelids fluttered.

"Kiukiu?" said Gavril. "Kiukiu, can you hear me?"

"Take care, Grandma . . ." mumbled Kiukiu. She blinked. Her eyes had lost that deathlike glassy stare. She gazed up into his face.

"Gavril?" she said wonderingly.

He tried to reply, but found his voice was choked in his throat. He nodded.

"I'm back?"

"You're back."

"And you're here. With me." She was smiling now, a shaky, uncertain smile. She raised her hand and touched his face. "Look at you. You're a mess. All cuts and bruises." She tried to sit up, but fell back against him. "But where's the Magus? And the princess?" She made no effort to move again this time, resting her head against his shoulder.

"Don't say that cursed man's name in here ever again," said a disgruntled voice. Malusha had come back to herself and was sitting up in her chair, stretching and groaning as she did so, as though stiff and tired after a long and arduous journey. "And you," she said to Gavril. "I should turn you out, if it weren't for the fact that you brought my girl back to me." But the hatred had gone from her voice and he thought he almost caught a glimmer of a smile.

"I'll make tea," Malusha said, pushing herself out of her chair. As she came toward the fire, she stooped down and gazed into Kiukiu's face. And she let out a little cry.

"What is it, Grandma?"

Malusha reached out to touch Kiukiu's face, threading a lock or two of her hair through her fingers. "How long were you in the Realm of Shadows?"

Gavril heard the concern in Malusha's voice.

"I—I don't know. A few hours, maybe more. Maybe days . . ."

"Your lovely hair. Look at your lovely hair."

"What's wrong with my hair?"

Malusha brought over a little looking glass and held it for Kiukiu to see.

"Oh!" cried Kiukiu, and then hid her face in her hands. "Don't look at me, Gavril. Please don't look."

In the few hours since he had brought her from Swanholm, the last of the gold had faded from her hair. Now it was all grey.

She began to weep silently, her shoulders trembling, her face still hidden in her hands, the tears trickling down between her fingers. He watched, stricken that she should be so upset.

"Don't cry, Kiukiu," he said. Gently, he prized her fingers from her face and kissed her wet cheeks. "All that matters to me is that you're here. That you're safe. That we're together."

CHAPTER 37

Eugene opened his eyes. He was lying on his own bed at Swanholm, and the shutters were open to let in the early morning light.

Had he been dreaming? Fleeting images flared in his memory and vanished before he could remember them clearly. There had been a girl . . . And then nothing but a muddle of confused, violent fragments: the moist, marbled red of torn flesh, the screaming of a wounded creature in pain, and then a warm, delicious, salty taste in his mouth, his throat . . .

He unlatched a window and breathed in the crisp, sweet air. The parkland was bathed in rising mists and the birds were singing. He could see a party of men with sticks and hounds on leashes in the far distance; his gamekeepers, he guessed, out searching for deer straying too far from the deer park.

"You're—you're awake, highness!"

Gustave stood in the open doorway. He was staring at Eugene as if he were amazed. And Gustave was never amazed by anything.

"I hope the noise outside has not disturbed your highness. A young servant girl was found on the grounds; we can't be sure, but it looks as if she was attacked by a wolf. Perhaps one of the Magus's Marauders has returned."

Echoes of his dream: a defenseless girl attacked and savaged by a wild creature . . .

"How long have I been asleep?" he asked. His whole body ached as if he had been sleeping rough on campaign. His back and shoulder muscles felt as if they had been strained to bursting.

"Nearly two days and nights, highness. Shall I call your valet to shave you?"

"Two days?"

"And I expect your highness will want breakfast?"

"Water," Eugene said. He realized now he was desperately thirsty. Gustave brought him a jug of water, which he drank straightaway. And as he drank, a memory pricked at the back of his mind of another devastating thirst that could not be quenched by water alone.

Had he been sick? He had no memory of the past days. A high fever would explain his memories of thirst and burning heat.

He set down the empty water jug and pensively ran a hand over his thickly stubbled chin. . . .

He looked down at his hand in amazement: The skin was smooth and unmarked. And his face felt soft beneath the two days' growth of beard. Best of all, there was no longer any pain.

A mirror. He must make certain it was not a delusion.

He gazed in the cheval mirror and his memory returned. The last time he had looked at his reflection, he had seen a Drakhaoul-daemon with wild, windswept hair and fierce eyes that gleamed green and gold in the gloom. And a horrible possibility gripped him. *Was I the creature that attacked the young servant girl? And what else has happened here at Swanholm in my absence?*

He flung open his bedchamber door and ran down the palace corridors, not caring who saw him in his nightshirt, making for the Magus's laboratory.

Guardsmen from the Household Cavalry saluted him as he crossed the courtyard, and Lieutenant Petter came hurrying up. He looked flustered.

"What's wrong, Lieutenant?" demanded Eugene.

"It's—it's the Magus, imperial highness. It seems as if he's gone. Or someone has abducted him."

"What do you mean?" Eugene crossed the cobbled courtyard in his bare feet, Petter hurrying at his heels.

He knew instantly that Linnaius was gone. There was no invisible barrier blocking their way; all the Magus's wards had been destroyed. And the door to his rooms had been torn off its hinges. Inside, everything was in total disorder. Books and papers lay everywhere, flung down as if whoever had broken in had been searching for something in haste.

"It's worse in here, highness," said Petter, opening the door to the laboratory.

Everything that could be broken had been, and the floor glittered with broken glass.

"The Azhkendi experiment," Eugene said, casting a quick look over the scene. "Someone was after the firedust."

"And the Magus too," said Petter.

"Isn't it possible he's gone in pursuit of the thieves in his craft?"

Petter pulled a wry face. "Unlikely, highness. We found his sky craft on the grounds."

Eugene had begun to put the clues together. First, King Enguerrand's demand that Linnaius should stand trial for his heretical crimes, then the earlier foiled attempts to break into the laboratory—

"Francia!" he cried, clenching his fists. Where were the rubies? The Tears of Artamon? He had given them to Linnaius on Ty Nagar. Whoever held all five rubies was entitled by ancient law to rule the five princedoms of Rossiya. "No; Enguerrand would never dare."

"Highness?" Petter glanced at him uncertainly.

"Send out to all the ports that no Francian vessel is to be allowed to sail until it has been thoroughly searched."

"I'll supervise the searches myself," cried Petter, hurrying away.

An ominous feeling of pressure was building in his head, like an ache presaging a migraine. Eugene went to the Vox Aethyria room where several undersecretaries were at work monitoring reports from around the empire. They all jumped up nervously when he came in.

"What's the latest news from our agents in Francia?"

"F-Francia?" said one. "Hasn't Gustave found you, highness? He went to look for you about ten minutes ago."

This did not bode well. Gustave only delivered intelligence of the most sensitive nature.

"I'll be in my rooms." Eugene set off, back toward the state apartments, only to encounter Countess Lovisa.

"Forgive me, highness," she said, her head bowed. Her voice was oddly constrained, as though she had been weeping. "I failed you."

"Not now, Lovisa," he said, striding onward.

"But, highness, she's gone!"

He stopped and turned around.

"Who's gone?" His voice rasped with tension. Did she mean Karila?

"The Empress," she said in a voice so soft he could hardly hear her.

"Astasia?" He came back along the corridor toward her. "What do you mean, gone? Gone where?"

"The whole palace was in an uproar. It seems the Francians—"

"The Francians kidnapped my wife?" Surely they would never dare touch his wife?

"No." Lovisa's pale blue eyes widened with fear at the rage in his voice. "It seems she may have sailed for Francia of her own accord. She is thought to have boarded a Francian ship with a dark-haired young man."

"What?" Eugene said, his voice low and dangerous. Had Astasia betrayed him after all? He caught hold of Lovisa by the wrist, pulling her close. "Was he the one at the secret assignation? Who is he, Lovisa?"

"We—don't know for sure," Lovisa said, "but several people who saw them at the quayside remarked on the striking likeness between them. And one said she called him 'Andrei.' "

"Her brother?" Eugene let go of Lovisa, who retreated, rubbing her wrist. He had expected to hear of a lover. Not this. "But it can't be. It can't be . . ."

He hurried back to their rooms, all the time trying to make sense of this information. So Andrei Orlov was still alive? What had he told Astasia, to make her leave with him? Or had she seen him return in Drakhaoul form, and been so terrified that she had simply fled?

He flung open the doors and started to search for clues. Here was the romance she had been reading, abandoned on the chaise longue. He picked it up and the card she'd been using to mark her place in the text fell out. He bent down to retrieve it and saw it was a little calendar, decorated with a colored engraving of a wreath of flowers to symbolize the seasons of the year. And then he saw that dates were encircled in pen and little numbers had been added under each month, one to nine, ending in late autumn.

"Could she be? . . ." he said out loud. "Is that why she has been so?"

He sat down heavily on the sofa. He had been so busy with his own concerns of state that he had never thought to ask Astasia if all was well with her. He had seen her laughing in the company of Celestine de Joyeuse and he had assumed she was happy. And now she had fled, carrying his unborn child, to Francia.

Bitterness overwhelmed him. Even though she was gone, the room still smelled faintly of her fresh, light perfume. He found himself lifting her lilac silk robe, left draped over a chair, and stroking it against his cheek. Everything here reminded him of her, from the slim volume of Solovei's latest verses to the little pot of violets on her dressing table. He had sent her violets before they were married. . . .

"Highness!" Gustave came running down the corridor, waving a dispatch. "Thank God I've found you!" He handed over the paper and then bent double, clutching his sides, trying to catch his breath.

Eugene snatched the paper and opened it, wondering if it were some communication from Astasia, but it was an intelligence report from Francia.

> The Francian war fleet has set sail. Heading northward up the
> Straits . . .

Eugene staggered as if someone had just punched him hard in the stomach. "Toward Tielborg?"

An undersecretary came hurrying down the corridor, another paper in hand.

"We've just received this communiqué from the Francian court!"

"By Vox Aethyria?" Eugene gave Gustave a frowning glance. "We were not aware the Francians had access to our communication devices. They are all individually tuned, aren't they, Gustave?"

"Well, yes, highness," said Gustave, wiping his brow. "But you recall the time Gavril Nagarian used our own device to contact us . . ."

Eugene put out his hand to take the communiqué.

> To Eugene of Tielen,
>   We have in our custody the heretic scholar known as Kaspar
> Linnaius. He will stand trial before the ecclesiastical courts for heresy,
> soul-stealing, and daemon-summoning.
>   Know also that we have in our possession the five rubies known as
> the Tears of Artamon. Ancient law decrees that whosoever holds all
> five stones is entitled to govern all five princedoms of Rossiya. We
> therefore assert our right to be called Emperor and impose our holy
> law upon all five princedoms, as well as Francia.
> Enguerrand of Francia, Commander of the Order of Saint Sergius
> and the Francian Commanderie.

Eugene slowly let the hand holding the paper drop to his side.

"What order shall I send to the fleet, highness?" said Gustave.

Eugene looked at him. For the first time in his career as military commander, he was utterly confounded.

"Stand by," he said mechanically. "And call the council."

"Stand by to defend the empire?"

"With whatever means we have left at our disposal." He would never give in to Enguerrand's demands. He would never let the religious fanaticism of the Francian court destroy the enlightened ideas that shaped Tielen life and philosophy. He no longer had the Magus's skill with alchymical weaponry to help him defend his people. And now that he knew too well the terrible price he would have to pay if he called on Belberith to aid him, he did not want to risk using his daemonic powers. Not yet. He would just have to rely on his skills and experience as a commander.

He let out a long sigh of resignation that shuddered through his whole body. He squared his shoulders.

"*Use me, Eugene,*" breathed the voice of his Drakhaoul. "*Let me help you.*"

"Gustave," Eugene said, ignoring Belberith's seductive tones, "get my old uniform ready: Colonel-in-Chief of the Household Cavalry. Let the Francians come. I'll be ready for them."

ABOUT THE AUTHOR

SARAH ASH, who trained as a musician, is the author of four fantasy novels: *Lord of Snow and Shadows, Moths to a Flame, Song-spinners,* and *The Lost Child.* She also runs the library in a local primary school. Sarah Ash has two grown-up sons and lives in Beckenham, Kent, with her husband and their mad cat, Molly. She is currently at work on the third book of the Tears of Artamon.